The

"*The Dark of Day* is Parker's best one creates an unforgettable protagonist—a smart lawyer who is up against Miami's politicians and power brokers, and the demons of her own secret past. The suspense is hotter than South Beach."

—LINDA FAIRSTEIN,
New York Times BESTSELLING AUTHOR OF *Killer Heat*

"Parker captures the dark side of South Beach—the glamour, the bling, and the night creatures who glide through the club scene with a drink in their hand and a malicious glint in their eye."

—HARLAN COBEN,
New York Times BESTSELLING AUTHOR OF *Hold Tight*

"No one writes like Barbara Parker about the sun-drenched gritty glamour of sinful Miami Beach. And her heroine C.J. Dunn is so well-drawn you want to reach into the pages and pull her back from the brink of disaster."

—P.J. PARRISH,
New York Times BESTSELLING AUTHOR OF *South of Hell*

"Best Summer Reading for 2008."

—*Miami Herald*

"Another sizzling thriller. . . . Almost every scene is filled with the flavor of South Beach, from the glitzy hotels on Collins Avenue to the trendy boutiques on Lincoln Road."

—NPR.ORG

"Parker has her fans, and female lawyers are a hot commodity in the genre at the moment."

—*Booklist*

"This tantalizing novel of suspense . . . zings with rich subtext."

—*Publishers Weekly*

"Filled with twists on both a personal and professional level, *The Dark of Day* is an exciting suspense thriller . . . the story line is action-packed from the onset as the spins and revelations keep on coming, making Barbara Parker's tale an engaging read."

—HARRIET KLAUSNER

"The characters come alive in this intensely plotted mystery where everyone carries a secret and appearances can be deceiving. Great characters, good pacing and lively action keep readers guessing until the very end."

—*Romantic Times*, 4 STARS

"*The Dark of Day* moves at a brisk pace as Parker imbues her plot with an insightful look at politics, greed and entitlement. Parker shows her prowess at character development as she . . . has shaped another appealing character in C.J."

—*The Sun Sentinel*

THE DARK OF DAY

Also by Barbara Parker

IN MEMORIUM

A Note from Vanguard Press

Dear Reader:

Vanguard Press published *The Dark of Day* initially in hardcover and then in this mass market paperback format. Just before the publication of this paperback, we heard that Barbara had passed away due to cancer, and we were incredibly saddened by the loss of such a talented, vibrant, and loving woman and author.

The Dark of Day is the only Barbara Parker book that Vanguard Press has published, but in the process of working with Barbara, we came to respect and admire her, we were proud to be her publisher, and we were looking forward to a long and fruitful relationship. Sadly, it was not meant to be, but we will always cherish our memories of working with her closely on *The Dark of Day* (and with Barbara, work was always fun). She served her readers well and was a total professional—an exemplar of a writer who truly cared about her craft.

We will miss her as an author, but even more as a friend.

the dark
of day

Barbara Parker

Vanguard Press
A Member of the Perseus Books Group

Hardcover edition first published in 2008 and mass market
paperback edition first published in 2009 by Vanguard Press, a
member of the Perseus Books Group

Books published by Vanguard Press are available at special
discounts for bulk purchases in the United States by corporations,
institutions, and other organizations. For more information, please
contact the Special Markets Department at the Perseus Books
Group, 2300 Chestnut Street, Suite 200, Philadelphia, PA 19103,
or call (800) 810-4145, ext. 5000, or e-mail
special.markets@perseusbooks.com.

Designed by Timm Bryson
Set in 10.5 point Electra by the Perseus Books Group

Library of Congress Cataloging-in-Publication Data
    Parker, Barbara (Barbara J.)
    The dark of day / Barbara Parker.
        p. cm.
    HC ISBN 978-1-59315-461-5 (alk. paper)
    1. Women lawyers—Fiction. 2. Miami (Fla.)—Fiction. 3.
Private security services—Employees—Fiction. 4. Murder—
Fiction. 5. South Beach (Miami Beach, Fla.)—Fiction. I. Title.
PS3566.A67475D37 2008
813'.54—dc22
                                                      2008007371

Mass Market ISBN 978-1-59315-518-6

10 9 8 7 6 5 4 3 2 1

For Nick and Andrea

chapter
ONE

t he third glass of champagne. Or the fourth. If you're alone at a party where you don't know anybody, you need something in your hands. You move around a lot. You look across the room like you see somebody you recognize and you walk in that direction. Or you stay in one of the bathrooms until someone knocks, or you look at the paintings on the walls, or you sit on one of the long sofas and pretend to be listening to the five-piece band and the woman singer. She was supposed to be famous, but Kylie had never heard of her.

The party had been okay—until Alana disappeared.

Kylie could look across a huge living room with polished marble floors and see the owner of the house in his tuxedo shirt with the cuffs rolled up, talking to a bunch of his friends. Probably his friends, but on South Beach, do you ever know who your friends are? Do they bring you to a party and then dump you? She thought about going over and saying hello and it's a nice house, but he might ask who are you? Were you invited?

The images split and drifted apart. Kylie mumbled, "Oh, shit, I'm wasted."

She walked to the buffet table near the windows, the lights of Miami a mile west, reflecting off the low-hanging clouds. It was all fuzzy without her glasses. The window reflected blurry candles, trays of food, flower arrangements, and a thin girl in a short black dress. Kylie flipped her hair over her shoulder and ate a miniature quiche.

When she turned around, she saw someone familiar. She squinted. Jason. His curly blond hair and red shirt had grabbed Kylie's attention. His friends were obviously flamers, not that she cared.

She walked over and tapped him on the shoulder. "Hi."

"Hey! How are you?"

"I can't find Alana. She's been gone for like an hour. Have you seen her?"

"Don't worry, Ky, she'll turn up. She always does. Why don't you find a place to sit down and wait for her?"

"I guess I will. Thanks."

He returned to his friends, and Kylie took another flute of champagne from one of the servers walking around with trays, obviously a model, so gorgeous you had to wonder what planet people like that came from.

Steadying herself on the walls, she went through the house again, in and out of rooms she had already seen. A dining room with a long table; a media room where people were playing Guitar Hero on a flat-screen TV; the kitchen with caterers running back and forth. In one of the bathrooms she saw some girls cutting lines of coke on the vanity. They offered her some. Kylie shook her head and went out.

She found a narrow staircase in the hall behind the kitchen. Sipping her champagne, steadying herself on the handrail, Kylie went up. At the top, a man in a black T-shirt and pants stepped in front of her. She stared at his hair and thought of a red brick. His shoulders were square, too. He said, "Can I help you?"

"I'm trying to find a friend of mine." She hiccuped. "Her name is Alana Martin. Do you know her?"

"I don't think so."

"She's a little taller than me? Long brown hair and a black halter dress? I came with her, and it's late, and I have to leave. She's not—" Kylie hiccuped again. "—anywhere else in the house, so logically she *has* to be upstairs."

"Sorry. The upstairs is Mr. Medina's private area."

"Please? I have to find her."

The man shook his head. "Girl, if she was up there, I'd tell you. All right?"

"Thank you." She held on going down, trying not to catch her stiletto heels on the carpet, Alana's Jimmy Choo knockoffs, which were too big. Why had Alana lent her this dress and helped her with her makeup if she was just going to take off, leaving her friend, *supposedly* her friend, at a party where she didn't know *anyone*, with five dollars in her purse? It was rude.

Making her way again through the crowd in the living room, even more people now, Kylie knew that if she didn't get some air she would faint.

She walked through one of the sliding glass doors, left open so people could go in and out, air-conditioned air pumping through it. Past midnight, still hot and sticky outside, even with the fans and the misting machines hissing out clouds of vapor. The bartender, a tall blonde girl, was wiping down the bar, nothing else to do except look good. Kylie walked over to the pool and leaned on a chair. She counted four people swimming in their underwear. No Alana. A transvestite had passed out on one of the chaises in her polka-dot dress. Her wig was crooked.

None of this surprised Kylie. Six months in Miami, you learn a lot. You see things, somebody hooks you up with a job, you get to know people, and you feel like you're fitting in, if you have a friend like Alana. And then she dumps you.

"Bitch. Where *are* you?"

The music faded as Kylie walked down the steps and around the side of the house. She looked to see if Alana was standing out front. Headlights swept around the portico as a Porsche convertible came to a stop. The parking attendant ran over to take the keys.

With a sigh, Kylie went back the way she had come. She would lie on a chaise next to the trannie until Alana came back and started wondering where *she* was. Kylie took off the shoes and walked barefoot across the thick, cool grass. A breeze came off the water. She could see boats docked at the seawall. A sailboat. Some yachts. Must be nice, being rich. She walked past a trellis of jasmine, and its sweet scent filled her head. Tiny lights shone into the palm trees by the seawall.

Kylie went slower and slower and finally stopped. On the way down, she thought how strange it was that time dragged out long enough for her to set the shoes and the champagne glass carefully on the path and then to lie beside them in the grass and close her eyes.

She woke when she felt something moving on her bare thigh. A hand, going up her leg, under her skirt. She grabbed for it. "No. Don't."

Two blurred, grinning faces moved into view. "Hey, baby. What you doing out here all by yourself? You need some company?"

She formed the words carefully. "Not . . . particularly. I'm studying the clouds."

One of them brushed her hair off her face, then a finger went along the low neckline of her dress. "I think the girl needs some company."

"I prefer to be alone, thank you very much."

"She definitely needs something. I have it right here for you, baby." He rubbed his crotch.

"Go away!"

The other guy looked around. "Over there. The boathouse. Help me pick her up."

"Don't." Kylie pushed against his chest.

Another voice said, "Hey!"

Their heads swung around.

The voice came again, getting closer. "What's going on?"

"Who the fuck are you?"

"Security, that's who. You guys clear out. Now."

Laughter. "Security, my ass. I know Billy's security guys."

The man holding Kylie said, "Turn around and keep walking before I kick you over the seawall."

Shadows moved. He let go of her, and she fell limply into the grass. She heard a thud, a grunt of pain. Then somebody saying, "Forget it, man. Let's go." Footsteps faded into the darkness.

A big man crouched beside her, a silhouette.

Kylie struggled to sit up. "Leave me alone!"

"It's okay, they're gone." He picked up her shoes. "Come on, let's get you back inside." He put an arm under her and she seemed to float up.

"I'm going to puke!" Turning, she leaned over the grass. When she was done, the man gave her a handkerchief. Her hands were shaking as she wiped her lips and chin. "I'm sorry. I want to go home now, please."

"Do I look like a cab driver? Who'd you come with?"

"A friend."

"Tell him it's time to go."

"Her. She's a girl. Do you work here? Maybe you know where she is. Alana. Long hair. Beautiful. She's sort of dark. From Venezuela."

"Alana Martin?"

"Yes! Where is she?"

"Don't know. Well, well. Small world. Friends of Alana."

"How could she just *leave* me here? Shit! How am I going to get home?"

"You have a cell phone? Call a taxi."

"I don't have enough money for a taxi." She started to cry.

"Come on. Stop that." He let out a breath. "Okay. It's your lucky night. I was leaving anyway. I'll take you home, but if you throw up in my boss's Cadillac, you can walk."

"Thank you so much. Thank you." She stumbled, and he held her up with an arm around her waist.

Then she was in a car, leaning against a side door, and cold air blew on her face. She opened her eyes. The man was going through her purse. She grabbed for it, and he pulled it out of her reach.

"I only have five dollars!"

"Just finding out where you live, sweet face. I asked, and you couldn't seem to tell me." He pulled out her driver's license and held it under the dome light, which shone on his shaved head. He had a short beard and a mustache. "Kylie Ann Willis. Lansing, Michigan. Twenty-one years old. Not bad. I should have had one like this back in the day. Looks almost real."

"It *is* real!"

"With that cracker accent, no way you're from Michigan. How old are you, kid? Are you even eighteen?"

"Yes!"

He shoved the license back into her purse and tossed it to her lap. "I doubt that. Your folks know where you are?"

"Of course. I . . . I'm a student at the University of Miami."

"Yeah? Studying what, nuclear physics?"

She closed her eyes. The seat was so soft.

"Wake up." He patted her cheek. "Where am I taking you? If you can't remember, I'll have to drop you at the Miami Beach Police station and let them figure it out."

She forced her eyes open, forced them to bring the two images of his face together. She moistened her lips. "Twenny-six, east of Biscayne. Windmere Apartments."

"Windmill?"

"Wind . . . mere."

"Good. Have you there in ten minutes."

They passed a long line of cars from the party, huge houses with gates, then the guard house at the entrance. The striped arm went up, down. They went over a short bridge and took a right on the MacArthur Causeway. The streetlights came faster and faster.

She moaned a little.

"Are you all right?"

"Uh-huh."

Downtown Miami. Lights going in and out of the car. The man held a cigarette, its end glowing orange. He blew smoke toward the window, which was open a few inches. He was a big man with big hands and a heavy stainless-steel watch on his thick wrist. He had taken off his suit jacket and rolled up his cuffs.

He glanced over at her. "So. Kylie. You're a friend of Alana's."

"Uh-huh."

"Good friend?"

"I thought so. She dumped me. She went off to see somebody and didn't come back."

"Like who?"

"Somebody, I dunno."

"You and Alana hang out together?"

"I guess. She's my best friend. A model. I'm going to be a model too."

"How long have you girls known each other?"

"Since . . ." Kylie frowned. "After I got here."

"When was that?"

"March?"

"What'd you do, come down from Cornpone, Alabama, for spring break and decide you liked South Beach?"

"I do like it. I like it a lot."

She closed her eyes against the streetlights that were coming too fast, turning into strobe lights, and in the darkness she began to spin backward. She dug her fingers into the seat and held on.

chapter

TWO

the judge's gavel came down, and the former defendant, Harnell Robinson, put a kiss on his lawyer's cheek. He hugged his family, his sports agent, and the teammates who had sat behind him during three days of trial. Swinging her tote over her shoulder, C.J. Dunn signaled her young associate to follow with the files and turned her client toward the exit. A sheriff's deputy pushed open the double doors while another held back the spectators. Robinson stopped to sign his autograph and shake a few hands.

In the corridor, reporters converged on Robinson, shouting. How did he feel? Was he relieved? When would he return to practice?

Arms around his family, Robinson smiled for the cameras.

"Good. I feel real good. I feel like, you know, like somebody up there was looking out for me. Justice prevailed!"

Before the trial, C.J. had sent him to Macy's for some blue suits. Leave the custom-tailored Armani at home with the Rolex. Wear a cheap watch, your wedding ring, your Super Bowl ring, and that's it. Lose the braids and the diamond ear stud. No miniskirts on the wife, belly shirts on the daughter, or drooping pants on the son. For the three days of the trial, his mother had carried a Bible and worn a hat, gloves, and a below-the-knee dress, a bit of overkill that C.J. had decided to let pass.

Last New Year's Day, at three o'clock in the morning, Harnell Robinson had been arrested at a club on South Beach for aggravated battery on one of the bouncers. A felony conviction on top of a previous skirmish with some fans could have ended Robinson's career. But C.J.'s private investigator delivered good news: the bouncer had served time in Illinois for possession of meth, carrying a concealed firearm, domestic battery on his girlfriend, and a string of DUI's. A copy of his rap sheet found its way to Channel Seven. The judge instructed the jurors not to watch the news, but it was too late.

C.J. motioned to her associate, Henry. When he came closer, she dropped her keys into his coat pocket. "Go get my car. I'll meet you outside." He backed up and steered the rolling briefcase around the crowd, which had grown as people stopped to see what was going on.

The woman reporter from Channel Eight's *Justice Files* elbowed the *Miami Herald* sports reporter aside. "Harnell, what's next for you?"

With a smile, C.J. stepped into the frame. "Mr. Robinson has been vindicated. What he wants now is to go home and be with his family so he can start putting this ordeal behind him. On Monday morning, eight A.M., he's reporting for practice with the rest of the team."

"Yeah, it's gonna be good, you know, to get back in uniform."

The reporter said, "Your accuser has filed a suit for damages. Do you think he has a better chance in civil court?" She shoved her microphone at him.

That brought a scowl. "No! Uh-uh. I'm gonna beat him there, too. You put me in front of a hundred juries, it's all the same."

C.J. gripped her client's elbow and pulled him away. They walked in a moving blaze of light toward an elevator that his friends held open for him. When the doors slid shut, C.J. found herself squeezed among men so tall that even in four-inch heels she couldn't see over their shoulders.

Robinson's wife had stopped crying. She stood stiffly with her arms crossed. Robinson stroked her hair. "Baby? You all right?"

"If you put me through this one more time, I will rip off your face." The chuckles in the elevator stopped when she whirled around and glared at the men behind her.

The group crossed the lobby and exited the glass doors of the fading, 1960s-style courthouse. A black Range Rover pulled up at the curb just as reporters and cameramen came out of the building and ran down the steps. People stopped to stare.

Spots of light shone on Harnell Robinson's wraparound shades. He bent to give C.J. a hug. "Girl, I appreciate everything you did for me."

On tiptoes she whispered into his ear, "I want the rest of my fee, Harnell. Cashier's check, my desk by noon on Monday. It had better not bounce this time."

"No problem."

His friends cleared a path, and Robinson and his family waved as they climbed into the vehicle. Through the open front passenger window he gave a thumbs-up. Reporters chased the car, which quickly picked up speed, heading for the expressway.

Alone on the sidewalk, C.J. opened her tote bag and found her sunglasses. The shadows from the palm trees didn't reach this far, and already she could feel the prickle of perspiration. Her lightweight wool suit was fine for an air-conditioned courtroom, but it soaked up the sun. She lifted her long, blond-streaked hair and scanned the parking lot for a silver BMW moving among the acre of cars and the support pilings of the expressway that arched over the river.

"Ms. Dunn!"

The *Justice Files* reporter was racing toward her in sneakers. Her cameraman trotted behind, shouldering his heavy camera. Black-haired, smooth-skinned Libi Rodriguez, showing her cleavage. She spoke into her cordless mike. "We're here with celebrity lawyer C.J. Dunn, who just came out of court with her client, Miami Dolphins running back Harnell Robinson, after a surprising victory. C.J., our viewers want to know. How did you pull it off, when so many witnesses testified that it was Robinson who started the brawl?"

C.J. didn't like to look into a camera wearing sunglasses, but if she took them off she would squint. She said, "The prosecution witnesses were mistaken."

"Some say the jurors were swayed by stories leaked from your office in the weeks before the trial. Do you have a comment?" She thrust the microphone at C.J.

Maintaining her smile, C.J. said, "Libi, I think you're just mad that you didn't hear about them first."

She walked away and noticed her car making the turn at the end of the block. The single line of traffic moved slowly. When Henry was in front of the building, he swung the BMW close to the sidewalk and waited for C.J. to get in. But her eyes had shifted to what was behind him, a Mercedes-Benz limousine, vintage 1956, with bulbous front fenders and a heavy chrome grille, glinting in the sunlight. She knew that car, and she knew its owner.

The driver's door opened, and a young man with blond hair got out and hustled around the long hood. He didn't look like a chauffeur; he wore a blue button-down shirt with the sleeves rolled to his elbows. "Ms. Dunn? Mr. Cahill wonders if he could have a few moments of your time."

The tinted glass gave no view of the man inside. She held up a hand, then walked back to her own car and motioned for Henry to lower the window. "Looks like I have a ride. Go ahead and take the files back to the office."

Henry turned around to see behind him. "Who is *that?*"

"In the limo? Milo Cahill."

"Milo Cahill the architect?"

"Right. I won't be long. Go on, we're holding up traffic."

The driver opened the rear door of the Mercedes, and C.J. peered inside the dim interior, making out a white Panama hat and a tropical print shirt. "Milo? What are you doing here?"

"Waiting for you. Get in, will you? It's an oven out there."

C.J. got in, and the door closed with a solid thud. They exchanged a quick kiss on the cheek. "You look fantastic as ever," he said in his honey-sweet Carolina drawl. He took her hand. "My word. Is that blood on your claws? My spies told me you won, and I ran right over to congratulate you."

She folded her sunglasses into their case. "Thank you for sending Harnell to me, but he still owes me twenty thousand dollars."

"But think of all the publicity!"

"My partners at the firm would rather have the cash," she said.

"Stop complaining. You should be happy. C.J., why don't you return your calls? I've been trying to reach you for days."

"I know. I'm sorry, Milo, it's just been crazy. You didn't say it was urgent, so—"

With a dismissive wave, he settled into his corner as the limo glided away from the curb. A glass panel separated passengers and chauffeur. "Kick off your shoes if you want to."

"May I?" They were ankle-strap Pradas, lovely and lethal. She dug her toes into the plush carpet. "Sweet Jesus, that feels good." She slid her hand over the faux leopard-skin rug on the seat. "You are getting too, too decadent."

"I would only confess this to my dearest friends, but the upholstery is so worn out I can't bear to look at it anymore. I'm having it replaced with red leather. This old rattletrap surely needs some TLC. I am speaking of the car, so don't make any jokes." Milo reached over to open a cabinet between the jump seats. A mahogany shelf dropped down, revealing a row of crystal glasses, a silver martini shaker, and cocktail stirrers. "I'd have brought champagne, but I wouldn't want to lead you astray." He lifted a Perrier from the cooler and handed it to her with a napkin. "Happy Friday, darlin'."

"I adore you, Milo." She twisted off the cap, and as she raised it to drink she saw a lamp bolted to the ceiling in place of the dome light. There were six antique doll's heads with curly blond hair, dimples, and small white teeth. Small halogen lights were wired to spirals of silver-colored metal. "Oh. My God."

"Like it?"

"It's insane. It's so . . . you. Where did you find it?"

Round cheeks pushed his eyes into inverted curves when he grinned. "Picked it up in Berlin over Christmas."

Milo Cahill looked younger than the late forties she knew him to be, with his wide blue eyes and small rosy mouth. His tan came from a high-priced salon. He usually wore a hat, and C.J. suspected it was not an affectation but vanity: hiding his bald spot. People assumed he was gay. The truth, C.J. had found out, was more complicated: he didn't like the physical act of sex; it was enough to surround himself with beauty, or the oddities that he judged to be beautiful.

Born to faded gentry in Charleston, Milo had gone to Duke University on scholarship. A genius, undeniably offbeat, Milo was a man who could glide without a ripple among the wealthy and cultured as easily as among drunks and addicts, sports stars and models, artists, actors, and various other cheerful wackos who drifted at the edge. It was they, he had once told an interviewer, who gave him his creative kick.

Before he was thirty, *Time* magazine named Milo Cahill one of the "Top 50 Future Leaders in the Arts." At forty-one he had been short-listed for the Pritzker Prize for his contributions to architecture. But Milo's plans required immense budgets, and he refused to compromise. Jobs dried up. He was reduced to designing furniture made of recycled plastic for a discount chain. Deep into a bottle of bourbon, he had confided to C.J. that he nearly wept with shame every time he cashed a royalty check. She hadn't seen him in a while, but she'd heard he was doing a big project in Miami, something about a residential tower with solar panels or windmills.

They had met in Los Angeles when C.J. had been living there, married to a TV anchor and working at her first job out of law school for a top-rated criminal defense firm. Milo Cahill had been the lead architect on a civic center in Malibu. Driving through a thunderstorm, he swerved to avoid a car and skidded into a tree. He came away with a broken arm, but his passenger, a thirteen-year-old boy he'd picked up hitchhiking, died at the scene. The boy's parents sued. This was C.J.'s first big case. She won the trial, saved Milo Cahill's reputation, and became a celebrity herself when he swept her into his glittering circle of friends. She moved to Miami and for years didn't hear from him, until one day he phoned to announce he'd just bought a house on Miami Beach, come on over, have a drink.

Milo smiled at her. "Would you like an early dinner? We could go to my place and call out for Thai."

"It sounds wonderful, but I'd better get back to my office. You're not in trouble, are you?"

"Me? No, it's just a favor for someone. Well, for myself too, in a roundabout way." He leaned toward the intercom and pressed a button. "Jason? We're going downtown to Ms. Dunn's office. The Met Center."

"Jason is gorgeous," she said.

"Brains, too. He has a degree in architecture from Princeton."

"If he's that smart, why is he driving your car?"

"He's just thrilled to be working for Milo Cahill. He'd take out my garbage if I asked him to."

"You have no shame," C.J. said.

The driver skipped the exit to the expressway and continued straight on Seventeenth Avenue, crossing the river. C.J. guessed they would go through East Little Havana, then north on Brickell Avenue, cross the river again, and finally arrive at the seventy-six-story skyscraper that dominated the Miami skyline.

"Who's the someone you need a favor for?" she asked.

"Have you watched the local news in the last couple of days?"

"I've been in trial."

"Well, it seems that a young lady by the name of Alana Martin vanished after, or during, a party at Billy's house last Saturday night. Alana is one of those girls on the fringes of the club crowd. Pretty little thing. Twenty years old. Venezuelan, I think."

"A party at Billy's house? Which Billy?"

"Yours. Guillermo Medina. It was an after-party that got going around ten o'clock. The main party earlier was a reception at the

Sony studios for Yasmina. She's from Lebanon. She was nominated for a Grammy last year. Have you met her? Why am I asking? You've been locked in your law office for months. We never see you anymore."

"Were you at Billy's?" she asked.

"Not for long. I ducked out as soon as I could. I can't stand those pointless millings-around. Alana Martin wasn't at the reception because it was invitation only, but she showed up at the after-party. And . . . poof! Gone. It's been almost a week. Her parents were on the news last night, asking for help locating her. She prob'ly ran off with a man she'd just met. She could have overdosed in some crack house in Overtown. They say she was doing drugs."

"Billy hasn't told me about this." She added, "Not that I've seen him lately."

"He isn't involved. He can't tell you if she was there or she wasn't. You know how people come and go at Billy's. He's in the clear. The person I need the favor for is Congressman Paul Shelby. One of his employees was at the party, supposedly the last person to see this girl alive. If that's true, it could look bad for Shelby."

C.J. finished the Perrier and screwed the cap back on. "I'll tell you up front, I'm no fan of Paul Shelby. Since when did you ever care about politics?"

"I *don't*. I care about The Aquarius. Please don't say you haven't heard of it. The Aquarius is revolutionary. It uses almost no energy, and it'll be a snap to hook it up to a desalination system. Problem is, there's not much waterfront left at a reasonable price, so we're looking into some unused federal land that's just sitting there, going to waste. Paul Shelby is on the Finance Committee, and he's pushing it for us. He says if the Committee approves, which it will, Congress will go along."

"What federal land?"

"About fifty acres down in the south part of the county, off Card Sound Road. Back in the sixties, the Navy used it for a listening post. Right now it's just weeds and rocks."

"So how is this a problem for Shelby? Or for you?"

"I'm getting there. He's up for re-election this fall, and the Democrats want his seat. They're looking for anything against Paul, *anything*. He was at the party, too—just dropped in and out long enough to thank Billy for that nice article he published in *Tropical Life*."

"Is Billy investing in The Aquarius?"

"Sure. He's staking his last dollar on it, so he's biting his nails like the rest of us. He didn't tell you? Oh, well, that's Billy." Milo put an imaginary key to his lips and turned it. "You didn't hear it from me."

C.J. lifted her brows. "And what is Shelby getting out of it? Or should I even ask?"

"No, no, not a dime. Honestly, C.J., he isn't. The tricky thing here is the girl. She disappeared from a party attended by Paul Shelby, at which the main entertainment was a woman from the Middle East who openly opposes our foreign policy. Then someone on Shelby's staff is suspected of—of kidnapping? Or murder? The Finance Committee will abandon him. There goes the project. It's enough to make me want to cut my wrists."

"And Paul Shelby has no financial interest?"

"He doesn't need to. He's loaded."

"That never stopped a politician. Tell me why he's supporting a project in green architecture when he has one of the *worst* environmental voting records in Congress."

"He's had a change of heart," Milo said.

"Try again."

"It's true! Well . . . it's probably true. Go ahead, accuse him of paying attention to which way the wind blows. The voters want green. The Aquarius would do a lot for his image."

"So it's just a public relations issue for Paul Shelby?"

"*Just?*" Milo closed his eyes and laid a hand over his heart.

"Whose idea was it, getting me involved? His?"

"No, it was mine. I haven't told him yet. They think they can handle it. They can't. They don't see the potential for disaster. It's not a big deal yet, and if it's managed correctly, it won't be."

"If something happened to this girl, it's a big deal to her family."

"Yes. All right. But so far there's no national media interest. A girl is missing. It happens. But she did disappear from a party on South Beach, with all the connotations that go with it. I'm sorry for her folks, but she's not a girl who will generate much sympathy."

C.J. shook her head. "I think what you need is a very quiet, well-connected public relations adviser. Want me to recommend someone?"

"I want *you*. This could blow up, and who else could I trust to handle it as well as C.J. Dunn? She's brilliant. She's beautiful. The media love her."

"Don't try to sweet-talk me, Milo."

He stared out the window as they paused at a stop light. The brim of the hat put a shadow on his face. On the opposite corner, men lined up outside the little window of a bodega. How they drank Cuban coffee in this heat, C.J. could not understand. A matron waddled across with her shopping bags. Past four o'clock, traffic getting heavier. A few blocks on, the chauffeur turned left onto Brickell Avenue. Soon they would arrive at her office.

He sighed. "I swear to you, if I have to go back to designing cheap bed frames and wall units, just shove me out of the car now and run me over."

"Milo." She squeezed his hand. That brought another sigh. She set the empty bottle into the cup holder on the bar. "Who is this person working for Shelby? What's his name? What does he do?"

The car headed north on a boulevard shaded with banyans. Sunlight reflected off the windows of the bank buildings and flickered through the trees.

"His name is Richard Slater. He drives the congressman and his wife to events and things. He takes their kids to soccer practice. He picks up the dry cleaning."

"So he's a chauffeur. Good. We're not talking about the inner circle. Did he take Paul Shelby to the party at Billy's that night?"

"He did."

"Shelby stayed only a little while, correct? Did his driver take him home?"

"No, Paul let him go and took a taxi."

"But the driver stayed. How long was he there?"

"Who knows?"

"He could have left with Alana Martin."

"I hope not," Milo said.

"Was he involved with her sexually? Or in any other way?"

"He denies he knows her at all."

"He might be lying," C.J. said. "Has he made any statements to the police?"

"He's managed to avoid them so far."

"Is that so? Maybe he's had prior experience with the cops. Who actually hired him?"

"Paul Shelby approved it. Slater was recommended by a security company."

"Fine." C.J. returned to her corner of the backseat. "Here's what you do. Tell Shelby to let Mr. Slater go. Fire him. If the media or the police ask questions, direct them to the company that sent him."

Milo chewed on his lower lip. "Well . . . some of the folks on his staff would agree with you, but Paul doesn't want to do that. What if this man doesn't like being fired?"

"Tough. Give him a severance check."

"I said, Paul won't do it." Milo's voice rose. "Are you being obtuse on purpose? He's in a delicate position. He can't just go around axing people. No telling what would happen."

Surprised by this outburst, C.J. was silent for a moment. "The congressman doesn't trust Richard Slater to keep his mouth shut. Is that it? What would he say, I wonder?"

Milo slumped into his seat. He took off his Panama hat and held it on his lap, bouncing the brim on his knees. "He could make up anything. Paul Shelby wears women's underwear. His wife beats their kids."

"You want me to get the police off Mr. Slater's back, is that it?"

"I think some degree of loyalty is called for." From Milo's wounded expression, C.J. could only believe he was talking about her.

"Who's going to pay for this? Not Slater, not on his salary."

"Paul Shelby will. I'll tell him he has to. He's sticking by his loyal employee." With a smile, Milo added, "You can charge him whatever you feel it's worth."

Tires hummed over the metal grid of the short bridge across the Miami River. She picked up a shoe. Crossing her legs, she fastened a buckle. The angled blue glass surfaces of the Met Center filled the windshield. The limo turned, circling around to the entrance.

"I'm going to pass. I've been running flat out for weeks. There are several excellent lawyers who could do this. I promise, Mr. Slater will have one of Miami's best holding his hand when he talks to the police. Paul Shelby's name won't come up."

Milo shook his head. "C.J., my love, it's a big mistake, saying no. You need a case like this. Ask me why. Go on."

She smiled. "Why do I need this case, Milo?"

"To get your pretty face on TV."

"Who said I wanted my face on TV?"

"You did, last time you deigned to cross the causeway to raise a glass with poor old Milo."

"I don't drink anymore." She buckled the ankle strap of her other shoe.

"You don't do a lot of things anymore." He set his hat aside and turned toward her. "Being a celebrity is hard work. It requires being out there, getting known, taking on the right jobs so you can keep on being known. There are other lawyers snapping at your heels, ready to snatch it all away."

The limo stopped under the curving portico of the Met Center. Tropical plants in massive pots cast shade on the sidewalk. She took her sunglasses out of her tote. "I just won an acquittal for Harnell Robinson. You'll see my face on TV tonight, if you're interested. My practice is in damned good shape."

The chauffeur's door came open. Milo scooted forward to press the intercom button. "Stay where you are, Jason. We're still talking."

"I have things to do," C.J. said.

As if confiding a secret, Milo scooted closer and whispered, "You only got the Harnell Robinson case because I gave him to you. What else do you have in the pipeline? Anything good? Before Harnell, you were doing a divorce for a Chevrolet dealer. Is that what you are now? A divorce attorney?"

"Stop it, Milo."

"Running flat out. Poor little thing. It sucks. Work, work, work. Never go to parties or see your friends. Have your dinner standing up at the sink. Never any time with your sweetie-pie. How long is he going to wait?" Milo lunged across her and grabbed the door handle to keep her from opening the door. "Come on, now, don't be like that. Milo knows what you want. He can help you get it."

His arm lay across her lap, blond hair on golden skin. His shirt was a pattern of yellow and blue surfboards. She smelled expensive cologne, felt the heat of his torso on her legs. "Milo, get off."

He smiled up at her, his light brown hair falling away from his forehead. He smiled and his cheeks pushed his eyes nearly closed, leaving a narrow glimmer of blue. "Couple of months ago, one of the producers at CNN contacted you. They had an idea, a show about celebrities on trial for murder, and they needed an attractive woman lawyer to host it. Billy told me. Don't get mad at him. He was proud they asked you."

"Well, I haven't heard back."

"'Course not. It takes time. You know Donald Finch? You know who he is? He's married to Paul Shelby's mother, Noreen. Donald Finch's sister is an executive at CNN. Isn't that something? I'll bet you a dollar that if I talk to Paul, he could pull some strings. Paul and I were fraternity brothers at Duke, did I tell you? He won't turn me down. What do you say?"

C.J. took a breath. Her chest felt tight. "I don't know."

"You do too. You'd be perfect. Beautiful, smart, fast on your feet. And no pushover. No, ma'am." Milo reached up and pinched her cheek, then swung around and sat beside her. "That's how it goes in the world. It's small at the top. Everyone's connected. Sideways, up, down. Membership is restricted, though. You're rich or you're famous, or you know somebody."

He held her hand and smoothed her fingers over his. He played with her diamond-and-pearl ring. Her nails looked good, and she was glad, and then she wondered why she cared. She shouldn't. Milo was a friend. And yet it did matter.

He said, "How old are you?"

"Have you forgotten?"

"No, but say it."

"Thirty-seven. What's your point?"

"Three years till you're forty. You've got intelligence and depth and a great voice and tons of poise, but what else do the TV folks look for? Youth. Energy. They want lovely young people with good complexions and tight bodies. It's not fair, but that's what it is. You should grab this job before it's too late. Don't let it go by."

C.J. felt dizzy. The possibilities burst in her head like fireworks. She did want it. She had never wanted anything as much.

chapter
THREE

ischman Farmer and Bates occupied a full floor halfway up Tower One of the Metro Miami Center. The view was impressive, the furniture sleek, and the walls paneled with rosewood. In the hush of the lobby, one would not hear the clatter of the engines of litigation, the crash of multimillion-dollar deals brought to earth, or the twenty-four-seven hum of the billing department.

As C.J. Dunn strode down the corridor, a ripple of applause followed in her wake. Paralegals and secretaries stood up at their desks. A senior partner in the civil litigation division came out to see what the commotion was about. He nodded to her. "C.J.! Heard you kicked butt today. Can you get me season tickets for the Fins?"

She laughed. "I'll see what I can do."

Henry was waiting outside her door. His wide smile said he'd been the one to deliver the news: a verdict of not guilty for Harnell Robinson. She took his hands. "We did it."

"We? You were terrific."

"Modesty, Henry, is not a virtue in this business." She patted his chest and went into her office. "I want you to do a letter to Harnell. Thanks for allowing us to be of service, *et cetera*. We'll both sign it, but it doesn't go out until we get paid. Grab a pen. I have some other stuff for you to do."

Henri Jean Pierre, whom everyone called Henry, was of Haitian descent, two years out of Harvard Law, a good-looking man, fluent in four languages. His father had been tortured to death by the Ton-Ton Macoute. His mother, pregnant with Henry, had fled in a wooden fishing boat with twenty-six others. Spotted by the Coast Guard a hundred yards short of Miami Beach, the boat captain forced everyone overboard. Half of them drowned, but Henry's mother crawled ashore. C.J. made sure this story found its way into Sunday's edition, the day before trial started.

She stepped around a file box and over a stack of ABA journals to be tossed. Nobody was allowed to rearrange the mess: papers, books, CDs of depositions, framed photos of the desert still to be hung, and oddball gifts from clients. Across one arm of the sofa lay a Mexican blanket she'd brought from California. She had spent the night on that sofa more than once, too exhausted to drive home.

C.J. tossed her tote and jacket into a chair and went over to the windowsill and picked up her orchid mister. It was a lovely little thing, brass with a wooden handle. As she walked along spraying her orchids, she gave Henry a list of instructions. Going out, he nearly collided with her secretary coming in with a mug of herb tea and a stack of phone messages. The mug had been a promo item for *War of the Worlds*. One of the producers back in L.A. had said sure, take it. C.J. thought the title nicely summed up her average work week.

She leaned over to examine the stem of a phalaenopsis orchid. After one gorgeous burst of yellow petals three years ago, it had stubbornly refused to bloom. She misted the thick roots that snaked across the top of the pot. "Shirley, could you find me a copy of today's *Miami Herald?* Just the first section and the local news, never mind the rest of it."

Shirley Zuckerman, nudging retirement age, had flame-red hair and a shape like a matchstick. Silver and gold bracelets slid up and down her skinny arms when she moved. Unmarried, childless, and petless, Shirley could spend sixty hours a week at the firm without a complaint. C.J. had gone through five secretaries before finding one who could keep up with her.

Shirley had put the messages in order of priority, most important on top. Calls from prosecutors on current cases. One from a judge's office. An inquiry from a potential client in Palm Beach. Two requests for interviews, but not about the Robinson case, unfortunately. C.J. stopped at the next slip of paper. She saw an area code from north Florida. And a name. Fran Willis.

"Oh, Christ, now what?"

"She called about five times today asking if you were in yet. She wanted your cell phone number. She said it was important. Should I have text-messaged you?"

"No. It's always important with this woman, you know that."

She flipped through the rest of the messages. Request to speak at a bar association luncheon. A deposition rescheduled. Her suit was ready at the tailor's. As Shirley wrote down instructions, C.J. took off her high heels. She knelt and reached under the sofa, feeling around until she found a well-worn pair of pink suede Chanel flats with black patent toe caps.

"Do a letter to Judge Ritter at the Third DCA. Yes to the bar association. No to the women's club, but say it's a scheduling conflict."

With a quick glance at her watch, Shirley gasped, and her penciled copper brows shot up. "Yikes. It's almost five o'clock."

C.J. smiled. "That's right, you're sneaking off to Orlando for a wild weekend with the girls. This can all wait till Monday. I'll do the letter to Judge Ritter myself. Just one thing before you go. *The Miami Herald?*"

"Be right back." Shirley rushed out in a flutter of tie-dyed Indian skirt and jangle of bracelets.

The message from Fran Willis was still on C.J.'s desk. *Urgent.* Shirley had put the word in quotation marks.

Frances Willis used to belong to the same church as C.J.'s mother in a small town thirty miles south of the Georgia border. Fran was living farther west now, in Pensacola, Florida. Several months ago, Fran's teenage daughter and a friend had driven to a cheap hotel on Miami Beach, where the friend's car had collapsed and died in the parking lot. They had decided, with the wisdom of youth, that they could blow off their final semester of high school and make up the credits in summer school. Both sets of parents drove six hundred miles, one end of the state to the other, to bring them back, but Kylie refused to leave. She wanted to get a job and an apartment and take her GED. And then what? The ultimate goal was still fuzzy, but at seventeen, did she care?

Since C.J. Dunn was the only person Fran knew in Miami, she had presumed upon an old connection. Fran was afraid something terrible would befall her daughter. Miami was a dark and dangerous city with drugs and illegal aliens everywhere. Drivers would run you over if you got in their way. You couldn't go into a store and expect to get waited on in English.

Not really wanting to get involved, because how do you ever escape once you're pulled into this sort of thing, C.J. called Billy Medina for suggestions. On his way to Antigua or Aruba or wherever, he turned it over to one of his assistants, who made the arrangements. A room in the apartment of Rosalia Gomez, who used to keep house for Billy's aunt in Puerto Rico. A job at the offices of *Tropical Life*, where Kylie would run errands for ten dollars an hour. Perfect.

C.J. had gone to the hotel where Kylie was staying. She was a tiny thing, couldn't have weighed more than ninety pounds. Long brown hair framed a delicate face, and gray eyes peered out from behind wire-rimmed glasses. The girl admitted to having less than fifty dollars in her wallet, so C.J. gave her fifty more and drove her and her backpack to the old lady's apartment downtown. She handed her a bus schedule and directions to the magazine's offices and told her she ought to be grateful.

Surely it wouldn't be long, C.J. had thought at the time, before the girl got tired of living like a pauper and slunk back to Pensacola. That hadn't happened. Her mother would call periodically and expect C.J. to do something about it. What C.J. always told her: Kylie was fine. If not, someone would have raised an alarm.

At the moment, there were other things to attend to, starting with her newest client, the chauffeur—assuming that Milo Cahill hadn't been blowing smoke. C.J. reached for the phone and punched in a local number.

She heard a *hello* against a background of light classical music. Judy Mazzio turned it down and said she was parked outside a love motel on South Dixie Highway, waiting for her client's cheating husband to come out, and with luck she'd catch him and the girlfriend on video. Judy was a private investigator in business with two former bail bondsmen, who provided the muscle if need be. She asked how the Robinson case had turned out. Was there a verdict? Judy Mazzio had an interest because she'd provided the unsavory details on most of the state's witnesses.

"Not guilty," C.J. told her.

"Way to go!"

"Thanks. And you too. What I'm calling about," C.J. said, "is the girl who disappeared from a party on South Beach last weekend, Alana Martin. Have you heard about it?"

"It's been all over the news."

"I may have a new client. Supposedly he was seen with this girl. His name is Richard Slater. He's a chauffeur for Congressman Paul Shelby. That's about all I know. I have no address, DOB, or social on Slater. Could you call your friend with the Beach P.D.? If they're trying to talk to him, they'll be able to provide enough so we can do a background check. See what you can find out."

"How soon do you need it?"

"Tomorrow if possible. I might be meeting this guy over the weekend, and it would be nice to have some info in advance."

"Sure, I can call right now," Judy said. "All I'm doing is keeping my nose pointed at room number six. Listen, it's Edgar's night to host the poker game, and he wants me to come too. He's ordering barbecued ribs. You should join us."

"Ribs? I can barely fit in my jeans as it is."

"Oh, shut up. I'm the one with the big ass. So, do you want to play some poker tonight?"

"And let Edgar clean out my wallet again? I don't think so. I'll check with you when I get home, probably around eight o'clock. I've got some things to finish here first."

Edgar Dunn, age eighty-seven, was her late husband's uncle. Edgar lived in a cottage behind her house, originally meant for maids' quarters. He had known Judy Mazzio in Las Vegas. She'd been a blackjack dealer, and Edgar loved to gamble. He used to fly out there with his friends several times a year. When Judy got tired of the scene, he suggested Miami. C.J. thought Edgar probably had a crush on Judy, which she found cute.

Just as C.J. was hanging up, Shirley brought Friday's paper, neatly folded. C.J. shooed her out. "Thanks. You'd better run before traffic gets too snarled."

"Have a good weekend," Shirley said from the doorway.

"We live in hope," C.J. muttered. Sipping her tea, she unfolded Section A. There was nothing about Alana Martin. She turned pages. Nothing. She picked up the local section, saw the story below the fold: *Woman Still Missing on South Beach.*

There was a photograph, a snapshot of a young woman with dark hair and a big smile, the face made pale by the camera flash. It had been clipped out of a group shot, other people's shoulders at the edges of the photo.

Alana Martin, 20, was reported missing last Tuesday by her employer after she failed to report to work at China Moon, a women's clothing boutique on Lincoln Road. According to neighbors, Martin had gone to a party on Saturday night at the Star Island home of Guillermo Medina.

Medina, 48, is the publisher of *Tropical Life.* He stated that Martin was not on the invitation list and that he did not recall seeing her among the more than 150 guests.

Martin, born in Venezuela, moved to Miami in 1997 with her family. She is described as 5'3", 100 pounds, with brown hair and eyes. Anyone with information is asked to contact the Miami Beach Police.

C.J. opened her desk drawer for some scissors and cut out the article. There had been no mention of Paul Shelby's driver, which she considered a positive sign. On the other hand, it could mean the police weren't interested in him anymore, in which case Milo had panicked over nothing . . . and she could kiss the job at CNN good-bye.

Her watch showed just past five o'clock. She shoved the paper aside and grabbed the remote for the television, which sat on a credenza across the office. The lead story on all channels was not the Robinson case, as she'd hoped, but the drought and tougher water restrictions. Reporters stood in front of browning lawns, and the owner of a car wash complained about cutbacks.

"Come on, come on."

C.J. put two channels on the screen at the same time, hit the mute button, and returned a couple of phone calls, walking around with the remote in her hand, one eye on the television. Libi Rodriguez appeared, big brown eyes, glistening lips, and teeth so white they fluoresced. She was standing in front of the gate across Billy Medina's driveway. C.J. apologized to the attorney on the line and quickly ended her call. She aimed the remote at the screen.

"—no leads in the case so far, and Alana's parents fear the worst."

They had been posed side by side on their living room couch, with a girl and two boys huddling close to fit into the shot. The mother, short and plump, wore a knit top, the father a blue shirt with his name over the pocket. They spoke through a translator. The text at the bottom said Luisa and Hector Martinez.

On her knees, the wife held what looked to be an eight-by-ten high-school graduation photo. Alana Martin—originally Martinez, no doubt—smiled with one side of her ripe little mouth, a combination of sexuality and boredom. Libi prodded to get them to say how much they loved her.

Then another view of Billy Medina's mansion, daytime file footage shot on his pool deck, Billy among his guests, wearing sunglasses and a white linen shirt, cocktail glass in hand. He had his other arm around the waist of a lanky blonde in a sarong tied at her hip. C.J. had been there. The event had been more than two years ago, but to hell with relevance.

"Just say it, why don't you? Billy Medina has Alana Martin chained in his bedroom as a sex slave."

Libi reappeared. She seemed intensely concerned. "Where is this young woman? Where could she have gone? Which of the celebrity guests at this exclusive Star Island mansion was the last to see Alana Martin? If you have a lead, call the Action Team at Channel Eight."

"Work it, Libi."

"When we come back, an exclusive interview with Dolphins star Harnell Robinson, acquitted today of aggravated battery. Did the jury reach the right decision? You decide. Keep it right here. This is Libi Rodriguez, Channel Eight News, your inside connection."

C.J. knew that after dissing Libi on the courthouse steps, she would see no reference to Robinson's attorney. She went through the other channels and caught a glimpse of herself walking out of the courtroom with her client. She hit the record button on the TiVo. A producer at CNN might want to see what she looked like. C.J. studied her new hairdo. It looked great. It should, for three hundred dollars. She watched herself speaking, the camera coming in close. The woman on the screen had blue eyes, full lips, and high cheekbones.

At the firm in Los Angeles, her boss had said one reason he'd hired her was that he didn't want a dog sitting next to him in court. Far from being offended, C.J. learned what to wear, how to do her hair and makeup, when to smile, when to show outrage. It was a game, and she was good at it.

The screen spun into wild gyrations, then an ad for a local car dealer. C.J. turned it off.

She went over to her desk, picked up her phone, and dialed the number that Billy Medina didn't give out to just anyone. His voice mail picked up.

"Hola, Señor Medina. It's me. Weren't you supposed to be back in Miami today? I hope you bring some rain. We're turning into the Sahara. Listen, I need to talk to you. It's about that girl at your party, the one they can't find. I may be getting involved. Milo roped me into this, and it could work out well. Have you ever heard of Rick Slater? He's Congressman Paul Shelby's driver. He could be my next client, and I know nothing about him. Call me as soon as you can, all right?"

No kiss into the phone. Billy wasn't the warm, cuddly type.

In Miami only seven years, C.J. had risen to an equity partnership, head of Tischman Farmer's three-attorney criminal division. She had arrived with the sparkle and flash of a big-name Los Angeles practice. Though her division didn't rack up the monstrous profits of the banking and litigation divisions, the executive committee liked the good PR, the free advertising, and the occasional spin-off client who believed that paying large fees was a confirmation of his manhood.

Flip back the calendar twenty years, most people would have said Charlotte Josephine Bryan was destined for hard times. The only thing her father had left her was a taste for alcohol. Her mother tried to keep her on the right path with prayer, and, when that didn't work, the back of her hand. They hadn't spoken since C.J. flew back from L.A. for her father's funeral. Her mother informed her she was damned to the eternal flames of hell. In those days, it may have been true. The last C.J. had heard, her mother was living in Knoxville, Tennessee, with her second husband, a Baptist minister.

On her desk, C.J. noticed the pink message slip with Fran Willis's name on it. She was tempted to let the message sit there until Monday, but the word *urgent* tugged on her conscience. She punched in the number, shook back her hair, and waited. Tapped her fingers on her elbow.

Three rings. Four. A faint voice came on the line. "Hello?"

"Fran, it's C.J. Dunn returning your call."

"Oh, my goodness, I've been trying to reach you for three days. They said you were in trial, but I thought maybe if you had a break, you could—"

"I'm so sorry. I was completely tied up. If you're worried about Kylie, you shouldn't be. They know to call me if anything happens."

"No, I spoke to her myself the other day. She says she's all right. What we want, her dad and me, is for her to come home. I've talked to the principal at her high school. If she enrolls this fall, she can graduate in January."

"Great. What does Kylie say?"

"Well, I think she's finally willing to give it another try. I told her it's important to finish school. You know about that, I mean, with all your education, and going to law school and everything. I said to Kylie, you're such a smart girl, don't you want to make something of your life? I *think* I got through to her, but it's hard to be sure. Sometimes you might as well be talking to a tree stump."

C.J. paced with the phone at her ear. "Fran, my secretary just signaled me. I have a call waiting. What is it you want me to do?"

"I'm sorry to take up your time, but I don't know who else to turn to. You promised to look after her."

Promised? C.J. bit her tongue, then said gently, "What do you want me to do, Fran?"

"Okay. What I wanted to ask you. Kylie has to get home, but we're so strapped right now. They laid Bob off at the gas company, and he can't find anything else, things being like they are up here, and with school around the corner, and the kids needing clothes and things, well . . . I checked all the airlines to find something cheap, but at the last minute, they really stick you!"

"It's all right. I'll buy the ticket."

"We'll pay you back. I'm sorry I have to ask. Seems like I'm always asking for help for Kylie, and I shouldn't."

"Fran, stop. It's okay. You don't have to pay me back. I would be happy to help."

"All right. Thank you." Fran Willis's mood seemed balanced between gratitude and anger. She made a nervous laugh. "Lord, if I added up all you've given us, I'd be paying it back a long time." She hesitated, then said, "Can you make sure she gets to the airport?"

"I suppose so."

"You'll take her yourself, right?"

C.J. tapped her nails along the edge of the desk. "If I'm not able to, I'll have someone else do it. Don't worry, Kylie will make her flight."

"Well, I'd rather you took her. That way I'd be sure." Fran laughed again. "Last thing we ask you, I swear to God."

"All right. I'll drive her to the airport myself."

"But she has to get on the airplane."

"Why don't I just tie her up and ship her UPS?"

The silence stretched out. Then she heard Fran Willis let out a breath. A screen door slammed somewhere in the house. Finally she said, "If I could go there and pick her up, I would, but I can't.

I can't. It's not like you have no responsibility. You said you'd take care of her. You distinctly said that."

C.J. swung around and paced in the other direction. "On Monday I will have my secretary arrange for a flight. Meanwhile, call Kylie. Tell her I'll take her to the airport. If she signs up for high school, I will send her a check for five hundred dollars. All right? I'm sorry, but my other call is still waiting. I have to go."

She disconnected and took a breath.

Her hand was still on the phone when it started ringing. She was tempted to ignore it, grab her purse, and walk out the door. It rang again.

"Yes?" she said sharply.

A man's voice said, "Ms. Dunn?"

"Who is this?"

"My name is Paul Shelby. The receptionist put me through to this number."

A rush of blood went to her head so fast that C.J. had to lean against the desk. She cleared her throat. "Yes, this is C.J. Dunn. My secretary just left, and I don't usually pick up this phone after five o'clock." She paused. "I'm going to assume that Milo Cahill has spoken to you."

"Yes, he has. You and I have never met, Ms. Dunn, but I've heard many good things about you. You might be in a position to help one of my staff."

"Possibly so."

"That would be great, just great. My wife and I are going downtown tonight for a concert, and I was wondering if you could meet me beforehand at the Everglades. Say about six, six-thirty? We're having a pre-concert dinner before going over to hear Arturo Sandoval. Diana is Cuban, you know, and a big fan of Latin jazz. There will be some people with me, but I believe you and I can find a few minutes to talk. Would that be acceptable?"

She had seen Paul Shelby on television more than once, but not face to face in a long time. A very long time. He didn't know who she was. How could he? She wasn't the same person anymore. *You and I have never met. . . .*

Her voice was calm, unhurried. "That's fine. I'll be there at six-thirty."

chapter
FOUR

t he humid blast of summer didn't reach into the Everglades Room, where the air was cool as early spring. Light filtered through palm fronds, mahogany-bladed fans slowly revolved in the high ceilings, and orchids decorated the tables. Huge backlit photographs of water birds in their habitat, of mangroves and sawgrass, swamps and sloughs, created the illusion that one might have wandered into the wilderness at dusk.

Following the hostess past tables and banquettes, C.J. could see through one of the fresh-water aquariums that served as room dividers. Shelby and his party had been given some privacy. When she stepped into view, they turned to look at her. The men rose, and Paul Shelby extended his hand. "Ms. Dunn. Thanks for coming on such short notice. It's a pleasure to meet you in person. Let me introduce everybody. My wife Diana. My mother, Noreen Finch. Her husband Don."

Hands were shaken all around, and Shelby pulled out the vacant chair between him and his mother. He was shorter than he appeared on television, but the wavy brown hair was the same, the gray eyes with lines at the corners, the downward-slanting brows and quick smile. He asked the waiter to bring a menu.

"Just a club soda," C.J. said.

Diana Shelby leaned around her husband. "Oh, have something. An appetizer?"

"Thanks, but I have plans for later. Please go ahead, finish your dinner."

Diana Shelby's gray silk dress and neat brown hair reminded C.J. of a nesting bird. Mrs. Shelby was eating salad, and if she was fighting to stay slim, she was losing the battle.

The congressman's mother had devoured her meal, and only the bones remained of what appeared to have been a whole red snapper. Her platinum blond hair looked sculpted into place. She had to be in her sixties, but a good surgeon had shaved off a decade or so. As she set down her wine glass, her diamond bracelet caught the light.

"How do you like Miami, Ms. Dunn?"

"Very much. After seven years, it grows on you. I have no plans to return to Los Angeles." She realized that they thought California was her home; she didn't correct them.

"Weren't you married to a reporter on Channel Ten? I forget his name."

"Elliott Dunn. We met in L.A. When he was offered the job in Miami, we decided to relocate. Elliott was born here, and he'd always wanted to come back."

"I was real sorry when he died. I liked his style. He had a heart attack, wasn't it?"

C.J. nodded. "Three years ago."

Quick sympathy appeared on Diana Shelby's face. "I remember him. He was an excellent reporter."

"Yes. He was."

"It's Miami's gain that you decided to stay," Paul Shelby said. "Ms. Dunn's a partner at Tischman Farmer."

His mother smiled at C.J. "Donald and I saw you on TV this afternoon. I figured Harnell Robinson would do time, but you sure pulled his fat out of the fire." C.J. couldn't place the accent, but the phrasing said country.

"Don, don't you think she's pretty in person?"

"Very." A smile passed over her husband's thin lips. Donald Finch held onto a rocks glass—probably not his first, judging from the level of his eyelids. The Finches were patrons of the concert hall. C.J. seemed to recall a million-dollar gift.

Noticing that his wife's glass was empty, Finch lifted the wine bottle from the standing ice bucket. "A refill, sweetheart?"

"Just a tad."

C.J. asked, "Are you and Don from Miami, Noreen?"

"No, I can't claim to be a native. Ha! I've only been here forty-five years. I was born in Worland, Wyoming. Give you a dollar if you can tell me where that is. My family had horses, used to rent them out to dude ranches. I grew up shoveling horse shit. Paul did his share of it, too, when we'd go visit." Chuckling, she nudged C.J.'s shoulder. "I think that's what got him into politics."

The line had to be an old one, but C.J. laughed obligingly.

Noreen turned to pinch her husband's lean, tanned cheek. "Donald here is a snotty Upper East Side brat, aren't you? But he's fun. He puts up with me."

"You know it. I like 'em hot."

She playfully slapped his arm. "Don!"

Donald Finch looked to be north of fifty, but he was still attractive, in a dissolute sort of way, with the shaggy, sun-bleached hair of a yachtsman, a square jaw, and a long, narrow nose. His sport coat draped perfectly, and his tie was a sumptuous yellow silk — the same color as his wife's pantsuit, C.J. noticed.

Squinting slightly, he focused on C.J. "Ms. Dunn, I understand you're in the running for a job at CNN. I have a sister who works there. She's on a project in Central America right now, but I think she might come see us. We should invite you over to meet her."

"That would be lovely," C.J. said.

"Do you have a card?"

She took one from her wallet, wrote her cell phone number on the reverse, and slid it across the table. "Call me anytime. What is her name?"

"Sarah Finch. She uses her maiden name. She married a friend of mine from New York. Playwright. Talented guy."

Noreen Finch dusted bread crumbs from her fingers. "Don knows everybody. You wouldn't believe it to look at him, but he studied at the American Film Institute. Heck, you and he could've bumped into each other on the street. He got his master of fine arts degree from there. Oh, let me brag on you a little, Donald."

The waiter brought C.J.'s club soda in a tall glass. Paul Shelby leaned back as the waiter took his plate away, then set his elbows on the table and propped his chin on his fists. So far he had said next to nothing.

Noreen Finch tilted her head. "C.J. Now, that's interesting. Do you mind me asking what that stands for? Not many women have initials as their names."

"I don't use my real name. I don't like it."

"Oh, come on."

C.J. made a dismissive wave. "Not on my life."

After a quick laugh and a glance around the table, Noreen said, "Well, Miss C.J., they say you're a damned good lawyer. Is that true?"

"So they say."

Finch murmured, "Ms. Dunn would like to be another Nancy Grace."

Paul Shelby leaned closer to C.J. "Don't pay any attention to Don."

Noreen said, "It's a compliment! C.J. is famous. She's been on *Larry King Live*. But I'm thinking . . . for a chauffeur, do we want a celebrity attorney? People are going to ask why the big gun? Then you get reporters crawling out of the woodwork, asking questions that don't matter a damn."

This was going in the wrong direction. C.J. set down her glass. "I'm sure the media aren't that interested in me."

"It isn't you I'm worried about; it's my son. They go after anybody in politics these days. It's a blood sport. God help us if this turns into a piece on *Entertainment Tonight*. Some smartass with a cell phone could be watching right now, and we'll see it on YouTube."

"Mother, that's not going to happen."

Donald Finch pulled up his cuff to check the time. "If you keep talking, Noreen, we're going to be late to the theater."

"We have a box. What difference does it make?"

"I happen to like Arturo Sandoval, and I want to see the whole show. Diana doesn't want to be late either, do you, Diana?"

C.J. turned to Paul Shelby. "The police are like anyone else: they respond to power. Call it celebrity if you like. They know me, and they know I don't let anyone step on my clients. If I offer proof that Richard Slater was elsewhere, or that he had no motive to harm Ms. Martin, the police will pay attention. I believe this can be wrapped up within a few days."

"Wouldn't *that* be dandy?" Noreen said.

Diana touched her husband's arm. "Paul, hadn't you better go talk to Ms. Dunn?"

"We can talk here," he replied. "Everyone knows the situation. Ms. Dunn—C.J., we're all sorry about Alana Martin, and equally so for her parents. Diana and I have two boys, Mike and Matthew, and if something happened to one of them—I can't imagine. Of course the police have to question anyone who was at the party that night. They even talked to me, and that's fine. I'm happy to cooperate, but there wasn't much I could tell them. I don't know Ms. Martin, and neither does Rick Slater. That's what he tells me, and I believe him. Rick was in the Army, and I hired him, or one reason I hired him, was to give a fellow veteran a break. Between college and law school, I served as a lieutenant in the Navy for four years, so I feel a kinship to some extent. What I don't do is get rid of people on my staff, good people, just because the police ask to interview them."

Noreen broke in. "You know my position. I'd have fired his ass already. His background is spotty. I don't trust him."

"Oh, Noreen, you can't mean that," Diana protested. "He's wonderful with the boys. He's reliable and courteous. I agree with Paul. Rick had nothing to do with that girl's disappearance."

Shelby said, "I'm not going to fire him."

His mother smiled tightly. "Then you're definitely going to need Ms. Dunn."

C.J. said, "Whether I take this case or not is up to Mr. Slater. Have you spoken to him, Mr. Shelby?"

"It's Paul. Please. I haven't talked to Rick about you yet. He's going to pick us up after the concert. I'll have a few words with him then. As a lawyer myself, I believe I can explain to him how important it is to have representation, even when you've done nothing wrong. He'll make the right decision. Should I give him your phone number? Or would you rather call him?"

"Tell him to call me in the morning. I can make myself available this weekend." C.J. put her folded napkin on the table. "I'm going to leave now, but first I'd like to offer a couple of suggestions. You don't have a *chauffeur*; you have a *driver*. Miami traffic is terrible, and you're concerned about the safety of your wife and children, so you hired someone to help out."

"It's true, I hate to drive," Diana Shelby said. "When I was a little girl, someone crashed into our car, and ever since then—" She gave a little shudder.

"You see? It's dangerous out there. Mr. Slater drives your boys to school and you and your wife to your various appointments. He is always there when you need him. But he's not a bodyguard, no. That has negative connotations. He's a loyal member of the staff. He's gentle, good with the kids."

"He's a golden retriever," Donald Finch said.

C.J. ignored him. "You trust Rick Slater because he's a veteran, a brother in arms. He served his country, and now he is serving a United States congressman and his family."

"Excuse me." C.J. felt a tap on her arm and turned. Noreen said, "Were you at the party at Guillermo Medina's house, the night that girl went missing?"

"No, I wasn't there. Why do you ask?"

"I thought you would be. There's been photos of you and Guillermo Medina in the local pages. Are you a couple? I'm only asking because if you are, it's one more thing for the media to get their grubby little hands on."

After a second, C.J. said, "Mr. Medina and I are friends."

A chilly smile was returned to her. "Well, let's just keep everything low-key. The first priority is to protect Paul. Get this over and done with. No interviews. No appearances on *Larry King*. All right?"

C.J. held her gaze. "You can trust me to do whatever is best for my client." She stood up. "It was a pleasure to meet all of you." Hands were extended again. "Mr. Shelby, could you walk me out?"

Halfway across the restaurant, he stopped to say hello to a man who wanted to introduce him to friends. C.J. walked on, crossing the spacious foyer, moving as far as possible from the crowd gathered around the reservations desk. She found a dim corner past some potted palms. The street was visible through wooden louvers. Sunlight hit the top of the buildings.

She took a breath, and her chest trembled with tension. He didn't know her. She had sat next to him, had spoken to him, had let him shake her moist hand, and he didn't remember her.

If there had been any hesitation when he looked at her, the faintest echo of a memory that just maybe they had met before. . . . She took a breath. "It's fine. It's going to be fine."

She heard footsteps behind her and turned.

With a smile, Paul Shelby said, "I think my mother might have gotten under your skin. I'm sorry about that. She gets a little carried away sometimes."

"No need to apologize." He stood too close, and she shifted away. "But in the future, I'd rather not have to explain myself to four different people."

He held up his hands. "Without question. You know, Noreen was my first campaign manager. I'd have been happy following in my father's footsteps in the insurance business, but she pushed me toward politics, and she was right. I love this job. Mom can be a bulldog, but she's great. Her dad and Ronald Reagan used to go hunting together out west, and she's been to Crawford, Texas, a couple of times. She's pretty well plugged into the Washington scene. I wouldn't be where I am without her."

C.J. smiled. "She wants to see you in the White House."

"That's true, she does." The corners of his eyes crinkled. "Something tells me you're a registered Democrat. No, I don't hold it against you. There's a lot of room in the center, and that's where I want to be, working for the American people. Noreen believes that the way politics are now, any little thing can jump out and bite you, and she's probably right. I have a good feeling about you, C.J. I'm glad you're on the team. You don't have to worry about getting paid. We need to talk about that, don't we?"

"Not at all," C.J. said. "If Mr. Slater wants to hire me, I'll charge him expenses. If you want to take care of it, that's up to you. If you've spoken to Milo Cahill, you know why I'm here. What I would like to know, before committing to anything, is where I stand with Donald Finch. Back in Los Angeles, I used to be able to lift a telephone and get to the right people. I even had an agent. Here, it's not that easy. I would like to have Mr. Finch's help, but I get the distinct feeling that he couldn't care less."

"No, no, Don's just that way. You have to know him. Look. I'll make sure he follows through. That's a promise." Paul Shelby held out his hand. Soft, warm fingers closed around hers. "Deal?"

"Deal." C.J. quickly shook his hand, then pulled away. "Milo tells me you and he were fraternity brothers at Duke."

"Oh, goodness. Yes, that's true. Milo's a character, isn't he? Well, C.J., it's been great meeting you. You have a nice evening, and keep me posted. You'll be hearing from Rick tomorrow."

"One moment." When he stepped back in her direction, C.J. said, "Tell him not to call me before noon. I'd like for you to call me earlier, no later than ten o'clock. There are some things I'd like to ask you."

"Such as?"

"When and why he was hired. Who recommended him. His background. That sort of thing."

"Of course."

From the depths of her tote bag came a melodic chime. "I also want you to send me copies of any documents relating to Mr. Slater. Résumé, employment application, pay records. Monday morning, if possible."

"All right." He glanced down at her tote. "I think your phone is ringing."

"It will stop." She smacked the side as if that might work. "Could I ask why you went to Mr. Medina's party?"

"Why? He invited me. I wanted to hear Yasmina. I'd have gone to that big bash Sony Records threw for her on Lincoln Road, but I was stuck in West Palm Beach giving a speech. Billy said come on by afterward, and I did."

"I wasn't aware you knew Billy Medina."

"Absolutely. He's always been a supporter. He's a great guy. You know, C.J., politicians don't spend all their time making speeches and sniping at each other. We occasionally like to get out and have a little fun. And before you ask, Diana was stuck at home with a bad cold. She knew I was going over to Guillermo Medina's house. Is this important?" He looked at his watch.

"Just one more thing. Richard Slater dropped you off, didn't he? Then what? You told him he could leave?"

"Yes. It was late. I said I'd find my own way home. I didn't think it was fair to make him stick around waiting for me after he'd been on duty for twelve hours."

"Did he tell you he was going to come inside?"

"No, I didn't see him. Later, when I asked him about it, he told me he'd just wanted to take a look around, see what the party was all about."

"How has Mr. Slater managed to avoid talking to the police for this long?"

"Well . . . I think they're extending me a courtesy."

"Power has its privileges?"

He acknowledged that with a smile. "Sometimes it does, but I try not to overstep." He lowered his voice. "What are the chances this thing could blow up?"

"I hope not, but yes, it could. It has all the ingredients. A missing girl. Miami Beach. Money, celebrities. And a link—tenuous, but it exists—to a wealthy, attractive, and very well-connected Congressman with presidential ambitions. The tabloid press are not known for extending courtesies."

Shelby's lips tightened. "I should have fired him. It's not too late."

"No. I think your first instincts were correct." C.J. added, "You're confident he told you the truth?"

"So far I have no reason to think otherwise. If you learn anything different, I'd like to know about it."

"I can't do that. He's my client."

"Of course." Shelby nodded. "Just take care of it, the sooner the better."

"I'll certainly try. Please rejoin your family. I'll talk to you tomorrow."

From her position behind the palms, she watched him walk toward the crowd near the entrance. Watched someone call to him, Shelby not responding until the man grabbed his arm, and then the photogenic smile, laughing, putting his hand on the other man's back. More introductions, more handshakes.

Expelling a breath, C.J. leaned against the wall. "What a phony. What a fucking politician."

She was aware of what she wanted, and that Shelby could snatch it away. Aware that she'd have nothing if his chauffeur told her to get lost. No, not *chauffeur*. Comrade in arms, a brother veteran, who would be left to rot if he became inconvenient.

Finally remembering that someone had tried to call her, she reached into her bag for her cell phone.

The screen glowed with white light. *Billy.*

chapter
FIVE

a yellow sliver of moon hung over the city. The sky had turned dark enough to admit the first pinpricks of stars. Along the seawall behind Billy Medina's house, up-lights skimmed over the trunks of the date palms and illuminated their pale green crowns. The pool glittered as Billy cut through the water, doing his laps.

C.J. hadn't counted; he was already swimming when she arrived. She sat on the edge with her skirt halfway up her thighs and her bare feet on the steps. Billy hadn't greeted her, but their eyes had met as he made a turn, taking a breath, pushing off, his body rippling under the surface.

They had been lovers for almost a year. Before that, their worlds had intersected at cultural events or, more often, the South Beach club scene—the late nights, the hangovers, the tired and trivial chatter, the crowd casting their razor eyes on newcomers, deciding if they were worthy. Billy had never been like that. He wasn't out to matter to anyone. He didn't care. This alone drew people to him, never mind the fact that he was rich and threw A-list parties.

He lived alone, except for the shifting group of friends who came and went. If he had other women, they weren't in Miami. C.J. had never heard any gossip. His ex-wife lived in Boston with their two teenagers. They rarely visited. Billy didn't seem to mind.

Billy dove under, coming closer. His right arm extended. A hand went around C.J.'s ankle, pulling hard, and she laughed and grabbed the handrail. Billy stood up in a cascade of water, raising his arms, pushing back his hair. It was prematurely gray, a contrast to black brows and dark eyes. He had a flat belly and long limbs. Not bad for a man of forty-eight.

He waded closer and kissed her on the mouth with cool, wet lips. Droplets of water fell on her cheek and dotted her silk blouse. "Welcome back," she said.

"How have you been?"

"I won the Harnell Robinson case."

"Of course you did. Let's go in."

He went up the steps and under the palm-frond thatch of the cabana, where he stripped off his swim trunks, careless of anyone going by in a boat. He tossed the briefs aside and ran a towel quickly over his body. He put on shorts and a loose linen shirt and slipped into his sandals. "My flight was delayed, so Maria put my dinner in the refrigerator. I have enough for two. Are you hungry?"

"Starving."

He let her go first through a sliding door, and she felt the air-conditioned chill on her face. A wall of glass overlooked the terrace. The floor was polished marble, and low tables and furniture upholstered in black leather formed several seating areas. Quiet, uncluttered, perfectly clean.

As they passed the dining room, C.J. heard a splashing noise and looked around the corner to see a red-haired man squeezing water out of a sponge into a bucket. He had a perfectly square crew cut, and longer hair in back that touched the collar of his plaid shirt. The tiles under his knees were wet and shiny, and an old beach towel bore the residue of grout that he had apparently been cleaning from the cracks. He was working in a small area in the corner. His name was Dennis something, and he did odd jobs for Billy. Dennis Murphy.

"Hello, Dennis."

He nodded in her direction, then said to Billy, "I'm about done here."

"Looks good. I left you some cash in an envelope on the table."

"Yeah, I got it. Thanks." He folded the towel and went to work drying the floor.

Billy continued toward the kitchen, and C.J. followed. She said quietly, "You didn't hire him for his charm."

"I hired him because I trust him to keep his hands off my stuff," Billy said.

"Why is he replacing tiles?"

"There were some rust spots where that flower thing used to be."

She remembered the metal sculpture, a five-foot-tall burst of flowers planted in a polished plaster base. "What did you do with it?"

"I threw it out. Why?"

"Billy! If you didn't like it, you should have said so before I bought it for you. Don't you remember? The Coconut Grove Arts Festival last February. I said it would look nice in your house."

"You did? I'm sorry, C.J., I completely forgot. How much was it?"

"Six hundred dollars. I don't want the money back. Forget it."

"Awww. You can help me pick out something else."

"I wouldn't dare. Your tastes are way too refined for me."

He laughed. "Come on, you need dinner. We have roast beef on the menu tonight." He went into the refrigerator for a stack of covered plates. "All I have to do is nuke it."

"I don't think I can wait that long." She rummaged through the cheese drawer. "When I saw Milo today, he took me for a ride in his limo. He says the interior is getting ratty, so he's going to have it re-upholstered in red leather."

"That's our Milo."

C.J. found a box of crackers in one of the cabinets. "He told me you're investing in The Aquarius. I assume it's not a secret."

"No, it's not a secret." Billy punched numbers into the microwave.

"Are you in trouble, Billy? With money."

He turned around.

She said, "Milo seems to think you are. Don't give me that look. I'm your lawyer. If you're taking chances on a project that in this market could just as easily go down the tubes, I wish you had sought my advice before you dug yourself further into the hole than you already are."

He held up his hands and laughed. "Not to worry. It's all good. We're golden. This project will take off, and when, not if, that happens, yours truly will be rolling in cash. And here's the best part. I'll have first dibs on a casino. I predict it's going to be on the ballot next year, and this time it's going to pass."

"You're sure," she said.

"Yes, indeedy."

"Well. Great. Would you hand me a cheese knife, please?"

"Don't pout. I'll hire you as general counsel." Billy gave her a knife and went back for silverware and napkins. He set two places at the granite-topped island in the middle of the kitchen. Halogens in frosted glass shades hung from a rail, and his hair gleamed as he went in and out of the light.

"You're insufferable," she said.

"I know," he said.

Watching him move, C.J. cut a small wedge of brie. "Paul Shelby told me you and he are good friends."

"Shelby has a lot of friends. I support him because he's pro-business."

"He's up for re-election this fall."

"Are you asking if we're buying his influence in Congress?"

"Let's just say you're supporting a pro-business candidate."

"But I'm not contributing to his campaign. Do you know why?" Billy leaned his arms on the granite top.

C.J. fed him a bite of cheese. "You don't want Shelby's opponents to start making snarky comments about this deal."

"Exactly."

"What are those?" She had noticed the bottles on the other end of the island, one in a brown wrapper with ornate lettering, the other a squat bottle with an old sailing ship on its label.

"Those? I brought them back from Aruba. I am on a hunt for the world's finest gin." He slid the bottles closer. "This is a Van Wees, from Holland, fifteen years old. The other is Martin Miller's, distilled in London, then shipped to Iceland to be blended with spring water." He slid off his stool and crossed to the refrigerator. "However, for a truly superlative gin and tonic, you need the right tonic." He presented a chilled bottle. "From India, Fever Tree tonic water. Cures you of malaria, dengue fever, and impotence, I expect." He squinted at the label. "What does this say?"

She read, "Bitter orange from Tanzania, African marigold, Sicilian lemons, pure cane sugar."

"I was going to do a taste-test tonight. Want to join in?"

"No, thanks."

Black brows rose. "This gin cost me a hundred and twenty dollars a bottle."

"I'll try the tonic."

"Suit yourself." He brought her an ice-filled glass with a lime wedge, then opened the tonic and poured.

She tasted it. "Nice."

He set out two shot glasses and filled the first with the Dutch gin. "It's not for you. Just taste mine. One drop won't hurt. Don't be a pussy. I need your opinion."

"One sip." She lifted the tiny glass, sniffed, then wet her lips. "This is the Van Wees? Smooth. But worth that price? I don't think so."

He finished it off, then breathed in. "Oh, yes. Good stuff." He filled the next with the gin from London. "Now. Let us try the Martin Miller's."

C.J. turned her head. The longing had come on her so fast she felt dizzy. "Billy, I'd rather not."

"You don't go to meetings anymore. I haven't seen you take a drink in a year. What are you trying to prove?"

"This is bad for me, what you're doing."

"Sorry." He picked up the other shot glass. He sipped, rolling the gin around in his mouth. She could see it wasn't fun for him, drinking alone. He said, "I vote for the Van Wees. Since you're being a Girl Scout, what can I get for you?"

"I'll have a Diet Coke or something."

"On the rocks?"

"Ha-ha." She cut a few slices of cheddar. "Why do you think Shelby wants me to take this case? Milo says he has no financial interest in The Aquarius. Is that true?"

"As far as I know," Billy said as he brought back her cola.

"You think he's trying to ingratiate himself with the environmentalists?"

"I'm sure that's part of it, but he believes this project will be good for Miami, good for development statewide."

"Since when did you trust a politician?"

"Since never. So what?"

"Tell me about Donald Finch," she said.

"Don produced a little comedy set on South Beach a few years back. It wasn't bad, got into the Miami Film Festival. I see him around occasionally, when he can sneak away from the ball and chain." Billy eyeballed his glass and poured in a practiced ounce-and-a-half measure of gin, then filled the glass with tonic. He squeezed the lime wedge and let it drop.

"Is he rich?"

"He used to be. The Finches were prominent in New York City, but Don left town after a dispute with his father, who is now dead. Jesus, this is good. Nearly perfect. I give it a ninety-seven out of a hundred. I don't suppose you want to—"

"No," she said. "Back to Donald Finch. Noreen told me he studied film in L.A."

"That he did. Donald took his inheritance and went to Hollywood. He lived large for a while but didn't accomplish much. That was before you went west. He slunk back to New York, I believe, bounced around on various low-budget productions, and finally wound up in Miami doing PR for the tourist board. Then he met Noreen Shelby. She's older. She's ancient, in fact, but he had what she wanted, a pedigree. He'd like to do more independent films, but Noreen controls the funding. She wants him to do a project on Paul Shelby's rise to fame and glory. So far, it's pretty short."

C.J. asked, "Where did Noreen get her money? Her family raised saddle horses in Wyoming."

"Her first husband, Paul Shelby's father, was big in commercial real estate. He left a very rich widow."

"As rich as you?"

"More. I'm still fighting with Uncle Sam."

"Noreen wants her son to be president."

"He could get there," Billy said.

"Yes, why not? He has money, connections, good hair and teeth, a lovely wife and two sons, and a mother who keeps a copy of Machiavelli's *The Prince* under her pillow."

"What have you got against Paul Shelby?"

"I have nothing against Paul Shelby, particularly." C.J. sipped her cola, which had all the flavor of water. "I just want to know what we're dealing with. You could be drawn into this case, and I'd like to prevent it if I can."

"Me? I've done my duty. I talked to the police. I told them I didn't see the girl here. I gave them a list of guests, those I could remember. They said thank you and went away."

"If they can't find her, they may be back."

"Fine. They'll get the same answers as before. I don't know dick."

"What about Richard Slater?"

"Who? Oh, Shelby's driver. Your new client."

"Maybe—if he lets me represent him. Did you see him that night?"

"Christ, C.J., I don't remember. There were tons of people here. Yasmina was here. She sang. I hired a band for her. Everyone had a good time. You should have come."

"I was in the weeds with the Robinson trial."

"Wait a minute. Now that I think of it, I have met Slater. He was driving when Paul Shelby and his wife took me home from a cocktail party at Milo Cahill's place a couple of weeks ago."

"What's he like?"

Billy let out a puff of air. "What's he like? He speaks in monosyllables. He's about five-ten, big through the chest. Thick neck. Shaved head, a mustache-and-beard combo. He stares right through you."

"Oh, wonderful. I can't wait."

"You prefer clients as handsome as me," Billy said.

"There aren't any." She wound a strand of his silver hair through her fingers, thick and soft as animal pelt. "When did Shelby leave the party?"

"Are we talking business tonight?"

"For now," she said.

"He left a little before midnight, I think."

"But his driver stuck around. I wonder why."

"Drinking my liquor and ogling the models, probably."

"I'm surprised your security people didn't ask him to leave."

"They don't, unless they notice somebody causing a problem."

"I wonder what he was doing with Alana Martin."

"Can't help you there," Billy said.

"Do you know Alana?"

"Until about three months ago she worked for my magazine. She sold advertising. I don't go in more than once a week, you know, just making sure it's still there, but I expect to see people at their desks, not hanging all over the VIPs and celebrities who drop by. I told personnel to get rid of her. She's a fame-fucker."

"For God's sake, Billy, don't say that to a reporter."

"It's true."

"Listen to me," C.J. said. "This is serious. A very pretty twenty-year-old girl was here, then she wasn't. If this turns into a major media event, you're going to see satellite trucks lined up on the street."

"They won't get past the guard at the entrance."

"It's a public street," she said.

"Technically, yes, but the residents of Star Island have an excellent relationship with the chief of police. There's the microwave. Dinner is served."

He brought the food over, a bottle of red wine, and one glass.

They ate in silence for a while. Then he told her about a restaurant on Aruba. He and a couple of his business partners had gone to Aruba to look into investing in a hotel. C.J. assumed nothing had come of it, but, then, he didn't talk much about his work. Just another day at the office. Billy had bought South Florida real estate when it was cheap, then a hotel on Antigua that had a small casino attached.

He said, "Why do you want to do a show on CNN anyway? Those talk shows are inane."

"Mine wouldn't be. I'd have intelligent guests with something to say."

"You'd be famous," he said.

"I could learn to live with that."

"You think so? People in your face all the time. No privacy."

"I'll hire bodyguards to keep the crowds back when I get into my limo."

"Who is that sexy blonde behind the sunglasses?" Billy's smile deepened the lines at his eyes. "C.J. Dunn. Yes, I know her. She slept with me last night, doing unmentionable things."

"Would you still like me if I were rich and famous?"

"I might like you more. Right now, you're only beautiful." He poured himself more wine, and the deep red liquid swirled and made streaks down the glass. The blood-heavy scent of it zinged into her nostrils.

"There's dessert," Billy said. "Some kind of pie."

"God, no, I'm full." She helped him carry things to the sink. The maid would wash them in the morning.

"Are you going to stay tonight?"

"Do you want me to?"

"No. I was asking to be polite."

"Fine. I won't, then," she said.

"It's your loss."

She laughed. "You're horrible. You really are."

He slid his hands up her arms. "Of course I want you to stay."

"All right, but I'm leaving early. I have things to do in the morning."

"Love your enthusiasm," he said.

"I love yours." She kissed his cheek, rough with a day's worth of stubble. The bridge of his nose was slightly out of line, but you had to look hard because a plastic surgeon had done a good job putting it back together.

A year ago, with a blood-alcohol level of one point eight, Billy Medina had crashed his Maserati into a guardrail, his second DUI. Billy's attorney worked out a deal: no jail time if he went to AA meetings for six months. He came to the same small group C.J. had joined, a Methodist church in a nowhere residential district on the Beach. She was avoiding the downtown groups, the lunchtime or after-work meetings where there were far too many other lawyers with alcohol problems. She hadn't recognized Billy at first, with the bandage over his nose, but soon they were going out for coffee after the meetings, or having a late dinner, C.J. stifling her laughter as Billy imitated the sappy stories they'd just heard. They started moving around to other meetings, not wanting to be known, not wanting to get involved with the real drunks, who might ask for favors.

Billy did his six months. C.J. stayed for a while, but she didn't have time, or she didn't like opening herself up to strangers, or maybe it was just too boring without Billy. So she quit too. She had stopped drinking, so what was the point? Her sponsor kept calling for a while, then gave up and wished her well.

The longing to drink still came on her, but not as often, and she was always able to fight it off. What she liked about Billy, among other things, was that he didn't nag her about it. What he liked about her was that she didn't expect him to save her. Whatever she chose, it was up to her. Billy made no demands. He never pushed. If she wanted to be with him, fine. If not, he wouldn't hold her. It was liberating. Sometimes a little lonely, but as Billy would say, if you don't like the view, move on. She had tried to do that. She had tried. She had given up alcohol, but she couldn't give up Billy.

chapter SIX

j udy Mazzio put the handicap tag on her rearview mirror and gave forty bucks to an off-duty cop to let her park beside a fire hydrant down the street from the concert hall.

As people streamed out the main exit doors, a line of cars moved under the brightly lit portico. Judy spotted the congressman and his party coming down the steps, stopping from time to time to greet friends. Handshakes, air kisses, slaps on the back. A big smile on the older woman with platinum hair, the man with her watching the line of cars. Judy raised her binoculars. This would be Noreen Finch, Shelby's mother.

A couple of minutes later, a silver-blue Cadillac sedan approached. Noreen Finch signaled the others, and they went down to the driveway. Shelby paused to shake another hand.

A bearded man with a shaved head got out of the car. Dark suit, open-collar shirt, big shoulders. No wasted motion. But Shelby had already opened the back door, putting the women and his stepfather inside. The congressman got into the front, and the car pulled away.

Pointed the same direction on the one-way street, Judy followed. C.J. hadn't asked her to do this. In her phone call three hours ago she had only mentioned that Shelby's driver would be picking them up after the concert. When the poker game at Edgar's ended early, Judy thought there might be time to take a look at the guy.

What had she learned? Not much.

She followed the Cadillac up the interstate on-ramp, heading south, the mirrored spires of downtown on the left, the low apartments and tree-lined streets of Little Havana on the right. The expressway arched over the river, curved past the turnoff to Key Biscayne, then dumped traffic onto South Dixie Highway. Judy turned up the volume on her satellite radio, the classical station, and settled into her seat. There were no classical stations in Miami, which said something about the culture, but she wasn't sure what.

She stayed just close enough not to lose them. Her gray Camry was as invisible a car as existed, but it had a six-cylinder, turbocharged engine and racing shocks. A couple of miles farther on, the Shelbys' car slowed at a light, then turned north on Riviera Drive. Here in Coral Gables, banyan trees met over the narrow streets and traffic thinned out. Riviera curved right, but the Cadillac went straight on to Biltmore. Judy slowed as its brake lights flared. The Caddy paused at a low, vine-covered wall on the left, waiting for a gate to slide back.

Judy cruised by the house, a sprawling, two-story mansion with a red tile roof and a fountain. She caught a glimpse of the older couple getting out and quickly did a U-turn at the end of the block and parked in someone's driveway with her lights off. When the Cadillac reappeared, she followed it back to South Dixie.

Through the usual heavy Friday-night traffic she kept her eyes on the Caddy's taillights. The driver maintained a steady pace, going the speed limit, signaling before changing lanes, a real Eagle Scout. He cruised past the University of Miami and took a left on Red Road, due south, into narrower streets and heavier foliage. Judy fell back.

They went over a bridge and toward a landscaped traffic circle. As she'd expected, the Cadillac went around, heading toward the low illuminated sign that marked the waterfront subdivision of Cocoplum, where the Shelbys lived. At the guard shack a gate arm went up. Judy kept going around to the small parking area near the bridge, which overlooked a canal. She turned off her lights, slid down in her seat, and adjusted the rearview.

Ten minutes later headlights approached the exit lane, and the gate went up. A dark blue Audi appeared. The side windows were tinted, but the light from the guard shack shone through the windshield. When the Audi had gone around the circle and over the bridge, Judy put her car into gear.

Heading north on Dixie Highway he picked up speed to fifteen miles over the limit, like everyone else. At Twenty-Seventh, he slowed as the light turned yellow, then whipped around another car and blew through the red light.

Caught by the car ahead of her, Judy watched the taillights on the Audi getting smaller. When the light turned green, she gunned the engine and zigzagged through traffic, but he was gone.

She hit the steering wheel and laughed out loud. "Damn. You're good."

chapter

SEVEN

fter two tries on the doorbell, Kylie stepped off the front porch and walked around to the side of the house. The only car under the portico was a twenty-year-old Buick sedan. She had come all this way for nothing. She hadn't called first because it would have been too easy for C.J. to say no on the phone.

She heard a noise from behind the house. It sounded like an electric saw. Kylie followed a mossy brick path to a gate, looked through the bars, and saw shade trees, an arbor with hanging baskets of orchids, and, beyond that, a stucco cottage painted the same white as the main house. A power cord came out the screen door of the cottage, down the steps, and over to the back wall, which Kylie couldn't see from where she stood.

The saw started up again. She tried the latch. It opened.

A long ladder reached the second floor, and a skinny man in a straw hat stood near the top holding a jigsaw against a PVC pipe coming out of the wall. Bits of white plastic flew everywhere. He turned off the saw, hung it on an S-hook, and brushed off the end of the pipe.

Kylie stepped closer. "Excuse me? Sir?"

The straw hat turned. Under the brim she could make out a pair of thick glasses, a small gray mustache, and a face lined with wrinkles. "We're not buying anything."

"I'm looking for C.J. Dunn. This is her house, isn't it?"

"Yep."

"Is she home?"

"Not right now. And who might you be?"

"Kylie Willis. My mother is a friend of hers."

He nodded slowly. "Seems I've heard the name."

"Will Ms. Dunn be back?"

"I expect so. She lives here." He reached into a bucket hanging off another hook and took out a short piece of pipe with a ninety-degree angle. "Said she'd be here about nine o'clock. You're free to wait."

With a sigh, Kylie sat on the bench under the tree. She checked her watch: ten minutes past. A breeze came through, cooling her bare arms and legs. She took off her glasses and cleaned them on the hem of her T-shirt. Five minutes ago, getting out of her borrowed car, she had seen how the street came to a dead end at the water, with a little park at the turnaround, the kind of street she'd live on if she had the money.

"Dad-drat it!" The old man stared down at the grass. "Girl! Get that for me, will you? That little can of PVC cement."

Kylie put her glasses back on, found the can, and went up the ladder. "What are you doing?"

"Diverting water from the shower drain to that barrel there." He unscrewed the cap and painted glue around the end of the pipe coming out of the wall, then daubed the brush into the angled connector. "We're in a drought, in case you hadn't noticed. We used to have dry spells, but not like this."

"Global warming," she said, going down the ladder again.

"No! It's too many idiots moving down here. Greed. Stupidity. We're paying the price now, boy-oh-boy, are we. When I was your age, Miami was a paradise. Pure spring water bubbled right up through the aquifer into Biscayne Bay. There were rapids in the Miami River, till they blew it up with dynamite and dredged it. Bet you didn't know that, did you?"

He pressed the connector onto the end of the pipe, grunting, then reached into the bucket again and came out with a red-handled valve on a threaded piece. He screwed the piece into the connector. "Now give me the hose. It's over there, by the barrel."

He pointed toward a blue plastic barrel lying on its side under a window. She couldn't see into the house; the blinds were closed. She picked up the coil of two-inch-diameter black hose lying in the grass and carried it up the ladder. The man slid it over the pipe, off and on. The uncoiled hose reached nearly to the ground.

She said, "An O-ring might work."

He reached into the bucket and came out with a shiny metal ring. "Like this?" He found a screwdriver and went to work.

"Why do you have a valve on it?"

"If it rains, we don't need the water, do we?"

"But if you close the valve, won't the shower overflow?"

"You're pretty smart for your age."

She put a hand on her hip. "I'm seventeen."

"No kidding." He finished with the clamp, let go, and tossed his screwdriver into the bucket. "It won't overflow. I installed a float and a shutoff valve in there. When the water rises too far, it goes back into the main pipe. I've got it all worked out."

"Sounds good," Kylie said.

"I'm glad it meets with your approval." He put the saw into the bucket and lowered it by a rope. "Hold the ladder, I'm coming down." He took one step at a time as she steadied the ladder. Flecks of paint dotted his scuffed work boots and his loose khaki pants. He wiped his face with a bandanna, which he folded neatly and stuffed into his pocket.

Stooping down to see her through his glasses, he said, "My name's Edgar Dunn." He reached out a big, veiny hand, and she shook it.

"Are you Ms. Dunn's father?"

"No, her husband's uncle. We're not blood kin. She was married to my nephew, Elliott. He passed away. His heart, only forty years old. Damn shame. Are you thirsty? Want some cold apple juice?"

"All right. Thank you."

He picked up the bucket, and she followed him up the steps of the cottage. He opened the screen door for her. Kylie said, "I'll just wait out here."

"Sure, have a seat," he said.

"Holy shit!" A huge green reptile with curved claws on its feet lay on the other end of the porch. Spikes stuck up from its skull and ran down its scaly back and tail. Its eye socket rotated toward her. It opened its mouth and hissed. Kylie backed up a few steps.

"Sorry for cussing." She glanced at the old man. "What is that thing?"

"An iguana. Name's Iggy. They're not native. I reckon somebody let him go when he got too big. He showed up one day with a bite out of him. The vet wanted to put him down, but C.J. wouldn't hear of it. She has a soft spot for strays. Iggy's only got three legs. We feed him good. He won't hurt you."

The old man went inside, and the iguana closed its eyes.

Looking through the screen door, Kylie could see wood floors, an old sofa and armchair. A fan whirred in an open window, lifting the curtains. She sat on the top step and looked across the yard to the main house. Blue-and-white-striped awnings shaded the windows on the second floor, and the back porch had been screened in. A cat lay on a chair looking at her. French doors led into the house, but the lights were off.

The old man—Mr. Dunn—came out with a glass of juice. "I'd join you, but I stink and I need a bath. I can't do much with the water in my place, need to rig a pump. C.J.'s bathroom has gravity going for it." He gestured toward the car port. "Speak of the devil."

The hood of a BMW was visible through the fence. Kylie quickly finished the juice and gave him the glass. "Thanks."

She picked up her bag and headed toward the gate, intending to go around and ring the bell again. She stopped when the back door swung open. C.J. Dunn stood on the top step. "Kylie?"

Designer sunglasses were pushed into her long blond hair. She wore a pink sleeveless blouse, a short gray skirt, and black high heels with ankle straps. Kylie had only seen her once before, when she'd dumped Kylie off at the apartment she'd found for her.

The old man waved from the cottage porch. "The girl's been helping me with the irrigation project."

"Hello, Ms. Dunn!" Kylie walked across the terrace with a bright smile. "I hope it's not a bother, me coming over. I wanted to talk to you personally."

C.J. put a hand on her hip. "Would this have anything to do with the fact that your parents want you home, and you don't want to go?"

"Not exactly. Do you have a few minutes?"

"Barely. I'm expecting a call from a client. All right, come in."

When she turned, she saw the ladder, then the hole in the back of the house. "Edgar? What is this?"

"I'm diverting waste water for the yard plants. I told you about it."

"You were *thinking* about it."

"Well, you take two showers a day," her uncle said. "That's a lot of water. Don't worry about the hole. I'll seal it up this afternoon. In the rainy season I can disconnect the hose and leave a little plate up there for future access."

"You went up that ladder? You could have fallen! You could have killed yourself!"

"Well, I didn't, did I?"

"Promise me you'll stay off the ladder. Tomorrow I'll have a plumber come over."

"And do what, exactly?"

She took his hand. "Edgar, we can't run sewage into the yard."

"Sewage? No, it's just the bathtub. I didn't tap into the toilet. Stop talking to me like I was a child. We've got to do something. If this drought keeps up, we'll run out of water."

She remembered Kylie was standing there. "We'll talk about it later. Kylie, would you come with me, please?"

Kylie wasn't sure what she had expected, but as they went inside she saw dishes in the sink, a dining table strewn with papers, and mismatched furniture in the living room. High heels, bedroom slippers, and empty mugs had been left by the rattan sofa, under the coffee table, and next to a toppling stack of magazines. There was a fireplace and a painted stucco chimney that rose to a high ceiling where two fans hung from extension poles, lazily twirling.

"This is a lovely home," Kylie said.

"It's a freaking disaster. I've been in one trial after another for six months." C.J. didn't offer a seat. She took the sunglasses off and tossed them toward her tote bag on the sofa. "Did your mother call you? I told her I'd fly you back to Pensacola on Monday."

"Yes, she called me."

"Did she mention that I will give you five hundred dollars toward your school expenses if you enroll this fall?"

"That's sort of what I wanted to discuss with you."

"Five hundred dollars is very generous, don't you think?"

"It is, and I really appreciate it." A knock came at the front door, but C.J. didn't notice. Kylie spoke quickly. "I've decided that what I really want to do is attend college at Miami-Dade."

"College? You haven't graduated from high school. You can't stay in Miami. You can't support yourself, your parents haven't got the money, and if you think—"

The doorbell rang. C.J. went over to the window. She glanced through, then walked into the foyer, high heels clicking on tile. The door opened. A woman's voice said, "Sorry I'm late. Did Shelby call yet?"

"No, not yet. I just got home."

"So how was it over at Billy's last night?"

C.J. made some hushing noises as they came around the corner. The other woman was taller and about ten years older, with black hair piled on top of her head and shiny pink lipstick.

"This is Kylie Willis," C.J. said.

The woman seemed to think that was amusing. "Well, hi there, Kylie. I'm Judy Mazzio, a friend of C.J.'s."

"Hello," Kylie said. She was about to ask C.J. if they could finish their conversation when the phone on the end table rang.

C.J. looked at the caller-ID screen. "Why don't you take Kylie over to Edgar's for a while? I have to get this."

"Sure thing. Come on, Kylie."

Kylie looked up at her companion as they crossed the yard. She wore a tight purple top and black crop pants. High-heeled sandals showed off her red nail polish. There was a rose tattoo on her ankle.

"So. You're the girl from Pensacola." A smile crinkled the corners of her brown eyes.

"Yes, ma'am."

"Call me Judy."

"Are you a lawyer too?"

"No, I'm a private investigator. C.J.'s one of my clients." She rapped on the screen door. "Edgar? It's me."

"He might be in the shower." Kylie added, "I met him before Ms. Dunn got home."

"Edgar, you have company!" Judy opened the door and motioned for Kylie to follow. "You want something to drink, honey?"

"No, thanks."

Judy dropped her bag on the dining table and walked into the tiny kitchen as if she owned the place. Kylie glanced around the room, everything neat and tidy, like a dollhouse. She noticed a box sitting open on the floor and looked into it. Photographs. She straightened her glasses and knelt for a closer look. She saw old cars with running boards, a dirt street, a seaplane, men in suits and hats, a woman in a white dress to her ankles.

A door opened, and she stood up. The old man had put on fresh khaki pants and a clean shirt. His gray hair was still damp. "All that stuff's going to the Historical Museum, soon as I finish organizing it, if I live that long." He looked through the bottom of his glasses to see the photograph she held. "My kid brother took that one with a Brownie. He died in Korea. Our dad was the real photo nut. He photographed everything that didn't jump out of his way. Here. Look at this one."

Kylie saw an alligator tied up in ropes. Indians stood alongside, dressed in patchwork clothes.

"Are they Seminoles?"

"Miccosukees. They caught that gator for their tourist camp.

That picture was taken on the other side of the river from where we lived. My brothers and I used to row over there and watch them wrestle gators. Not much of a show. Cost a dime." He turned the photograph over. "Go there now, you find a gas station and a Cuban strip mall. Why oh why don't people write down names and dates? That littlest Indian, the boy, his name was Sam Osceola. Pal of mine. I can't remember the others. You think you'll remember forever, but you don't."

Judy came back from the kitchen stirring a glass of iced tea with a straw. "Edgar, are you boring that girl with your old photos?"

"They're interesting," Kylie said. "You were friends with the Indians?"

"Sure. We used to throw rocks across the river at each other. They didn't go to school. I think we were jealous. When was this? Nineteen-thirty? I need to write it all down before it's too late."

Judy sat in a chair and crossed her legs, swinging her foot. "Edgar thinks he's about to croak. He's been saying that for twenty years."

"Here I am in my army uniform, W-W-Two, the Stone Age. I used to be a good-looking fella."

"He still is," Judy said, and winked at him.

Edgar showed Kylie a photograph of the Orange Bowl Parade. The colors had turned brown, and the faces were fuzzy. "My nephew Elliott was the drum major for the Miami Edison High School marching band. He's dead now. But I told you already. My brain is going."

Judy laughed. "Ask him how much he took off his poker buddies last night. I'm surprised they didn't shoot you."

"They were too drunk to hit the side of a house."

Kylie put the photograph back into the box. "These are really good. You ought to scan the color ones before they're totally gone."

"How's that?"

"You could make digital images and correct the color, not perfectly but a lot better. There are programs for that. But you'd need a computer," she said.

"I have a computer." He pointed at a desk across the room. "I use email and go online. I'm not your typical old fart."

Kylie went over to look. The boxy beige monitor had a twelve-inch screen, and the computer was a kind she'd never heard of. "It's kind of old. If you had a new one, you could make a DVD slide show for your family and friends. You could put your photos online."

He sucked on his upper lip, biting his mustache. "I don't know. Seems like a lot of trouble for something I won't be around to enjoy."

"Why not do it?" said Judy. "It sounds like fun. I'd look at your damned pictures."

The old man looked at Kylie. "How much?"

She shrugged. "Computer, scanner, DVD burner, a printer . . . two thousand?"

"Jesus, Mary, and Joseph."

A cell phone chimed, and Judy pulled hers from a pocket and put it to her ear. She listened, then said, "Kylie, I'm going to hang with this old fart a little longer. C.J. wants you to go on back to her place."

Kylie hadn't slept at all last night after her mother called. She had sat on her bed staring through the tenth-floor window at the dark water of Biscayne Bay. She had seen the streetlights go out and the sky turn pink, then silver blue as the sun rose over the hotels and condos on Miami Beach. She had pictured herself back in Pensacola, wearing a red smock at that part-time job at the Dollar Store, or dating some asshole whose idea of fun was smoking a joint and getting laid, or hearing her father, who was a good man basically, say he wouldn't go to France if you paid him. These thoughts had pulled like weights on her heart, and she wanted to scream and grab her stuff and run somewhere, anywhere. And then what?

She had to admit she'd been stupid. Skipping work, drinking till she puked, borrowing money from Alana because hers always ran out so fast. Last night Kylie's mother had said no sane person would want to live in Miami, but it wasn't Miami that was so bad; people in general were fucked up. If it was bad everywhere, you might as well pick a place that didn't make you want to shoot yourself. There were times when you had to take a chance, and if you didn't, it would be too late. You wouldn't even have a box of fading memories, because you never did anything worth remembering.

"What I have decided to do," she told C.J. Dunn, "is get my GED this fall, then register at Miami-Dade College in January. If I get good grades my first two years, and I will, then I can apply for a scholarship or a loan and transfer to the University of Miami. They have a program in journalism, and I could intern at *The Miami Herald*. My goal is to work at a newspaper or magazine where they cover political issues. I plan to learn Spanish, of course, which is extremely useful in Miami, and I also want to study Mandarin Chinese. In fact, I've already bought some tapes at a used book store. China will surpass the United States in fifty years, and that's not just my opinion."

They sat at the dining room table. C.J. had shoved aside some of her files and papers to make room. She had her forehead in the palm of her hand. Her eyes shifted to Kylie, and she stared at her a long time before she said, "A journalist. Have you ever written anything?"

"Not for a newspaper. I'm still in high school."

"What kind of grades do you get in English?"

"I *know* I can do it. I have a plan." Sliding forward on her chair, Kylie said, "First thing, you need a budget. Miami's expensive, but if you rent a room instead of an apartment, and you don't eat out, and you shop at thrift stores, you can survive. A lot of people are so into, like, buying *things* and having the perfect shoes or an expensive car . . . I don't mean you, of course, but some people. I'm just not into that."

C.J. kept staring at her. Kylie heard the grandfather clock ticking in the corner of the dining room and felt the moment slipping away.

"Okay. My budget. I can work part-time and go to school, but there's a shortfall of five hundred dollars a month. Tuition and books are about four thousand dollars for one semester. If you could lend me enough for my first year, I think I could get a school loan after that. I'll pay you back when I graduate, with interest, of course, more than you would earn from your savings account."

"Kylie." Now C.J. was making little squares in the dust on the table. "You go home, you finish high school, and you attend a local college like other girls your age. It's going to take commitment and patience, which I think you're lacking. There are no shortcuts. I wouldn't be doing you a favor to—"

"It's an investment. You've given money to my mother, and she never paid you back. I will."

"I can't go against what your parents want. They love you. They miss you."

"I know that, but—"

"I'm sorry. This is not open for discussion." She held up her hands. "I promised Fran I would send you home. You have to go."

As the words went on, Kylie felt the weight in her chest again, worse than before. She said, "I will kill myself if I have to live in Pensacola. You don't know how it is up there."

Blue eyes fixed on her. "Yes, Kylie, I do. I was born in Mayo, one traffic light and a water tower. My father couldn't keep a job, and my mother didn't even graduate from high school. Nobody gave me a damned thing. I worked my way through college. I got scholarships. I did it *alone*." She let out a breath. "All right, I'll make a deal with you. When you have your high school diploma, I will pay your first two years at . . . whatever college they have in Pensacola. Then, if you do well, we can talk about the University of Florida. It's a wonderful school."

Kylie said, "But if you're going to help me, why can't I stay *here*?"

"It's not up to me. It isn't my decision!"

"What if my parents say it's all right?"

"They won't."

"They would if you talked to them."

"I can't do that."

"Well, I'm not going back to Pensacola."

"Don't be such a whiny brat. What made you so entitled?"

"That is so hateful!" Kylie stood up so fast her chair nearly tipped. "And you call yourself our *friend*."

C.J. followed her out of the dining room. "I know the publisher of the magazine where you work. You will be out of a job on Monday."

"Too late. They already fired me." She slung her bag over her shoulder. "Good-bye. Thank you for caring whether I live or die. I guess I'll just hitch a ride back downtown."

"Wait." Heels tapped on the wood floor and went silent on the carpet in the living room. "I'll have Judy take you."

"No, don't worry about me. It's easy to get rides, especially from men. They think I'm cute."

"Kylie, stop."

"Why? I have to start looking for another job, don't I?"

"Go ahead, do what you want, but I'm not letting you leave this house and accept a ride from a stranger!"

Kylie went into the foyer and stopped at the door, staring at the dark, heavy wood. It was curved at the top, with a crystal hanging in the fan-shaped window, catching the sun. Kylie bowed her head. Her hair fell around her face like a curtain. "Actually, I drove here."

"Drove what?"

"A friend's car." She stared at the floor. "I'm sorry I said you were hateful. I didn't mean it."

"We were both upset," C.J. said.

"Can't I stay another week? It won't make any difference."

"What about Wednesday? That gives you time to say good-bye to your friends. It's not the end of the world, you know. You can always come back. Miami will still be here." C.J. had a smile so phony that Kylie wanted to shove her. "Well. Is there anything you need? Do you have enough cash to last until then?"

"Actually, no." Kylie put on her own smile. "I need some gas for the car. It's running on empty. And I have to drop it off on South Beach. Could you lend me enough for a taxi?"

"Of course. I'll just get my purse." She went over to the sofa. "You do have a valid driver's license, don't you?" When Kylie said she did, C.J. nodded. She took a twenty-dollar bill out of her wallet, then another one, then all of them, including a fifty. She tossed the wallet back into her bag. "Be careful, borrowing somebody else's car. If you get into an accident, and you're under eighteen, the owner could sue your parents for the damage."

"I doubt it. The owner's been gone for a week, and I don't think she's coming back."

Blue eyes opened wide, and the hand with the money froze as Kylie reached for it.

Kylie tugged it away. "Thank you very much, Ms. Dunn. I really appreciate this."

"What are you talking about, the owner is gone?"

She slid the money into her shorts pocket. "The car belongs to

Alana Martin. Nobody can find her. It's been on TV. She and I were friends, and I think . . . well, I'm pretty sure she went to Hollywood. She told me she had a friend out there or something."

C.J. tilted her head as though she hadn't heard correctly. "You knew Alana Martin? What are you doing with her car? Kylie?"

"I borrowed it." Kylie wished she hadn't said anything.

"From Alana? When?"

"Somebody was fixing the transmission, and they dropped it off at her apartment a couple of days ago. When I went by there yesterday to ask her roommate if she'd heard anything, I saw Alana's car, and then . . . I needed some way to get here, so I took a bus over to the Beach early this morning and borrowed it. She kept a spare key under the rear bumper." Kylie added, "I'm going to take it right back."

"You knew her. You knew Alana Martin. How do you know her?"

"From the magazine. Alana was working for the advertising director. She quit just after I started there, but we would go out together. Parties. Dancing. Alana got me a fake ID. She knew most of the bouncers, so we didn't have any trouble."

"A fake ID. Oh, God."

"It's not a big deal."

"No? Tell me that when you get arrested. When did you last see Alana?"

"The night of the party. There was a party on Star Island. We went there together. She said she had to talk to someone, and to wait, but she never came back. I waited and waited and finally hitched a ride home."

"You hitchhiked?"

"It was somebody from the party. He was all right."

"What is the matter with you? My God, Kylie, anything could have happened!"

"I couldn't find Alana, and I didn't have any money. What the fu—What was I supposed to *do?*"

C.J. took her arm and put her on the sofa while she sat on the edge of the coffee table, facing her. "We need to take that car back before someone reports it stolen. I'll ask Judy. She can do it. You and I are going to talk. I need to know everything about Alana Martin."

After some seconds went by, Kylie said, "Why?"

She shook her head. "It's related to a case I'm doing. I can't discuss that with you, but it's extremely important that I know what happened that night. Why did she go to the party? Who was she going to meet? She must have said something to you. What can you tell me about her friends and the men she knew? Don't move. I'm going to call Judy." Crossing the room, C.J. picked up the phone. "You need to give her Alana's address and the key to the car."

The key was in the pocket of Kylie's shorts. She could almost feel it vibrating against her hip. A feeling of lightness was rushing through her, and everything suddenly seemed so clear, so perfectly obvious. Sliding her bag over her shoulder, she went around the coffee table, past an armchair, then toward the foyer. "This is so interesting. You have this big important legal thing you can't talk about, and I have information you want. I might know a lot about Alana. It depends."

C.J. turned around with the phone in her hand. "What do you mean, it depends? Depends on what?"

Kylie sent her a little smile. "I can't talk to you if I'm not here, can I?"

As C.J.'s mouth dropped open, Kylie ran for the door. "Stop! Where are you going? Wait!"

She slammed the door on her way out, leaped off the porch, and sped across the yard. She skidded to a stop at the end of the brick walkway and dug the key out of her pocket as the front door swung open.

"Kylie! Stop!" C.J. almost tripped in her high heels. "Come back!"

Kylie spun around. "I am *not* going to Pensacola! If you want something from me, you can pay for it!"

She sprinted to where she had parked the car, unlocked it, and got in, slamming down the lock. The tires screeched when she stepped on the gas. Before she turned onto Bayshore, she looked in the rearview and saw C.J. Dunn standing in the middle of the street fifty yards back with her hands in her hair.

chapter
E I G H T

j udy Mazzio said, "You couldn't stop her?"

"*You* try to catch a teenager in sneakers with a head start." C.J. threw one high-heeled Prada, then the other, at the sofa. "I hope she gets arrested for car theft."

"Do you really?"

"No." C.J. fished a pair of scuffed flats from under the coffee table. "I'd have to go get her skinny little butt out of jail. You should have heard her. 'Thank you for caring whether I live or die.' That's something you expect out of the mouth of a thirteen-year-old. I thought she'd be . . . I don't know. Nicer."

"Edgar likes her. He says she's spunky."

"Edgar likes everyone. I need some coffee. I need it *bad*. Let's talk in the kitchen."

"Better make it decaf," Judy said with an arch of her brow.

Standing in the doorway, C.J. sighed at the mess, then spotted one of her three cats on the counter. "Get down, you!" He leaped off and walked calmly to his dish, tail switching. "When I have a spare minute, I'm going to interview housekeepers." She waved Judy away from the sink and retrieved the coffee carafe herself. "I'll do it. Go have a seat."

Judy pulled out a chair at the bistro table under the window and shifted aside a week's worth of newspapers. "Have a good time last night?"

"Yes, I did, thank you."

"And how is Señor Wonderful?" Judy's attitude was showing. She thought that Billy Medina had the morals of an alley cat, that he would dump C.J. one day, and that she deserved better.

C.J. grinned over her shoulder. "He climbed out of the pool and took off his Speedo. That was pretty wonderful."

"I'll bet."

"I like going over to Billy's. He keeps a very neat house. It's inspiring."

"That's the reason?"

"Well, the sex. There is that."

Judy swung her foot. Changing the subject, she said, "What are you going to do about Kylie?"

"If she knows anything, I have to get it out of her."

"It's going to cost you."

"I'll send Paul Shelby the bill."

Judy smiled. "You admire the kid's *chutzpah*."

"Please."

"You do, admit it." With a chuckle Judy set her chin in her palm. "Not often someone gets the better of C.J. Dunn. Even worse, a smartass teenager. How much for a year in college these days?"

"She's going to school in Pensacola." C.J. measured coffee into the filter. She turned on the coffeemaker and stared at it, letting out a long breath.

"What's the matter?"

"How did Kylie get involved with people like this? Drugs, drinking. A fake ID? And she got fired from her job, too." Pushing away from the counter, C.J. said, "I can't think about this now. What did you find out on Richard Slater?"

"A couple of things. First, tell me what Shelby had to say."

"Not much. It was basically a repeat of what I told you last night." C.J. found some mugs in the sink and washed them. "Shelby hired Slater two months ago. He doesn't remember where Slater lives or how much they pay him."

Judy brushed some crumbs into her hand and sprinkled them into a potted geranium on the windowsill.

"That was on my list," C.J. said. "You're making me feel bad."

"Sorry." Judy grinned.

Pouring the coffee, C.J. said, "Billy met Slater once. He thinks he's basically a muscle-bound dimwit. Now it's your turn. He's going to call me at noon. What should I know about him?"

"Well, for one thing," Judy said, "Billy Medina is dead wrong."

C.J. looked at her from across the kitchen as she stirred in the milk.

"I followed the Shelbys' car from the concert last night. Just curious, you know? Slater dropped the Finches off in Coral Gables and took the Shelbys home to Cocoplum, where he picked up his own car, an Audi with dark tints on the windows. I don't know when he made me, but he did. Coming back up Dixie, he took off like a rocket and left me stuck in traffic. Very slick move. I was parked on the circle at Sunset Drive, and I bet he read my license plate."

C.J. brought the mugs. "It doesn't matter. You work for me. I wanted to know who my client is. So tell me about him."

Judy rummaged in her bag, found an envelope, and took out

some pages. On top was an enlarged color copy of a Florida driver's license. Richard A. Slater. All the charm of a mug shot. The man's hair was shaved close to his scalp. Brown or hazel eyes—it was hard to tell—stared through narrowed lids. A small scar made a pale line above one of his straight, dark brows. His jaw and lips were obscured by a closely trimmed mustache and short beard. His collar seemed too tight, and his shoulders looked massive. Five-ten, 200 pounds, age thirty-eight, living in a Latino neighborhood west of downtown.

She grimaced. "My new client."

"It's a driver's license photo. You should see mine. I think he's kinda sexy. Check out the birth date. He's a Scorpio. Same as me. Passionate, intelligent—but secretive and stubborn. You're a Leo. You might get along with him."

"I'm sure." C.J. sipped her coffee. "What else have you got?"

Judy unfolded a pair of purple-framed reading glasses. "I ran his name, DOB, and social security number through a national database. No criminal record, no traffic tickets. No record of real estate bought or sold. No record of car loans. He bought the Audi here in Florida two months ago, used. No outstanding debts. One credit card, a Visa, zero balance."

"Does he exist?"

Consulting her notebook, Judy said, "I talked to a friend with the Beach police last night. Marla. She's in property crimes, but she said she'd find out what she could. The lead detective on the Martin case is George Fuentes, who I think you know."

"Yes, he's a decent guy."

Judy went on, "Slater lives alone. Never married. Born in Kentucky. Dad was in the military, so they traveled around a lot. He served eight years in the Army, earned a college degree, was honorably discharged, then went into private security work overseas. He applied for a job with Atlas Security, and they sent him to Paul Shelby." Looking over the top of her glasses, Judy said, "It's not unusual if he's been out of the country most of his adult life. Do you want me to dig further, or do you want to just ask him?"

"I'll ask." C.J. pushed her coffee away. The acid was giving her heartburn. She opened the bag of potato chips she'd left on the table. They were stale, but the grease and salt made her mouth water.

"Didn't Señor Wonderful have breakfast sent up?"

"Stop calling him that. No, he was still asleep when I left."

"You're going to make yourself sick." Judy snatched the bag away and threw it in the trash. Opening the refrigerator, she found some yogurt and looked at the expiration date. She tossed that in the trash as well. "Oh, this is pathetic. At.least you feed the cats."

"I've been busy lately," C.J. said. "The witnesses who allegedly saw Slater with Alana Martin. Did you get any names?"

"Marla doesn't know." Judy came back. "I'm not giving up, but you could ask Paul Shelby to find out, couldn't you? He has some influence, is all I'm saying."

"I do that, and we'd start hearing stories about Congressman Shelby meddling in a murder investigation. That's how it would play if reporters like Libi Rodriguez got ahold of it."

"And so . . . bottom line, you protect Shelby. If not, he might pull the rug out from under your chance to get on TV."

"I deserve that job," C.J. said. "You know I'd be good at it."

"Oh, definitely, but as they say, be careful what you wish for." Arms raised, Judy poked a loose strand of black hair into the knot on top of her head. "I had my little moment of fame, and, honestly? It was a drag, except for the money, which went out as fast as it came in. I made a few friends, I guess, but when you're paying the bills, everyone's your friend. I'm not complaining. I was a featured dancer at Caesar's Palace. I flew to Paris in a private jet." She made a crooked smile. "Big deal."

"You've done all right." C.J. smiled across the table. "Best P.I. in Miami."

"Yeah?" She winked, a sweep of long lashes. "They never suspect a thing."

C.J. said, "You know, I might ask Billy to find out who the so-called witnesses are. He knows the mayor."

"You think he would lift a finger? Great. Make him do something useful. Meanwhile, I'll keep asking around."

"Judy, you have the wrong idea about Billy. He's not as shallow as you think."

"Now, there's a sterling recommendation."

The phone rang on the other end of the kitchen counter, and C.J. glanced at her watch. Nine-forty-five, too early for Rick Slater to be calling.

"Are you going to answer it?" Judy asked.

"No, it's probably a salesman." But the thought came to her that it might be Kylie Willis. The girl had raced out of here, and she had crashed the car, or had been pulled over for speeding. C.J. crossed the kitchen. The screen on the wall phone said unknown caller, but by the time her mind registered that fact, she was already lifting the handset. "Hello?"

The male voice on the other end said, "Ms. Dunn? This is Richard Slater."

She glanced over at Judy, then said, "Good morning, Mr. Slater. I didn't expect to hear from you this early."

"Sorry about that. Are you busy right now?"

"Just doing some paperwork. We need to talk. If you could meet me at my office later today—"

"No good. The police just dropped by my place with a search warrant. I need you to come over here."

chapter
NINE

Rick Slater had a ground-floor apartment in The Banyan Tree, a two-story, L-shaped complex on the fringes of Little Havana. The initial wave of Cuban refugees had been diluted by successive floods of other Latino groups, evidenced by the Nicaraguan market on the corner and a Brazilian steak house across the street. A black metal picket fence surrounded the apartment building, accessible through a wide rolling gate that apparently was left open during the day. The namesake trees put some shade over the rows of tenant vehicles baking in the lot.

As she pulled into a vacant guest space, C.J. noticed a Miami patrol car and two unmarked sedans clustered at one end of the building. The duty of serving a search warrant fell to the police in the local jurisdiction, the city of Miami. She guessed the unmarked cars would belong to detectives from the Beach.

At number 108, a uniformed officer was posted outside. She told him what she wanted. A minute later, Raymond Watts came out, a big man with a stomach he counter-balanced by placing his feet apart and leaning backward. This produced a view of a double chin, short nose, and a fringe of gray hair.

"Well, lookee here. It's the famous C.J. Dunn. I'm all excited."

She had last seen Watts on the witness stand three days ago, when she sliced him apart on cross-examination. Poor Raymond. His best days were over. After Gianni Versace was shot dead on Ocean Drive, Watts was giving updates at press conferences and statements for the nightly news. Since then, he had become just another ageing cop with an eye on his pension.

C.J. looked at him through her sunglasses. "Good morning, Detective. Are you going to let me in, or do I have to stand out here listening to your pointless sarcasm?"

"Don't get your panties in a wad. Officer, this is the lady, if I can call her that, who screwed us over on the Robinson case. It's really disgusting, don't you think, the way some lawyers get away with playing the race card? Harnell Robinson beat the crap out of somebody. He deserves jail time, and I don't give a rat's ass what color he is or how much money he makes."

"Where's the warrant?" C.J. said. "I want to see it, and I want to speak to my client."

Another figure appeared at the door. "Ray, I'll handle this."

Watts stepped back inside, and George Fuentes said, "Morning, Ms. Dunn. The warrant's inside. When you get a chance, come talk to me." They went in and he closed the door. Fuentes was a good cop; he simply went about doing his job, like most of them.

C.J. took a quick look around. The apartment was up to date but generic, the kind you rent if you don't intend to stay for long, furnished with a brown sofa-armchair combination, lamps, a small flat-screen TV. The coffee table held yesterday's newspaper, a pack of Marlboros, an overflowing ashtray, an empty pizza box, and at least . . . she counted them . . . nine empty bottles of Rolling Rock beer. Through the open bedroom door, she saw the end of a neatly made bed with precise corners on the dark green duvet. A plain-clothes officer was going through dresser drawers.

They had put Slater in the dining area, out of the way. He stood up as she approached, a solidly built man with a shaved head and the muscled arms of a boxer. He might have been sleeping when they knocked on his door. He was barefoot. His cheeks were stubbled past the edge of his beard, and it seemed he had pulled on the first pieces of clothing he could find, a rumpled shirt printed with palm trees and a baggy pair of jeans. This made C.J. feel slightly less grungy, wearing the same clothes as yesterday. She had grabbed her jacket, run out the door, and touched up her lipstick in traffic.

Her hand vanished into Slater's. "Glad you could come," he said.

"A pleasure to meet you, Mr. Slater. Sorry it's under these circumstances, but we'll sort it out." She picked up the warrant from the table and read it. The search was relying on information from unnamed sources who alleged that Richard Slater was the last person seen with Alana Martin, and another who stated that the two had an "intimate relationship." This didn't fit Slater's assurances to Paul Shelby that he had never met the girl. C.J. had long ago lost the capacity to be shocked by a lie. The only question was, whose lie?

"Have you said anything to them beyond 'What do you want?' and 'I'm calling my lawyer'?"

"No."

"Good. As soon as they leave, we'll go downtown to my office and talk."

Raymond Watts came over to Slater. "I need your car keys. Your vehicle is next."

Slater said, "On the kitchen counter."

Watts went to get them. A muscle tensed in Rick Slater's jaw as he watched the detective walk away.

"The paperwork is in order," C.J. said. "There's nothing we can do except wait. Have a seat. Sergeant Fuentes wants to see me. I'll be right back."

A short hall led to a bathroom, where a uniformed female officer in blue latex gloves was going through the medicine cabinet. She glanced over at C.J. as if a movie actress had suddenly showed up, then remembered where she was and went back to her duties.

Inside the bedroom, another officer felt the pockets of slacks in the closet, pushed aside hangers, and turned over shoes to see the tread. Sergeant Fuentes stood at a desk going through papers. An ethernet cable lay on the desktop, connected to a wireless router. There was no computer attached. Unless Fuentes was blind, he had noticed too.

C.J. asked, "Find anything interesting?"

"A forty-five çal Smith and Wesson M-and-P pistol. That's military and police issue. He's licensed, so he can keep it." Fuentes thumbed through some papers. "Other than that, not much so far."

Like the rest of the apartment, there was little in this room to distinguish the occupant. A stack of paperback crime novels on the nightstand. Some CDs beside a portable stereo on the dresser. C.J. walked over and looked at one of the albums. Saima Khan, a dark beauty with jeweled earrings, a gold ring in one nostril, and a yellow silk head scarf about to slide off. She turned the CD over. Recorded in London. The singer was Pakistani. C.J. put it back and saw Radiohead, Mexican *ranchero* tunes, and a collection from The Buddha Bar in Paris. The man had eclectic tastes.

Fuentes balled up his gloves and stuck them in a pocket. A

thin, dark man, he favored brightly colored knit shirts tucked into khaki pants. Jackets were for court. His badge was clipped to his belt holster.

"What can I do for you, George? Mr. Slater didn't know Alana, despite what you may have heard."

"Uh-huh. He told me that, too, but I have two witnesses who put your client with Ms. Martin the night she disappeared. She was passed out drunk in the backyard of Guillermo Medina's house. They went over to see if she was all right, and Slater came along and told them to get lost. They saw him leave with her. We have another witness who tells us that Alana was intimate with Slater."

"Do these people have names?"

"Sorry, C.J., can't go there, not yet."

"What possible motive would Richard Slater have to kidnap this girl? And then what? Rape and murder her? Really, George, you can't believe that. Rick works for a United States congressman. He was thoroughly vetted. His record is spotless."

Fuentes held up his hands. "I gotta run down my leads, doesn't matter who or what. See what your client has to say. I'd be curious to get the real story. Maybe we can stop all this dancing around."

She nodded. "I'd love to get it resolved, believe me. They say that Alana Martin was quite the party girl. I imagine you have a long list of people to interview."

"A few. Call me if and when he wants to make a statement. You know the number."

When they went back into the other room, Raymond Watts was tossing Slater's car keys onto the dining table. "Damn. That is the cleanest car I've ever seen. When was the last time you had it detailed?" The heat had reddened his heavy face and put circles of perspiration under the arms of his sport shirt.

Slater said, "I'm just a very neat guy."

"Don't talk to him, Mr. Slater." Watts wasn't asking because he was curious; he wanted to know if Rick Slater had disposed of trace evidence.

Watts kept his eyes on Slater. "Oh, wait. I forgot. You were driving Congressman Shelby's Cadillac the night Alana Martin disappeared. When did you have it cleaned?"

C.J. stepped closer. "That's enough. Mr. Slater? Let's just walk over here so they can finish their work." She crossed the living room and stood by the front windows, which were shaded by the usual beige mini-blinds. The trees shifted in the wind, sending dappled light into the courtyard.

Quietly she said, "Your cell phone is mentioned in the search warrant. Did you give it to them yet?"

He turned his back to the room. "I couldn't. You know, I think I must've left it at the convenience store when I bought some cigarettes." Hazel eyes flecked with green fixed on her with a look of such fuddled embarrassment that it sounded almost plausible.

C.J. looked through the window into the parking lot. "How did you call me?"

"One of the officers lent me his."

"Well, you'll have to buy another phone, won't you?"

"I guess so, if mine doesn't turn up."

She put a finger between the blinds. A motion had caught her attention, a man in sunglasses and a dark blue ball cap running across the street between the cars. He stopped just outside the fence and lifted a camera, its long lens going through the pickets, aiming at the window where she stood. She doubted he could get a clear shot.

"Mr. Slater, do you see that little man taking pictures? There, near the gate."

"I see him. Who is he?"

"His name is Nash Pettigrew. He's a tabloid photographer."

"Why is he out there?"

"Oh, I think he's just sniffing around so far, waiting to see who comes out. His interest has been piqued. A beautiful girl, gone. A party on South Beach. A congressman's driver questioned by police. There could be something to it. Pettigrew sells to the sleazier publications, rarely the national media, though he did get some of his photos of the Anna Nicole Smith saga into *People* magazine. He came to Miami for that, and it looks like he's back. I knew him in L.A. He's the sort of photographer who takes those embarrassing pictures of stars walking on the beach, showing their hip bones. 'Angelina Jolie Anorexia Scare.' He will wait outside nightclubs for someone to trip on the curb in her high heels, and then you see the headline, 'Celebrity Lawyer Loses Case, Gets Smashed.'"

Rick Slater's smile creased his cheek. "Personal experience?"

"The funny thing is, it was my partner's case, not mine, but I have better legs. My car is parked in plain sight, so he knows I'm here."

"How did he find out they were serving a warrant?"

"Nash has contacts in the major police departments, and he pays them for leads. It's like seeing that first buzzard circling over the desert." She stepped away from the window and twirled the rod to close the blinds. "Is there another way out of here?"

"There's a back door in the kitchen."

"We're going to my office to chat. Do you mind driving?"

"I do it for a living," he said.

Five minutes later, the police were done. Sergeant Fuentes asked Rick Slater to sign a form that nothing had been removed from or damaged in the premises. They said thank you and left.

Slater locked the door behind them and sat on the couch to slide his feet into a pair of woven leather sandals. He put his cigarettes in his shirt pocket and walked to the table to pick up his car keys. On the way through the kitchen, he stopped and opened the refrigerator's freezer compartment. He lifted the door on the ice-maker

and rummaged through the ice cubes. He retrieved a cell phone in
a small zip-lock bag.

C.J. closed her eyes. "I didn't see that."

"Do you want to tell the cops to come back?"

"Let's just go," she said.

chapter
TEN

riving across the parking lot, Rick Slater told C.J. to scoot down in the seat if she didn't want her picture taken. The Audi slowed at the gate and turned left. Sitting up again, C.J. looked through the back window. The photographer was running toward a small brown sedan parked along the curb. "He's following us."

Slater said, "Hang on."

Her body was slung sideways into his shoulder as he made a fast right at the end of the block. She had just recovered when he hit the brakes and turned into the alley behind a discount furniture store, came out on Twenty-Second, and headed north. He zipped around a car slowing for a yellow light on Calle Ocho and took a left on the red. A truck gave a long blast on its horn.

"Slow down! Are you trying to get us *killed?*"

He calmly glanced over to the passenger seat. Dark wraparound shades covered his eyes. "You should fasten your seat belt."

She did so, then raked her hair off her face. "We're going the wrong way. My office is in the Met Center."

"There's a good Cuban diner up the street. I'll buy you some *café con leche.*"

She wanted the sleek corner conference room at Tischman Farmer, not a diner. "Thanks, but I've had my coffee. I'd rather we talk at my office."

"Later," he said. "I haven't had breakfast. I get cranky."

"Fine."

He shook a cigarette out of his pack and grabbed it in his lips, then reached for a lighter in the console. He paused. "You mind?"

"Yes, actually, I do. It gives me a headache."

He hit the button to send the window back up and returned the cigarette to his shirt pocket. "I don't smoke that much. Five or six a day. And those beers in the living room? They aren't all mine. I had a friend over. Just so you know."

"I wasn't asking," she said.

Slater planted his right elbow on the arm rest. "Paul said you can take care of this for me, the police and so forth. He said you're not charging me the regular rates."

"That's correct."

"You look expensive."

"I am. Let's say five thousand for my expenses. I believe Mr. Shelby will pay it."

"Five thousand dollars? I'm definitely going to respect you in the morning."

"Excuse me?"

"It was a joke." Slater accelerated around a city bus, then said, "I thought Shelby would fire me. Why hasn't he?"

"He's loyal to his employees."

Slater made a little twist of his lips. "That's good to know."

"You could find another attorney," C.J. said.

"You'll do. You did the job for Harnell Robinson. I saw you on the news last night. I thought for sure Robinson was going away." Slater stopped at a red light. "What does C.J. stand for?"

"I don't like my real name. I never use it."

"Cordelia?"

"God, no."

"I bet I could find out."

"You probably could, but it's C.J."

"Calamity Jane?"

She had to smile.

Slater made a six-gun out of his thumb and forefinger. "You could start with the photographer."

"That's so tempting," she said.

The street took them past small storefront businesses, a *botanica* with a life-size statue of San Lazaro on crutches out front, and a Walgreen's announcing *descuentos* on school supplies. Slater held on to the top of the leather-wrapped steering wheel. As he turned the wheel to go around a slower-moving vehicle, his sleeve pulled up, and on the heavy muscle above his elbow she noticed a pale, shiny scar about the size of a quarter.

He saw her curious gaze. "It was a swordfish."

"A what?"

"The fish with a long, sharp bill."

"I know what a swordfish is, I just thought . . . it looks like a bullet wound."

"Yeah, it does, but it was a swordfish. Cut the artery. Son of a bitch leaped right out of the water. A friend of mine owned a charter boat on Isla de Mujeres, Yucatan. We took a bunch of American doctors out for the day." He smiled. "Good thing they weren't lawyers."

She looked at him for a few seconds more, doubting the story but unable to think of a reason for him to lie about it.

Slater put on his signal and turned into a shady parking lot. He braked, then skillfully backed into a space between two SUVs that hid the Audi from view. He walked around to open her door, but she was already getting out.

He shrugged. "Habit."

The restaurant was crowded, a brightly lit place with red-covered stools at a long counter with tables in another section. While they waited, Slater took a copy of *El Herald*, the Spanish edition of *The Miami Herald*, from a stack of them and left some coins beside the cash register. He slid out the local section and dropped the rest in a trash can by the door.

"Let's see what we've got. They've been running stories about Alana Martin all week." He turned the A Section over to see below the fold. "Here it is. Yesterday it was in the local section. The *Venezolana* is still missing. The parents are asking the community to contribute reward money. Here's something new. They deny that she was stealing from her employer. She worked in a dress shop on South Beach. She's an angel. Never a problem. A beautiful daughter. A model. She dreams of being a movie actress."

He turned the article so she could see it. C.J. asked, "Who alleged she was stealing?"

"It doesn't say."

"I'm sorry for her parents," C.J. said quietly. "I've represented parents of missing children. It tears your heart. It's bad when they find them dead. Worse if they never know."

"Someone killed her," Slater said. "The police are waiting for the body to turn up."

"I think so too."

A young hostess appeared with menus. He folded the newspaper. "*Por favor, una mesa al fondo.*" With a nod and a smile she led them to a booth in the back. When they were seated with menus, Slater took off his sunglasses and said, "What do you want? I'm buying."

"Nothing. Juice. Maybe some wheat toast."

"How about a ham-and-cheese omelet? You look a little underfed."

"Two scrambled with one piece of bacon," she replied.

"You're not skinny. I didn't mean that."

"Where did you learn Spanish?" C.J. asked.

"Here and there. Mexico, mostly."

"What were you doing in Mexico besides fishing?"

"Playing bodyguard for rich ex-pats. Tending bar. Basically wasting time." He spoke as though what he said didn't matter in the least and her inquiries were only an attempt to make polite conversation.

Before she could probe further, the waitress came with her notepad. Slater ordered for both of them, sending her off with a flash of white teeth and a *gracias* that put a smile on the woman's face. He wasn't ugly at all, C.J. thought. He had a good face for the camera. With the right sort of clothes and some polishing, he would look rugged, not rough.

C.J. said, "Your criminal record comes up clean, but . . . have you ever been arrested?"

"Not really. The Philippines, does that count? It was a bar in Manila. This whore, excuse me, a woman at the bar approached me, I declined, and her pimp and another guy tried to take my wallet when I went to the men's room. The cops threw me in jail till it got sorted out. I didn't put it on my résumé. What I tell you is in confidence. Am I right?"

She stared at him for a while, then said, "I should probably be careful what I ask you. Can you meet me at my office later? Say two o'clock?"

"Can't." He looked at his heavy watch with its three smaller dials.

"I'm taking Paul Shelby and his chief of staff to a luncheon in Boca Raton, some kind of fundraising thing. We're talking now, aren't we?"

She leaned forward. "This is going to take more than a few minutes over eggs and toast, Mr. Slater. What I need, if I'm going to—"

"Call me Rick." He smiled.

"Fine. Rick. If I'm going to do my job, I need to know everything about you. I want your autobiography. I have a written list of questions you can use for a guide—"

"Hold it." He glanced into the restaurant, then leaned closer to speak in a heated whisper. "I didn't kidnap that girl. I had nothing to do with it. They say they have witnesses. Bullshit. What witnesses? You're a hotshot lawyer. Explain it to them. They searched and came up empty. They should back off."

She locked eyes with him. "Yes, why don't I just tell them to leave you alone? You know, when an adult is missing, the police don't usually serve search warrants on marginal suspects. They don't have the time. But when a case hits the news? They're on it. I predict there's a better than even chance that you're going to find yourself under a very bright spotlight. I'll do what I can to deflect it, but my credibility is on the line too, and I don't like surprises. So far, Mr. Slater, you've shown a remarkable ability to lie. Don't let me turn on the news one day and find out something you didn't tell me first. I will drop you flat."

He looked at her in silence, his expression flickering from puzzlement to hostility before settling into a neutral stare she couldn't see into. "Mr. Slater? Do you understand me?"

"Loud and clear—Ms. Dunn." He shifted condiments to make room for his elbow on the table, or to have something to do with his hands.

"It's not Ms. Dunn, it's C.J. I don't need to jump on you so hard, Rick. I apologize. Just be straight with me, okay?"

"Sure."

The waitress brought two coffees with milk and two large glasses of orange juice, then rattled off more Spanish before going away, ending with the words *ahorita, mi amor.*

Slater said, "The food is coming right out."

C.J. drank some juice. "About that cell phone in the freezer? I'm going to guess that you have names and phone numbers stored on it that you'd like to keep private."

He acknowledged that with a shrug.

"Then I suggest you commit them to memory. Where's your computer? I saw a wireless router on your desk."

"I think that belonged to the previous tenant."

C.J. asked, "Is that what you told the detectives?"

"No. I said my lawyer just told me not to talk to them. I don't have a computer. I have email, though, and whenever I want to check it, I go over to a friend's house."

"All right. Try not to lie to the police. Or to me." She spoke quietly. "You told Paul Shelby you had never met Alana Martin. Tell me the real story."

"I know her slightly." He stirred extra sugar into the sweet, caramel-colored coffee. "I met her when I first got to Miami. I was over on South Beach and asked for directions. We got to talking. I wanted to know the area, and she showed me around. I took her to lunch a couple of times."

"The police have a witness who says you were intimate with her."

"That's a lie."

"Any idea who this witness might be?" C.J. asked.

"No, but I'd like to find out."

"Stay away from the witnesses. No exceptions. I have a private investigator. That's what she's for."

A smile lifted a corner of Slater's mouth. "Judy Mazzio?"

"Judy said you might have seen her license tag. How did you run it so fast? Of course. You work for a security company."

"It comes in handy." He leaned back when the waitress reappeared with their plates, massive amounts of eggs and bacon and long wedges of toasted white bread slathered with margarine. When C.J. didn't pick up her fork, he said, "What's wrong?"

"I'll never eat all this."

"Doesn't matter. I'll help you. All right—C.J. What's next? What's the plan?"

"They want you to make a statement, but that won't happen until we have enough information to put you in the clear. If you had an alibi witness, your worries would be over. But you would have said so already. Nobody?"

He shook his head.

"Then our best option," C.J. said, "is to dig into Alana Martin's background and find someone else who makes a better suspect than you. We have to work quickly, because once this hits the national news, you're part of the story. I want the media to see a good man unjustly suspected. You served our country. Now you work for a respected congressman. You wouldn't snatch a girl from a party and kill her. Of course you want to cooperate in every way, but your lawyer is bitchy and overprotective. Nobody gets to you, nobody interviews you, except through me. I won't allow lies and negative innuendo to pass unchallenged. *I* take the heat, not you."

Slater cut a large chunk of omelet, ate it, then wiped a napkin across his mustache. "So you want five grand in expenses, and Shelby's going to pay for it, right? What about fees?"

"Don't worry about it. It's taken care of."

"How much would the check be for, if I were writing you a check? Twenty thousand? Thirty?"

"Probably, but I said you don't have to worry about it."

"When people do me a favor worth that kind of dough, I like to know why." He waited for an answer. "Are you a political supporter of the congressman? A friend of the family? Or what? I mean, are you working for me or for somebody else?"

"Of course for you. You're my client. Paul Shelby asked me to help you, and I said yes because, well, he's running for re-election, and I want to do what I can for him."

"That's a pretty big favor."

She bit into a piece of toast. "I suppose it is. So what?"

Rick Slater laughed without humor. "This is surreal."

"I need to caution you about something else," she said. "People are going to approach you for interviews. They might ask you about Paul Shelby. Keep in mind that he's doing you a big favor, too."

"I make my living being discreet, lady." He laid down his fork. "Your job, correct me if I'm wrong, is to protect Paul Shelby, and I'm part of the game plan. That's okay. I sure as hell can't afford your services, but I'll accept the favor. I'm not trying to be a pain here. I just want to know how it is."

C.J. met his steady, unblinking gaze. She sat back and folded her hands in her lap. "Mr. Shelby might be paying the freight, but you're my client."

"And if it comes to a choice, me or him?"

She repeated what she had said before. "You are my client. That comes first. My integrity as a lawyer is worth a great deal to me."

He finally nodded. "Okay." And dug into a pile of hash-brown potatoes.

"Tell me about the night of the party," she said. "Did you go there to meet Alana Martin?"

"Absolutely not. I wanted to check it out. I don't usually get inside houses like that. I'm the guy waiting in the car with the AC on, working a crossword."

"Paul Shelby didn't mind?"

"I didn't ask him."

"So you avoided him at the party?"

"There were a lot of people. It wasn't hard. He left about midnight. Took a taxi, I guess. That's what he said he'd do."

"When did you leave?"

"About a quarter to one."

"And you went where?"

"I took Mr. Shelby's car to his house."

"Was he home?"

"Lights were on. I didn't ring the bell. We have a place to leave keys. I left his car in the driveway and took mine."

"Where did you go after that?"

"Home. I got there about two in the morning. It's a hike down to Cocoplum."

C.J. let these facts settle in her mind before she said, "Did Sergeant Fuentes mention to you that they have witnesses who saw you with Alana Martin?"

"He told me. I'd heard about it already. They're either lying or mistaken."

"They say that Alana was passed out drunk in the backyard. They were trying to help her, but you told them to go away. They saw you pick her up and leave with her."

"That's news to me." Rick Slater's blank expression had returned. "What else?"

"That's all he told me. Can you explain it?"

His eyes drifted upward. "I left with a girl, but it wasn't Alana Martin. They're right, she was drunk. I was leaving and saw two men messing with her. Young, mid-twenties. One of them pushed me, so I dropped him, then punched the other one. They were both pretty well lit, so maybe I got lucky, but they took off. I couldn't leave her there. She asked me to take her home. She didn't have any money for a taxi." He laughed and put his forehead on his fist. "This is so screwed. You can see why they're lying. They want to get even."

C.J. blinked to put his face into focus. A terrible thought had occurred to her. But it couldn't have been Kylie. Or could it? "Who was she?"

"The girl? I don't know."

"You don't know?"

"I didn't get her name."

"What did she look like? Height, weight, age?"

He lifted his shoulders. "Those girls all look alike. Long brown hair. Young. Thin."

"You said you took her home. Where does she live?"

"I dropped her outside some apartment building."

"Be more specific."

"I can't remember. It was late, and I was in a hurry to get the car back to Shelby."

"And she never told you her name?"

"I wish I'd asked," said Rick Slater. "She could be my alibi."

C.J. sensed a lie. She looked at him steadily, but he didn't blink.

chapter
ELEVEN

eaving Rick Slater's building, C.J. circled the block twice to spot anyone tailing her car, but the photographer had given up for the time being. She caught Thirty-Seventh and headed south into Coconut Grove. On slower, narrower streets, she pulled out her BlackBerry, scrolled to voice dialing, and spoke into the microphone. "Call Kylie Willis."

After four rings she heard, "Hi, Kylie's not here. You know what to do." *Beep.*

"Hello, Kylie, this is C.J. again. We really do need to talk, sweetie. Please call me back as soon as you can." She hit the disconnect button. "Damn." That had been the third message.

Rick Slater hadn't provided much of a description. Young, thin, long brown hair. He'd been right: this could be every other girl on

South Beach. But if it was Kylie, and Kylie could identify Rick Slater and say that she'd left the party with him, Slater's problems would be over. At the very least, George Fuentes would start looking further down the list of suspects.

It would have to be done quickly. C.J. could feel the first rumblings of a case about to explode into the national media, like the first tremors of an impending earthquake. Through experience, she knew that when people like Nash Pettigrew started showing up, events were about to reach a critical stage. She didn't care what happened as long as she could pull Rick Slater out of the way before it blew. That was what the congressman wanted. If C.J. succeeded, she could soon be in negotiations with the producers at CNN. She would need an agent. There were several in L.A. who would remember her.

Not twenty-four hours had passed since C.J. had sat in the back of Milo Cahill's limousine, getting seduced. She and Milo would never have been friends if they had not, at the innermost core, shared the same desire to make their lives matter, or seem to, which in the end could be the same thing.

Deep in thought, C.J. heard an impatient driver lean on his horn. The light had turned green. She pressed the accelerator and shot ahead.

She would have to persuade Kylie. The only problem was, would Fuentes believe her? A seventeen-year-old girl who had passed out at an after-party on South Beach. A girl with a relationship to Richard Slater's attorney. Would he not question her credibility? But what alternative was there?

After she and Elliott had bought the house in Coconut Grove, they

had converted the two spare bedrooms upstairs to home offices, his
and hers. Late at night they would tap on their keyboards, a com-
panionable rhythm that had not carried over to the bedroom. They
were busy: his new job as anchorman at the CBS affiliate; hers at
Tischman Farmer. Cocktails at home, parties on weekends, a carnival of faces and laughter, Elliott doing cocaine — just enough to
keep going, he said. *You're a drunk, so get off your fucking high
horse.*

Elliott wanted to stop. He found them a counselor, but C.J. was
in trial. Then there was another trial. On one fresh, blue spring
morning, she glanced out her office window and saw Elliott in his
bathrobe picking up the Sunday paper from the lawn, but he stayed
bent over, standing there like a question mark. Then he dropped to
his knees as if he was praying and slowly, so slowly, fell into the
grass. She ran downstairs screaming his name, but it was too late.
At his funeral she realized he was gone, truly and forever. She sank
down beside his coffin and sobbed, and they had to carry her out.
One day, after she'd gone blank during jury selection in a murder
trial, the judge called her into his chambers and said if she didn't
get help, he would report her to the bar. That should have worked,
but it didn't. A month later, Edgar found her unconscious in the
kitchen and called 911. Judy Mazzio took charge and saw to it that
C.J. spent two weeks in a locked facility in Boca Raton. Her law
firm told the press she was recovering from pneumonia.

Sober now, C.J. missed drinking. She couldn't lie to herself
about that. Billy Medina could take one drink and walk away, and
maybe now she could too, but she didn't have the guts to find out.

The fluffy gray cat, Dylan, jumped onto her lap. She stroked his
warm fur as she waited for her computer to connect to Tischman
Farmer's mainframe downtown. Her senior partner at the firm in
Beverly Hills had come up with a list of topics for hot-button clients
to think about, and C.J. still used it. Questions about money, prop-

erty, business relationships, overseas accounts. Have you ever been sued? Extramarital affairs. Long-term affairs: how did they end? Homosexual relationships. Have you ever used drugs? Alcohol? Ever under the care of a psychiatrist? Is there anyone who could reveal embarrassing events in your life? God help her if she was ever forced to answer the questions herself.

Slater had supplied his Hotmail address, the initials RAS with a string of numbers. C.J. composed a message asking him to send the answers back as soon as possible, preferably before their next meeting. She attached the document.

It was possible that none of this would be needed, though she had to admit to some curiosity about the man.

She hit SEND.

Next: a letter to Kylie. From a desk drawer C.J. took a sheet of buff-colored note paper embossed with her initials and uncapped her Mont Blanc. The salutation—Dear Kylie? C.J. realized she had never written to the girl. No birthday cards, no Christmas cards, only the occasional note to Fran Willis that accompanied a check. She didn't have a photograph of Kylie, had never asked for one. Until this morning, C.J. had never really looked at her. Behind the wire-rimmed ovals of her glasses, Kylie's eyes were wide and bright. Her center-parted hair framed a face with a small chin, rosebud mouth, and freckles across her cheeks. A few tiny moles dotted her slender neck.

C.J. took her pen and wrote, *Kylie—*

She crushed the paper, tossed it into the basket, and started over.

> *Dear Kylie, I would like very much to talk to you. I'm sorry that we argued. You deserve a good education, and I understand why you want to attend college in Miami. . . .*

She hesitated. Make no promises.

Let's try to work something out. Please call me as soon as you read this.

She signed it . . .

Sincerely, C.J.

. . . and sealed it inside a matching envelope.

After a shower, she pinned up her hair in a clip to keep her neck cool, changed into pale pink linen pants and a matching top with heeled sandals. Gold earrings, gold-faced watch with a white leather strap, and a white bag. Downstairs she poured more kibble into the cats' bowls, gave them each a treat and a pat, and went over to the little table under the window.

The papers Judy Mazzio had brought were still there. C.J. found the copy of Rick Slater's driver's license photo and held it up. "You're not going to make my job easy, are you?" She folded the page and stuck it into her purse, in case she connected with Kylie. She wanted to see if Kylie recognized him.

The iguana was asleep next to the cottage in a patch of shade, keeping cool. She turned on a spigot and refilled his water dish. She set the dish on the porch and picked up the pie tin of cat food that Edgar had left there. She rapped on the screen door. Edgar kept the cottage closed up in the heat of the day, with the window unit running.

He opened the door and said through the screen, "You're back."

"Not for long," she said. "I've got to run out again. Edgar, we can't leave Iggy's leftovers out all day. We'll start attracting raccoons."

"Yep, yep, I forgot." He took the pan from her. "Where you headed?"

"I have to talk to someone. It's on the Alana Martin case."

"Oh, sure, they were talking about her on the news at noon.

Sounds like a wild scene that night. Drugs and drinking and all sorts of carrying on."

"Don't believe everything you hear, Edgar."

"The same house as the fella you're dating," he observed. One of his tangled eyebrows went up. "Medina."

"Yes, unfortunately, it was his party. Billy's horrified, as you can imagine."

Edgar stepped onto the porch and shut the door to keep the cool air inside. "Listen, I've been thinking. That girl, Kylie, had some nifty ideas about scanning my photos. I'll bet she could help me pick out a new computer and show me what to do. I'd pay for her expertise."

"What a marvelous idea, but—" C.J. shrugged. "I'm afraid Kylie will be leaving Miami soon, going back to Pensacola to finish high school."

"Well, that's good. Nice girl. Smart as a whip."

"Isn't she, though? I'll help you. I'd like to."

"That'd be great. Say, why don't we grill out tonight? If you don't have a hot date, I mean."

She had heard nothing from Billy Medina, though sometimes he called at the last minute, and too often she would go flying over to Miami Beach instead of telling him she had plans, which would have been a lie but satisfying all the same.

"I'd love to cook out," she said. "I'll pick up some steaks."

"Take a gander at that." He pointed toward the back of the house. The black hose still hung from the PVC pipe protruding from the hole in the wall, but now it went through the lid of the big plastic barrel. He had attached a soaker hose to a valve in the bottom of the barrel and laid it in a circle in the backyard. "You just took a shower, am I right? You watered the grass."

Repressing a sigh, she said, "Genius." She stood on tiptoe to kiss his cheek, pat his shoulder, and say a prayer for rain.

She was forced to consult her address book for the building where
Kylie lived, having been there only once, the day she had delivered
Kylie into the hands of Rosalia Gomez, the retired housekeeper for
Billy Medina's aunt. A mile north of downtown, C.J. cut over to
Biscayne Boulevard. The new performing arts center had started a
wave of redevelopment that was sweeping away tiny stucco houses
and rundown apartments. The wave washed up against the box-like
condominiums that had staked out a place in the 1970s, now terribly un-chic but too expensive to tear down just yet. The Windmere,
with its faded beige paint and aluminum railings, occupied a prime
spot overlooking the bay.

In the lobby, C.J. put her sunglasses into their case and told the
man at the security desk she was here to visit Mrs. Gomez in 1015.
He called up, then buzzed her through to the elevators. Rosalia
Gomez had moved to Miami, C.J. remembered, to be near her
only relative, a sister. C.J. had been sending Mrs. Gomez a hundred
dollars a week so Kylie could live in her spare bedroom. It had all
been arranged through Billy Medina's assistant at *Tropical Life*.
Billy himself had never met Kylie. How fortunate to have people to
relieve you of the messy details of life.

The woman who answered the door was short, gray-haired, well
past seventy. "*Entra, señora, por favor.* Come in." Clear plastic covered her living room furniture, and family photographs fought for
space on a glass étagère. It was very clean, very quiet. Not the lodg-
ings of choice for a seventeen-year-old with any say in the matter.

"Hello again, Mrs. Gomez. It's been a while. How are you?" As
the woman fumbled with her hearing aid, C.J. repeated, "How are
you? *¿Cómo está?*"

"*Ay*, not so good, I have the *artritis*. You are here for Kylie, no?"

"Sorry to disturb you, but I can't seem to reach her on her cell phone." C.J. took the envelope out of her bag. "Would you give her this note when she comes home?"

"She is no here."

"I see that, but could you make sure she gets it? *Por favor.*"

"Kylie is gone."

"What do you mean?"

"Gone." Mrs. Gomez emphasized this with a sweep of her hand. "*Hace dos horas.* Two hours ago. Yes. I show you." She took C.J. down a hall and opened a door at the end. "Kylie say, 'Good-bye, Rosalia, thank you very much, I going for stay with a friend.' That's all. *Se fué.*"

"What friend? Where did she go?"

The old woman shook her head. "I'm sorry. I don't know. I ask her, but she don't tell me."

Still not believing it, C.J. walked inside the small room. Kylie had left the sheets and pillow stacked on the end of the single bed. Coasters and plastic drink glasses from night clubs littered the dresser. C.J. opened the closet to see empty hangers. Small white squares on the wall marked where posters had hung, and the posters themselves were folded and crammed into a paper grocery sack. With no chair in the room, Kylie would have sat on the side of the bed to look out the window. The blinds were open.

In the distance, Miami Beach lay twinkling in the sun.

chapter
TWELVE

rs. Gomez didn't know any of Kylie's friends. No, there was one, a girl who spoke Spanish. She had come only once or twice, and had gone into Kylie's room and shut the door. Her name? *Lo siento, señora.* Mrs. Gomez didn't remember.

"When was this? When did you see Kylie with this girl?"

"I don't know. Two weeks? Three?"

Her eyes fell once again on the grocery sack by the door. A scrap of black fabric spilled over the side. She crossed the bedroom, removed the discarded posters, and pulled out a dress more air than substance. The quality of the fabric, the design, and the finishing said this little rag must have cost more than Kylie could ever have afforded. The bodice was slashed to the waist, and a light puff of wind would be enough to lift the gauzy skirt. Had Kylie worn this? Kylie, with her flat chest and narrow hips? In the bottom of the bag, C.J. found a pair of shoes with stiletto heels and red soles. Cheap fakes. But with such a dress, who would notice?

C.J. put the clothes back into the bag and asked Mrs. Gomez if she could have them.

In the parking lot, she sat in her BMW with the engine running, staring through the windshield at the bay, which sparkled like broken glass. Kylie had been fired, so C.J. wouldn't be able to find her at work on Monday. Did she have a place to stay tonight, tomorrow? Her money would run out soon, and then what? C.J. hadn't felt so unsettled in a long time. Where the feeling had come from, she didn't know. She couldn't really describe it, except that it was something like dread.

She took out her cell phone, scrolled through the directory for Milo Cahill, and found nothing. Resting her forehead on the steering wheel, she tried without luck to think of his private number. It was written down somewhere in her office at home. It had been so long since she'd called him. *Hey, guess who? It's your California girl. We're at Crobar, and it's dead here, can we come over? . . . Listen, listen, everybody. Milo's having a party for Puff Daddy! . . . Milo, sweetie? We're so smashed. Can you send the car?*

C.J. dialed Judy Mazzio, who picked up on the second ring. She was at her office doing paperwork and having a late lunch of takeout Chinese.

"Kylie's gone."

"Gone? Gone how?"

Judy listened without comment as C.J. related the facts. "Judy, do me a favor, will you? Find out Alana Martin's address and get right back to me. I believe there's a roommate. I'd like to talk to her."

"By yourself? Don't do that," Judy said. "I should go."

Defense lawyers did not, as a rule, interview potential witnesses, in case they themselves could be called to testify. C.J. said, "I'm not going as Rick Slater's lawyer. I just want to find Kylie. That's what I want to do. The roommate might have some information."

Judy said, "The way it usually works is, people get in touch when they're ready to talk. Kylie seemed pretty savvy to me. I don't think she would put herself in danger."

"Yes, we all tell ourselves that at her age, don't we?"

Judy was silent for a while, then said, "What's up with you?"

"What do you mean?"

"You don't even like this girl. She's been here for four months, and now you're worried?"

"Can you get the address for me or not?"

"I'm on it." Judy asked, "What about Rick Slater? Did the cops find anything at his apartment?"

"No, nothing. I'll tell you about it later."

"Look, hon, sorry to be a pain in the ass, but if you're emotionally involved in something, you shouldn't be the one to ask the questions."

C.J. considered that. "All right. Come with me, then. How long do you think it will take?"

"To get the address? Give me an hour. I'll meet you on the Beach."

"That's fine. I have something else I need to do."

Ten minutes later she was dropping quarters into a meter just south of Lincoln Road. The street had been turned into a pedestrian mall years ago. Shade trees cut the heat, and there were plenty of people strolling from shop to shop. By nightfall, every outdoor table would be taken. The bars wouldn't clear out until two or three in the morning. She noticed that one of the bars had a new name, and another was gone entirely, replaced by a gay-themed gift shop. Giving up drinking had kept her away from the Beach. It seemed strange to her now.

She found China Moon between an art gallery and a gelato shop. The windows of the boutique were starkly beautiful, with orchids in cloisonné vases and manikins dressed for seduction. C.J. grasped the polished brass door handle and went inside.

A middle-aged Asian woman stood behind a glass case arranging wispy bras and camisoles in confectionery colors as alluring as French pastries. Her straight black hair was chopped at her jawline, and she wore retro psychedelic print pants and a bright yellow top.

"Ms. Chu?" When the woman looked around, C.J. said, "I called you a little while ago. I'm C.J. Dunn."

"Yes, I'm Marilyn." The woman's eyes went to the piece of black silk draped over C.J.'s arm. "This is the dress?"

C.J. laid it on the display case. "Is it yours?"

Marilyn checked the label and turned it this way and that. "Yes, it's mine. We noticed it missing a week ago. Oh, my God. Somebody used blue thread to take it in! The waist is ripped. And what is this stain on the skirt? It's ruined!" She looked at C.J. "Where did you get this?"

"I'm sorry, I can't share that information, but I believe that one of your former employees, Alana Martin, might have taken it."

The small, crimson mouth tightened. "Why did you bring it back? I can't sell it."

"I'd like to ask you a few questions about Alana." C.J. produced a business card, which Marilyn Chu made no move to take. "I'm a lawyer, and I'm looking for a friend of hers."

"I can't talk to you now. I'm very busy."

"When would be a better time?"

"There's nothing I can tell you. The police have been here, reporters, all of them with questions. Yesterday I threw a photographer out of my shop. He was sneaking pictures and asking my salesgirls about Alana. I don't like this. It isn't good for business."

Reaching across the display case, C.J. put her hand on the other woman's wrist. "I need your help. The girl I'm looking for is the daughter of an old friend of mine, and we can't find her. Her name is Kylie Willis. She's young, seventeen, about five-feet-two, with gray eyes and long brown hair. She wears glasses."

"I'm sorry, I don't remember anyone like that."

"She left the place she was staying without a word. Now she's somewhere on South Beach, and we're afraid of what might happen to her. She and Alana had the same circle of friends. Anything you could tell me might be useful. Please."

Marilyn Chu looked at her steadily, then said, "This dress was stolen from my shop, and now it's a total loss. Someone should pay." She arched her brows, the implication clear.

C.J. asked, "How much did it cost?"

"Twelve hundred and fifty dollars."

"What? That's insane."

"Would you like to see the invoice? You can have it for seven. No, I'll give it to you for six-fifty."

"You just said it was ruined. Of what value could it possibly be to me?"

Marilyn Chu said, "Well, then, if you'll excuse me, I need to get back to work."

"Three hundred."

"Five. Not a penny less. The seams can be fixed. You can have it cleaned."

C.J. nodded. "All right. Five hundred."

Marilyn Chu's little smile put dimples in her cheeks. She turned and called out, "Debra! I am going into my office. Watch the store, will you?" She motioned for C.J. to follow. They went through a workroom lined with racks and boxes, then into a cluttered office, where Marilyn put on a pair of half-glasses. "Your charge card, please?"

C.J. opened her wallet, silently cursing.

Marilyn sat at her desk to write. "This is not an easy business. I have a shop in SoHo, but Miami is the worst. People steal you blind. You are continually disappointed. Have a seat, Ms. Dunn."

C.J. pulled a chair closer. "How long had Alana been working for you?"

"About three months. She wasn't reliable, but she turned out to be one of my best salesgirls. You know, I hired her as a model. She was a perfect size two. Gorgeous skin and hair and a lovely body. Men sometimes come to China Moon to buy gifts for their wives or girlfriends. Alana would model for them. They rarely said no. It was something to watch."

Marilyn turned the charge slip around and gave C.J. the pen. "Your phone number also, please." When C.J. was finished, Marilyn tore off the duplicate and gave it to her.

"You wouldn't have any photographs of Alana, would you?"

"Yes, I do. She gave me her portfolio when she applied for the job." Marilyn crossed the room to a filing cabinet and opened a drawer, returning with a large envelope.

C.J. looked through a dozen or more color closeups and full-length shots of Alana Martin in various types of clothing, from white fur to a minuscule swimsuit. Front view, back view, reclining with her back provocatively arched. The pose didn't match her small breasts and thin limbs. The makeup had been professionally done: glossy lips, immense brown eyes, and slashes of color on her cheeks, but all wrong for her upturned nose and baby-doll face. It was creepy somehow. The name of the photographer—Carlos Moreno—was printed on the bottom edges. The name sounded familiar, but C.J. couldn't think why.

She asked, "May I have one of these?"

"Take them all if you want. I don't need them anymore." Marilyn sighed. "Tragic."

C.J. set the envelope on the floor beside her purse. "A story in today's *Herald* referred to an allegation that Alana had been stealing. Is that true?"

"Apparently so. Things went missing, and one of the clerks told me that Alana was taking them. I confronted her, but she denied it. She was so convincing. She was an actress, you know."

"I've heard that," C.J. said.

"She told me she'd had a part in an action movie shot in the Bahamas."

"Was it true?"

"Oh, who knows? She couldn't tell me the title or the director or anything about it. It could have been a walk-on in one of those low-budget productions that go right to DVD. I put her in touch with a friend of mine, an agent for TV commercials. They paid her a few hundred dollars to model back-to-school clothes. The director told her he could use her again, but she didn't want to be known for commercials. No, Alana was going to be a star in Hollywood. Where do they get these ideas? Oh, I suppose she had some talent, but not enough. Not nearly enough to compete against so many other girls with the same dream. Maybe on some level she knew it. She always seemed a little desperate to me. The kind of girl people take advantage of, the kind who get all used up, and you try to make them see, but they won't. They can't. They need their illusions. Otherwise, their ordinary little lives wouldn't be tolerable, would they?"

C.J. only gazed back at her.

Crossing her legs, Marilyn Chu took off her glasses and slowly twirled them, happy to expound on Alana Martin's poor prospects. "The last time we spoke, Alana told me that she'd soon be working in Hollywood. Again, no details, but this time she was certain. She had someone who would make it happen for her."

"Did she say who?"

"An agent, a producer, someone like that. I didn't try to pin her down because, well, it sounded like another of her stories. I told the police about it. They thought at first it might be true, and she'd turn up on a movie set, but I don't think she will ever be found alive."

"Do you have any theories on what happened to her?"

"She was careless. Money, sex, drugs, good times. Always a party going on. It attracts the wrong sort. You're right to be concerned if your girl is part of that crowd."

"Was Alana taking drugs? Did you see any indication?"

"My dear. If I required drug testing, I would have to fire half my staff. How do you think they get by on three hours of sleep a night?" She passed a long, French-manicured nail under her nose. "What they do outside the shop is not my concern."

C.J. decided that she loathed this woman. She opened her purse. "I want to show you a photograph." In her lap, she folded the copy of Rick Slater's driver's license to hide everything but his face, then held it up. "Have you ever seen this man?"

Marilyn leaned closer. "No, but the police showed me the same picture. He looks like a felon. Who is he?"

"If you don't know him, his name doesn't matter." C.J. put it away. "Did Alana ever go out with any of the men she met here at the shop?"

"I wouldn't know."

"Did she have a boyfriend? Did she ever talk about anyone?"

"Not to me. I don't encourage trivial chatter. Please don't disturb my salesgirls, asking them about her. It wouldn't do you any good. They didn't socialize with Alana."

Marilyn picked up the black dress and went over to a work table. She unfolded a shopping bag imprinted with the name of the store. The paper was gold, the handles red rope. She found some sheets of matching gold tissue paper, which she gently tucked around the dress. "You've bought yourself a treasure. This dress was originally designed for Paris Hilton."

"Oh? How exciting," C.J. said.

Turning around, Marilyn held up a hand. "Wait a minute. There was someone. Tall, blond, very handsome. He had blue eyes. They perfectly matched his shirt, really stunning. He came in and asked for Alana. I think it was late. I don't usually close the store myself, but my manager had just quit."

"Who was he?"

"His name? Oh, what was it? I don't remember. I told him Alana was working, to come back after nine o'clock. We close at nine on weekdays. Alana was with a customer, a man who was in the middle of making a large purchase, so I wasn't about to break in. Her friend said they had reservations somewhere. Well, I told him that's just too bad, wait for her outside. I could see him out there, walking back and forth, trying to signal Alana. She finally rang up the sale, grabbed her purse, and went right out the door. Her boyfriend was still waiting, and I could hear him yelling at her."

"Did you mention this to the police?"

"I only just now thought of it. Oh, yes. She called him Jason. I'm sure that was it."

"You referred to him as her boyfriend. Did she use that word herself?"

"Oh, yes, the next day she did, and if you'd seen them, you'd say they had a relationship." Marilyn finished wrapping the dress, securing the tissue paper with a gold seal.

"When did this happen?"

"Oh . . . about a week before she turned up missing. I wouldn't say it was unusual. Alana had a temper, and she was hard to deal with."

"But you kept her on," C.J. said.

"My dear. She could sell." Marilyn placed the package into the shopping bag. "She had a gift for it. I'm going to lose some good customers now that she's gone."

"Yes, it's a shame," C.J. said.

Marilyn led her toward the door. "Good luck finding your friend's daughter. And Ms. Dunn? Do have the dress repaired. You're a little heavy in the hips for it, but a dressmaker could let it out."

C.J. smiled at her. "No, I think I'll just donate it to Goodwill."

chapter
THIRTEEN

arked under the trees on Jefferson Avenue, C.J. kept her eyes on the apartment building at the end of the block. The car's air conditioner blew cold air on her face and ruffled the edges of the photographs that Judy Mazzio was shuffling through.

C.J. said, "You should've seen the underwear at China Moon. Gorgeous. I've never had a pair of fifty-dollar panties."

"You feel deprived?"

"Definitely."

"I've had a few pairs. They make you want to lift your skirt. I didn't buy them for myself, you understand. I bet Señor Wonderful would give you some."

"He probably would." C.J. added, "By the way, I asked him about getting me the names of the witnesses against Rick Slater. He said yes."

"Get out."

"True. As soon as he delivers, I'll let you know who they are."

"Well, damn."

The building was a long rectangle that extended back from the street, six units under a flat roof. Ocean Reverie. The white concrete letters marched diagonally up fading turquoise paint. Glass-louvered windows were cranked tightly shut against the cloudless, ninety-two-degree heat. There was space for cars out front. Alana's wasn't among them.

Arriving earlier, Judy Mazzio had spoken to the landlord, who had come over to repair a faucet. He told her the car had been towed an hour before from a no-parking zone. Judy asked about Alana. The landlord had met her but didn't know her, the same thing he'd told the reporters and police who'd been bugging him about it all week. The name of the roommate? Tisha Dulaney. She'd been living here two years, worked nights, slept days, paid on time, kept to herself. There was a lot of turnover in the tenants. She was home, as far as he knew. Her car was there.

Judy slid the photographs of Alana back into the envelope, except for a head shot. "Can I keep this?"

"Keep whatever you need," C.J. said. "Does the name Carlos Moreno ring a bell? He did Alana's portfolio. You work with photographers. Do you know him?"

"No, but he's probably local, so it won't be hard to find him. Why?"

"I'm curious what he can tell me about Alana Martin. Some of those pictures are fairly provocative."

"Yeah, she could've posted them on a soft porn site."

"That makes me feel so reassured about Kylie."

"Do you have a photo of Kylie? I'd like to show the witnesses both pictures. Which of these girls did Rick Slater leave the party with?"

"I don't have any, but you could probably get one off her driver's license."

Judy said, "I'd rather take one with my camera, assuming we find her."

"Oh, we'll find her. I'm going to see if she can ID Slater, and if she can, we'll talk to Fuentes, and then I'm sending her home if I have to drag her there myself."

Judy slid Alana's photos into the envelope. "I cannot believe that Marilyn Chu forgot to tell the cops about the boyfriend."

"If he is the boyfriend."

"Lucky for you if he is. He killed Alana in a fit of jealousy."

"Jason is an architect," C.J. said. "He graduated from Princeton. Milo has him running errands."

"The boy's really coming up in the world," Judy said.

C.J. turned off the engine. "Let's see if the roommate is awake yet."

There was a handwritten note taped to the door of Number Five. *If you are here about Alana Martin, go away!* Each word was underlined twice, the last line so emphatic it had torn the paper.

Judy and C.J. exchanged a glance. Then Judy rapped loudly on the glass louvers. Waited. Tried again, longer this time.

Finally the louvers tilted open, and from the dark interior a woman's voice said, "Can't you people fucking *read?*"

Judy went up the two steps to the door and peered in. "Miss Du-laney? My name's Judy Mazzio. We're looking for a friend of Alana's, Kylie Willis. I'm a private investigator, and this lady here is a friend of the family. They can't find her, and they're worried." Judy held up her private investigator's license. She looked the part: beige slacks and a white top, low shoes. "Have you seen Kylie today?"

"No, and I don't know where she is."

"Do you mind if we come in? It's hot as blazes out here."

"Good-bye." The glass slats in the door began to roll shut.

Judy grabbed hold of one to keep them open. "We need some help, hon. The girl's a runaway, and she might be in danger. Five minutes, I swear."

A face appeared. The eyes were on C.J. "Excuse me? Do I know you? Oh, wait. I've seen you on TV. You're a famous lawyer, right?"

"I'm C.J. Dunn." She stepped closer. "The girl we're looking for is the daughter of an old friend of mine. The smallest detail could help us find her. May we come in and talk to you? We won't take much of your time."

The face stared out for a while longer. "Okay, wait there. I'll be right back." The glass louvers closed.

Judy murmured, "Open Sesame."

"Where's she from?" C.J. asked.

"Jersey? Brooklyn?"

After a minute, the chain rattled, and the door came open. The occupant stepped aside. Dim light filtered around the edges of a blackout shade in the living room and through a curtain over the kitchen window. A counter littered with take-out containers sepa-rated the two areas.

"Ignore the mess, okay?"

A torchiere in one corner illuminated an L-shaped faux-leather sofa that faced a flat-screen television. A couple of DVD cases lay open on the coffee table. There were some dark rings on the glass where wine bottles might have been, and ashes but no sign of cigarettes or—more likely—the joint she'd been smoking the night before. Not she, *they*. A pair of men's alligator shoes had been left on the brown shag carpet.

Tisha Dulaney was a pretty woman in her mid-thirties with a rat's-nest of blond hair and mascara smudges under her eyes. Her lips had been shot full of collagen. Full breasts jutted through the thin fabric of a zebra-print satin robe that came to mid-thigh.

She shook C.J.'s hand. "Wow, I'm meeting C.J. Dunn. I watched that trial on Court TV, the one you did in Palm Beach, John Winterhouse? You were really great. I apologize for being rude, but I am so tired of people knocking on the door. The police have been here twice, and some of her friends, and fuckin' reporters every morning and every night. Excuse me. I'm getting sleep-deprived."

"What kind of work do you do?"

"I'm in the travel industry. Cruise ships, resorts. We get a lot of famous people from the entertainment and sports world. Some lawyers, too. You might be interested. I can give you girls my card."

"All right, thanks." C.J. said, "Let me ask you about Kylie. If she had friends other than Alana, I don't know them. Anything you could tell us might be helpful. She's only seventeen, and this is her first time away from home."

"Seventeen? Ha. She told me she was twenty-one, like I'd believe that. I wish I could help you. The last time I saw her, she and Alana were getting ready to go out. It was the same night Alana went missing, Saturday a week ago. They were trying on clothes and doing their makeup. I had to go out too, and I couldn't get in the bathroom. I finally told Alana this is my damned apartment, so wait your turn. I left about eight o'clock, and that was the last I saw of either of them."

C.J. heard a toilet flush, then a door close. "We woke someone up."

Tisha said, "Don't worry about it. He should be up already. Do you want some coffee?"

"No, thanks, we're fine." She asked, "Did Kylie ever talk about modeling? Did she ever mention an agency or any jobs she had?"

"No jobs, but she talked about it a lot. She wanted to earn money for college, and Alana put the modeling idea in her head, but really. It wasn't gonna happen. Now, Alana had the looks, but please. Five-foot-three? Nuh-uh."

C.J. saw Judy checking out the DVDs on the coffee table. "Alana was also an actress. I believe she was in a movie?"

"No, she *tried out* for a movie. Never made it. She had the talent, but she needed more on top, you know what I mean?" Tisha cupped her breasts. "Maybe not like this, but something. Alana told me to keep my opinions to myself. It got so we hardly spoke. She's my last roommate. That's it. I need my privacy, and my gentleman friend—" Tisha rolled her eyes in the direction of the bedroom. "He and Alana didn't get along. What can I say? He's kind of older and didn't like her attitude."

"How did you meet Alana?"

"I knew her from around the Beach, the clubs and parties. She was selling advertising for *Tropical Life*, you know that magazine? I said sure, my company will buy an ad. But they downsized her, and she lost her apartment. I offered to rent her my spare room. I like to help people. But you gotta be compatible, and she wasn't. The exact same day I asked her to leave, she told me she'd be moving out anyway at the end of the month. She was going to Hollywood. Some friend of hers knew people out there."

"Did she say who this friend was?"

"Never. Most roommates like to talk, you know, but her? Forget about it."

"Do you think she was telling the truth about Hollywood?"

"Sure. I said good for you, Alana, I hope it works out. I did hope that. I never wished her ill. Now she's probably dead." Tisha shuddered, and tightly crossed her arms. "This world can be so, so cruel."

C.J. said, "Do you know a friend of Alana's named Jason? He's blond, late twenties." Tisha shook her head. "Did she bring men around? Did she have a boyfriend?"

"She dated, sure, but nobody stayed over. She kind of kept to herself."

"Was she doing drugs?"

"Nooooo." Tisha lifted her hands and raised her shoulders. "I mean, maybe some weed, but not here."

"Did you ever suspect cocaine? Not here, of course."

"She might've. It's all over."

C.J. opened her bag. "I wonder if you've ever seen this man." She held up the folded paper she had already shown to Marilyn Chu. "It's a driver's license photo."

Tisha nodded. "Yeah, I know him. I mean, I don't *know* him, but he was here. He came to take Alana out. His name is Rick. Am I right? The police showed me the same picture."

"And you ID'd him?"

"Sure. That's a terrible picture. He's a lot more attractive in person."

"What happened when he was here?"

Judy Mazzio came back across the room to listen to Tisha's reply.

"Well, he sat over there on the sofa and waited for Alana to get ready. They were going out. We talked about the clubs and where to go. I gave him my card."

"Did he say how he met Alana?"

"I don't remember."

"When was he here?"

"About a month ago. I never saw him again."

"Did Alana say anything about him?"

"Yeah. The sex was real good. He had her every which way, and he was huge."

Judy said, "I thought you two didn't talk."

Tisha rolled her eyes toward Judy. "Well, that is exactly what she told me."

C.J. put away Slater's picture. "Would you mind if we saw Alana's room?" When Tisha hesitated, C.J. said, "There may be some clue to Kylie's whereabouts. You'd be doing me a great favor."

"Just a second." Tisha went to a door down the hall and opened it far enough to stick her head in. Voices murmured. She shut the door and said, "Okay, but please don't take too long."

She reached into Alana's bedroom and turned on the light. Most of the small space was taken up by a bed with a disorderly pile of blankets and pillows. A life-size stuffed toy rabbit lay at the foot. Other stuffed animals filled a wicker basket. Clothes littered the carpet. A TV sat on the dresser.

Tisha leaned against the door frame with her arms crossed. "What a mess. Her parents are supposed to come over sometime and pack her things. This is going to be my meditation room and library. I do yoga."

Judy slid back one of the closet doors. C.J. tugged on the top drawer of the dresser, whose wood-laminate top was strewn with hairbrushes, a jar of coins, makeup bag, cologne, a bill from Macy's, an iPod, and a recent issue of *Cosmo*. The drawer was empty, except for a few pens and a box with a stapler, paper clips, stamps. She opened the next drawer, finding silky underwear and lace camisoles.

The next drawers were taken up with shorts, tops, swimsuits. The drawer in the nightstand held a paperback romance novel, nail polish, and a throwaway camera that hadn't been used. Overdue bills. A checkbook whose balance hadn't been figured in months.

Judy sat on her heels to go through shoe boxes. "Tisha, did the police take anything with them?"

"Not really. They made me show them my room, and they went through everything. C.J., did they need a search warrant for my room? They said they didn't."

"They lied. You could have said no." C.J. got on her hands and knees to lift the bed skirt. "But they'd probably have done it anyway and said you'd given them permission." Under the bed she saw only a stuffed toy panda and a clear storage box with sweaters in it. She got up and brushed dark lint from the knees of her pink linen pants. "Tisha, who had a key to the front door? You and Alana. Anyone else?"

"The landlord has a set."

Judy glanced around from the closet. "You should think about changing the locks."

"Why?" Tisha pulled in a long breath, and her pillowy lips remained parted. "Oh, my God. Whoever killed her has the keys. Oh, my God." She rushed across the hall. "Hal? Are you up? Hal! You know how to change a lock? . . . Well, you can fucking learn. Get dressed; we're going to the hardware store."

Judy slid the closet door shut, and she and C.J. went into the hall.

C.J. said, "Tisha? Thanks for talking to us."

She came out of the bedroom. "Sure. It was really nice meeting you. I should ask for your autograph. Never mind." Tisha laughed as she led them toward the front door. "Sorry for going all nutso on you. He says he'll get a locksmith over."

Tisha opened the door and with a little yelp she jumped back, clutching the front of her robe. A group of people were coming along the walkway from the street. Leading the pack was a man in a suit, trailed by a short, middle-aged couple; then, a few paces behind them, a man with a video camera on his shoulder followed by a black-haired woman in her twenties with a cordless microphone.

C.J. said, "I don't believe this."

Judy looked past her. "Hey, it's your favorite reporter. Who are the others?"

"Alana's parents. Libi interviewed them yesterday. The man in the suit . . . I don't know, but I'd bet they've hired a lawyer." C.J. pulled Tisha back by an elbow. "It's your choice whether to let them in or not, but my advice is, don't say anything on camera." As she and Judy went down the two steps to the walkway, she heard the door slam and a lock turn.

Libi snapped her fingers in the cameraman's direction, and he looked into the view finder, the same man who had been at the courthouse yesterday. C.J. remembered the round face and thick gray mustache.

The man in the suit stepped forward. Sweat was putting a shine on his forehead. He frowned, then enlightenment hit. "Ms. Dunn? I'm Oscar Enriquez, attorney for the Martinez family. They came to get their daughter's belongings. May I ask why such an eminent attorney as yourself is here?"

"I'm so sorry that you came all this way, Oscar. If the family wanted to collect Alana's things, they should have called first to make arrangements."

"Are you representing Tisha Dulaney?"

"No, I'm simply pointing out that most people prefer the courtesy of a phone call, rather than seeing strangers turn up at their door. Why don't you wait a day, then let Mom give Tisha a call?"

Enriquez smiled. "If you aren't Ms. Dulaney's attorney, why do you speak for her?"

"Fine. Ms. Dulaney can speak for herself. Go read that sign on the door." C.J. went over to Alana's parents. "*Señor y Señora Martinez, lo siento mucho.* Please accept my sympathies for your daughter. I pray that Alana is found safe."

They nodded numbly.

She and Judy Mazzio started toward the street.

"Ms. Dunn!" Sneakers pounded on the walkway. "We're here at the South Beach apartment of Alana Martin, and well-known defense attorney C.J. Dunn has just come out." The microphone appeared in front of her face. "Ms. Dunn, how are you connected to the case?"

"I have no comment." C.J. kept walking.

"Tisha Dulaney is Alana's roommate. Does she have any words of encouragement for Alana's parents?"

"You'll have to ask her yourself."

The cameraman lowered the camera. "Libi, forget about it."

They found an empty booth at the Eleventh Street Diner. When the waitress came back with their iced teas, Judy said she'd have a Reuben sandwich and fries.

C.J. said, "Didn't you have barbecued ribs with Edgar last night?"

"I missed lunch, thanks to you." Judy reached into her bag for her compact and lipstick for a touch-up. The uncompromising light through the window showed the fine lines that forty-six years had sketched on her face.

"If you're interested," C.J. said, "we're grilling steaks tonight. They say we'll get a breeze. I'm so tired of this heat."

"You should try Vegas." Judy blotted her lips, now shiny plumred. "We'll get some rain soon."

"It won't be soon enough." C.J. unwrapped a straw. "Richard Slater. My goodness. 'How well do you know Alana Martin?' 'Oh, hardly at all. Just bumped into her by accident and asked for directions. Had lunch with her.'"

"Had more than that," Judy said. "Bad boy, lying to his lawyer."

"They all do. I shouldn't be surprised."

"I wonder how huge he is?"

"Oh, stop." Stirring her tea, C.J. said, "Did you see Alana's parents? I wish I could tell them. They're going to be used up by people like their smarmy attorney, and Libi Rodriguez, and whoever else wants a free ride to five seconds of fame."

"Maybe they want it too," Judy said. "It sort of keeps her alive in a way. As long as people are talking about her—"

"It never lasts. People will stop talking. The reporters move on to the next story, and Alana will be even more dead than she is now."

"Aren't we in a mood," Judy said.

C.J. suddenly smiled. "Carlos Moreno. I know who he is. Libi Rodriguez's cameraman."

"Who?"

"The photographer who did the portfolio for Alana."

"No way. You sure?"

"Positive. I thought the name sounded familiar. I've seen him around the courthouse." C.J. paused. "He used to work for a big news agency. AP, Reuters, something like that. One of his pictures from Afghanistan made the cover of *Newsweek*. Now he's with Channel Eight. I can't imagine he's happy tagging along after Libi Rodriguez."

"Another guy coming up in the world," Judy said. "Here's a question. If it is the same Carlos Moreno, why aren't we seeing those sexy photos on Channel Eight? I mean, if you listen to Libi Rodriguez, Alana was this sweet, innocent kid who was snatched for no reason at all, just another night of mayhem on South Beach. You get what I'm saying?"

C.J. nodded. "Moreno knows Alana Martin, and he's keeping it from Libi. But why? Find out what you can on him, all right?"

"Is Rick Slater's five grand going to stretch that far? Which he hasn't even paid you yet, if I'm not mistaken."

"If it runs short, I'll get it from his boss. So. What's your impression of Tisha Dulaney?"

"Barrel of fun, that girl."

"She said she's a travel agent. What do you think? An exotic dancer?"

"Maybe at one time," Judy said, "but she's a little old for it now. No, I think she was telling the truth. And she said travel industry, not travel agent. How about *adult* travel industry? There are sex cruises where you can meet your favorite porn stars. Live demonstrations. Ping-pong-ball contests."

"Judy, for God's sake."

"What? You haven't heard about this?"

"Yes, it's disgusting."

Judy smiled around her straw. "Did you notice the DVDs on the coffee table? They were watching *Bambi Gets It On*, and it wasn't the Disney version. That's okay. I don't care what people do in the privacy of their own homes and so forth, but it got me to thinking: What about Alana? I took a good look at her wardrobe. Most of it's ordinary stuff, you know, but some of it? She must've bought it from Skank and Co."

"What is that?"

Judy gave her a patient smile. "I made it up, hon. It's not a real company. So if you look at the clothes, and the fact that she was a quote-unquote actress who couldn't remember what movie she was in—" Judy shrugged. "I'm thinking X-rated. The industry is worth billions, not just DVDs but the stuff you download on your computer."

"She told Marilyn Chu it was a feature film."

"Sure. What else would she say? Want me to run a check on Tisha? Find out what she's into?"

"Why not?" C.J. laughed. "This just keeps on getting better and better. Where is Kylie in all this, I wonder?"

"Why do you think she's in it at all?" Judy said, "I didn't pick up on anything like that. She's a good girl. She is. She comes off tough, but she's still innocent."

"Kylie? Innocent?"

"Basically, yes. I mean, compared to Alana Martin, and forget Tisha. I think I can read people pretty well. Kylie's got ambition. She wants a life. That's why she came here. You're not wrong, though, worrying about her. I think she's right on the line. She could go one way or the other."

"Where she's going is Pensacola. Why the hell doesn't she call? One phone call. That's just plain rude. Do you think I should notify the police?"

"How long's she been gone? Five hours? Relax. She's letting you steam, that's what she's doing. She'll call you. You're her ticket to getting what she wants."

"Conniving little witch, isn't she?"

Judy returned her smile. "I won't even tell my priest what I was into at her age."

"You and me both."

"Okay, then. We survived. Kylie will too." Judy looked up as the waitress arrived with her Reuben and fries. "Talk about huge. C.J., you have to help me with this." Holding it delicately with her long nails, she cut the sandwich in half.

"It's possible," C.J. said, "that I won't need to use Kylie. If Jason is what Marilyn Chu suggested, I can point Fuentes in his direction. That's all I have to do."

"You'd make Paul Shelby happy," Judy said. "Not so sure about Jason."

"That's not my problem. He should've stayed away from Alana Martin." C.J. slid her cell phone out of its pouch.

"Who are you calling?"

"Billy. He has Milo Cahill's private number."

chapter
FOURTEEN

after the trip to Boca Raton with the congressman, Rick Slater dropped by Carlos's house to check his email. He had been keeping his laptop and personal papers over there ever since the police had first requested to talk to him.

Rick kept everything in a metal suitcase with a lock, which Carlos stored for him on an upper shelf in a closet in the master bedroom. Before coming over, Rick would call, and Carlos would carry the suitcase into the family room. Rick had a key in the event no one was home. Inez didn't like this arrangement. She had worn a permanent crease between her brows ever since Rick had shown up three months ago, and her husband's refusal to explain didn't help matters. But Inez was loyal; she would have had her fingernails pulled out before she talked. Rick had to give her that.

He set his laptop on the card table and attached the power cord. Out in the backyard, teenagers splashed in the pool, their laughter mixed with music, some kind of rap or hip-hop that he failed to appreciate. Carlos was sitting on the other side of the table with a beer, bringing Rick up to speed on the events at Tisha Dulaney's apartment.

His back was to the kitchen. Inez was putting dinner together, pretending not to care if Rick Slater was in her house. Carlos spoke quietly, and his eyes danced with merriment.

"There was a note on the door. 'If this is about Alana Martin, go away.' Libi was going to knock regardless, but the Martinezes' lawyer said no, please. He said it would be bad for the parents. If Tisha got mad, she might throw away their daughter's things, and it's all they have left of her. The guy almost got on his knees. He didn't have the chops to order Libi to back off, and he knew it, so he was begging. His clients didn't know what the hell was going on. The mother started crying. I told them, don't worry, you can come back later. Libi says, 'Be quiet, Carlos. You're the cameraman. You don't talk.' But that was it. We left."

Rick said, "I think I'd have decked her."

Carlos's laugh turned into a sigh. He took another swallow of beer. "I have my résumé out."

"You going to stay in Miami?"

"What else can I do?" He tilted his head toward the backyard. "It's not so bad, Rick. The family. A steady job, the insurance. But I think about it. Maybe some day, after the kids are gone, and if I'm not too old. . . ."

Rick said, "I haven't been shot at in a while. Can't say I miss it." He raised the screen on his laptop.

"I should let you go to work," Carlos said.

"That's okay. Just want to see what my lawyer has sent me."

Carlos said, "There was another woman with her today. She was tall, about six feet. Black hair. Mid-forties."

"Must've been her private investigator, Judy Mazzio." Rick asked the question he had already asked without getting an answer. "Why was C.J. talking to Tisha Dulaney?"

"Don't know."

"And how the hell did she get through the door?"

"Don't know that either."

"What does 'C.J.' stand for?"

"I never heard." Then Carlos smiled and said in Spanish, "*Cojones*. That woman has a set of balls. You have to see her in trial sometime."

"Glad she's on my side . . . if she is."

Rick leaned over to plug the cord into the wall. He became aware that a telephone had been ringing, and that it had stopped. On the other side of the pass-through, Inez called out, "*Carlos! Te llaman, mi amor.*"

As Carlos headed across the room, Rick gave Inez a little wave. She saw it but went back to cooking dinner, or whatever domestic duties would allow her to keep an eye on her husband. She was afraid that he might suddenly get a notion to pack his camera bag and take off for places where it would be wise to wear a Kevlar vest and a helmet.

At fifty-one, Carlos Moreno had a son in high school, two stepkids, a new grandbaby, a house with a pool, a voracious mortgage, and a motorboat he used for fishing in the Keys, about as far away as he got these days. It was a second marriage, and Inez had put her foot down. Ten years ago, Rick and Carlos had been on the Afghan–Pakistani border, bullets whining past, knocking chunks out of the wall, somebody moaning in Pashto for Allah or his mother. The moans had ended when a mortar hit their position. It had been two weeks before Rick got his hearing back. Carlos had bitched about his broken lens. Fun times.

Rick drank some of his beer as the computer went through its startup routine. He logged on and checked his Hotmail account. More trash had leaked through the spam filters. Would he please reply to a Christian lady from Zimbabwe needing to transfer cash to the U.S.? Did he want to clean out his colon, buy stock at a discount, increase his potency? Among these, he saw a message from C.J. Dunn. He clicked on it. She was sending the questionnaire she'd mentioned over breakfast. He opened the PDF, scrolled down, went to the next page, then the next. She wanted it ASAP.

"Jesus." His fingers quickly tapped out a reply: "So many questions, so little time. Easier if we talk. Call me." He paused then wrote: "Old hand injury, too hard to type." He hit send.

He scrolled down through more junk mail, then saw a message from SoBeGrl227. A lot of girls on South Beach. Only one had his email address. He opened the message. She had written: "Hi. I will answer Qs about Alana but what about $? Pls e me back."

He wrote: "Kylie: Money possible but depends on what you have for me. Let's talk. I'm tied up tonight, can meet you tomorrow, early is best. Tell me where, when. Text me. You have my phone number."

Carlos came back and stood over the table.

Rick looked up. "Problems?"

"That was Libi. She's covering a reception downtown tonight for The Aquarius. I told her I have things to do, but there isn't anyone else. She said wear a suit."

"I might see you there," Rick said. "I'm taking Shelby and his wife to the same event. Look for the dark-green Ford hybrid SUV. People these days don't want their congressmen driving Cadillacs. They still have it, though. It's in the garage, along with the Excursion."

"Ay-yi-yi-yi." Carlos finished his beer. "Let's you and me load up the boat and head for Key West."

"Sounds like a plan."

chapter
FIFTEEN

Calling Billy Medina for Milo's phone number, C.J. learned that Milo would be at the Royal Palm Hotel at a reception in his honor, as the architect of The Aquarius. The real goal was to seduce investors. Every business leader, major real estate broker, and environmental activist in South Florida had been invited, along with more than a few from the arts crowd. Billy said it sounded boring. C.J. had tossed away her invitation two weeks ago.

Billy wanted to load a dozen friends on his boat and cruise over to Monty Trainer's for a lobster dinner, one of those spur-of-the-moment ideas he was famous for. C.J. would go, she told him, only if they could stop off at the hotel, which was on the way. After hanging up the phone, she went over to Edgar's cottage to apologize for canceling the cookout. Edgar said good, it was too hot, and anyway he wanted to work on his old photographs. C.J. quickly showered, put on a strapless dress with splashy tropical flowers, and added the coral necklace and earrings that Billy had given her for her last birthday. Thirty-seven. How had that happened? She leaned closer to the mirror.

The water was like oiled satin, the sky full of thin, barren clouds drifting north. Everyone stayed below in the air-conditioned salon because it was just so damned humid on deck, and the women didn't want their hair blown to bits. Billy was playing bartender. He had hired a man from the marina to drive the boat. Billy put on a Jimmy Buffet CD and made drinks in the galley as the *Lucky Lady* glided across the bay.

He was gorgeous in pale green slacks and an ivory linen shirt. A strand of his hair put a silver-gray comma across a black eyebrow. With every seat taken, he stood behind C.J. and sipped his gin-and-tonic, shifting his weight with the easy movement of the boat. Across the salon, the toffee-skinned Jamaican girlfriend, or wife, of the owner of some car dealership or other crossed her long, bare legs, giving a glimpse to the man seated opposite, who nudged his neighbor. C.J. held her club soda and focused in the general direction of the woman with spiked blond hair, who was talking about the wretched food at her hotel in Croatia.

Somewhere in the bubbling chit-chat, the man from London, who may once have been Elton John's arranger, leaned over and grinned at C.J. He had large, moist lips and brows like inverted Vs. "Billy says you're going to have a show on CNN."

"I wish it were that certain," C.J. said. "They haven't decided on a host."

"Nonsense," Billy said. "Who else is there?" He stroked her bare shoulder and played with the necklace. She felt his fingers gliding across her skin.

The man from London bounced on his seat. "Ooooh! Could I be your first guest?"

C.J. said, "You'll have to murder someone to qualify. The topic is celebrity trials."

"Oh, Christ! I have to murder someone to get on her show!"

They shouted out suggestions for a list of victims and methods of whacking them. C.J. got up and walked over to the galley to find the club soda. A bottle of Gray Goose sat next to the sink. If it hadn't been flavored with cranberries, she might have poured herself a shot.

Billy followed with two empty wine glasses and took a bottle of white from the below-the-counter refrigerator. He spoke quietly. "What's the matter with you tonight? They're going to think you don't like them."

"I don't."

"Well, do me a favor—fake it. This boat ride is for Mark. I owe him."

"Which one is Mark again?"

"My accountant. Striped shirt, far right." Billy refilled the glasses. "You've met him twice already."

"Billy, did you get the names of the witnesses?"

"What?"

"The witnesses who allegedly saw my client with Alana Martin. Don't tell me you forgot."

"Jesus. Give it a rest." He pushed her against a cabinet and his hips pinned her there. "I want to fuck you blind."

"Billy! Shhhh." She looked over his shoulder at the others.

"I'm going to pull your skirt up right here." Laughing softly, he tugged on the hem.

A wave of heat flooded through her traitorous body even as she pushed him away. "Don't."

Before he could reply, the engines slowed and C.J. gripped the edge of the sink. Billy looked through the window. "Land ho, everybody. We're making a brief stop. Grab a quick one at the pool bar, or you can stay on the boat and get shit-faced. Either way, the gangplank goes up in thirty minutes, that's eight o'clock sharp. Stragglers will be taking a taxi."

"Aye-aye, sir!" came a few voices as the line formed. The Jamaican woman and the car dealer were in a clench, obviously not going anywhere. C.J. picked up her purse and followed everyone else up the steps to the open deck behind the helm. Billy stepped off the side, caught the lines, and wound them around the cleats. A yacht twice as big was docked farther on, the occupants idly watching the new arrivals.

The Royal Palm and half a dozen luxury condominiums soared from a small island at the mouth of the Miami River, the skyline of downtown to the north, more condos and bank buildings to the south. The sky was still blue, but fading. The low sun pushed the hotel's shadow out over the water. Chattering gaily, the small crowd moved forward.

"C.J.!" Billy held out his hand and helped her to the dock. He was saying to his accountant, "I'm looking at a sixty-two-foot Hatteras. They're willing to make me a deal. I could easily get down to the islands in that. But could I deduct it?"

"No problemo. You go down there, you check on the casino, hold some meetings on board, take your partners fishing—" Their conversation ended as the accountant's girlfriend, or whoever, took his arm and led him toward the pool bar.

"A new boat?" asked C.J. "That's risky."

"Stop being my lawyer, will you, baby? I told you, everything's golden. And they'd give me a good trade-in on the *Lucky Lady*."

"Well, at least you aren't going to throw it out in the trash."

"Are you talking about that sculpture again? Why do you keep bringing it up? Didn't I apologize already?"

"I don't care about the damned sculpture. It just seems that when something bores you, you get rid of it."

He came closer. "Are you afraid it will apply to you?"

"I was simply trying to make a point."

"One thing about you, C.J., you're never boring." She could feel his breath on her lips. "Let's just have a good time. Aren't you having a good time?"

"I'll have a better time after we dump your tedious friends."

He smiled. "Me too. Now go, find Milo. I'll be at the bar."

"Billy, what about the witnesses?"

"Oh, the witnesses. Sure. I'll find out for you first thing in the morning." He patted her fanny as she walked away and called after her, "Hurry up."

The party was being held on the second floor in a room overlooking the pool and an acre of landscaped gardens, bedraggled from lack of rain. Music and voices floated down. C.J. picked her way carefully over a brick bath. The straps on her shoes were so narrow they gave the impression of walking barefoot on tiptoes.

With a glance around to make sure Billy was out of sight, C.J. opened her bag for her BlackBerry. She was hoping for a message from Kylie. She had kept it on vibrate mode in the boat. She hadn't told Billy anything about Kylie. If he remembered at all, the girl was an annoyance, a minor favor to be handled for some old acquaintance of C.J.'s mother. Billy knew where C.J. had been born. He thought it was amusing. He'd faked a Southern accent until she'd screamed at him to shut up.

C.J. was praying not to get a call from Fran Willis. When is Kylie's flight home? Did you talk to her yet? C.J. had no idea what to say. She should have called Fran already, gotten it over with.

The screen showed that email had come in. She clicked the icon. Scrolling through messages from friends or colleagues, she saw one from Rick Slater. Curious, she clicked on it. He had blown off the questionnaire. He suggested she call him instead. She laughed in disbelief. "Buddy, you are on thin ice." She put away the phone, checked her lipstick, and snapped her compact shut.

On the second level, she opened a glass door and strode into the crowd. Her attention was drawn to a large, square table that held the model of The Aquarius Residences and Resort. The glassy blue bay was dotted with sailboats, and the swampy, waterfront acreage on Card Sound had turned into the landscaped surroundings for three glass towers that resembled columns of water rising from the sea. There were pools, fountains, a marina, shopping, a conference center, and—just as Billy Medina had wanted—plenty of room for a Vegas-style casino. All the surfaces were pale turquoise, smooth and liquid, with solar panels everywhere, positioned to catch the sun. An empty rectangle at the edge of the property indicated the location of a desalination plant. Someday. When they invented a method that wouldn't cost a fortune.

Milo had been right: The Aquarius depended on getting fifty scrubby acres of abandoned government land. Again, she wondered why Paul Shelby would take such a political gamble. Because he wanted an endorsement from Friends of the Everglades? "And sell me the Brooklyn Bridge, too," she muttered.

The architect stood in the light of a video camera being interviewed by a reporter from the local CBS affiliate. He wore a white dinner jacket with black silk trousers, cowboy boots, and his Panama hat. He spotted C.J. and opened his arms. "There she is! The beautiful and very talented, formerly from Hollywood, celebrity attorney C.J. Dunn."

The reporter, a man with a bit too much base makeup, asked if she'd had a chance to see the model and what she thought. The microphone shifted toward her. C.J. smiled at Milo. "I think it's just brilliant. We're all so excited that a project of this importance will be built in South Florida."

A camera flashed. Someone said, "One more? Smile. Big smile."

When the lights went off, and the reporters moved on, Milo said, "This is a surprise. I thought you weren't coming."

"Of course I'd come, Milo, but listen, I don't have much time. Billy's waiting for me. You know that young architect who works for you? He was driving when you picked me up at the courthouse. Jason. What's his last name?"

"Jason Wright. Why?"

"He was a friend of Alana Martin, and I want to talk to him."

"Well, I don't have his number on me."

"Is he here?"

"Yes, but I can't help you look. It's just one interview after another. The burden of fame."

C.J. slid her arm around Milo's waist. "Milo, sweetie, I need to talk to you sometime. Not now, tomorrow. Early. Say elevenish?"

"Whenever you call me 'sweetie,' I am immediately suspicious. What's it about?"

She spoke into his ear. "Oh, just this thing I'm doing for your friend, Mr. Shelby. But now I have to fly."

He stuck out his lower lip. "Are you deserting poor old Milo already?"

"Afraid so. Oh, wait. You know all the gossip. Have you heard anything about Alana Martin being in adult movies?"

His wide blue eyes opened further. "Adult movies? You mean porn? My goodness. Who told you that?"

"Nobody. I've been talking to people who knew her. She claimed to have been in a movie but didn't want to say which, or with whom, or anything about it. She led a fairly free lifestyle, to say the least. I was just wondering if you'd heard anything."

"Not a word."

"Find out for me? But don't say who's asking. You're so good at that." She put an air kiss on his cheek. "I'll call you in the morning." She backed away, and within seconds he was surrounded again.

Her watch said 7:42. When she lifted her eyes, she noticed a woman handing out brochures at a table by the door. C.J. pushed through the crowd. Reaching the table she said, "Excuse me. Don't you work for Milo Cahill? I'm looking for Jason, but I have no idea where he went to."

The woman pointed to one of the bartenders' stations, and her mouth moved, but the jazz quartet was playing again, and C.J. couldn't hear. She nodded and thanked her. It took C.J. five minutes to find a young man who resembled the one she had seen yesterday. This specimen was six feet tall, with tousled blond hair and the deepest blue eyes. His indigo suit skimmed his body, and the open-collar white shirt set off his tan. He was holding a drink, laughing with some other men.

Touching his shoulder, she said, "I'm sorry to break in like this, but aren't you Jason Wright? May I talk to you for a minute?" When they had moved to a quieter location near the windows, she introduced herself. "Do you remember me? You were driving when Milo picked me up outside the courthouse."

"I know who you are," he said, "and I am not Milo's chauffeur. I'm an architect. I specialize in structural engineering."

Jason was having trouble pronouncing his words. C.J. smiled at him. "I know. You're a graduate of Princeton, too. How long have you been with Milo Cahill?"

"Two years."

"Must be great experience for you, being on the team for The Aquarius."

He focused on her. "What do *you* think of it?"

No one, she thought, ever asked a question in that manner unless they wanted a negative response. "Well . . . it's not really to *my* taste, but . . . I have to admire the technology."

"Yes, yes, let's admire the technology."

She said, "And I really don't think it fits the location. It's too . . . cold."

He narrowed his lovely eyes. "Ha. At last. One person in this room not totally full of crap. I'm sorry. That wasn't nice." He laughed. "Oh, God. If Milo was here, he'd have my head. You won't tell him?"

"Of course not."

"May I get you a drink?" He held up his glass.

"Thank you, but I don't have time. Did Milo tell you why he wanted to see me yesterday?"

"No."

"He asked me to take on a client, a man who was at Billy Medina's party the night Alana Martin disappeared. The police are interviewing everyone. My client had nothing to do with it, but when the police show up, it's good to have a lawyer on your side. To do my job, I need to discover as much as I can about Alana and hopefully discover the reason. . . . " C.J. stopped. "I'm sorry about Alana."

"Who says she's dead?" Jason turned his back to the room. "They say that, but where's the body?"

"They may never find her, but that doesn't stop the police from investigating or the media from turning it into a circus and possibly ruining several lives in the process, including that of my client."

Daylight was turning to dusk. The arch of lights on the bridge to Key Biscayne had come on. Some of Billy's guests were back on the boat, sitting on the bench seats behind the helm. Billy was nowhere in sight.

"Jason, I need to know about Alana. Who she was, what she wanted. Her friends, and those who were not her friends. What I need, to be honest, is a motive. If I have that, I can point the investigation away from my client. He's an innocent man. But I'm handicapped because I just don't know where to start. You're busy now, but could I meet you somewhere tomorrow or Monday?"

The lights in the room put his pale reflection on the window. "Let me ask you a question. You're a criminal lawyer. If the police want to talk to me, and I don't want to, will they suspect me?"

"Well, they shouldn't, but it does arouse their interest. It's human nature, isn't it?" C.J. concentrated fully on Jason's face. He had something on his mind. The proper thing would be to walk away, tell him to find a lawyer immediately and to keep his mouth shut. But she said, "Have the police contacted you?"

"They showed up earlier today at my apartment. I wasn't there. They left a card in the door. Sergeant George Fuentes. He wrote me a note to call him."

"I know Fuentes. He'll be back."

"So should I call him? I don't know what happened to Alana. What should I tell him?"

C.J. said, "He will probably ask if you saw her leave the party with anyone."

"I didn't see her leave at all. She was just gone."

"When was the last time you saw her?"

"Only once, when I got there at ten-thirty."

"Did you speak to her?"

"No, I saw her across the living room. She was talking to some people. I don't know who they were. I didn't see her after that."

"When did you leave?"

"About one o'clock. I came with some friends, but I was tired, and they wanted to stay, so I left early."

"Where do you live?"

"South Beach, Twenty-Second Street."

"How did you get home? A taxi?"

"You can't get a taxi on Star Island. You call and it takes forever, that time of night. I had my own car. Why?"

"A taxi driver could confirm when you left."

Jason leaned down to speak to her, and she smelled the alcohol, the tangy-sweet aroma of scotch. He said, "What difference does it make when I left? Alana was gone around midnight. That's what they're saying on the news."

"They don't know for sure," C.J. said. "Where were you around midnight? Are there people who can swear you were with them continuously between, say, eleven p.m. and one o'clock in the morning? Do you have an alibi witness? The police will ask you." She waited for an answer. "Jason?"

"Everyone was coming and going! I can't prove where I was. How do you *prove* something like that?"

"It's not easy," she admitted. "They'll be looking for a possible motive, too."

"I had no reason to—to—" He ground his teeth together. "I can't believe she's dead."

"You cared for her."

"Of course I did."

"Were you very close?"

"Yes." He wiped his fingers across his mouth. "She . . . she was a special person. She lit up everything she touched."

"You were . . . intimate with her?"

His eyes had reddened. "I—Yes. No. We . . . we were friends. But I did love her. Who could help but love her? I'm sorry. This is so hideous."

"Yes. I understand." C.J. put a hand on his arm. "Could you tell me if she had enemies? Someone who was jealous of her? Or angry? Or afraid she might reveal a secret? Did she mention any threats?"

Taking a deep breath, he glanced back at the crowd, which had grown even larger. "I should go. I'm supposed to be over there kissing ass." He cleared this throat and finished his drink. "You didn't hear that either."

C.J. held on to his arm. "Could we talk sometime?"

Jason was edging away. "Sorry. I have to go."

"It would be so helpful. Please. Anything you tell me would remain between us." As she spoke, she fumbled in her purse for a card. "Take this. Wait. Call my cell phone in the morning. Or anytime." She found a pen and quickly jotted it down. "Will you call me?"

He slid the card into his coat pocket as he turned away and vanished into the crowd.

She had lied to him. She felt bad about it, but not so bad she had stopped herself. There was no attorney–client privilege between them. Jason Wright was not her client. If he implicated himself, she would use it. Her duty was to Richard Slater.

A glance outside told her she was running out of time. The sea had turned gray, and the trees were dark silhouettes. Swiveling quickly toward the door, she took a step and collided with someone, a man, who grabbed her arms to keep her from falling. She gasped and put a hand to her heart.

With a slow smile, Paul Shelby said, "I don't usually scare people like that."

"Sorry. It's fine, I just. . . . " She pushed back her hair. "I was just leaving."

"Let me walk you out."

As they went out to the terrace, C.J. said, "I dropped by to congratulate Milo. It's a marvelous design."

"Yes, I'm proud to be associated with it," Paul Shelby said. "You may have heard, I'm sponsoring a resolution in the House to sell an old naval base to the company building The Aquarius. The land's no use to anybody, just sitting there. We've scheduled a press conference for Monday to announce that and some other things. My candidacy and so forth."

With the temperature still nudging ninety, sweat was breaking out on her neck. As Shelby talked, she moved slowly toward the stairs and put her hand on the tubular white railing that curved to the gardens below.

"C.J., would you mind? I asked to speak to you for a reason."

She stopped and turned, the low wall of the terrace at her back. "I'm so sorry, but there are people waiting for me. Is it something that could wait till tomorrow?"

"No, it's not. I think you can afford to give me a minute of your time." Shelby spoke softly, although the nearest people were several yards away at small tables, having hors d'oeuvres and cocktails. "Rick told me you want five thousand dollars for expenses. What I'd like to know is, what expenses could there be? I thought you'd have this all wrapped up in a few days."

"I'm hoping to." C.J. wandered toward the side overlooking the gardens, and Shelby followed. She fanned her face. "My God, this heat. Where is our ocean breeze? Mr. Shelby—"

"Paul."

"Paul. I don't discuss my cases except with clients or members of my staff, but since you're paying the bill . . . the expenses are primarily for my investigator. We're doing background checks on everyone involved. Mr. Slater, of course. Alana Martin and the people she knew. I regret I can't get into details."

"Why are you investigating your own client?"

"I always do in a criminal case. I investigate everyone connected with it."

"That seems a tad excessive."

"It's how I do things. Look. Any lawyer who can accomplish what you want is going to incur some expenses. You're lucky I'm not charging fees." She said, "By the way, did you have a chance to talk to Mr. Finch's sister about my interview with CNN?"

She doubted it was the heat that had caused color to rise in Paul Shelby's face. He looked distinctly annoyed. "Yes. I mentioned it. Sarah is flying through Miami this weekend. There's a possibility she'll have time to see you. Don't worry, C.J. I'm a man of my word. You'll get your part of the bargain. There's one other thing. I've been told the police searched Rick's apartment this morning and found nothing of interest. Is that true?"

"Yes. I was there."

"Then can you explain why a producer for *The Justice Files* is requesting an interview with me?"

She shook her head. "Are they? Someone is fishing. You should decline."

"Oh, we did. Our schedule is jammed. My mother, whose advice has always proved right on the money, wants me to reconsider my decision to keep Rick Slater on. He's becoming a liability. Any thoughts?"

"It would raise questions."

"It would save me five thousand dollars."

"Give me a few days," she said. "I'm on to some good leads about Alana Martin."

"What leads?"

"Sorry, Paul, you aren't the client."

"No, but you owe me some consideration, don't you think?"

She relented. "There might be a jealous boyfriend. Alana dated Jason Wright, a young architect who works for Milo Cahill, but I don't want to speculate. Also, we're tracking down the witnesses who claim they saw Alana with Rick Slater. I believe they will change their minds when they think about it more clearly."

"What's your strategy to hold off the media?" Shelby asked.

C.J. checked her watch and saw with a start that she was late. "Forgive me, but I really must run."

"Would you keep in touch with me about this?" He reached for her arm, and she jerked away.

"Don't!"

He smiled quizzically. "What did I do?"

"Nothing. Nothing." Her hands were raised, palms out. "I'm just in a hurry." She turned and ran for the stairs. Her hair flowed behind her, and her skirt belled out. The staccato of her heels matched the quick tempo of her breathing. She reached the sidewalk and without stopping took a smaller, straighter path leading to the dock. A row of palm trees marched along the seawall, with tables and chairs between them. The planter to her left, filled with flowers, had white metal sconces to light the way.

The path was made of bricks, and she did not notice the sandfilled separations between them until her high, narrow heel had plunged into one. She staggered and barely stayed upright. She jerked on her right foot, and a strap across her instep tore loose from the sole. She hopped to keep her balance. The shoe was pinned by its heel. "Goddamn it! Oh . . . *fuck!* Four hundred dollars, and you do this to me, you piece-of-shit shoe!"

She also noticed, too late, a bald man with a short beard slouched in one of the chairs, smoking. "You cuss pretty good for a girl."

Rick Slater. His shirt sleeves were rolled up, and his jacket lay folded on the table beside him. She closed her eyes. "What are you doing here? Of course. You brought Congressman Shelby."

"And the missus. Just your friendly chauffeur. I saw you up there with him. In a hurry?"

"I have some friends waiting for me on a boat." She crouched down and grabbed the shoe and pulled. *"Come on!"*

"Here, let me get that." He pushed himself out of his chair and walked over. With a sharp tug it came loose. He dangled the shoe from a finger and squinted through cigarette smoke. "I think it's a goner."

C.J. took it and turned it over. The strap could be repaired, but the bricks had shredded the heel. "Marvelous." She sat on a chair and brushed the sand off her foot.

"Nice dress, though." He made a clicking noise with his tongue.

She didn't look at him. "Mr. Slater, I want you to call me tomorrow morning at home. I read your email. You refuse to answer the questions. That is not acceptable. Hand injury? Give me a break."

"Whoa. Whoa. What's biting your ass?" He crushed out his cigarette in the planter.

"I don't have time to talk to you." She slid her foot into the shoe. The remaining straps would hold it in place if she walked carefully. "No, I will ask you one thing, and I'd like the truth, if that is remotely possible. You told me you barely knew Alana Martin. You'd had lunch with her a couple of times. Correct? I spoke to Alana Martin's roommate today. She told me that you and Alana were having a sexual relationship."

"We were?"

C.J. looked coolly at him for a second, then said, "Call me tomorrow." She started to get up, but Slater put his hands on both arms of the chair. His face was inches from hers.

"Let me get this straight," he said. "Tisha Dulaney claims she saw me having sex with Alana Martin."

"No. She reported what Alana told her. I would rather not describe it."

"Must've been good. Did I like it?"

"Get out of my way."

"Somebody is for damn sure lying, and it ain't me, lady."

They both looked around when a man's voice came from a few yards away. His silver hair and white shirt emerged from the dark background of foliage. "Excuse me? C.J.? What is going on here?"

"Hello, Billy." She pushed Slater's arm aside and stood up. "I'm sorry to have kept you waiting. It took longer than I expected." Billy had his eyes on Rick Slater. "This is a client," she said.

"Yes. It's . . . ahhh . . . what's-his-name. Paul Shelby's chauffeur." Slater said, "Glad to meet you too, whoever you are."

"Guillermo Medina. A friend of your boss."

"Richard Slater." He smiled. "That's my name."

"Did I ask?" Billy motioned with his fingers to C.J. "Let's go."

She said, "Give me a minute, all right?"

"Everyone is waiting for you."

"I know. Start the engines. I will be there in one minute, after I finish with Mr. Slater."

"We have reservations," Billy said in a singsong voice. "It's Saturday night. If we're late, they'll give away our table."

"So call them. I will be there in one minute!"

"I told you, stragglers take a taxi."

Rick Slater laughed softly and leaned back with his hands in his pockets.

Billy looked at him. "You have something to say to me?"

Slater shook his head.

"No, say it."

Still smiling, Slater looked out over the bay.

C.J. said, "Billy, leave it alone. I'll be right there."

"No, I want to hear what this asshole has to say to me."

"I'll be darned," Slater said, furrowing his brow. "Richard A. Slater. My mother never told me the A was for asshole."

C.J. stared at him. "Stop it."

"What I was going to say was . . . butt out. My lawyer and I are having a conversation here."

"Ms. Dunn sees clients during working hours."

"Isn't that sort of up to her?"

A glint came into Billy's dark eyes. "C.J., we're leaving. Right now."

She said quietly, "Both of you can go to hell. Mr. Slater, I will see you on Monday, my office. Call my secretary. Billy, please give my regrets to the others. Enjoy your dinner."

"All right," Billy said with a shrug. "Sorry you can't make it."

She hesitated for a moment, thinking he might say something more, but he didn't. With a final hard look at Rick Slater, she turned and walked back toward the hotel, clenching her toes to keep her shoe from falling off.

chapter SIXTEEN

as soon as Medina was out of sight, Rick secured his holster to his belt, put on his jacket, and headed for the hotel. It wasn't hard to spot the pink-and-orange dress and blond hair. She went straight through the carpeted lobby and out the front door. As she passed, people turned their heads like they recognized her, or maybe because of her looks. If she hadn't been his lawyer, he would have been interested. Or not. The woman was a hundred and ten pounds of attitude.

He stood beside her. She kept her eyes on the cab pulling under the portico. A man got into it. She was next in line, as soon as another one came along.

"I'm sorry about that scene back there," he said. "I put you in a bad spot with your boyfriend. I guess he's your boyfriend. A man doesn't speak that way to a stranger."

She signaled the doorman, who nodded and held up a hand to wait.

"I never slept with Alana Martin. She might have said it, but that doesn't make it so."

"You know what? I don't care. Call me on Monday." C.J. stepped off the curb as a taxi appeared at the bottom of the driveway. "And when you come, be sure to bring a check."

Slater took her elbow, swung her around, and smiled at the couple behind her. "Go ahead. She's with me."

"That was my taxi!"

He quickly moved in front of her. "Where are you going? Home? Let me drive you. The Shelbys are here till at least nine o'clock. I'm parked right over there, got a VIP spot." He added, "You don't really want to wait till Monday to hear the truth. Do you?"

Her blue eyes fixed on him. He counted off five seconds before she said, "My car is at Billy's house. You can take me there."

A short bridge led to Brickell Avenue, and he turned north toward downtown, keeping the SUV under the speed limit. It would be a quick ride over to Star Island, fifteen minutes at most, unless the Saturday-night party crowd heading for South Beach had clogged the causeway. C.J. crossed her arms. The breeze from the air conditioner lifted the hair around her face. He reached over and angled the vent the other way. She was wearing a light, flowery perfume that made him want to lean closer and sniff her neck.

He said, "I've been trying to figure out why Alana lied to her roommate about me. I went over there to pick Alana up for lunch, and she wasn't ready, so I waited. Tisha was home, and we talked a bit. You saw her. She looks like a hooker, right? She was never in the business, according to her, but she said she could show me some fun. She asked if I was a swinger. Multiple partners and all that. I said no. Alana came out, and we left. And then Alana asks me if I was hitting on Tisha. Maybe she told Tisha what she did to get one up on her. You know what I mean?" Rick looked over at C.J.

She gave a little shrug. "I suppose it could have been that way."

"So are we square?"

"Thanks, but that wasn't really what I wanted to know," C.J. said. "Did Alana ever mention the name Jason Wright?"

"No, who's he?"

"He works for Milo Cahill. He's an architect, twenty-eight years old. I just talked to him at the hotel. He may or may not be Alana's lover. Jason says he was at Billy's party the night Alana disappeared. He says he left at one o'clock, but he can't prove it. I have the feeling he's hiding something. I've no idea what. The police want to talk to him. It's probably routine, because they're talking to everyone, but Jason is nervous." After a pause that stretched out a while, C.J. said, "I don't think he knows where she is, but he makes a nice suspect. The media would snap him up in a second. I could spin it that way. But. . . . "

"But what?"

He couldn't see her clearly until the vehicle went under a street-light. She said, "I don't think he did it. The problem with practicing law is, what's right doesn't always match with what's right for your client."

"A lawyer with a conscience."

"Most of us do have one, believe it or not."

Past the towers of the Met Center, where C.J. Dunn had her office, the street turned north, becoming Biscayne Boulevard. He stopped at a red light, Bayside Marketplace just ahead, tourists crossing the street to browse the souvenir shops or catch dinner at the Hard Rock Café.

C.J. scanned the neighborhood as if she'd never seen it before. "That girl you dropped off after the party. Where was her apartment? Which way did you turn when you came off the causeway? North or south?"

He shook his head. "I don't recall. When you put on as many miles as I do, it all runs together."

She looked at him as though he'd change his mind and say something more helpful. After a while she let out a sigh. "We may not need her. Someone is getting me the names of the two young men who saw you that night. My investigator will interview them and show them Alana's photo. We're hoping they tell the truth. You could be home free."

"Excellent," Rick said.

"There are still a lot of if's," she amended. The next question surprised him. "Did Alana ever mention being in a porn film?"

"What?"

"Alana was in a movie shot in the Bahamas, but she would never give details. I wonder what kind of movie it was."

His conversations with Alana Martin went through Rick's mind. He could answer this one truthfully. "She never said anything about porn films. She wanted to get the hell out of Miami and go to Hollywood. That's where her mind was."

"You don't just go to Hollywood and get a part in a movie unless you're stunningly beautiful, incredibly talented, or you know someone." C.J. turned toward him, and the safety belt across her chest did interesting things to her cleavage. She saw where his eyes were and shifted in the seat.

Rick looked toward the road. "That's a pretty necklace. Coral?"

"Yes, it was a birthday present." She added, "From Billy."

"Great."

"Did Alana talk about how she planned to get into the movies? Did she have any connections? An assistant producer, a casting agent?"

"Damned if I know." He checked the rearview and moved into a line of traffic slowing for the entrance ramp to the causeway. "What makes you think she was a porn actress?"

"It's a feeling I get. The trashy lifestyle, the drugs, the people she knew, her disinclination to talk about her past experience in the movie business even though she was eager to get into acting. Alana gave her modeling portfolio to the owner of China Moon, and I have it. Aside from the usual head shots, there were some that could have been lingerie shots for an escort service, except that she looked like a child wearing her older sister's makeup. In one, she has her finger in her mouth, pouting."

Rick kept his eyes on the road. "She's twenty years old."

"I said she *looked* like a child. Here's something else. The photographer who did the portfolio is a cameraman for a local TV station. His name is Carlos Moreno. Do you ever watch *The Miami Justice Files* with Libertad Rodriguez? She calls herself 'Libi' on air. She hates my guts about as much as I hate hers. I'd love to ask Moreno about Alana, but I doubt he would talk to me." C.J. held up her hands. "But I can't even ask him. Lawyers don't interview witnesses. I shouldn't have been talking to Tisha Dulaney, but you know, I just couldn't help myself. I'm going to ask my investigator to check out Moreno."

"What's the point of that? What are you trying to prove?"

"I want a credible reason why Alana Martin disappeared. Do you know anything about the porn business? I don't mean pornography, I mean the people behind it, the investors, and the cash they produce."

"Not really. I know it's worth a lot of money."

"Enough to kill for," she said.

"Speaking of money. I caught some heat from Paul Shelby about your expenses."

"Don't worry. He said he would pay for it."

The road went past Jungle Island, big sign out front decorated with parrots and monkeys. South Beach lay about a mile ahead, traffic already getting heavy. Rick asked, "Is that what you and Shelby were talking about up there on the terrace?"

"Basically. He wanted to know about your case, and I said I couldn't discuss it with him."

"You looked angry."

"I wasn't angry."

"Your body language said you were. You didn't want to be there."

"I was in a hurry," she replied.

"Well, try not to piss him off, okay? I don't want to lose my job. I'm hearing rumblings. His mother doesn't like me."

"It's the potential for bad publicity she doesn't like. If this all goes away, she'll leave you alone."

"If," he said. C.J.'s profile was backlit by the lights of the Port of Miami, a couple of cruise ships at the dock, ready to head out in the morning. Rick moved to the left-turn lane, the bridge to Star Island ahead. "Do you want to hear some more about Alana?"

She turned to look at him. "Tell me."

"You say she's trashy. That's true to some extent, but you have to understand where she came from. The family lived in Caracas, Venezuela, blue-collar folks. Life is tough down there. Mr. Martinez had actually been born in Miami, so it wasn't too hard to bring the family to the U.S. Alana was the third child of four, the second daughter. Her sister was three years ahead, got A-plus report cards, went to church, played the piano, everybody loved her. The parents doted on this girl. When Alana was seven, an older cousin started fondling her. It went on for about five years, until he joined the Marines and moved away. Alana tried to tell her mother, but mom didn't believe her and didn't want to hear about it. Said she was dirty. When the sister graduated from high school, mom and dad gave her a car. One night the girls went out riding, and Alana asked if she could drive. First time behind the wheel. She ran through a guard rail into a canal. She got her seat belt loose and tried to save her sister, but the car sank too fast."

C.J.'s eyes were fixed on him, and her lips were parted, the images working in her mind.

"After that," Rick said, "Alana tried to take her sister's place with the school and the church, and so on, but of course it didn't work. She moved out, got a job on South Beach. Had some dreams. And a lot of baggage to drag around. One more hard-luck story."

They had arrived at the gatehouse. The guard leaned out to see what they wanted. Rick told him who he was and said they had come to pick up Ms. Dunn's car from Guillermo Medina's house. Then he waited while the guard took down the number on his license tag. This was a public road, but the residents didn't want the public to know that.

The gate arm went up. Rick said. "Which way, left?"

As if waking, C.J. blinked. "Yes. The street will curve. It's about halfway up the island."

"Are you okay?"

"I had no idea."

"You've probably heard worse," he said.

"All my clients have a story. I'm sure you do too."

"Not like that."

"It's why I keep doing my job," she said. "The stories. They make my clients into human beings. If I succeed, the jurors find out that the person on trial isn't all that different from themselves. There, but for the grace of God. Except child molesters and rapists. They have to prove to me that they're innocent before I'll take their cases. Otherwise, I've done it all. People accused of murder, aggravated battery, theft, conspiracy, political crimes. And pornographers. Some of those too."

Rick said, "What's your story?"

"Mine?" She shook her head. "Very boring. Only child, raised in a small town. I left to seek my fortune, found it, got married, moved to Miami. He died of a heart attack, and I stayed. *C'est tout.*"

"That's all, huh? Somehow I doubt that."

The narrow road took them past one mansion after another, most of them tucked behind walls or heavy foliage. C.J. pointed to a row of lights inset into a white stucco wall, shining down on the neatly trimmed grass. Rick parked on the grass outside the open gate. The house was modern, two stories under a flat roof, part of it extending out to make a portico, everything bone-white except for the front doors, which had been painted shiny red. Half a dozen cars filled the circular driveway, but C.J. would be able to maneuver her BMW sedan out of the pack.

"Who's home?" Rick asked.

"Nobody, as far as I know. They all got on the boat." C.J. had her keys in her hand. She tossed them back into her purse. "Show me where you saw the girl."

"What girl?"

"What girl? The one you found passed out in the backyard."

"Why?"

"Humor me." She tilted her watch toward the lights in the portico ceiling. "It's only eight-twenty. You have time."

A slate walkway led around the side of the house. The trees cut the ambient glow from the city, but landscaping lights helped, and the back patio had some security lights. The place seemed unnaturally quiet. Last time, music had been blaring out the patio doors. The long, narrow pool was sending a pale wash of turquoise up into the palm trees. Another island lay a hundred yards west, more big houses, and, beyond that, the causeway, the port, the city. The sky had faded to purple, stars coming out.

"When I was here," he said, "there were some boats at the dock."

"Friends of his who came to the party, I suppose. Billy only has one."

"Only one. Imagine that." Rick said, "I have a friend with a boat. That's better than having one myself. I kick in for the fuel, and we share the fish. Sweet."

The path forked, and he led her around some traveler's palms. The boathouse was at the back corner of the property. A vine-covered wall separated the Medina house from the one next door.

She said, "You know people in Miami? I thought you just moved here from Mexico."

He thought: *This is what you get from not paying attention, dumbass.* "He's a guy I met in the military. Settled down now, a wife and kids, the whole nine yards. We go fishing, but I don't have much time for it." Rick pointed to a patch of grass between the walkway and the boat house. "That's where I saw the girl."

"Tell me what happened," C.J. said.

"I heard her telling them to stop, so I came over to see what was going on. The men had their hands on her. Far as I could make out, they were going to carry her over to the boathouse. She was so drunk she could hardly stand up."

"Where were you when you heard her calling out?"

He jerked his head toward the water. "Over there, near the dock."

C.J. looked in that direction, then at him. "But you told me this morning that you were leaving, going home."

He said, "I was. I wanted to have a cigarette first."

"I see. You heard her call, you chased the men away. Then what?"

"She asked if I'd give her a ride. I said yes."

"She was too drunk to stand up," C.J. said, "but you dropped her off downtown, alone, at one o'clock in the morning?"

"She was fine by the time we got there."

"In ten minutes? Obviously *not*. Did you wait until she was safely inside or leave her standing on the sidewalk?"

"Why are you cross-examining me?"

"I'm trying to understand what happened."

"I just told you what happened. I wasn't her baby-sitter. Don't give me the look from hell. You don't even know this girl. I wouldn't have left her if she hadn't been okay."

"All right. Fine. Let's go, then."

He looked past her at the boathouse. The back half extended out over the water, room for a small boat to pull in for shelter. He hadn't noticed before, but the dock ran along the seawall the entire width of the property, about seventy-five yards. On the south side, only a few yards separated the boathouse from the wall at the property line.

"Rick, let's go," she said. "What are you looking at?"

"Give me a second." He walked toward the corner of the property. C.J. slipped off her shoes and followed through the grass. He reached the end of the wall and stepped down to the dock, heavy planks of wood lit dimly by a row of small lights on the pilings. The dock ended abruptly. He peered around the end of the wall and saw the hulking shape of another big house. Hurricane shutters had been pulled across every window and door. There was a dock over there too, but a smaller one in the center of the property. No boats. Nothing.

"Does anybody live next door? It looks vacant."

"He owns an Italian tire company. They come here in the season."

"It's a lot bigger than your boyfriend's place," Rick said.

She gave him a look.

"And what's beyond that?"

"Another house."

"Owned by?"

"Harnell Robinson."

"Your client, the Dolphins running back?" C.J. nodded, and Rick said, "Damn. All sorts of celebrities in this neighborhood. Wait. I thought Robinson lived in Miami."

"He does. He invested in this house when the market was up. Now it's down, and he'd love to sell it, if you're interested. It's a small one, only three bedrooms, and a bargain at one point five million."

"Location, location. Check this out." He stepped easily around the end of the wall to the other side. He heard C.J.'s voice asking him what he thought he was doing.

"It's easy to get over there. You want to try it?"

She said, "The police searched every property on this street. They found no trace of Alana."

"Oh, well." Slater stepped back up to the grass on Medina's side. C.J. Dunn stood there waiting for him. He looked at her bare feet. "I thought you were about five-seven till you took your shoes off."

"No, I'm a shrimp. I wear heels to intimidate my enemies."

"Calamity Jane," he said.

She turned and walked up the slope the way they had come, her hips swaying nicely. They had just passed the boathouse when a spotlight caught them in its powerful beam. It came from the direction of the traveler's palms, about ten yards away. The light glinted on the barrel of a shotgun.

Rick automatically put out an arm, swept C.J. behind him, and calculated how fast he could get to his pistol. A man holding a high-powered lantern and a long gun at the same time wouldn't be able to manage both.

A voice came from the darkness. "Don't move. Stop right there."

Rick raised one hand and used the other to shield his eyes. "Take it easy. We weren't stealing anything. We came to pick up the lady's car."

"So what're you doin' all the way down here?"

C.J. looked around him, a hand at her eyes. "Dennis Murphy? Is that you? It's just me, C.J. Dunn."

"Who's the guy?"

"His name is Richard Slater. He works for Congressman Paul Shelby. I wanted to show him the view."

Rick still had his hands up. "How about pointing that thing in some other direction? It might go off."

"I fucking know how to handle a shotgun."

"I can see that, but oblige me, okay? Just in case."

C.J. said, "Dennis, for God's sake. Put it down, and get that damned light out of my eyes!"

The barrel dropped toward the ground, and he shifted the lantern, which made a pool of light at his feet. He was wearing paint-spattered sneakers. The calves needed some work, but he had the thighs of a power lifter and a chest like a bulldog.

"I'm sorry for not ringing the doorbell," C.J. said, "but I didn't think anyone was here."

"I was in the garage. Billy didn't say you'd be over."

"I had to pick up my car. Call him. I'm sure it's all right."

"I'll definitely call him." The pool of light jerked toward the front of the house. "You better go." Finally Rick could see the man's face: a short nose, heavy cheeks, and red hair standing straight up. The top of his head looked like a paintbrush.

"We were leaving anyway," C.J. said, bending to put on her shoes.

"Uh-huh." He stared at her chest, maybe hoping she'd fall out of the dress. She lifted one foot, then the other.

Rick moved in front of her. "Nice haircut. And they said mullets were over. Guess not."

Murphy didn't growl, but he lifted his lip. He followed them across the yard. Rick took C.J.'s arm, as she was having some trouble with one of her shoes. He held her with his left hand in case he felt like using his right to punch out the man behind them, who had his eyes on her ass. When they reached the driveway, she tossed her hair off her face and dug into her bag for her car keys.

Now the guy was looking at her legs. He was holding the lantern in one hand and the shotgun across the other arm; it looked like a semiautomatic Browning 12-gauge. A little out of his price range, but you never knew.

Rick took her keys and opened the driver's side door of the BMW. "Hop in." She sat and swung her legs around. Before he closed the door, he leaned down and said, "I'm going to follow you out of here. Stop when you get a chance. The driveway of Harnell Robinson's place. All right?"

The engine purred to life. C.J. turned on her headlights and went through the gate. Rick took out his own keys. "Does Mr. Medina like you drooling on his girlfriends?"

Murphy's pale blue eyes narrowed. "How about I shove this shotgun up your ass?"

"No, you go first."

"Fuck you."

Rick had to make a three-point-turn to head back south, Murphy watching from the other side of the gate as it rolled shut. Brake lights flared farther up the street, C.J.'s car pulling over, waiting for him. He felt a vibration in the breast pocket of his shirt. He'd left his phone there, not to miss the call from Paul Shelby. He had a mental image of the congressman and his wife standing out front of the hotel, wondering where their driver had gone to.

But the screen said something else. Moreno.

He hit the button. "Yeah, Carlos, what's up?"

"They think they found her."

As the SUV drifted along about five miles an hour, Rick listened to what Carlos Moreno had to say. He pulled in behind C.J.'s car and sat there with the engine idling, parking lights on. He could see her opening the door, getting out, wondering what was going on. She was barefoot again. She closed her door and walked toward him.

"Carlos, I have to go. Call you right back."

He slid the phone into his pocket and got out of his vehicle.

C.J. looked up at him, her face in shadow, the streetlight behind her. "Well? Why did you want me to stop?"

It took him a second to think how to tell her. "That friend I mentioned was watching the news. The police have cordoned off a section of Fort Lauderdale Beach. A body—correction, body parts—washed up on shore. It's a young woman. They think it's Alana Martin."

"Oh." Her hands went to her mouth. "Oh, no. Oh, my God. What did they *do* to her?"

"You should go on home. If I hear anything else, I'll call you." Rick walked C.J. to her car. "The congressman is expecting me."

chapter
SEVENTEEN

from the sidewalk, Carlos Moreno could see a circle of floodlights fifty yards away lighting up the breakers, and, beyond that, empty black ocean. Libi Rodriguez was leaning into the open door of Channel Eight's live truck, speaking with the operator inside. The truck had just arrived, parked on the east side of A1A, close to the curb, and raised its 45-foot mast. The police were squeezing northbound traffic to one lane and keeping onlookers back. Red and blue emergency lights swept over the fronts of the fancy condominiums across the street, and people watched from the balconies. Carlos had brought all his gear, but the tripod would be useless in the sand.

Thanks to a contact in the Fort Lauderdale P.D., Channel Eight had arrived first on the scene. Libi had seventeen minutes to get her story together. They would go live with footage of the crime scene, assuming the police let them get that close. Libi leaned into the truck.

"Manny! *Escúchame bien.* I want that piece with me and the detective, then go to the interview with the tourists. The Taylors? Right. Don't cut the part where the woman looks like she's going to barf. I want that in. We'll be back in ten minutes. When you get the tape, I want thirty seconds of whatever Carlos shoots plus my comment and any good quotes from the cops on the scene. We'll go live from there. *¿Me entiendes?*"

Carlos heard the *thwop-thwop-thwop* of rotor blades and looked at the sky. Channel Six had arrived, the others sure to follow.

Libi stepped down to the sidewalk and grabbed his arm. "They just called from the station. CNN wants the story for their ten o'clock news hour! Carlos, I'm going national!"

"Will CNN use it, though?"

"Fuckin' A, they will!" She heard the helicopters—two of them now—and looked up. "Oh, shit. Come on, let's go." Holding her microphone in one hand, her reporter pad in the other, she went through the opening in the long, curving white wall. A light breeze rattled the palm trees. Carlos hugged his camera close to his chest as he plowed through the sand.

"We're the first ones here! Can you believe the luck?" Libi was practically skipping with happiness. "What should I lead with? The mysterious disappearance of a beautiful young woman has finally been solved with the shocking discovery of a dismembered body in the surf on Fort Lauderdale Beach."

"That's fine for *Court TV*," he said.

"You're right. How about this? The body of a young woman drifted ashore tonight on Fort Lauderdale Beach, putting an end to a week of speculation, and so forth."

"Better, but how do you know it's Alana Martin?"

"Who else could it be?"

"But you aren't sure it's Alana, and you shouldn't say she's been dismembered. The medical examiner hasn't had a chance to look at the body yet."

"Carlos, they haven't found the head, and the legs are missing below the knees. One of her arms is gone, and they found the other down the beach. Someone obviously cut her up."

"Not necessarily." He was getting short of breath. "If you're in the ocean a week, it can do things to you. A shark could have come along."

"Sharks do not eat dead flesh." Libi was an expert on everything.

Carlos could deal with bombs going off around him, but he didn't like filming death scenes, the exposed bone and the blood. In this case, there wouldn't be any blood left, and the body would be covered by now. Just after dark, the Taylors, a young couple from Ohio, had been walking barefoot in the surf and had noticed something at the edge of the water. The only light had come from the street, so they couldn't see clearly. The woman thought it was a sea turtle, because turtles nested this time of year, but as they walked closer they saw it was too pale, and it wasn't moving. The man noticed long, gray tendrils that floated around the thing as the waves went in and out. He leaned over it, and as the next wave went out he saw shoulders and ragged white flesh where the head should have been. His wife screamed, and they ran to call 911. Later the police explained to Libi that the tendrils had been strands of silver duct tape, floating free.

There was not one station on Planet Earth that would show it, even if the police let them tape it, which was highly doubtful. Carlos planned to shoot at a distance, put a sense of desolation into the frame. But Libi Rodriguez would be chattering in the background.

She was doing it now. "Our chopper is on the way. After we finish and give the tape to Manny, let's see if we can catch a ride back to Miami. We'll get the car later. I want to interview the parents before anyone else gets there. They know me. They trust me. I want their reaction."

"But we aren't sure it's her," Carlos said, "and even if it is, we shouldn't be the ones to break it to the family."

"Don't be so squeamish. Everyone has heard by now. It's been on every station."

Someone passed him, falling into step with Libi, a short man in a ball cap with a folded tripod on his shoulder and two cameras with long lenses, the straps making a black X across his back. "Ms. Rodriguez? Nash Pettigrew from Los Angeles, freelance photographer. I admire your work." He looked around at Carlos and gave him a quick nod.

Libi picked up the pace. If he had been a TV reporter she would probably have tripped him. "We're on a deadline," she said.

"I was hoping we could work out a trade," he said. "Some footage of the tourist couple for some shots of the dead girl. I got inside a sixth-floor apartment, great view. I have a good one of the waves breaking over the body, before they pulled it farther onshore and covered it up."

Libi finally looked at the man. "What's she wearing? The girl on the beach. Did you see any clothes?"

"It looked like a little black dress. She was wrapped in duct tape, and I guess that kept the dress from coming off her."

"Ah-ha." Libi looked around at Carlos. "It's definitely her, then. Alana Martin was wearing a black dress the night she disappeared."

Pettigrew said, "Are you interested in a trade?"

"Why should I be?"

"We're not in competition. You're video, I'm print." He grinned up at Libi as he trudged beside her. "I've been told you have footage of the lawyer, C.J. Dunn, coming out of Alana's apartment today. I have shots of her at China Moon, talking to Alana's employer. I also have her talking to Alana's boyfriend, Jason Wright, two hours ago. Same party you were at."

Libi didn't stop but she slowed down. "Why are you interested in C.J. Dunn?"

"She's all over this case. Follow her, you find who the cops are looking at. See, I know her from L.A. She doesn't get into a case unless it has high publicity value, and usually the person she represents is guilty as all get-out. She's been hired by someone you'd never think was connected to Alana Martin."

"Who?"

"Not yet." Pettigrew wagged a finger.

Libi walked along a few more paces before she said, "If you had something on C.J. Dunn I could use, I might be interested. I mean something personal."

Pettigrew's front teeth had gaps between them. He passed his tongue over his lips. "Okay, this is for free. She's not from L.A. She's a redneck from a podunk town in North Florida. Her father died in prison. Her real name's Charlotte Josephine Bryan. Oh, there's more, but we share it, see? What about a deal?"

Libi stopped walking. "Go back there to the Channel Eight truck and wait for me."

"Okey-doke."

As Pettigrew turned toward the street, Carlos said, "I wouldn't get involved with a man like that."

"Well, Carlos, that's why God made you a cameraman and me a reporter." She headed again toward the lights, double time.

He caught up and asked, "Why do you want something on C.J. Dunn?"

Libi was smiling. "Did you know that C.J. Dunn is up for a job on CNN? Hosting a show on homicide by the rich and famous. She's too aloof for that gig. People don't like that. And I'm younger and hotter, anyway."

"It doesn't sound like an entertainment show," Carlos said.

"Of course it is. It's all entertainment. Even this." The glare of the lights cut across her face. She clamped her microphone and reporter pad under her arm long enough to take a compact out of her jacket pocket and check her lipstick. "Okay, let's do it. Get the police activity first, then swing over to me. Wait. I want to stand so my hair isn't against the sky. Let's have some backlighting. How's this?"

"Good." As Carlos panned over the scene, Libi pushed her hair behind her ears and straightened her collar, opening her shirt to show some chest. He turned on his camera light and put her in the right side of the frame.

Her image said, "I can guess what Nash Pettigrew will tell me. Want to hear it?"

"Sure."

"Congressman Paul Shelby is the one who hired C.J. Dunn. Why else would he blow off my request for an interview? I happen to know that homicide detectives have been questioning his chauffeur. I can't remember his name, but I wrote it down. Don't you think that's interesting, Carlos?"

"Not really. They're questioning a lot of people."

Libi said, "A mere chauffeur wouldn't be able to pay her exorbitant fees, but Shelby would. I saw her with Shelby tonight. They went outside to talk. I'll bet it was about this case."

The viewfinder framed the circle of lights blazing on the beach, the yellow crime-scene tape, and two men approaching with a stretcher. Carlos said, "They're going to take the body away."

Libi looked around. "We got here just in time. Are you taping it? I want that."

They carried a stretcher with metal rails and a heavy black bag in the center, neatly folded. Someone ought to be calling the family, maybe bring a priest to the house.

"Carlos!" Libi looked into the lens. "I'm going to give you a couple of openings. They can use whichever fits. Ready?" She had a slight frown on her face, which was appropriate, he guessed, for a pickup of a death scene by the major networks. "This is Libi Rodriguez for CNN, reporting from Fort Lauderdale Beach." She paused, then said, "This is Libi Rodriguez for Channel Eight News."

Gesturing toward the activity behind her, she went on, "Speculation over the disappearance a week ago of a beautiful young Miami woman, a model and budding actress, seems to have ended tonight when an Ohio couple, taking a romantic walk on the beach, stumbled upon a grisly sight."

For the small thrill it gave him, Carlos let his finger touch the button that would turn off the sound. He wondered how soon he could get to his phone to call Rick Slater.

chapter

EIGHTEEN

I n her bedroom, C.J. turned on the television and scrolled
   through the local channels for the gruesome scenes of a body
   washing ashore. Or worse: parts of a body. She saw game
shows and sitcoms. She hit the mute button and left the picture on.
One of the stations, probably all of them, would break in at the top
of the hour.

What chilled her to the core was the thought that the girl on the
beach wasn't Alana Martin at all, but Kylie Willis. Highly improbable, but all the same she felt anxious, and the muscles of her chest
quivered when she took a deep breath.

"What an *idiot* you are," she told an absent Kylie as she flung
her dress over a chair and jerked open drawers for shorts and a

sleeveless top. "Friends like that. Alana and her bunch. Sex, fake ID's, drugs, alcohol. The road to ruin, my little darling." C.J. slid the top over her head and shook her hair free. Tomorrow, she decided, she would call Fran and admit that Kylie had run away. "I hope you have some magic formula for getting her home, because I sure as hell don't."

Then guilt settled down on her, heavy and gray, and she heard a woman's voice. *You've been a disappointment to me from the day you were born.* C.J. slammed the drawer shut with her knee. She hadn't spoken to her mother for ten years, and a hundred wouldn't be long enough.

When C.J. turned around, she saw Taffy on her bed, licking his paws. He had limped into the yard last winter, bleeding, and, nine hundred dollars later, the vet said he'd make it. Useless old cat. She walked over and scratched the pale orange fur on his belly, and he hissed at her, his love song.

Her cell phone chimed, and she dug it out of her purse and saw Billy's name on the screen. She let it ring twice more before she answered it. "Hey, sailor. Where are you? Still at Monty's?" There were noises in the background, conversation, a laugh.

"Great dinner," he said. "Sorry you missed it. We're about to get back on the boat. Dennis Murphy just called. He said you and Slater were at my house wandering around the backyard. How did you hook up with him again? And what, may I ask, were you doing?"

"Picking up my car, and then I wanted to look at the place where my client was supposedly seen with Alana Martin. Dennis pointed your shotgun at us. Did he tell you that?"

"Did he? I'm sorry. He thought you were burglars. He was cleaning out the garage. He should've left already. He said you and Slater were pretty chummy. What's going on?"

"Nothing is going on. Mr. Slater is my client. Are you jealous, Billy?"

"Not of him, unless your standards have slipped. But you'd like me to be jealous, wouldn't you?"

"You sound a little drunk," she said.

"I am, a little. C.J., don't be mean. Come over tonight. I miss you. My friends are tedious, you are absolutely right, but you shouldn't have walked out on me. It was hell to explain."

She sat on the edge of her bed and petted the cat. Taffy grabbed her hand and gummed her fingers. He was nearly toothless. "Have you heard the news? A body washed ashore on Fort Lauderdale Beach. They think it's Alana Martin."

"What did you say? A body?"

"Pieces of a body, to be exact. I don't have any details. I thought you might have heard—"

"*Coño carajo.* We've been sitting here having dinner. I haven't heard a thing. Pieces of her body?"

"She might have been dismembered, or the body could have come apart."

"Ugh," said Billy.

"The medical examiner will be able to say which, but either way, it's terrible. Her family will be devastated."

"Christ, let's not talk about this. Will I see you later?"

C.J. played with Taffy's torn ear. A woman and her cats. Something sad about it, but not sad enough to send her running to Billy. Not tonight. If she went over there tonight, there was every chance of waking up with a hangover.

"Thanks for the invitation, but I need to look halfway rested this weekend. Donald Finch's sister is in town. I might be seeing her if she has time. The producer at CNN. Remember?"

"Sure. A job interview. You choose fame and fortune over me?"

"Alas, yes," she said. "I also have to see Milo in the morning. I asked him to find out for me if Alana Martin was doing porn films. Milo hears everything."

"Milo is an old lady," Billy said.

"Do you know Jason Wright?" C.J. asked. "He's an architect who works for Milo. Tall, blond, good-looking. Do you know who I'm talking about?"

"Jason. Sure. Why?"

"I spoke to him tonight. Supposedly he and Alana had something going. He says they're just friends, but if you'd heard him— He really cared for her. I pressed him to tell me about her, and he shut down. There are things he wanted to say, I'm sure of it. I did get this much: he has no alibi for the time Alana disappeared. He left the party in his own car. Alana's body could have been in his trunk."

"How convenient for you," Billy said. "You could close your file."

"Yes, but I'm not going to the police, not without more. You could find out for me, couldn't you, Billy-boo? I need to know the real story with Jason and Alana. I don't want to ask Milo."

"No. Turn it over to the cops and let them handle it. I promised you the names of the witnesses. That's my good deed for the day. Let's not talk about it anymore. I think it puts you in a bad mood. Body parts washing up on shore. It's depressing. Come see me. I'll cheer you up." He must have cupped his hand around his cell phone, because the background noises faded, and all she heard was the rumble of his voice, smooth as velvet.

She lay on her bed. "Persuade me."

Billy said, "I'm sorry we argued, baby. Let me make it up to you. We'll light some candles, get the Jacuzzi going. I'll take a Viagra."

She laughed. "I wasn't kidding, I really do have to wake up early."

"We'll set the alarm."

"You won't be home for hours."

"Meet me at the Grand Bay Hotel. I can walk there in ten minutes."

"What about your friends?"

"Fuck 'em. The guy from the marina can take them back. Come on. Say yes. I'll get us a suite with a bathtub for two. Bring your bubble bath."

The word hung on her lips—*yes, yes, yes*. But he would open the minibar and make drinks for himself and have a joint in his pocket for her, being considerate of her sobriety, and he would have some cocaine delivered at two or three in the morning, and argue when she said no, and the night would be a blur of sensation and regret. But she did miss him. It was a sickness.

"C.J.? Come on, baby. You're the only woman I want. You know it's true."

She finally heard the rapping noise that had danced at the edge of her awareness for the past several seconds. She sat up. "Someone's at the back door. It's got to be Edgar. I'll call you right back."

"How long is this going to take?"

"One minute."

"Uh-huh. Are you coming or not? I need to know."

"Maybe not. I'd better stay here tonight. If I met you—"

"All right. Suit yourself." The phone went dead.

She stared at it. "Prick." She dropped the phone and headed toward the door. Taffy jumped off the bed and followed her down the stairs, hissing. She turned on the light in the dining room, then the one on the screened porch, and could see Edgar through the French doors. She unlocked one and pushed it open. "Hey. I got home early. Is everything all right?"   .

"I guess so. I have company. That girl, the same one who came around this morning. Kylie. We've been working on my old photos all evening."

C.J. stared at him, then at the cottage. "Kylie is *here?*"

"Yep." Edgar spoke quietly. "Fell asleep on the couch. I heard you come in, so I thought I'd run over and ask you what to do."

"My God. I was so worried. Why didn't you call me?"

"You were out with that Medina fella, and I didn't want to bother you. I'm sorry."

"No, no, it's fine. How did she get here? Was she looking for me?"

Edgar shook his large, gray head. "I don't know how she got here. She knocked on my door and asked if I had some work for her, fifteen bucks an hour, cash. I could see something wasn't right, but I didn't ask questions, figured I'd wait for you. She got busy right away on my photographs. Said we ought to sort them into piles and write down who was who. I fed her some soup, and she closed her eyes, and that was that. Poor little mite."

C.J. hurried across the porch and stepped down to the dry grass, which crackled under her sandals. The air was heavy and still, with a distant chorus of air conditioners, crickets, and a passing jet plane. She quietly opened the door of Edgar's cottage.

Kylie lay with her head on a sofa pillow, glasses crooked, one foot on the floor, the other dangling. The coffee table was strewn with black-and-white photographs, and someone had been making a list in a spiral notebook. Creeping closer, C.J. leaned over her. Kylie was dressed exactly the same as twelve hours ago, shorts and a bright yellow T-shirt. She had the smell of someone who had been out in the heat all day.

C.J. started to touch her shoulder, but her hand stopped in midair. "I don't know what to do."

Edgar said, "Leave her there. I'll get a blanket."

She might have heard their voices. Her eyes came open. She

quickly straightened her glasses and sat up. "Hi, Ms. Dunn. I came over to help your uncle with his photos."

"That's what he told me," C.J. said.

"I didn't get much sleep last night," Kylie said. "I have insomnia, and then it catches up with me the next day." She looked around, then picked up her purse. "Well. I should be going."

"Would you like to stay here? I have a spare bedroom."

"I can catch a bus to the Beach. I have someone to stay with."

"Who?"

Kylie shrugged. "Friends."

Maintaining her smile, C.J. said, "But it's nearly ten o'clock. The guest room is all made up. There are towels and a new toothbrush in the guest bath. You don't have pajamas, do you? I can lend you something. It's no problem."

"Well . . . I suppose I could."

"Wonderful. Edgar, thank you for taking care of her. Come on, Kylie." C.J. motioned from the door.

Kylie threw her arms around Edgar's neck, and he chuckled and patted her shoulder. "Good night, then. Sleep well. I make pretty fair pancakes. We'll have some in the morning."

As she followed C.J. across the yard, Kylie kept her distance. "In case you were wondering, I took Alana's car back."

"Oh? That's good."

"I've been thinking. You don't have to pay my tuition. I shouldn't have asked you in the first place. My dad says, and I agree, that it's better not to borrow from friends or family. I have other ways to get the money."

"Like working for Edgar?"

Kylie stood on the porch, not moving when C.J. opened the French door. "I really was helping with his pictures. I didn't come over here to sponge money off him."

"I know." C.J. stood aside. This was like urging a skittish cat into the house. She guessed that Kylie had heard nothing about Alana. Edgar rarely turned on his television. Sooner or later she would have to know. In her mind, C.J. saw an image of an ocean wave falling back, revealing a body half buried in wet sand.

"Please come in. We're letting the cool air out." When Kylie stepped inside the dining room, C.J. closed the door and locked it. "Are you hungry?"

"Not really. No."

"Want some hot chocolate?"

"All right." At last a faint smile. "Thanks." Kylie followed her around the dining table stacked with boxes and papers. "I got your messages. You said if I tell you what I know about Alana, we could work something out. That's fine, and if you want to give me a loan, I won't say no, but what I really want is for you to talk to my mother."

C.J. turned on the light in the kitchen.

Kylie moved aside a box of crackers and set her purse on the counter. "My father is fine with me staying in Miami, but my mother's the problem. I'd like for you to tell her I have a job and a place to live."

"You want me to lie to her? I don't know where you're living."

"I'll get my own place this week. An efficiency apartment, or I might go through a roommate service, but a safe, clean neighborhood. Tell her that."

"Do you have the money for an apartment?"

"I will have. Don't ask me how. I'm not stealing it. I'm not doing anything illegal."

"I'll have to think about that," C.J. said. "How will you pay for school?"

"Well, some modeling, like I mentioned before. I mean, if it works out. And there's always waitressing. I have experience as a server. I put in three applications today."

"And what else? School is expensive."

"I'll manage. Don't worry about it. Listen, my mother was kind of upset, but I told her, I am not changing my mind. She might call you. She has the idea you're trying to talk me into staying in Miami."

"Hardly. You know where I stand." C.J. took the milk out of the refrigerator, the cocoa from a cabinet.

"Does that mean you won't help me?"

"It means we can talk about it." She turned on the hot water to wash a mug. The orange cat walked past Kylie and hissed. C.J. said, "He won't scratch. If he hisses, it means he likes you. His name is Taffy."

Kylie knelt to pet the cat. "Hey, Taffy. You're a fighter, aren't ya? Somebody took a bite out of your ear, big boy."

"The gray one is Dylan, and there's a little white cat named Lady Bell, but she's probably hiding under the sofa. Tell me about modeling. I think they want models to be at least five-eight."

"Junior models can be shorter."

"Do you have an agent? There are people out there who will take advantage of you."

Kylie stroked the cat. "I know how to look out for myself."

"If you're under eighteen, a parent will have to sign the contract."

"I'll get an ID. I've been getting fake ID's for years."

"Have you now?" C.J. set the mug on the counter and dried her hands.

"I had to. My parents don't have any money, and I needed to work. I didn't tell them about it, of course. They're sweet but clueless. I got my first part-time job when I was fourteen." She stood up, shook her hair back from her face, and leaned against the counter with her arms crossed. Her collarbones were clearly marked, and faint tracings of blue showed beneath delicate skin. The overhead lights reflected in her glasses. So serious, this girl. Rarely a smile.

C.J. folded the towel and set it aside. "Kylie, I have to tell you something. It's about Alana. The news isn't good. They believe they've found her."

Like a small animal hearing a strange noise, Kylie stiffened. "Where? Is she dead?"

"Her body was found tonight on Fort Lauderdale Beach. She must have been dropped from a boat shortly after she was murdered, then drifted north with the currents. They aren't sure, but it's probably her. I'm sorry. It's impossible to understand such violence, especially to someone you care about."

"Oh, Jesus." Kylie pressed her fingertips to her mouth.

"They'll have more on the morning news."

For a long moment C.J. stared at the girl's red and crumpling face before she closed the short distance between them, hesitated, then tentatively put her hand on Kylie's cheek. "I'm so sorry."

With a small moan, Kylie lowered her head to C.J.'s shoulder. "Oh, shit. I thought maybe she'd gone to California. She wanted to so much. It was her dream." Kylie sobbed, and C.J. stroked her back, feeling the wings of her shoulder blades, the warmth under her cheap yellow shirt.

"You see what a dangerous place Miami can be for girls on their own."

Kylie grabbed at a paper towel on its holder by the sink, ripped off an uneven piece, and wiped her cheeks. "Yeah, well, Alana was stupid. I am not like Alana."

"What do you mean? What was Alana like?"

"Some of the people she hung with. Lowlifes and druggies. I don't do drugs."

"Where did Alana get it?"

"From friends."

"Cocaine?"

"Yes. Other things. Pills. I'm not into that."

"Did Alana ever have sex for money?"

"She wasn't a prostitute," Kylie said fiercely.

"If not for money, for things? Drugs, clothes, rent?"

"No!"

"Would you have known?"

"I would have, sure."

"Did she ever have a part in an adult movie?" When Kylie hesitated, C.J. asked, "Do you know what an adult movie is?"

"Yes! God! Who doesn't? Alana tried out for one of those movies, *one*. They told her she could make a lot of money, but she had to talk like a little girl and wear short dresses and knee socks, and she hated it."

"She played the part of a child? Kylie, is that what she did?"

"Alana didn't know it was going to be like that. They didn't tell her! She said it was embarrassing and stupid, and she was going to get the tapes back so nobody would see it on the Internet. That would have ruined her career. She wanted to be a regular actress. She could have been a star! That's all she wanted, and now she's dead!"

C.J. put an arm around her. Last weekend, Alana's former roommate, Tisha Dulaney, had said the same thing: Alana had tried out for a movie. C.J. asked Kylie, "Did Alana ever get the tapes?"

"I don't know." Kylie blew her nose. "She was like totally wasted when she told me, and the next day she said if I ever opened my mouth about it she would never speak to me again."

"Who were these people?"

"She didn't say."

"Were you wasted too?"

Kylie stared at the floor and sniffled. "Sort of."

"When was this?" C.J. asked. "When did she try out for this movie?"

"I don't know."

"Well, when did she tell you about the tapes?"

"Like . . . two weeks ago?"

"Kylie, you told me she was going to meet someone at the party. Remember? Did she say who?"

"Yeah. A modeling agent from New York. That's why I wanted to go along. Maybe I could meet him too. Alana said I'd be good for junior fashions."

"An agent from New York? Didn't you think this was strange? Miami has no shortage of modeling agencies." When Kylie only shrugged, C.J. asked, "How do you know he was legitimate?"

"Alana said he was."

"Alana said."

Kylie blew out a breath and looked at the ceiling. "That's how it's done in the industry. A friend of a friend. It's all very informal."

"Are you *that* naïve? Alana Martin knows people who make pornography. You and she go to a party looking like junior hookers, and she's meeting a *modeling* agent? I saw the dress you wore. You left it at Mrs. Gomez's apartment. Alana stole it from China Moon."

"Alana *borrowed* it. The dress was torn, or I'd have taken it back. I don't steal things!"

If Kylie ran out the door, C.J. had no hope of catching her. She pressed her hands together, then said. "I'm sorry. Of course you don't. Let's not talk any more tonight. It's late."

"And I am totally not in the mood." Kylie looked at the paper towel wadded in her hand. "Where can I put this?"

"Here." C.J. crammed the paper into a trash can under the sink, which should have been emptied days ago. She closed the cabinet door. "You're tired. Come on, I'll show you to your room."

Kylie took her purse and followed her out of the kitchen. C.J. turned on a lamp in the hall. Covered in worn green carpet, the old stair treads creaked as they went up. The light from the street came dimly through the pebbled yellow glass in the small round window on the landing. She opened the first door on the left and flipped the light switch, revealing a double bed and white wicker furniture. The ceiling fan began to turn.

"It's a nice room," Kylie said.

"I'll get you something to wear to bed." C.J. went into her own room at the end of the hall and rummaged through the drawer where she kept her sleepwear, looking for something cotton, preferably demure, finally grabbing a pale blue gown with hand-embroidered lace trim. A gift from Elliott, but she hadn't worn it in years, and it was clean.

When C.J. returned to the guest bedroom, she lay the gown on the bed. "That should fit. Go ahead and take a shower. Towels are in the bathroom, and a new toothbrush in the cabinet with some toothpaste. There's a hair dryer, lotion, everything. If you put your clothes outside the door, I'll wash them for you."

"You don't have to."

"I don't mind. I have some things of my own to do anyway. You'll have fresh clothes for tomorrow. And I'll bring the hot chocolate right up and leave it on your nightstand."

"All right. Thanks. Well, good night." Kylie pushed her hair behind her ears.

They stared at each other. C.J. felt a sudden desire to embrace the girl, but her feet wouldn't move. "Good night, Kylie." She closed the door and went back downstairs.

In the kitchen she leaned against the sink and took a deep

breath. Then laughed. "Oh, God, would I love a scotch on the rocks about now."

She walked to the dining room table and lifted papers until she found the envelope Judy Mazzio had brought over early this morning. C.J. thought she had put Rick Slater's photograph back into it. She peered inside, making sure. In the morning she would show it to Kylie. Do you recognize this man? This is the man who took you home from the party, isn't he? Would you mind telling that to the police so I can get rid of this goddamn case and send you back to Pensacola?

With a start, she glanced at the clock, then ran back to the kitchen and turned on the little TV in the breakfast nook. The breaking news about Alana Martin was the top story on Channel Six. The remote in her hand, she saw the beach, black sky, glaring floodlights. She flipped from channel to channel, catching brief scenes. A neighbor of the Martinez family: "They're praying it's not Alana, but it would bring closure." A Coast Guard officer: "—possibility of calculating the point of entry, based on the currents and the tides." A Broward sheriff's deputy: "—about a hundred yards north, what appeared to be the arm. We're combing the entire beach area."

C.J. checked CNN to see if they had anything. She stared at the screen. "Oh, no."

Libi Rodriguez was wrapping up an interview with George Fuentes on a sidewalk beside the beach. He was saying, "We won't know for sure until DNA tests are done, but the clothes, the approximate age of the victim, and the changes to the body, consistent with being in the water for at least several days, all point toward that conclusion."

The camera focused on Libi, her black hair teased by the wind, her full, glossy lips. "There you have it. The victim is most likely

Alana Martin, who disappeared a week ago today from a celebrity-studded party on exclusive Star Island. Nobody is talking, but at least one of the attendees has hired high-powered attorney C.J. Dunn, one of America's top female lawyers."

Through her teeth, C.J. muttered, "*Shit!*"

The video switched to footage from a murder trial last year, C.J. in her sunglasses and spike heels, trailed by her associates, clearing a path through reporters at the courthouse, refusing to comment, bitch lawyer that she was.

Back to Libi: "As the investigation continues into a life cut brutally short, we'll be here to bring you the story. From Miami, this is Libi Rodriguez for CNN."

C.J. turned off the television and sat in the silent kitchen. She thought of calling Rick Slater. And saying what, exactly? Hang on, it's going to be a bumpy ride. But he could take it. He was that kind of guy. She laughed a little, remembering how cool he'd been with Billy back at the hotel, getting the better of him. She thought about Slater pushing her behind him when Dennis Murphy aimed the shotgun, then blocking Dennis's view when she put on her shoes, not letting him look down her dress. Billy liked it when she showed herself, and she felt both valued and cheapened at the same time.

With her forehead in her hands, C.J. heard noises upstairs, then water running and the groan of old pipes. She got up and finished making Kylie's hot chocolate.

She left the mug in the bedroom, as promised, and went out again, picking up the little pile of clothes by the door, which she carried back downstairs to the laundry room. The socks, T-shirt, and shorts could go in the regular wash, but the underwear—

She held the wispy bra in one hand and the tiny matching thong in the other. Leopard print on satin with a fine edging of black silk ruffles. The label said *La Coquette. Paris.* She thought of the polished mahogany display case at China Moon, the lingerie gleaming like jewels under glass. Kylie wouldn't have bought these for herself. Her friend Alana Martin had stuffed them into a pocket. She'd given them to Kylie, maybe after she'd worn them a few times. Or she had turned her back and let Kylie walk out with them.

At sixteen, C.J. and a friend had done just that at a mall in Gainesville. They had never been caught, but the friend had been fired for using drugs and a year later went to jail for selling meth.

C.J. balled the garments into her fists. When she opened her hands, the sumptuous fabric expanded like flowers. Her fingers began to tremble, and she flung the things into the laundry sink and went back to the kitchen.

A keen thirst had gripped her throat and turned her tongue to sand. She walked to the pantry, flipped on a light, and pushed aside some boxes, which fell to the floor. She had purposely put the wine on a shelf above her head, out of sight. She felt around and grabbed a bottle by the neck. It clanked against its neighbors. She took it to the kitchen and set it on the counter by the sink. The label seemed to glow in the under-counter lights. Marcassin Vineyards, 2002. Sonoma Valley pinot noir. Elliott had spent eighty dollars for this wine, and they'd planned to toast their anniversary.

"Just one glass. That's all. I will pour the rest out," she told herself. "One little glass. Three ounces."

Metal clanked and rattled as C.J. pulled open a drawer and rummaged for the corkscrew. She sliced the top off the seal and thrust the point into the cork. It broke coming out. "God *damn* it." She ran back to the pantry and opened the toolbox, finding a flathead screwdriver. She jabbed it into the cork and twisted until the cork was shredded into pieces.

Open a cabinet door. Slam it shut. Another. Another. Wine

glasses. Where the hell had she put them? On an upper shelf.
Never mind. Use a juice glass. Very elegant.

"Three ounces." C.J. picked up the bottle and held it over the
stainless steel sink, upside down. The bits of cork floated up and the
wine gurgled out. When the aroma hit her nose she wanted to weep.
She flipped it right side up, gauging it was half gone, then turned it
over again and let more go. And more. She watched the dark red liquid swirl across the sink. She watched it all go until nothing was left
but the soft tick of liquid in the drain.

She began to laugh. She put her head down on the counter and
laughed some more. Then she put her tongue to the mouth of the
bottle and retrieved a single drop.

That night she lay awake, every nerve buzzing. She thought of Kylie
just across the hall, twenty feet away. She would call Fran first thing.
And say . . . *You and Bob come get your daughter. I'll pay for your
flight. No, wait a few days, until she makes a statement to the police.
And that girl who washed up on the beach? Never mind her. Kylie
needs to come home. I think she's been hanging around a bad ele-
ment. Not that I have any right to talk.*

C.J. dreamed of being pursued, naked and alone, trying to run.
She awoke and watched the windows lighten to gray, heard the first
morning bird songs. She closed her eyes and drifted.

Then Dylan, as was his habit, was leaping onto her bed, batting
at her hair, demanding his breakfast. The clock said 9:15. C.J.
threw back the covers and put on a robe. In the hall she saw that the
clothes she'd left outside the guest room at midnight were gone.

The door was open. The sheets and blanket were neatly folded
at the foot of the bed, and the gown lay across them.

C.J. rushed downstairs. There was a note on the kitchen counter.

> *Dear Ms. Dunn, Thank you for letting me stay here last night. I had to go somewhere this morning. Edgar loaned me his car. Don't worry, I'll bring it back.*
> *Kylie*

chapter NINETEEN

She found Edgar in the front yard of his cottage with a pie pan full of cat food. Edgar was dressed for the day in his khaki pants and work shirt and straw hat. He rattled the pie pan. "Iggy! Breakfast is served. Oh, good morning, C.J."

"Kylie's gone. She left me a note in the kitchen."

"You just missed her. Left not ten minutes ago. She had to meet somebody."

"Who?"

"Didn't say."

"I can't believe you let her take your car!"

"What are you so hot and bothered about? I'm not going any-place today, and it's my damn car. She's a good driver. She ran me over to the store last night for a six-pack."

"You let her have a beer?"

"No, she's a kid! I bought her a Sprite."

"Where did she say she was going?"

"Didn't say. She was in a hurry, though. I offered to make her pancakes and sausage and she said she didn't have time."

"Did you give her any money?"

"I gave her what I owed her, thirty bucks. Two hours. Plus a little in advance. She'll be back." Edgar stooped to look under a bush. "Iggy! I see you. Come and get it. The boss doesn't like us leaving your food out all day. You snooze, you lose, little buddy."

C.J. stepped in front of him. "Edgar? Are you keeping something from me? Did Kylie ask you not to tell?"

He squinted through his heavy glasses. "C.J., I've never lied to you in my life. I told you before, she said she had to meet somebody, and if I knew who, I'd spill it."

Giving up, C.J. leaned against one of the porch roof supports and watched Edgar bend his knees, extend an arm, and set the pan under the bush. She said, "I have to leave soon, but I should be back by two o'clock. If she comes before I get home, will you please try to keep her here?"

"That won't be hard," he said. "There's plenty for her to do. We can finish going through the photographs. She's interested in 'em. Most people aren't. You aren't. That's the way it is. Unless it's your family, who cares? Toss it in the trash can."

C.J. walked over and put an arm around his waist. "I'm glad you're doing this, Edgar. I am. They're great photos."

"I'm going to ask her to help me pick out a computer and scanner. She says she's not going back to Pensacola for a while, so . . . Don't give me that face, C.J. I trust her. She's a good girl."

"I suppose she is. You're right, it's your decision." She put a kiss on his cheek and said she would see him later, and she would appreciate it if he would call her cell phone when Kylie showed up.

In her white terrycloth robe and slippers, C.J. went around the house to pick up the Sunday paper, which lay in its bright blue wrapper on the front walk. She pulled the paper from the wrapper, juggling for a moment to keep the circulars from sliding out. The story about Alana Martin was above the fold. *Body of Missing Woman Found on Fort Lauderdale Beach.*

Moving into the shade of a mahogany tree, she set the bulk of the newspaper on the grass and turned to the continuation. There were enough references to body parts to ensure that tomorrow's edition would fly off the racks. Written close to deadline, the article was short but accompanied by photos of the beach, the crowds behind crime-scene tape, and—no surprise—a stock photo of Billy Medina's house, where the victim had allegedly last been seen alive. The police refused to name suspects, only that "several persons" were being interviewed. C.J. Dunn's name was not mentioned, but Grammy-nominee singer Yasmina had entertained, and U.S. Congressman Paul Shelby had made an appearance.

"Oh, great."

A spot of light flashed across the dark foliage, then was gone. A reflection. C.J. looked toward the street.

The long lens of a camera was looking back at her. Nash Pettigrew. Turning away, C.J. stooped to gather the newspaper. She wanted to grab the camera and smash it over his head. She wondered if he had taken any photos of Kylie.

"Mr. Pettigrew. How long have you been lurking?"

"Just cruising by and I saw you come out. How's that for luck? C.J., look this way. Smile pretty. I like the outfit. Real sexy."

"Get lost, Nash. I'm going inside and calling the police."

"Am I on your property? I think not." As she walked away, Nash called, "I hear that your client is the Numero Uno suspect. Richard Slater. Is that right? He works for Congressman Paul Shelby. What have they got on him? Did he cut that girl up?"

The front door was still locked, so C.J. had to walk back under the carport, and she imagined that every step would be another image in Nash Pettigrew's camera. Her face without makeup would look washed out, she would be squinting in the sun, and the thick white robe would add ten pounds.

Her jaw was clenching when she went inside and slammed the newspaper on the kitchen counter. She should have known better. "Damn."

Nash Pettigrew had been out to get her ever since she'd had him arrested for trespassing onto her and Elliott's property in Topanga Canyon, back in L.A. If Pettigrew hadn't slid down the hill, and his gear hadn't tumbled out of his backpack, he would have gotten away with photos of them in the hot tub, smoking a joint. Completely nude, Elliott sprinted across the yard and caught the intruder, and C.J. took the memory stick out of his camera and threw it into the hot tub. Nash Pettigrew had her to thank for his criminal record.

She poured herself some coffee and went upstairs. She had planned to call a producer she knew at Channel Seven, the most tabloid of the TV news stations in Miami, and promise an exclusive interview, but it had gone beyond that. She needed to contact a friend on the staff of *People* magazine, or do a preemptive strike and call Larry King.

First she needed to let Rick Slater know what was going on. As she walked into her closet and slid out of the robe, she scrolled to his number. Phone at her ear, she flipped through the rack, deciding what to wear to Milo's house.

Slater's phone went to voice mail. "Rick. This is C.J. Dunn. Just wanted to warn you. Remember that little weasel following us yesterday? He was outside my house this morning taking pictures. He knows the police are interested in you. Call me when you get a chance. I have an appointment at eleven, so if I don't pick up, leave a message."

She held up a sleeveless turquoise dress on its hanger, then put it back for a more photo-friendly navy blue with a stand-up white collar, just in case. Walking past the full-length mirror, she noticed what she was wearing—a pink satin thong—and imagined Slater getting an eyeful of that. She slowly turned, checking her butt. Not bad for thirty-seven. Still tight. She put her hands over her breasts. Slater's hands would have covered them completely. A flash of warmth went up between her legs.

She grabbed a robe. "For God's sake, stop it."

She went into her office to paw through her desk for Milo's number. Of course he was still asleep, so she left a message with a man who said he was Milo's massage therapist, not his secretary, thank you very much. C.J. apologized, then said, "Would you please go into His Excellency's bedchamber and remind him that I'm coming over at eleven? Yes, he knows about it."

That done, she went into the bathroom and turned on the shower. Noticing the message icon flashing on her cell phone, she checked her voice mail. If it was a reporter, she would hang up.

The message was from Donald Finch.

He was sorry for calling at the last minute, but would she like to come over and meet his sister Sarah, who had come through MIA last night from Belize on her way home to CNN in Atlanta? They would have a chilled Bloody Mary waiting.

chapter
TWENTY

hey sat on a bench in Peacock Park in Coconut Grove, a patch of trees and gray dirt that led to a dried-out baseball field, a tangle of mangroves, and a pile of seaweed-draped rocks. It was already hot, and the dogs being walked had their tongues hanging out. But it wasn't bad in the shade, with the wind coming off the bay. Kylie could see the boats moored in neat rows behind the Coral Reef Yacht Club. The sailboat rigging sounded like bells.

She said to the man next to her, "I kept thinking she'd call. 'Hi, it's me. I made it. I'm standing right here on the Walk of Stars in Hollywood.' She said that's the first place she'd go. She said somebody was going to hook her up with a friend out there. She had it all planned."

"Well, she sure took a wrong turn." Richard stirred his frozen lemonade with the straw. He had bought them both one at the cart by the street before he looked around for the right place to sit, near the water with a fence at their backs. He could keep an eye on the park.

Kylie said, "Can you get any more information from your sources? Your friends, other reporters? Don't you have contacts with the police?"

"I'm working on it. I have a friend with a TV station in Miami. He's close to the story."

Richard wore baggy cargo pants, a tropical print shirt, sunglasses, and a Chicago Cubs hat. She hadn't recognized him until he tapped her on the arm, having seen him only that one other time. She had been walking to the bus stop on Biscayne Boulevard two days after the party and this man fell into step with her, a big man with a beard and shaved head. *Hi. Remember me?* She didn't until he told her he was a friend of Alana's, and he'd brought her home from the party at Billy Medina's house. He wanted to talk to her. He would pay for information.

She looked at him, trying to see past the sunglasses. "Do you think someone killed Alana because of your investigation?"

"Jesus, I hope not."

"I mean, if somebody found out she was working with you. . . . "

"If I find it had anything to do with me, I'd hate myself, but I can't see it. Alana could keep her secrets. We don't put our sources in danger. We don't ask them to wear hidden microphones or anything like that. Don't worry. Talking to me is not a risk. We're just two people shooting the breeze."

Kylie watched a sail puff out from the front of a sailboat, red and blue stripes. "Before we start, we need to discuss how much you're going to pay me."

He set his cup aside. "All right. What did you have in mind?"

"I need at least three thousand."

He started to laugh but could see she was serious. "You think reporters have unlimited expense accounts? That our publishers have big buckets of cash we dip into?"

"*The New York Times* is rich. Aren't they? And you said this story would be huge."

"I also told you we pay on the value of the information we receive."

"I want some of it up front. Or no deal." She sipped her frozen lemonade.

He looked at her for a while, then scanned the park. Under the brim of his hat, his eyes moved to the cars rounding the curve onto Bayshore Drive. He finally turned toward the water, and his body shielded any sight of his wallet coming out of the thigh pocket of his cargo pants. He said, "I don't want anybody to get the wrong idea." She saw his fingers walking over the tops of some twenties. He pulled out five of them and held them folded near his waist.

"A hundred dollars? It's worth more than *that*."

"Not so loud." He pulled out four more twenties. "That's all I've got on me."

She zipped the money into her purse. "How much did you pay Alana?"

"That was between me and Alana."

"More than this, no doubt."

"Why don't you use it for plane fare home?" he said.

"The money is for school," she told him.

"School?"

"College. I'm going to get a degree in journalism at the University of Miami. I decided just the other day. I'm a good writer, and I've always been curious about things. I guess you could say you're my inspiration."

"Really? That's nice."

"So I hope you don't screw me over."

He smiled. "Likewise."

"You travel a lot in your job, I suppose."

"All the time."

"That's what I want to do. Travel."

"It's great, if you like living out of a backpack and running for your life occasionally."

"You did that? Where?"

"Afghanistan." Richard turned his right arm so she could see the scar on the underside. "I took a round from a Kalashnikov. I was an embedded reporter with a unit of Special Forces in pursuit of the Taliban. They got the bad guy for me." He spread out his left hand and showed her a scar across the palm. "Souvenir of Peshawar, Pakistan. I was on a story about Ayman al-Zawahri." He smiled at her again. "It was rough. Time to come in out of the cold, so to speak. Where are you from, Kylie? You're not from Michigan. Come on."

"Pensacola."

"Naval Air Station. Dad in the military?"

"No, he works for a gas company, when he's not hung over."

"I've never been to Pensacola."

"Biggest town on the Redneck Riviera."

"Your parents know you're down here?"

"I'm not going back."

"They throw you out?"

"Not exactly. We had a difference of opinion," she said.

"Sorry to hear it. I hit the road at sixteen, but I went back."

"I'm adopted."

"Yeah?"

"My birth parents were from Miami. My mother told me. I was twelve and a pain in the ass, asking about them all the time. She said all she knew is that my parents were from here, and they died in a car crash. My brother and sister are adopted too. They came from the same family. They've met their birth parents. I never will. But I imagine sometimes, when I'm walking down the street, that my father walked there too, or my mother lived around the corner. I might have cousins here. I feel a connection to Miami."

"Is that why you came?"

"Sort of. Yes. And I wanted to see something different."

"That's understandable. Well, maybe you'll bump into your relatives some day."

"Maybe." She plunged her straw up and down through the lid. "What do you want to know about Alana?"

Richard reached into another pocket of his cargo pants and took out a folded white envelope. He hung his sunglasses off the pocket of his shirt. He had squint lines, but his eyes were wide open, sort of green with bits of brown. She felt like he was making contact on some level, and she made a note to herself: Never wear sunglasses when you're talking to a source.

"I'm going to show you a picture. I pulled it off the Internet." He passed it to her. "Does he look familiar?"

The photo had been cut from a larger page. She saw an ordinary-looking, middle-aged man in a suit with neatly combed brown hair, eyebrows that slanted downward, a small nose, and a wide smile. She shook her head. "I've never seen him before."

"You sure? Look carefully."

"I don't know him. Who is he?"

"Paul Shelby. He's a U.S. congressman. He lives in Miami. You never heard the name?"

"No."

"Alana never mentioned him?"

"No."

Richard put the picture back into the envelope. "Did Alana ever talk to you about politics, or politicians, or anyone on the take? Bribes, favors, that sort of thing?"

"I get it. The congressman is part of your investigation, isn't he? You think he's crooked. Big political scandal. Right?"

"Something like that." Richard put an elbow on the back of the bench and knitted his fingers. His stainless steel watch had three smaller dials. His nails were very clean. No rings. She wondered if he was married. Probably not. It would be hard to have a relationship as a journalist, never knowing where they would send you next.

"Let me ask you about the party at Billy Medina's house. Did you ever meet Billy Medina?"

"I know who he is. I've seen him a couple of times. He doesn't know *me*."

"Did he invite you and Alana to the party?"

"I don't know. I guess he did."

"Let's not guess. The right answer is, 'I don't know.' Aside from going to the party, do you know Medina?"

"I used to work for his magazine, *Tropical Life*."

"Used to?"

"Well, they laid me off last week. I'm looking for another job. I met Alana at the magazine, before she quit."

"Why'd she quit?"

"She had a hard time getting up early every day."

Richard scratched the side of his face, the edge of his beard. "Let's try something else. What about Milo Cahill? Have you ever met him?"

"Yes."

"What do you know about Cahill?"

"He's an architect. He lives on the Beach. He has a Southern accent."

"You've talked to him, then."

"Alana and I went to a few parties at his house. It's actually on the Intracoastal. He invites all kinds of artists and musicians and people like that. Why are you asking me about him? Is there some connection between him and . . . and Billy Medina or the congressman?"

"Let me ask the questions, okay? Were you ever alone with Mr. Cahill?"

"No."

"Were you always with Alana when you went there?"

"Yes, and there were always lots of other people too."

"What do you know about Milo Cahill? I mean the things that most people might not be aware of. Things that might have surprised you, maybe even shocked you."

"He wears a hat indoors," she said. "He lets his dog lick him on the mouth. It's really dark in his house, and his living room looks like an art gallery. He's actually very nice."

Richard nodded. "You've been to his parties. What goes on? Is it fairly wild, or do they serve tea and cookies?"

She smiled. "No, they're normal parties for the Beach."

"Loud music, drinking, lots of beautiful people?"

"Yes."

"Sex?"

"Not openly. Not that I saw."

"What do you do at the parties?"

"Dance. Listen to the music. Maybe just watch what goes on. Yeah, it's a circus here, that's for sure." She drank more of her lemonade, which had nearly all melted but was still cold.

Richard brushed a leaf off the bench. "Did Milo Cahill ever suggest to you or flat-out say, Kylie, there's this guy I want you to meet. He's looking for a little fun, and he wants to hook up. Did he ever say anything like that?"

"You mean like to have sex?"

"That's what I mean."

"No." She laughed. "He isn't like that at all."

"What about Alana? Did she ever want to hook you up?"

"Well . . . yes, but it didn't work out. I wasn't interested in the guy she picked out for me."

"Where was this?"

"At a dance club."

"No, I mean privately and possibly for money. The night of the party at Medina's house, did she say she wanted to hook you up with someone? Is that why she took you there?"

Kylie stared at him. "I don't know what you think I am, but I am not a whore, and neither was Alana."

"I apologize, but we have to ask uncomfortable questions sometimes. It's part of the job."

She nodded. "It's okay. I know. Ask me anything. I want to help."

His eyes were on the water. A catamaran flopped its sail over to the other side, turned, and went slowly out of sight behind the trees. He said, "You told me something the night of the party, when you were in the car and I was driving you home. You probably don't remember, but you said that Alana went to talk to someone, a modeling agent. Is that right?"

"Yes. She said wait here, I have to go talk to someone. She left, and she never came back. She said he was an agent from New York."

"You don't sound sure about that," he said.

Kylie sighed. "There are plenty of agents in Miami. And anyway, I don't think she was that good a model. She never got on any photo shoots. She only modeled for China Moon."

"So you never met the agent. Don't know who he was."

"If I knew, I'd go see him. Except I don't have a portfolio. Which is another reason I need some cash."

Richard slid his fingers down his mustache, then said, "What about other friends of Alana? Do you know her friends? Other girls I could talk to?"

"Not really. I remember first names, but not who they are, or how you could find them. Friendships on the beach are shallow. I'm sort of a loner anyway."

"So how did you get to be friends with a party girl like Alana Martin?"

"I was new, and she asked me if I'd like to go to lunch with her. She could be really nice. And a little bit crazy. She made me laugh. We went out together. It was fun at the time. But she wasn't . . . she wasn't the sort of person you could remain friends with forever, you know."

He put his elbows on his knees and looked at the water. After a while, he said, "Well, I guess that's about it."

"Don't you have anything else to ask me?"

"Sometimes a source doesn't pan out like you'd hoped."

"I'm not giving any of the money back. I answered all your questions."

"So you did." He patted her knee. "Listen, here's some free advice for an aspiring journalist. Smile. You don't smile enough. People respond to a friendly face. And get yourself a reporter's vest. That comes in handy, all the pockets."

"You're not wearing one."

"I'm undercover. Another thing, very important. Protect your sources and they will protect you. Understand?" His forefinger went back and forth. "You and me. I might need to contact you in the future and pay for more information, but if you blow my cover, I can't do that. Deal?"

He held out his hand. She wondered what he would do if she demanded extra for her silence, but she knew she wouldn't say anything, so what was the point? Her hand disappeared into his. "Deal."

Putting his sunglasses back on, he stood up and said, "You have my phone number. If you hear anything else, call me. And I'd like to hear how school turns out. Good luck with that. You take care of yourself, Kylie Willis. I'll be thinking about you."

"Will you let me know when your article gets published?"

"You bet." He looked down at her. "One more piece of advice. If I were you? I'd go back to mom and dad. Patch up your differences and let them take care of you. Like they say, there's no place like home."

"Sure."

He walked away, wide shoulders, muscular arms, the hat covering his head. He turned around and saluted, and she faked a smile and waved. As he continued his way toward the street, Kylie kicked at a root. The dust settled on her sneakers. She brushed them off, then put her head in her hands and stared at the ground between her feet. She had less than four hundred dollars, total. The rat-trap hotel where she was staying charged sixty a day, so it wouldn't last long.

C.J. wouldn't help. C.J. would send her back to Pensacola, no matter what promises came out of her mouth.

When Edgar had paid her this morning, she'd seen where he kept his cash, behind some old books in the living room, but she could never do that. Ever. She could work for him, fifteen dollars an hour, but after she finished his photographs, what?

Go home.

Her heart felt as heavy as it ever had.

The only person she could think of was Milo Cahill. He had money, no question about that. He liked her. He'd said she was an angel, pretty as a Carolina peach. Standing there in his white Panama hat, opening his arms, smiling so big his eyes squeezed shut.

Come here, sugar. Come on over here and talk to Milo.

chapter
TWENTY-ONE

"**O**h, but I make a world-class Bloody Mary."

"I'm sure you do, but just give me the kiddie version and an extra piece of celery."

"Did we overdo last night?" Donald Finch raised a sun-bleached brow.

With a grin, his sister waved him away, "Don, don't be a pain."

He went back to the wet bar in the corner, leaving C.J. to continue her conversation with Sarah Finch. Sarah had been in Belize to check on a wildlife special CNN was coproducing with *National Geographic*. Summoned back early to Atlanta, she'd arranged her connecting flight to give her the day with her brother and sister-in-law. She'd been wanting to meet C.J. Dunn.

"The decision will be made by the end of the month, I believe.

There are other people under consideration, but they're all light-weights. I've seen tapes of your interviews with Barbara Walters, Larry King, Bill O'Reilly—I think you'd be ideal for the show. It's not up to me, you understand, but I do have some input."

Warmed by the compliment and the sense that this was going her way, C.J. smiled. "Is there a name for the show?"

"Tentatively it's *Rich, Famous, and Deadly*."

"That's catchy. I've already been thinking of possible guests, people who can give a real insider's look at the system. We don't need more babble about the lifestyles of the accused."

"Oh, I agree completely," said Sarah. She had the same square jaw and prominent nose as her brother, but not his lethargy or well-oiled sarcasm. Her laugh was genuine, and her nervous energy kept her poised on the edge of her chair.

They were under the colonnade behind the Finches' Mediter-ranean-style house in Coral Gables, ceiling fans making a pleasant breeze, a tray of croissants, bagels, and fresh fruit on the table. The pool sparkled, and hot pink bougainvillea climbed the coral rock columns. The property sloped down to a canal, where a small cabin cruiser was docked. A plaque on the vine-covered wall out front an-nounced that the home was a city landmark. Hence the mildewed Spanish tiles on the roof and the streaks down the mustard-yellow walls. Donald Finch had explained, ushering C.J. to the patio, that the paint had been made using the original formula from the nineteen-twenties. He spoke as if he actually owned the place, though C.J. doubted his wife had put his name on the deed.

Noreen, in sun hat and dark glasses, was occupied in the back-yard, supervising the crew from her husband's production com-pany, who would be filming in the afternoon for Paul Shelby's campaign ads. Noreen pointed at the nude, poured-concrete cherub at the far end of the pool and said to move it and throw some floats into the water.

Finch came back with the drinks. "God, yes, let's have some family values in the shot. Paul and Diana and the boys will be over soon as church is out. Paul's PR guru suggested he teach a class at Sunday School, but Noreen nixed that idea. Not macho enough. I've heard Noreen lecture him on his haircut. It's too pretty. You look like the king of your high school prom. My wife is very good at this, actually. She studied Leni Riefenstahl, filmmaker to the Nazi Party."

"Really, Don." He sister threw him a look, but her eyes twinkled when she bit into her bagel.

"Noreen, sweetheart! Come take a break."

"In a minute."

Sarah speared a piece of mango. "Paul and I don't share the same politics, but I have to admit, he's taking the right position on green architecture. Do you know anything about The Aquarius? They say the design is getting lots of positive press."

"The architect is a friend of mine," C.J. said. As she described the project, she watched a powerfully built man in mirrored sunglasses grab the statue around the waist, lean back, and haul it toward the corner of the house. He seemed familiar. Yes. Dennis Murphy. The top of his head was the shape of a box, and sweat-soaked red hair fell past his collar. He set the cherub down and mopped his face.

"I know that man. He works for Billy Medina. His name is Dennis Murphy."

Finch lowered his head to look over the top of his sunglasses. "My company hired him when we needed someone to tote and carry. In the trade, he's known as a grip."

"Did you bring him from California? I remember Noreen saying you studied at the American Film Institute," C.J. said.

"Yes, but I acquired Dennis locally. He used to move furniture, I think."

"Do you still have many contacts in the movie business? Back in California, I mean." C.J. hoped the inquiry sounded innocent enough.

"A few, but we're going back twenty-five years." Finch grimaced. "Is that possible?" He turned to his sister. "Sarah, dear, do you know Billy Medina? I should introduce you sometime. Puerto Rican from New York. He owns a hotel in Antigua and publishes *Tropical Life*, all the latest glitz, glamour, and sin on South Beach. He hosted the party of the century last weekend. They'll be talking about it for years, and I'm afraid poor Paul is wishing he'd never gone. Please do not bring this up in front of Noreen." Finch retreated behind his drink. "Here she comes."

Sarah looked at C.J. "Medina. Is that the same man—I saw something on CNN last night."

"The same," C.J. said.

Noreen Finch, platinum hair pinned off her neck, fanned her face with her hat. Diamonds twinkled on her fingers. "Lord, will this heat ever let up? Don, go get me a drink, will you? Lots of ice." He stood to hold her chair, then hustled back to the bar. Noreen looked across the table through her big sunglasses. "Well, Miss C.J. How do you like this old shack?"

"It's lovely."

"Paul's granddaddy built it in nineteen twenty-six, and, God willing, my grandkids will want to keep it. Right now, I'm about ready to tie down the porch furniture and bring in the plants."

"Pardon?"

"There's a storm coming. Paul was mentioned in that article in the paper this morning."

"They said he was at the party. I wouldn't be concerned about it," C.J. said. She thought of her encounter with Nash Pettigrew, but only said, "Don't be surprised at the questions at Paul's press conference tomorrow. Someone might ask why I was hired to represent his chauffeur. They know you've turned down an interview with *The Justice Files* and that Mr. Slater's apartment was searched."

The lines around Noreen's mouth tightened, and for a moment she looked every bit of sixty-five. "Oh, my God. 'Congressman, can you explain why you've got a murder suspect working for you?'"

"Paul should simply respond that Mr. Slater had nothing to do with it, and the police are questioning everyone. He should stick to the topic, his reelection and his support for the environment."

Sarah said, "C.J., do you think you should be there with him? With Paul, I mean."

"No. It would raise more questions. Anyway, I'm not his lawyer."

Noreen was not mollified. "You didn't ask Libi Rodriguez to drop your name into her broadcast on CNN last night, did you?"

"Absolutely not."

Noreen turned to her sister-in-law. "Sarah, who can I talk to up there? How did that Rodriguez woman get on CNN? She ought to stick with local news. She acts like finding a murder victim in South Florida is the biggest thing since Nine-Eleven."

"I have no control over the news division," Sarah said, "nor would I intervene if I did."

Donald Finch brought his wife a Bloody Mary. She made a little kiss in his direction and stirred the drink with her celery. "They ought to interview C.J. She has a good idea who killed that girl."

C.J.'s mouth fell open. "Actually, I don't."

"That's what you told Paul last night, isn't it?"

"Excuse me, Noreen, but I said nothing of the sort."

"You told him you have a suspect, the dead girl's boyfriend. Makes sense to me. A crime of passion. I'm sorry she's dead, but if you lead a life of drugs, sex, and immorality, you're asking for it."

Sarah said, "No woman *asks* for it."

"You know what I mean. Actions have consequences."

C.J. silently cursed herself for having said one damned word to

Paul Shelby. She glanced into her lap and tilted her watch. Before leaving home she had called Milo to tell him she would be late. If she left now, she could get there by noon.

Noreen said, "I hope you've relayed your suspicions to the police."

C.J. looked up. Noreen had taken her sunglasses off, and cool blue-gray eyes were staring across the table. C.J. said, "First, I clearly told Paul that I'm not certain this person was Alana's boyfriend. And second, I'm sorry, but I can't discuss a case with anyone but the client."

"Well, Miss C.J., I think you need to remember who your client really is. If there's somebody the police ought to be talking to instead of a man who works for us, then why not tell them so?"

"I'm sure they're already aware." She smiled around the table. "Well. I hate to run, but I have a luncheon engagement. Thank you for the hospitality. And Sarah, it's been a pleasure meeting you."

Tall, lanky Sarah Finch rose to shake her hand. She gave it an extra squeeze, and a smile passed between them. She said, "I'll put in a good word for you."

"Thanks."

Noreen waved her husband back to his seat. "Oh, let me walk Ms. Dunn out."

The thunderclaps C.J. had expected broke as soon as the heavy front door closed. The women faced each other on the wide coral-rock porch under a jacaranda tree in full, purple bloom. Except for C.J.'s high heels, Noreen would have had the advantage. They were eye to eye.

"You told us on Friday this story wouldn't get into the national media."

Calmly C.J. replied, "That was before Alana Martin's body washed up on Fort Lauderdale Beach last night."

"Since you're spending so much of our money investigating

everybody involved in this case, have you been asking about Jason Wright? Paul says he works for Milo Cahill."

"I'm sorry, I can't—"

"Can't discuss the case. We're not the client. Don called you over here this morning to speak to Sarah. We're doing you a big favor, and to turn around and brush us off like you do—"

"Noreen, please don't tell me how to practice law. I will say it again. You are *not* my client." C.J. took her car keys from her purse.

"If you know somebody who might have killed her, why'n hell don't you say so?"

"Because I don't know that, and it is unethical to make unfounded accusations based on a mere assumption."

That brought a loud bark of a laugh. "My God. I don't know how you've lasted this long, taking that prissy attitude. Reporters have been calling Paul's house all morning. They're turning up the heat, and I don't like it. He's getting hives."

C.J. put on her sunglasses. "It's going to be fine."

"It had goddamn well better be."

She went down the steps, past the fountain—whose four brass porpoises were spouting jets of water into the air in blatant violation of current use restrictions—then to the gravel driveway, where she opened the door of her BMW and slid behind the wheel. Noreen was watching from the porch.

Turning toward the street, C.J. pressed the accelerator and heard the rear tires spinning and gravel hitting the wheel wells.

"Take that, you bitch."

chapter
TWENTY-TWO

t he downside of dealing with wealthy and powerful individuals, C.J.'s mentor had told her, is that the bastards expected to win. Don't show your hand too soon. In ten years dealing with all varieties of such people, C.J. had learned the lesson pretty well, or so she had thought. Occasionally one slipped up by being too sanguine in judging the probability of success. One could also commit other mistakes, like making assumptions based on incomplete evidence. Case in point: suggesting that a twenty-eight-year-old Ivy League architect had brutally murdered, dismembered, and dumped his girlfriend into the sea, without the lawyer's having first ascertained whether said architect was actually her lover, let alone whether he had a propensity toward violence and access to a boat.

C.J. hoped that Milo Cahill could shed some light. If not, C.J. would have to rely on Kylie Willis to establish an alibi for her client—if Kylie had been sober enough that night to remember who had taken her home, and if the police believed her. C.J. also hoped to confront the witnesses who claimed it was Alana Martin that Slater had taken from the party. Billy Medina had promised to find out their names, but he might be so ticked off at her right now that it could be a week before she heard from him, if ever.

Barring all that, there was very little that was going to make this case magically disappear. Still, C.J. knew she had made a good impression on Sarah Finch, and that the odds of landing the gig with CNN had definitely improved.

She automatically followed the Interstate north from downtown. The second exit to the beach would take her to Milo Cahill's house. She was so deep in thought that it took a while to realize her cell phone was ringing. She had left it in its cradle on her dash, plugged into the speaker system. The screen said "unknown caller," but she recognized the number. Fran Willis. How had she found out her cell-phone number? Well, from Kylie, of course.

She kept her hands on the wheel. After two more rings, the phone went silent. The message icon came on.

Sooner or later she would have to speak to the woman. *Fran, I swear I didn't tell Kylie she could stay. I will pay you to come here and take her back with you. How about it? A few days in Miami on me. Bring Bob. Bring Donny and Darlene, too. Go to Disney World on the way home. I'll take care of it. She's your daughter. Come and get her.*

The phone rang again. She was about to hit the mute button when she saw who it was from. "Rick, hello. I'm in traffic, but I have it on speaker. What's up?"

His voice surrounded her. "Got your message about Pettigrew. I was busy and couldn't get back to you till now."

"Have you been watching the news?"

"I'm on the road, but they had it on NPR."

"Damn. Then it has to be on all the talk shows," she said.

"I cruised by my apartment just now, and there was a TV crew outside my door, so I thought I'd find something else to do for a while. I called Shelby. He wants me to take him and the wife to his press conference tomorrow. I'm picking up vibes from the man, like I'm about to get fired."

"I don't think so," she said.

Rick asked, "If it happens, where does that leave you and me?"

"What do you mean?"

"I can't pay you."

"Don't worry about it. Just try to avoid the press until I get a few things nailed down."

"Like what?"

"Like . . . I'm working on it. I'd rather not say until I have more to report."

"Okay. I think I might take off and go fishing this afternoon."

"Good idea. See you tomorrow. Don't forget the check."

"You still want me to answer all those questions?"

Smiling, she settled into her seat. "No. We'll just chat. Come in the afternoon. Toward five."

"Depends on what the congressman has for me, but I'll try to see you then."

The words were forming on her lips. *Maybe we can grab some dinner after,* when she heard "*Hasta mañana*" and then the disconnect. She was glad she had not spoken. Another rule that she had almost forgotten: Unless they are persons to whom you could not possibly be attracted, do not meet your clients outside the office.

She hit the speed dial for Edgar's number at home. He didn't own a cell phone, refused even to consider it. He had the old-fashioned kind that would ring off the hook until answered. He finally picked up, a little out of breath.

"Edgar, it's me. Has Kylie come back yet?"

"I'd have called you if she had."

"What are you doing? You weren't up on the ladder again, I hope?"

"No, no. I was under my house taking measurements. I want to open the bathtub drain, but it's a pretty tight squeeze."

"Edgar, please don't do that. What if you got stuck? It's going to rain soon. I promise."

"If you have any influence, use it, but I think we'd have a better chance asking the Miccosukees to do a rain dance."

"By the way, have any reporters been by the house? Have you seen anyone?"

"Nope."

"Well, lock the gate, and don't answer the door unless it's Kylie. And don't forget to call me when she comes back."

It had been months since C.J. had visited Milo Cahill, but she saw the red tile roof of the tower above the trees on the narrow, curving street. C.J. parked next to two other cars on the bricked area outside the wall. The heavy wooden gate was closed, so she walked to a smaller door, pressed a buzzer, and a minute later an unfamiliar man in a white T-shirt and trousers let her in. His beard was a narrow line along his jaw, and his glasses were tinted blue.

"I'm C.J. Dunn. I've come to see Mr. Cahill. He's expecting me."

"Just so you know, I'm his massage therapist." He escorted her across the courtyard. The garage door was up, but Milo's Mercedes wasn't there. Another car, a Chrysler, was parked in its place.

"Milo is home, isn't he?"

"In all his glory."

"His car is gone, and I thought—"

"That's a rental."

"Oh, yes. Milo said he's having the limo reupholstered." She added, "In red leather."

"La-de-fucking-dah."

They walked up the steps. The rambling, two-story house was an Art Deco throwback that had been built in stages, creating a labyrinth of hallways and oddly shaped rooms. One of the previous owners had added a tower, accessible by a narrow, curving metal staircase. To the tower Milo had added oriental carpets, silk pillows, an antique Moroccan hookah, and a dumbwaiter to send drinks up and empty bottles down. He used the large living room as a gallery and place to mingle. There were black leather stools and a long red sofa shaped like lips.

A short, dumpy figure in an embroidered green silk turban stepped into view at the end of the hall. He opened his arms. "Well, butter my butt and call me a biscuit, look who's here."

She walked over and gave him a hug. "Hello, Milo."

"Forgive my attire." He brushed a hand over his baggy gray T-shirt and warmup pants. Leather slippers covered his feet. "Only my true friends are allowed to see me in this condition. But *you* look fresh as a daisy."

"I just came from Noreen and Donald Finch's house. I had a nice talk with his sister, Sarah."

"Do tell."

"I think I stand a good chance of getting the job."

"Of course you'll get it. Aren't you glad you took my advice?

Julio!" He looked around her to speak to the man still lingering in the hall. "C.J., you want some breakfast, don't you? Or lunch?"

"I've just eaten, thanks. I'll take some coffee."

"Coffee for Ms. Dunn, please, Julio. Cream, one sugar. You see, I remember how you like it. I'll have a pot of Earl Grey, some cranberry juice, and dry toast."

When Julio was gone, rolling his eyes, Milo put his arm through hers, and they walked. "We're being kind to Mr. Tummy this morning."

"You had a party," she guessed.

"Did I ever! Finally had somethin' to celebrate. Wasn't that a fabulous reception at the Royal Palm? Wasn't it perfect? Everybody came over afterward and didn't leave till the sun came up, and some of them are probably still asleep if you look in the corners. I was outside at dawn saying 'bye when the newspaper dropped at my feet. I made the mistake of looking at the front page. So they found Alana Martin. Most of her. It's too awful for words. I had to take a Xanax."

They entered the room he called his terrarium, half an octagon built on the back of the house. Tall windows looked out on a thatch-covered outdoor bar, a lap pool, and a dock where one could sit and look up and down the Intracoastal Waterway or at the mansions on the other side. But the cool air in the house had fogged the windows, and C.J. could only make out the plants pressing up against the glass. Roll-down bamboo shades cut the view even further, so that the room was dim and quiet, except for the trickle of water from a small fountain in the corner.

They sat opposite each other in rattan chairs upholstered in tropical print fabric from the 1940s, a teakwood table between. Its top was cluttered with antique wooden puzzles, some feather carnival masks, a dish of colored glass balls, and other things whose purpose was a mystery to her. C.J. stared at the collection, unable to decide if Milo's house had always been so bizarre, or if sobriety had altered her perceptions.

"Thanks for referring this case to me, Milo, but it's about to become a media feeding frenzy. When you turn on the news, you'll find out."

"Well, now you can get that pretty face in front of the public. You'll be doing all sorts of interviews. I know someone at *Vanity Fair*. A profile is in order. How a small-town girl became one of America's most glamorous attorneys."

"Thank you, but no."

"I don't understand that about you, C.J. You love love love to talk about the law, but never a word about yourself. People like those rags-to-riches stories. They do."

Milo's head turned toward the jingling noise coming across the room. As a small blur of brown and black leaped on him and attacked his face with its tongue, he laughed and raised his arms. The dog circled, jumped down, and bounced into C.J.'s lap. She got her hands around its belly before it could lick her too. She held it up and looked past the fur into bright black eyes. The Yorkie let out a high-pitched yap and wagged its thumb-sized tail.

"Christ, Milo, you need to train this thing."

He straightened his turban. "Princess just went to the groomer. Doesn't she smell pretty?"

"Take her, please."

"Come on, Princess. Come to Daddy." He reached across the table. "Auntie C.J. doesn't want to play. Sit. Be still. All right, C.J., you didn't come over this morning because you missed us. What's on your mind?" His mood had soured slightly.

"I'm sorry, I didn't sleep well last night," C.J. said. "First, Noreen Finch. She's not happy that I haven't wrapped this case up and tied it with a bow already. Don's sister is on my side, but I'm worried about Noreen. Do you think she'll be a problem?"

Milo stroked the dog. "Don't you worry about big bad Noreen. I'll talk to Paul. No, I won't say you asked me to. I know how to handle it. I think they all need to calm down over there."

"You and he were fraternity brothers at Duke," C.J. remembered. "Friends for a long time."

"Oh, it's just one of those connections you make when you're young, and it sticks. We were boys, practically. Almost thirty years ago. Am I that old? Wait, I remember why you came over. You wanted to know if Alana Martin was doing porno movies. Well, I did ask a few people last night who might have heard something like that, and—" He lifted his hands.

C.J. replayed in her mind what Kylie had told her. She raised her brows. "No?"

"Not that I know about, and I know everything."

"Well, if she never actually appeared in an adult film, did she ever try out for one? Or did she know or associate with people who made them?"

"My, you are on a tangent. Darlin', that kind are not welcome on the beach, at least not in Milo's house. We like to have good clean fun, don't we, Princess? Oh, Alana had no inhibitions. She liked to party, we all knew that. I told you before, I think she got mixed up with drug dealers or such. They're the people that tie a dead body to something heavy and throw it overboard." He shuddered, and Princess took that as a signal to leap up and go for his face again. Her pink tongue darted over his eyes and mouth. "Yes, yes, you love Daddy, but that's enough. Look, Julio brought you a cookie."

The man in the white T-shirt had come in with a tray, which he quickly unloaded. "If that's it, I have other appointments, and I'm already late."

"Enjoy your day. Thank you." Milo took the dog biscuit from a gold-rimmed saucer and gave it to Princess. "There you go. Yum-yum."

C.J. had spent hours in this house, part of Milo's circle, watching his courtiers come and go. In those days, she had even found his antics with his dog amusing. She had relied on Milo for fun, for never judging her, and to fix the little problems that arose. He knew she had spent two weeks locked away with other drunks and a few addicts, but he had kept it to himself. He was discreet. She felt some fondness toward him, and she doubted he would lie to her.

"Milo, has Donald Finch ever made adult movies?"

That brought an open-mouthed laugh. "That is funny. Donald Finch makes second-rate documentaries that wouldn't sell at all if he weren't so well connected. The smartest thing he ever did for himself was marry Noreen Shelby."

"He studied film in L.A., but he'd left by the time I arrived," C.J. said. "Does he talk about people he knows in the industry?"

"Yes, but I take it with a grain of salt. Why are you asking?"

"Alana Martin said someone was going to connect her with a friend in Hollywood."

"Oh, not Donald. I doubt he knew her, and he certainly wouldn't have offered to help her. Noreen would have had his balls on a platter."

"It wasn't you, was it?"

"Me?" Milo laid a hand on his chest. "Why, I'm so flattered you think I have any influence in Tinseltown. If Alana had come to me, I'd certainly have done what I could for her, though."

C.J. sighed.

"I'm sorry," he said. "I'm not being very helpful to you today, am I? Last night, did you have time to see the drawings of the interior of The Aquarius? We're doing something new there, too. Fiber-optic cable, which admits light but not heat."

She picked up her coffee cup, yellow Fiesta Ware pottery, and put it down again. "What I came over to talk to you about is someone on your design staff. Jason Wright. I need to ask you about him."

Milo closed his eyes and raised his brows. "No longer on my staff, as of about one o'clock this morning."

"What happened?"

Milo poured himself some tea. "I found out Jason was bad-mouthing me behind my back. Oh, we'd had our disagreements, but his attitude had become impossible. A master's degree from Princeton. An internship with Frank Gehry. That makes you smarter than Milo Cahill, who has been in this business as long as you have been alive? I don't think so."

"I'm sorry to hear it," C.J. said. "I spoke to him at the reception. He seemed unhappy."

"He's a deeply unhappy young man. That was part of our problem. I don't like mopes."

She leaned forward with her arms crossed on her knees. "Was he Alana Martin's lover?"

Over his tea cup, Milo's eyes narrowed with amusement, and his rosy lips turned up. "Hardly. Jason is gay. You mean you didn't pick up on it?"

"No. I didn't."

"Well, I should rephrase that. Jason is having difficulties accepting what he is. He hasn't told his family. He's the only son, mommy and daddy are in the country club, go to church, vote Republican. You know. I introduced him to Alana Martin, hoping she could push him off the fence, but . . . well, it didn't work. I tried." He smiled across the table. "Have a piece of toast?"

"No, I should leave."

"We're so glad you came to see us." He wasn't urging her to stay, she noticed. She had done the unforgivable, turned into a mope.

She leaned over and kissed his cheek, their customary parting. "Thanks, Milo."

He stood up with Princess draped over his arm. "Don't be a stranger."

When the door closed behind her, C.J. doubted she would ever be back. Something had changed. For years she had called him her friend, but she really knew very little about him beyond the surface glitter. After she moved from California, she never heard from him. When he came to Miami, he used her contacts to dig new roots. His money and his laughter attracted friends. He was generous, but the kind of generosity that served to keep him at the center of the circle. He was a fixer, but the price was loyalty. To those who crossed him he could be dismissive and cruel. How could she never have noticed? The world was not as pretty, sober.

As she went through the small door to the street, C.J. looked up at the sky. The heat and humidity had turned the blue to a featureless haze. Clouds floated tantalizingly west to east, holding on tightly to any rain.

One thing she knew: the week was gonna be hell.

chapter
TWENTY-THREE

It was 7:10 A.M. when C.J. opened her office door and turned on the lights. She had come in early to avoid the reporters who would soon be swarming the lobby. Her name had come up on CNN again. Well-known attorney C.J. Dunn had been hired by a person of interest in the murder of Alana Martin. Sources were suggesting it could be someone on the staff of U.S. Congressman Paul Shelby, who had been at the party that night.

The only possible source of that rumor, C.J. thought, was Libi Rodriguez. She had wanted an interview with Shelby, who had brushed her off. Libi had to know something was going on, and sooner or later she would leak Rick Slater's name, leaving it to the talking heads to draw the wrong conclusions. C.J. planned to grab the story out of Libi's hands and spin it her way.

Driving to work, half expecting an outraged phone call from Shelby or even his mother, C.J. had flipped through the talk-radio stations. The theory of a connection to drugs was getting some play, Alana Martin as a party girl who had crossed the wrong people. A person who called herself a friend of Alana was certain that a man she'd met at a bar had stalked and killed her.

At her desk, C.J. aimed her remote at the television and let it play in the background. She tossed her tote into a chair and flipped open her daily diary so see what could possibly be put off until later in the week or given to one of her associates.

At 7:25, her secretary knocked on the open door and came in, her dyed red hair a vivid contrast to a lime-green jacket and skirt. C.J. looked around from the window, where she had been spraying a little fertilizer on her orchids. "Aren't you the early bird?"

"Well, I kinda figured there'd be a lot going on today," Shirley said. "I saw your picture on *Good Morning America*. They talked about all the big cases you've done. I expect you'll get some phone calls."

"I expect I will."

"What's first?" Shirley scooted her jangling bracelets up her arm and poised her pen over her steno pad. "Coffee?"

"No, I'll get it. Put a note on Henry's door to come see me as soon as he gets in. And tell the front desk that if they get any calls from the media, we have no comment at this time." Ten minutes later, she had given Shirley enough to keep her busy the rest of the day. "So how was your weekend at Disney World with the girls?"

"Great, but I felt like I was playing hooky. The real fun is here." Shirley stuck her pen behind her ear and, with a swirl of her skirt, she was gone.

"Right. We're having a ball."

The corridors, empty and silent when C.J. had arrived, were coming to life. The girl from the printing room was making deliveries, and legal assistants were turning on their computers. In the kitchen, C.J. fixed herself a large mug of coffee and took a bagel from the tray, which would have to do until lunch.

Henri Pierre was waiting for her when she got back to her office. "Morning, boss. You wanted to see me?"

"*Bonjour*, Henry. That's a nice suit."

He shrugged, smiling. "On sale. You like it?"

"Very handsome. You look like partnership material. Come on in." She took a sip of coffee. "I could use some help. I'm jammed up with this Martin thing. Can you handle a federal bond hearing at two o'clock this afternoon? Basically, all you need to do is show up."

"I have a conference call, but yes, I can move it to later today. Where's the file?"

"Wait." C.J. aimed her remote at the screen to turn up the volume. The *Today Show* host was saying, "After the news at the top of the hour, we'll be talking to the parents of Alana Martin, the Miami woman whose body was found more than a week after she vanished from a celebrity party at the home of a wealthy Miami Beach publisher and socialite."

C.J. wondered about calling Billy Medina to warn him.

Henry said, "How can you go on national TV if your child was just found dead? Do they like the attention?"

"Everyone deals with it in his own way. This is the second daughter they've lost." C.J. looked at Henry. "Alana's older sister drowned when her car went into a canal. Alana was driving."

"My God. That is beyond tragic. How are they functioning?"

"I don't know." She handed Henry a thick file. "Here. If you have any questions, call me."

From behind her desk, C.J. scrolled through the channels, then backed up to CNN. She had caught sight of the beach, police standing in the glare of floodlights, and a tarp covering a body. The story was no different than what she had seen at home two hours ago. She turned it off and called her secretary.

"Shirley, don't we have a portable TV in the storeroom? I want you to put it on your desk and if you see anything on the Martin case, take notes. Let me know if they say anything I need to respond to. If they mention Paul Shelby or Rick Slater, drop everything and tell me what channel. I also want you to check the Internet and see what's coming through on the news blogs."

Shirley said she would. C.J. thanked her and turned to the files that she had hoped to get to over the weekend. She checked her watch. There were certain reporters she wanted to call, but it was too early.

At 8:05, she turned the TV back on and kept an eye on it. A few minutes later, the *Today Show* host, Scott Matthews, went to the Martin story, reminding the audience that the girl's body had been found on the beach two nights ago. He had the good manners not to describe the body's condition. The screen went to a view of the parents and their lawyer at a conference table, probably at Oscar Enriquez's office.

Matthews gave them his condolences, then asked if they had prepared themselves for this outcome.

"Stupid question," C.J. said.

Oscar Enriquez translated, then spoke to the camera. "They were holding on to hope of finding her alive. It's very painful for them, Scott. Alana's older sister died in a traffic accident, and to lose a second child to a murder, well, they are traumatized. Alana was a good student, a good daughter, an aspiring actress, a beautiful young woman. They want people to know that."

Matthews asked if the police were making any progress in the case.

Enriquez said, "Not fast enough. Luisa and Hector want to find the persons responsible, so if anyone has information, please come forward. They also want to thank the hundreds of people who have sent them messages of sympathy, and as soon as the medical examiner releases their daughter's body, they will see about a burial. They want to have a nice service for her. They don't have much money, but it's the last gift they can give their daughter."

"I can't stand this." C.J. aimed the remote at the television but was stopped by the faces of Alana's parents. They were drained. Stunned. Holding hands, they mumbled their thanks in heavily accented English.

The screen went dark when C.J. pressed the remote. Their daughter was dead. Whatever she had been, they had loved her. Their pain had poured through the screen. For a minute, C.J. rested her forehead on the heels of her hands, eyes closed.

She thought about Kylie. She still hadn't heard from her, even after leaving four messages. Kylie had returned Edgar's car yesterday while C.J. was at Milo's. She had come and gone, apologizing to Edgar for not finishing his photographs, but hoping to get to it in a few days. She had asked Edgar to drop her off at the bus stop on South Dixie Highway.

C.J. looked at her telephone. Taking a breath, she picked up the handset and from memory dialed the Willises' home number in Pensacola. Three days ago she had promised Fran to put Kylie on an airplane today, Monday, and fly her home. She expected to catch hell for it, but there was nothing left to do but admit she had failed.

Kylie's father answered.

"Bob, this is C.J. Dunn. I hope I'm not calling too early."

He said she wasn't, they were just finishing breakfast. "I guess you'll want to talk to Fran."

C.J. took a last sip of cold coffee from the mug and, a moment later, Fran came on. "Well," she said, "I was wondering when you'd get around to calling back."

"Fran, I'm sorry, I don't know where Kylie is. She spent the night at my house on Saturday—"

"I know. She told me. We had a talk last night. She's going to stay in Miami. Bob and I aren't thrilled, but there comes a point when you're just beating your head against the wall. She has a job and her own apartment—"

"Her own apartment?"

"An efficiency, one room and a kitchen. She has some money, and she got a little advance on her salary."

C.J. couldn't decide if Fran was angry at her or at Kylie. She said, "Where is she working?"

"In a gift shop on Miami Beach. They sell henna tattoos and crystals and things like that. She says she likes the owner, and she's making enough to live on, so I said, Kylie, if that's what you really want, there's nothing your father and I can do about it, as long as you call us every week and let us know you're okay, and she said she would."

C.J. said, "She's too young, Fran."

"Well, what am I supposed to do about it? You don't have to worry about her anymore. I was wrong to involve you in the first place. Kylie said you were trying to reach her, and I told her, no, just leave Ms. Dunn alone." Fran paused to take a breath. "I won't be calling you again, and you don't call here. All right? We won't be bothering you anymore. Kylie is my daughter, not yours." As Fran spoke, her voice had risen and become more clipped, until it seemed that the words came at C.J. like sharp pebbles.

Into the silence on the line, she said, "If that's what you want."

"It's what I want. And Bob too. I'm sorry it has to be that way."

"So am I. Good-bye, Fran."

C.J. slowly replaced the handset. She knew she ought to be relieved. Another task crossed off her list. A burden lifted. But all she felt was hollow, as if something precious to her had been irretrievably lost. She felt pressure behind her eyes, then the burn of tears.

"Stop it." She jerked a drawer open for a tissue.

At 8:30 she consulted her computer for her list of media contacts. She called an acquaintance who worked for Larry King. He said he would call the assistant producer for her and see if they could get her on the air tonight or tomorrow.

Next, C.J. put in calls to friendly reporters at *The Los Angeles Times*, *The Miami Herald*, *The Sun-Sentinel* in Fort Lauderdale, and the local ABC affiliate. Some were in, some not, but when she had them on the line, she told them she was representing a member of Congressman Shelby's staff, one of several persons being questioned by police. Mr. Slater, an Army veteran with a spotless record, had given his consent to a search of his apartment, and the detectives had found absolutely nothing to incriminate him. C.J. told the reporters about the men who claimed to have seen her client leave the party with Alana Martin, but it had actually been some other girl. No, sorry, she couldn't divulge the name of this girl just yet, but she expected to get statements soon to clear it all up.

After she had worked her way through as many reporters as she believed would report the story her way, she called Edgar. So far, the vultures had not landed on her front lawn, though Edgar had spotted a car driving by slowly, someone taking pictures through the window.

C.J. worked through the morning and ate lunch at her desk. The managing partner stopped by for a chat, making sure that the Martin story wasn't going to disrupt the smooth functioning of the office—it wouldn't—or to see if C.J. had any juicy details. She didn't.

Shirley came in waving some message slips. "Fox News wants a phone interview at four-fifteen."

"Sure, right in advance of Paul Shelby's press conference. Call them back, say not at this time but we'll be in touch."

"I already did." Shirley gave her a list of stories that had appeared on the portable TV set at her desk. "They're talking about a boyfriend of Alana Martin, a young architect named Jason Wright."

C.J. laid down her pen. "What are they saying?"

"Well, that he and Alana were dating, and she broke it off. They showed where he lives, an apartment on Miami Beach. They're not saying he killed her or anything." Shirley looked closely at C.J. "What's the matter?"

"Nothing." Someone had leaked this story, and C.J. could only think of one person: Noreen Finch. It wouldn't have been hard for Noreen to discover the name of the young architect Alana had been dating and, from there, to drop a few hints to the right people. The effect it would have on the poor schmuck she was accusing wouldn't have occurred to Noreen. And C.J. was painfully aware of where the blame lay: with herself.

"There are a couple other things," Shirley said. "*ET* is going to interview Yasmina tonight, the singer who was at the party."

"Yeah, I'll be sure to watch. Did Harnell Robinson's check arrive? He was supposed to have it here today by noon."

"Nothing yet," Shirley said.

"Dammit. He's not going to blow off twenty thousand dollars. I *will* sue him. His last excuse was, I had to make some back payments to my agent. Next time Milo Cahill sends me a client, I'm going to make sure they have the cash."

"Want me to call Mr. Robinson and see if it's on its way?"

"Please. If I do it, I'll scream at him."

"Oh, you got this." A large brown envelope was clamped under Shirley's elbow, and she handed it across the desk. "It's from Paul Shelby's office."

When Shirley had gone out, C.J. opened the envelope. She unfolded a letter from Shelby's chief of staff. *Per your request to Mr. Shelby, enclosed please find. . . .* He had attached the résumé and pay records for Richard Alan Slater.

Slater was earning $700 a week plus overtime. C.J. went to the résumé, expecting nothing unusual. Judy Mazzio had already supplied the basic information. Born at Fort Campbell, Kentucky, lived on bases in six different countries. High school and first two years of college in Chicago. Eight years in the Army Special Forces, various assignments overseas, discharged as a lieutenant. Paratroop training. Medal for expert marksmanship. Third-degree black belt in karate and tae kwon do. Graduated from UNC-Wilmington, near Fort Bragg, with a degree in political science.

C.J. turned to the next page. Private security work in Malaysia, Italy, Colombia, and Mexico. Most recently with Atlas Security, Miami. Licensed to carry firearms. Fluent in Spanish, had basic Italian, French, and Arabic.

Odd. Why would a man with that much going for him settle for $700 a week to be a chauffeur in Miami, Florida?

Her thoughts were interrupted when Shirley buzzed her on the intercom.

"It's Mr. Medina. I told him you didn't want to be disturbed, but he said you were expecting his call."

When she connected, C.J. said, "Billy, I was hoping to speak to you today. Have the media showed up?"

"Like flies," he said. "But what can I tell them? Yes, I had the party. Yes, she was here. That's all I know. Well, my lovely, I have something you want. I spoke to the mayor about the witnesses."

"Thank you, Billy. I wasn't sure you would."

"You should have more faith in me, *chica.*"

He gave her the names of two men and their addresses, one in

Miami, the other on the beach. He said, "I hope you get rid of this soon. It's making you a little crazy. You'll be easier to get along with when it's over."

"Probably true. Maybe we can see each other this weekend. Until then, I'm swamped."

"Really? How unusual. Whenever you break free, you know my number."

Click.

"Yes, and I would be so happy to see you too," she said.

She called Judy Mazzio's office and left the information on Judy's voice mail. She added, "See if you can get a statement out of these guys pronto. I need it yesterday. Threaten to break their legs if they lie. Oh, and I'm going to courier that black dress over to you. See if it improves their memories."

As she worked, she kept the TV on mute, two channels on the screen, NBC and CNN. She planned to watch Paul Shelby's press conference at four-thirty. He had timed it to give the reporters a chance to put his big smile and brilliant remarks into their five o'clock lineup. But she suspected they weren't going to ask many questions about The Aquarius.

Her intercom buzzed. Shirley told her that Mr. Slater had arrived. C.J. said to ask him if he wanted anything to drink; she would be with him in a minute. She hung up and raced around her office shoving boxes out of the way, straightening stacks of journals, and pushing three pairs of shoes out of sight under the sofa. She touched up her lipstick and went out to the twenty-first-floor waiting room to find her client.

He sat on the edge of one of the square-shaped armchairs, leaning over the large glass-topped table, feet planted apart, reading an issue of *Yachting Magazine*. The back of his dark gray suit coat stretched tightly across his shoulders. The halogens in the ceiling put a little shine on his head.

"Mr. Slater?"

His eyes went first to her face before doing the automatic male scan, starting at her open-toe, four-inch Manolo Blahniks, up her legs, over the above-the-knee skirt, lingering for a split second on her chest, then back to her face. He smiled politely and stood up, extending his hand.

"Ms. Dunn."

"Come on back."

In her office she closed the door behind him and said, "No comments on the clutter, please."

"Nice view." He walked over to the window. "I don't have much time. I dropped the Shelbys off at his congressional office for the press conference, and he expects me to come right back."

"Does he know you're here?"

Slater withdrew an envelope from inside his jacket. "He gave me a check for you. Five grand. I don't think he was too happy about it. He's been listening to the news, waiting for the other shoe to drop." Slater looked at the row of orchid pots on the windowsill. Three were in bloom, including a white vanda that was sending out double sprays of flowers, propped up on long sticks. "Green thumb," he said.

"I just feed them. They bloom when they get good and ready." C.J. put the envelope on her desk. "I had to give your name to some reporters whom I trust before Libi Rodriguez figures it out. She's good, I have to hand it to her. She smiles pretty and shows her cleavage. Do you want to sit down?"

"Sure." Slater sat on the edge of the sofa, feet apart, elbows on knees. He was frowning. "What are the chances of them coming after me? In my business, we don't like our faces on TV."

"Fifty-fifty. I'm doing the best I can. If they think you're just another Joe Schmoe at the party, they'll leave you alone." She told him that she had obtained the names of the witnesses who supposedly had seen him with Alana Martin. "My investigator is going to show them Alana's picture and encourage them to say they were mistaken. We'll give their statements to the police. I thought I had an alibi witness, but it didn't work out."

"Who?"

"The girl you took home from the party. I thought I could find her."

"How?"

"I have my ways, but it was a dead end. We won't need her. Somebody else's name has come up. Jason Wright. Remember him? The architect who works for Milo Cahill? Or he used to. Cahill fired him."

"Yeah, the guy you didn't think was guilty."

"I didn't tell them. I think Noreen Finch did. Shelby's mother. It was a rotten thing to do, but it's out in the media now, and if we can take advantage, so be it. That's how the game is played."

"Some game," Slater said.

"My job is to protect you."

"And Shelby."

"Screw Shelby." When Slater raised his brows, C.J. said, "Politicians."

"Shelby at the top of the list, seems to me," Slater said. "Saturday at the Royal Palm, he put his hand on your arm, and you nearly slugged him."

"I did not." C.J. picked up her remote. "Let's see if his press conference is being carried live. I doubt it. If anything, they'll just put some sound bites on the evening news."

She was wrong. Paul Shelby was live on two local channels, the Fox affiliate and Channel Eight. There were others taping it; he spoke into a cluster of microphones. His wife stood beside him in a neat blue suit, a smile on her pretty face. As background they had hung up large drawings of The Aquarius, glittering blue towers rising above a horizon of palm trees and turquoise water. Shelby was finishing his remarks, gesturing to a photograph of the land as it currently existed, scrubby and dry, useless as surplus government property, to be developed for the good of the people of Florida, for American energy independence, and for the future of the planet.

"Give me a break," C.J. said. "Slater, I know he's your boss, but can you honestly tell me he's not getting anything out of this but a good deed that warms his heart?"

"So he says."

When Paul Shelby was finished, the room erupted. Reporters were on their feet waving arms, shouting. A man with a Fox News microphone managed to get through. "Congressman, a question about the party a week ago where Alana Martin disappeared. Is it true that you went there to hear the Lebanese singer, Yasmina? Were you aware then, or are you now, of anti-American statements she's made against our policy in the Middle East?"

Rick Slater stared at the screen.

"Oh, that's a good one," C.J. said.

Paul Shelby chuckled. "No, I wasn't aware, but you can be sure I won't be buying any of her CDs."

The laughter was quickly drowned out by shouts for attention. A slender arm at the front of the crowd rose, and a woman called out, "Congressman Shelby, a question on The Aquarius!"

"Yes." He pointed.

The camera swung to Libi Rodriguez with her Channel Eight microphone. "The architect for the project is Milo Cahill. Mr. Cahill has a long relationship with celebrity criminal lawyer C.J. Dunn, going back at least ten years, when Ms. Dunn represented Mr. Cahill in a wrongful death case in California. Now Ms. Dunn is apparently representing you or someone on your staff. Why did you hire Ms. Dunn? Is it related to the disappearance and murder of Alana Martin?"

Shelby broke into a smile. "Well, that's a bait-and-switch if I ever heard one. A member of my staff was at the party with me, and police have been interviewing everyone. It's only wise to have advice of counsel in a situation like this, and I asked Ms. Dunn for her opinion. That's all it is. And I'm not going to give you the name of my staff member, out of consideration for his privacy. Next?"

Slater let out a breath. "I just heard a bullet go past my head."

C.J. said, "Shelby's good at this. Nothing hits him and sticks. He was born to be in Washington."

Slater looked at her. "You really don't like the man. What did he ever do to you?"

"Nothing, I hate them all equally."

"You look like you could use a drink."

C.J. laughed. "A double scotch on the rocks. We need to talk about this, but you should go. Call me after you're finished with Shelby."

"What if we meet later, say six-thirty? I'll buy you a hamburger at my favorite joint, the Killarney Pub."

She hesitated. "I can't. I've got too much to do."

"You have to eat sometime, and it's on your way home."

"I don't drink when I'm working. I have some things to finish tonight."

"I said eat. I'm not out to get you drunk, Ms. Dunn." He smiled, and his teeth flashed white in his beard.

She let Shirley escort him back to the elevators. She picked up her little brass plant mister and walked down the row of orchids in her window, wondering if they would be happier in her backyard, or if the heat would bake them. She lifted a leaf on the phalaenopsis and sprayed the roots. Leaning closer, she saw a tender green shoot that hadn't been there yesterday. She smiled and gently touched it. "Where have you been?"

chapter
TWENTY-FOUR

r ick sat in a booth on the side facing the door so he could
watch for C.J. Dunn. The windows were heavily tinted,
and neon beer signs reflected back into the bar. There were
three televisions going, but the sound was turned off, CNN on one,
the others showing a game between the Florida Marlins and the
Atlanta Braves, top of the eighth, Atlanta getting creamed. Not too
many people on a Monday, so Rick wasn't bothering anybody by
talking on his cell phone. Even so, he spoke quietly, his hand in
front of his face. Carlos Moreno was on the other end, calling to tell
him that in her next broadcast, Libi Rodriguez intended to mention
his name.

"What the hell?" Rick said. "What's she trying to do?"

"It's not you, man," Carlos said. "It's your lawyer. She says C.J.

Dunn is a menace to the media, but here's the story. They're both being considered for a job on CNN, hosting some show about murders by the rich and famous."

"Libi knows criminal law?"

"She covers the courthouse beat, and she thinks she has a shot because she's getting so much air time on this Martin murder. Hey, something else, Rick. A woman's been asking questions about me, an investigator named Judy Mazzio. Doesn't she work for your lawyer? What's going on?"

"C.J. thinks you're a cameraman for adult movies."

Carlos laughed. "*¡Ay, qué rico!* I wish. Why does she think that?"

"Tell you later. I have to sign off. She's coming in now."

He turned his cell phone to mute and slid it into his pants pocket. He had hung his jacket on the hook at the end of the booth and rolled up his sleeves. His pistol and holster were locked in the glove compartment of the Audi. As a general rule, he never took his gun into a bar that didn't serve pickled pig's feet and two-dollar beer.

She was walking past the window, reaching for the door. The sun, low in the sky, put some gold in her long blond hair. A nice-looking woman. Better than nice. Under other circumstances, if they weren't attorney and client, he might have asked her out. This didn't count, because she wanted to talk about his case.

C.J. took off her sunglasses and looked around for him. Rick stood up and raised a hand. She nodded and came over, shoved her leather bag over on the seat, and took off her jacket. Underneath, she wore a soft white blouse, so thin he could see the lace on her bra. He quickly put his eyes on her face and smiled. "You made it."

"Sorry I'm late." She scooted in.

"No problem." He handed her a menu just as the waitress appeared with his order of nacho chips smothered in cheese with bits of jalapeño peppers.

C.J. said, "In an Irish pub?"

"This is Miami."

The cheese stretched when she took a nacho chip. She bit into it and fanned her mouth. "Hot."

The waitress said, "What can I get you to drink?"

C.J. stared at her as if she'd spoken Chinese.

"On draft we've got Killian Red, Bass Ale, Harp, Sam Adams, Bud, Bud Lite—"

"I'll have . . . oh . . . Bushmills on the rocks. I'm in an Irish mood. But go easy on the pour. I have to work tonight."

"One Bushmills on the rocks." She wrote it down, and Rick ordered another Harp. "You folks know what you want to eat?"

"Give us a minute, please," Rick said. He pushed one of the small plates across the table toward C.J. "You changed your mind about working tonight?"

"I'm having just one, and promise to stop me if I ask for another." She opened the menu. "What do you recommend? I'm not up for a hamburger."

"Potato soup's good, if you're feeling Irish. Corned beef. Fish and chips."

"Soup, I guess. Oh, it comes with soda bread. That's a lot of carbs."

"What are you worried about? You don't have an ounce of fat." She smiled and kept reading. Rick leaned closer. "I found out something about you."

"What's that?"

"Your real name. What C.J. stands for." Her eyes met his over the top of the menu.

"Charlotte Josephine Bryan."

"Well, aren't you clever?"

"Charlotte's a nice name."

"I dropped it when I moved to California. When I was a kid they called me Charlie. I could've passed for a boy, skinny and flat-chested."

"You filled out nicely," he said.

She turned a page of the menu. "Just so we're even, I found out that you spent eight years in the Special Forces. Do you want to come clean about that scar on your arm? Swordfish?"

"Well, I don't like to scare people. I'm just a big old pussycat."

"Good thing for you I like cats, or we'd have some trouble." She set the menu aside. "You didn't lie to me about anything important, did you?"

"No. Scout's honor."

"Make sure you don't. Have you tried their fish and chips?"

"You'll like it, trust me." He signaled the waitress, and she came with their drinks. He told her what they wanted, two orders of the fish and chips. When she left, he noticed that C.J. was staring at her glass. "Did she bring the wrong thing?"

"No, it's fine." C.J. took a tentative sip. Her tongue came out and licked the liquid off her lips. She pressed them together as if she might find more of it.

Looking over her head, Rick saw Alana Martin's face on the television tuned to CNN. Live from Miami. He saw Libi Rodriguez standing in front of Paul Shelby's office on South Dixie Highway, a storefront with a sign in the window.

REELECT YOUR REPRESENTATIVE IN CONGRESS.
PAUL SHELBY, WORKING FOR YOU.

The sun was slanting across the building at the same angle as outside the bar.

C.J. turned around to see what he was looking at.

The transcription at the bottom wasn't keeping up with the reporter's mouth. *Richard Slater, chauffeur for Congressman Shelby....*

"Uh-oh," said C.J.

Rick saw himself in sunglasses and a dark suit, opening the door of the Ford SUV, helping Mrs. Shelby out, walking the congressman and his wife to the door of the office, then turning around, the camera doing a closeup and a freeze on his face. He looked like a hit man.

The words slid by. *Police say Slater is a person of interest in the Alana Martin investigation. Slater, thirty-eight, is a former member of the Army Special Forces who quit to join Blackwater USA. He relocated to Miami earlier this year and was hired by Atlas Security, a Florida-based company.*

Libi Rodriguez reappeared, her mouth moving silently. *Slater has been working as Shelby's bodyguard and chauffeur for two months. Sources tell CNN that Slater knew Alana Martin, though the nature of their relationship is uncertain. Slater has hired celebrity defense attorney C.J. Dunn. Ms. Dunn recently won an acquittal for Miami Dolphins star running back Harnell Robinson, charged with aggravated battery. This is Libi Rodriguez reporting for CNN.*

The video switched to one of the anchormen, some news about a typhoon in Asia.

When Rick looked back across the table, C.J. was staring at him. "Celebrity defense attorney. You're famous." As C.J.'s eyes narrowed, he said, "I spent less than a year with Blackwater, and that was back in oh-two."

"Which you omitted from your résumé."

"You know how it is. The controversies they're involved in lately—"

"And what did you do for Blackwater?"

"Security for press organizations in the Middle East and Central Asia. I quit when we went into Iraq. They wanted me to guard convoys, and it just didn't sound like as much fun as hanging around with reporters from the BBC or Reuters or *The New York Times*."

She lifted her glass and drank. "Bull. Shit."

"I am not lying to you, C.J."

Her eyes were drilling holes in him, but she took a breath and shook her head. "I must be crazy, believing anything you say."

He pointed at the television. "What now?"

"If you mean, are the police going to look at you more closely because of that report, no. If you're wondering if Shelby is going to fire you, I can't answer that. I have the feeling that Libi is too late. Most of the media's attention is turning to Jason Wright. As I told you before, Jason makes a better suspect because of his relationship with Alana. There's only one catch. He's gay. He hasn't come out yet, and as long as he stays in the closet, people will wonder if he's the boyfriend, which would be very good for you."

"So what's your advice? Wait and see?"

"Turn on the news at eleven," she said. "I'm also working on another theory." During the pause that followed, she seemed to weigh how much the client needed to be told about what his lawyer was doing. "Alana auditioned for the part of a young girl—very young—for a porn movie. There are perverts in the world who get off on that. The movie was never made, and she was trying to get the audition tapes back. If she had made it to Hollywood and they turned up on the Internet, it could have hurt her career. What if she had threatened to go to the FBI? Even if these people were using adult actors, an investigation could have done some damage. Did Alana ever say anything that, as you look back now, could refer to this? Did she mention any names?"

Rick slowly shook his head. "This is news to me. The subject never came up. Where are you getting this from?"

"Well, I can't really say, but I believe the information is accurate."

"Who was making the movie?"

"I'd love to be able to answer that one. It wasn't Libi's camera-man. I had him checked out, and he doesn't do porn."

"It didn't seem likely," Rick said.

"But it still doesn't explain why Moreno hasn't revealed the pictures in her portfolio. The tabloids would pay big money, but he's holding on to them. Why? What's he hiding?"

Rick said, "Alana was Carlos Moreno's client. Why would he want to make her look like a slut?"

"Maybe, but if you knew photographers like I do, you wouldn't be so trusting." As she talked, she drank, and the level in the glass was sinking. "I wish I could ask Jason about Alana's audition tapes. He might know. They were friends."

"Why can't you ask him?"

"If I thought he would talk to me, I would."

"Let me ask you something," Rick said. "It's about Milo Cahill. At the press conference, Libi Rodriguez said you represented Cahill in a wrongful death case in California. I wasn't aware you knew him."

She lifted a shoulder and drank some of her Bushmills.

"Did you win his trial?"

"Yes. It wasn't really his fault. Milo's car went off the road in the rain. His passenger was a boy he had picked up hitchhiking, and the parents sued. It was unfortunate, but they had no case. After-ward, Milo made sure his friends in Hollywood knew who I was."

"He was grateful." Rick rested his elbows on the table. "So . . . how did you actually get involved in my case? You said Paul Shelby called you, but I'm just curious if Milo talked to you first. He owed you a lot." C.J.'s eyes shifted to his. Rick decided to wait her out.

She took another sip of her drink. "Yes, Milo did talk to me first. I was busy, but it sounded like the kind of case I'd be interested in."

This was a different story than the one she'd given him two days ago. Then, she had taken the case because Shelby was up for re-election and she'd wanted to help him out. Not if she hated Shelby as much as it appeared she did. Rick smiled. "Lucky for me Cahill talked to you. I guess that Cahill wanted to do a favor for Paul Shelby. You know. Shelby is doing a big favor for Cahill, getting the land for The Aquarius through congress."

C.J. had gone silent again, looking at him.

Rick said, "They go way back. They were fraternity brothers in college in North Carolina. Duke. Did you know that?"

"Yes, I think I did," she said. "Why are you asking about Milo and Paul Shelby?"

Instead of an answer, he made a joke: "You think when Shelby fires me, Cahill will want a chauffeur?"

She laughed. "Believe me, you wouldn't want to work for Milo."

Rick had more questions, but he could see that it wouldn't get him anywhere to ask them. He had never known a lawyer who wasn't on the alert for ulterior motives. C.J. finished her drink and looked around for the waitress.

"You said just one," Rick reminded her.

"So I did. Thanks." She pulled a nacho chip off the stack. Then another, eating them with a greediness that left her fingers and mouth shiny. "Oh, God, this is good. Hot, hot. Jalapeño attack!" She grabbed his beer and took several gulps. She laughed when she put it back. "I think I owe you a beer."

"Waitress!" Rick held up his hand. "Could we get some water over here, please?"

C.J. wiped melted cheese off her fingers. "What were you really doing in Mexico, if you weren't catching swordfish?"

"I was catching swordfish. I'm a damn good fisherman. I was also tending bar for a friend, not making much money at that, and doing some security work in the American community, and . . . don't laugh. Writing a novel."

Her brows rose. "You?"

"Yeah, me. I'd written some nonfiction. I collaborated on a couple of articles with the reporters I'd met. My older brother had passed away and left me some money. I didn't touch it for a long time because I thought it would be like getting some use out of his death, but I was looking at forty on the horizon and said what the hell? So I rented a house on the beach and started on chapter one."

"What's it about?"

The waitress brought their water. Rick still had some beer, but C.J. ordered another drink. He said, "Do you want that? You said to stop you after one."

"Bring me the Bushmills, please." When the waitress was gone, C.J. said, "Your novel?"

"The main character is a charter-boat captain. The bad guys kill his best friend, and he seeks revenge and foils a terrorist nuclear attack." Rick laughed and had to cough to clear his throat. "It was the biggest piece of crap you ever saw. I tore it up and started over. The second draft was going along pretty well, but my girlfriend walked out on me, the people I worked for left town, and the money was running dry. I got a call from Atlas Security about the job for Shelby." He shrugged. "And here we are."

"Here we are." C.J. looked at him a while longer. Her eyes moved so closely over his face, it was making him nervous.

"What are you looking at?"

"You shave your head, don't you?"

"Yes, so?"

"Would you have a bald spot if you let it grow? I'm asking because I might need to make you appear less threatening. If we could grow your hair and shave off the mustache and beard—"

"No."

"I've studied emotional response to faces. Most people are leery of men with bald heads and beards. It's backward, you see. The accepted norm is hair on top and none on the chin."

"I'm not going to shave my beard."

"Well, what about the hair? Pattern baldness is associated with vulnerability, depending on the man. I think you'd look . . . reliable. Trustworthy."

"Yeah? What do I look like now?"

"Hmmm." She leaned closer on crossed arms. The neckline of her blouse opened up, and he could see the curve of her breasts. He brought his eyes back to hers, blue and warm, like the water off the beach in Mexico. She said, "When you get that serious expression on your face, you look . . . dangerous. Maybe a little sexy. That would be fine if you were the lawyer, but you're the client. Clients should look harmless and friendly. What if we get you a pair of wire-rimmed glasses and a plaid jacket?"

"Uh-huh."

"Oh, that's good," she said. "I like the smile."

"Harmless enough?"

"I wouldn't say that."

The waitress came with their dinners and C.J.'s whiskey on the same tray. C.J. reached for it before the waitress had finished putting the plates on the table. She settled back with the drink and left her dinner untouched.

Rick sprinkled some malt vinegar over his fish and chips. "Want some?"

"In a minute."

He put away a couple pieces of fish, then wiped his mouth and leaned across the table. "How long has it been?"

"What?"

"Since you had your last drink? How long?"

She tilted her head and pursed her lips. Shadows cut under her cheekbones. "Excuse me?"

"You sucked that first one down like it was water in the desert, and you're halfway through the second already."

She set her glass on the table. "There. Happy?"

He asked, "Were you ever in AA?"

"No. Why are we talking about this?"

"Then you don't have a problem."

C.J. seemed to search the ceiling for a response to such a stupid question. "I hardly think that two drinks constitute a problem."

She reached for her glass, but he got there first. He poured the contents into his nearly empty beer mug. Her mouth opened. He said, "You told me to stop you at one."

Her gaze turned chilly. "Call the waitress."

"Do you really want me to do that? Do you?"

"If I want another drink, I can damned well have it."

"Sure. It's up to you, but you're my lawyer, and I don't want to see your face on TV when they book you for a DUI. Want to give me your car keys now or before you leave?"

"You have a lot of nerve." C.J. crossed her arms, and her fingertips went white, like she was holding on.

"I apologize," Rick said. "My older brother, Tom, was an alcoholic. I know what it is."

"I'm not an alcoholic."

"He died of it, cirrhosis of the liver," Rick said. "I was in Pakistan when I got word he wasn't going to make it. It took me three days to get home. Tom didn't want to die in the hospital, so I took him to Illinois, where our grandparents lived. Our parents were both gone by then. He lasted two weeks. The morning he died, he wanted me to carry him out on the porch. It was the first warm day of spring."

Sympathy flooded across C.J.'s face. "I'm so sorry."

"What can you do?"

"It's been a year since I've had a drink," she said. "I was in AA, but I stopped going because I wasn't drinking anymore. I haven't touched it in a year, and . . . I don't know why I'm telling you this. Forget you heard it. Listen, I'm not mad at you for pouring out my Bushmills." She laughed. "Although it was awfully good. My father used to drink Black Jack by the quart. He was a real drunk."

"He passed away?"

"The same thing as your brother. I was in California. I came back for his funeral."

"That's rough."

"Not really. I hadn't seen him since I left home at twenty. He was in his own world, and he barely knew I was gone. My mother is still alive. She buried my father, told me I was going to hell, and a year later she married a fundamentalist preacher and moved to Tennessee. I'm sure she's very happy."

"No brothers, sisters?" Rick asked.

"Nobody. My husband was originally from Miami. His uncle lives in a cottage behind my place, and we've adopted each other. Edgar's a dear old thing, eighty-seven years old. I may have some cousins left in Mayo, but we've completely lost touch." She finally unrolled her napkin and picked up her fork. "And that's my life. You know more than most people."

"It's safe with me. Where's Mayo? Is that where you're from?"

"Where is Mayo? About an hour northwest of Gainesville near the Suwanee River, population one thousand. A nice little town if you like cows, pine trees, and not much to do except follow the Florida Gators. The name is from Ireland, speaking of things Irish." She ate some potato. "You were right, this is delicious."

"Glad you like it. We'll do dinner again sometime."

"Maybe, when this is over." She cut a piece of fish and ate it, then another, as though her desire for alcohol had switched to hunger. "I've made a decision. Even if Shelby lets you go, I'm not firing you as my client."

"That's good. Go easy on me with the fees."

"What fees? I'm doing it for all the free publicity."

"I could live without it," he said. "Reporters have probably staked out my apartment."

"I'm sure they have, after that report from Libi Rodriguez. You shouldn't go home right now. I'd rather you avoided the media. Is there somewhere you could stay until later on tonight?"

"Sure, I've got a friend I could stay with for a while."

C.J. finished chewing and patted her mouth with the napkin. Her eyes lit up. "Let's get out of town for the rest of the day. What about Key Largo?"

"I thought you had to work."

"I'm always up late. I don't sleep. There's a little place on the bay side I haven't been to in years, but it's still there. We could do dessert and coffee and be back before midnight."

He could read the question in her eyes, and it wasn't about coffee. He said, "We'd better not."

"Why?"

"You know why." Her hand lay on the table, white and smooth, the fingers gracefully curling. She wore a ring, pearl and diamonds. "Because if we do that, we'll end up in the same hotel room, and that wouldn't be smart." He drew a line across her knuckles, around her thumb. "Would it?"

"Well, I'm glad one of us is thinking straight." She dropped her hands into her lap.

"It's not that I don't want to," he said. "You know that, don't you?"

"Rick, when this is over. . . . " A smile slowly formed on her lips.

"When this is over, what?"

"Do you think you could teach a city girl how to fish?"

He smiled. "Count on it."

chapter
TWENTY-FIVE

On Tuesday morning a producer for Larry King called to say they would feature the Alana Martin murder that night, and they wanted C.J. to comment. They would go live from L.A. at 9:00 P.M., and do C.J.'s part of the show from local Channel Eight. After a sentencing hearing that afternoon, C.J. planned to go home and get ready, but when Judy Mazzio called, she decided to take a detour.

The two witnesses against Rick Slater had changed their minds. Judy had their signed statements at her office. She had shown the two men a photograph from Sunday's *Herald*, a group snapshot taken at Billy's party, Alana Martin in a black halter dress that left her shoulders bare. Judy took another black dress out of a bag, one with cap sleeves and a neckline slashed nearly to the waist. The girl you saw, Judy told them, was wearing this dress. She showed them Kylie's driver's license photo.

C.J. drove the few blocks from the Justice Building to Judy's office, a converted 1930s bungalow with shade trees in the yard and security bars over the windows. Mazzio Bail Bonds and Investigations. While Judy made copies, C.J. sat at a long table looking through the latest tabloids and news magazines. She could hear a television going in the next office, where one of Judy's bail bondsmen was working.

She picked up a copy of *The Globe*. The letters leaped off the page: *Alana Martin's Secret Life of Sex and Drugs* over a photograph of girls stumbling out of a night club. On the cover of *People*, Luisa Martinez held a graduation portrait of Alana: *Alana's Mom: It Could Happen to Your Daughter.* The headline in *The National Enquirer* blared: *Horror on the Beach! Exclusive Interview with Ohio Couple Who Found Alana's Body!* C.J. turned pages to find indistinct images of police officers pulling a tarp toward a shape in the sand.

In Touch featured a collage of the celebrities at the party that night, unflattering photos in which they appeared drunk or stoned. In a box to one side, C.J. saw a photo of herself without makeup, squinting. *Which celeb is lawyer C.J. Dunn's client? See page 22.*

She found the picture that Nash Pettigrew had taken in her front yard. With a laugh she held it up. "Judy, did you see this one of me in the bathrobe and slippers?"

"Yeah, great outfit," Judy said, stapling papers together.

"Thank God the public has a short attention span." C.J. read the article and found that she represented Richard Slater, the chauffeur for U.S. Congressman Paul Shelby. They didn't have Slater's photo and didn't imply he was guilty. So far Slater still had his job. Milo Cahill had promised to talk to the congressman, and it appeared he had done so.

The Sun reported *Alana's Boyfriend Denies Fight at Party.* The cover photo showed Jason with his arms around two girls, one of them Alana, obviously not taken at Billy's because Alana was wearing a blue top, and her hair was up. The flash had caught them laughing.

Judy said, "I marked one of the pages."

Inside, C.J. learned that Jason Wright was a spoiled rich kid who had graduated from Princeton and had come to South Beach to party. He had been fired by world-renowned architect Milo Cahill. Jason's parents lived in a wealthy area in Connecticut and spent the winters in Delray Beach.

"Every time I think the tabloids have gone as low as possible, they prove me wrong," C.J. said.

Judy came over and tapped a finger on the photograph of the Wrights' waterfront townhouse. "I'll bet you they have a boat."

Shaking her head, C.J. said, "Jason didn't put the body in his trunk, drive fifty miles north, then carry it in a boat all the way back to Miami and dump it. Alana was carried north by the currents."

"I know that, but you can't deny it helps your client," Judy said.

"Oh, look at this one," C.J. said, holding up a copy of *South Beach Insider.* "According to this, Jason is gay. A bartender at the Samba Room swears they had sex. Now why haven't the tabloids run that story?"

"Because they like him better straight." Judy went to her desk and came back with the local section of *The Miami Herald,* already opened and folded to a certain page. "Here, in case you're tired of reading about Jason."

The story was titled *Police Baffled by Metal Piece Found with Body.* The accompanying closeup showed a small plastic ruler alongside a piece of metal about three inches in length, a quarter inch in diameter. One end was straight, and the other twirled to a point. They had found the piece caught in the duct tape wrapped around Alana Martin's torso. It was believed that it could have broken from a larger object used as ballast to insure that the victim would sink, but which had failed to achieve that purpose. Detective Sergeant George Fuentes said the photograph was being released to the public in case someone might be able to identify it.

"I'd guess a corkscrew," Judy said, "but the metal is thinner."

C.J. turned the photo sideways, then upside down. "It's got to be one of those things that when somebody tells you what it is, you hit your forehead and say oh, sure, I knew that."

Judy said, "Does it look familiar?"

"Maybe I'm crazy, but it does." C.J. tossed the paper aside. "I've no idea."

Judy handed her the folder with the statements inside. "When are you taking these to Fuentes?"

"Tomorrow. I have a hearing in federal court in the afternoon, and I'll run over to the Beach after that."

Judy sat down and took off her reading glasses. They had zebra-print frames, matching her black top and tight white jeans. "Do you want me to find Kylie for you? How many New Age shops could there be on South Beach? I was thinking as long as you're over there—"

"Thanks, but Fran doesn't want me to contact Kylie."

"What a bitch. I don't understand it. What's her problem?"

"I'm a bad influence," C.J. said.

"How?"

"I don't want to get into it now. Do you have an invoice for me?"

"Sure." Judy went to get it. "We're only up to sixteen hundred dollars so far. Don't leave yet, though. I have something to put a smile on your face." She held up a business card. "Remember this? Tisha Dulaney, Excitement Travel, Miami Beach?"

C.J. took the card. "She gave me one of these too."

"Excitement Travel does ordinary bookings, but they also do porn cruises. What did I tell you? The owner and CEO is Harold

Vincent. He's sixty-seven, divorced, lives in an apartment in Surfside. He was born in Kansas City, made money in strip clubs, relocated in Vegas, then came to Miami in the late eighties."

"Harold Vincent. Wasn't that the man in Tisha's bedroom? I saw a pair of alligator shoes by the sofa."

"I wouldn't be surprised. He used to produce adult videos before everybody started downloading. He's always been in the adult entertainment industry. He has a company on Aruba that does on-line gaming and pornography. It's called Blue Wave, Limited. For twenty dollars a month, you get access to their catalog."

"Don't tell me. Harold Vincent is behind the movie that Alana auditioned for."

"I'm not sure yet, but give me a couple of days."

"You amaze me, Judy."

"When you're in this business you kinda learn who's who. I've met Harold Vincent. It was in Vegas. He was a tall, skinny man with a toupee and bags under his eyes. Not the best-looking guy in the world, but he dressed like a million. They always comped him a suite, and he'd bring his friends and order up two or three working girls." Judy swung a foot and twirled a strand of hair from her topknot around her finger. She laughed. "I gave him some lessons in blackjack, and he still lost. Small world, huh?"

They looked around when a man's voice at the door said, "Judy? You and C.J. ought to come look at this."

They got up and followed Raul into his office. He was Afro-Cuban, built like a pro wrestler. Raul specialized in tracking down bail bond skips in Miami's heavily Latin population. He turned up the volume on the television, tuned to *Celebrity Docket*. They were showing the usual South Beach scenes: stretch limos, lots of skin on smiling models, and night clubs with pounding beats.

A cheerful female voice said, "This is the world that Alana Martin belonged to."

There was footage of Billy Medina with his white hair and blazing smile, waving at the camera from the terrace of a restaurant on Ocean Drive. He was standing next to 3-Strikes, a rapper who later that weekend would be arrested for throwing a beer bottle at a police officer.

"I've seen it all before," C.J. said. "Sorry, Raul, but I need to go."

"Wait. They mentioned your name."

And there she was, staggering into the scene with a drink in her hand, catching herself on 3-Strikes's shoulder.

The voice-over said, "Glamorous attorney C.J. Dunn, formerly of Hollywood, was a regular on the South Beach party circuit until the lifestyle caught up with her. Our *Celebrity Docket* sources say that C.J. spent two weeks earlier this year in a court-ordered drug and alcohol treatment center known for its celebrity clientele. It must have worked. She's been hired by U.S. Congressman Paul Shelby of Miami to represent his bodyguard, who's being questioned by police in the strange and tragic murder of Alana Martin."

The host was back with her wide smile. "Stay tuned for more inside looks at the stars and celebs involved in this case."

Stunned, C.J. could only stare at the screen, which had turned into a blur of color.

"You ought to sue them," Raul said. "That's invasion of privacy."

C.J. smiled. "Unfortunately not. The story is true, and I am arguably a public figure. The court didn't order me to go to rehab, and I don't work for Shelby, but who cares about the details?"

"That sucks. Why do they have to say things like that?"

Judy said, "Because the jerk-offs have nothing better to do. Turn it off, Raul." When C.J. abruptly spun around and went back to Judy's office to collect her things, Judy followed. "C.J., wait."

"I need to go home. I have to get ready for my five minutes on *Larry King Live* tonight. Oh, that should be fun."

"Cancel it."

"I'm not canceling an appearance on CNN. I want that job, and by God I'm going to have it. You never cancel, you come out swinging or denying everything. Except I can't do that, can I? Yes, I was locked up for my own good. I had blackouts and was late to court. I lost clients, and if it weren't for my good friend Judy, I'd still be a drunk."

"Larry won't ask you about that. He's a gentleman."

"That's true, he is. I'll call you tomorrow."

Judy stopped her. "What son of a bitch told them? Who hates you that much? Does Libi Rodriguez know?"

"She does now."

"Tell me who it was so I can go break his neck."

"Who knows how these things get out? I'll survive. I've been through this kind of crappy situation before. Maybe not quite *this* crappy, where they're sticking their damned noses into everything I do."

Judy returned her smile, but lines creased her forehead. "Like you said, the public has a short attention span."

"I swear, if I hadn't gone sober, I would get so smashed right now."

"Oh, hon."

They exchanged a hug. C.J. finally broke away. "I don't mean that. I'll be a good girl."

The truth had come at her like the creak of footsteps outside her door in the middle of the night, leaving her hands trembling and her heart beating too fast. It was possible she was imagining things, but she didn't think so. Who had known about her two weeks in hell, losing her mind and finding it again, clean and sober for the first time in twenty years? The partners at her law firm, but they wouldn't be that vicious. Edgar and Judy, of course, but that was unthinkable. Only two other people had known. Billy and Milo. Her money was on Milo.

The topic on *Larry King* was the media's influence on perceptions of guilt and innocence, and C.J. had some things to say about that. Novelist-attorney Dan Hale was on a split screen with her, and together they pounded the tabloids and the paparazzi who fed them.

Relieved it was over, C.J. cruised into her driveway just as her cell phone rang. Rick Slater was calling. She let the car drift into the carport and turned off the lights but left the engine running.

"Rick, I just got home," she said. "I was on *Larry King*."

"I saw it. You did a great job."

"Thanks."

"And I want to thank you for keeping my name out of it."

"Generally they don't care how you answer as long as you say something halfway intelligent. How's it going with Shelby? Are you hearing any explosions yet?"

"Not yet, but he sits behind me in the car now, not in front. He catches up on phone calls. He sounds happy. His press conference went well, his poll numbers are up, and whatever you're doing, keep doing it. Listen, Charlotte Josephine, there's another reason I called."

"Forget you ever heard that name," she said.

"All right, C.J. I don't usually sit around watching TV, but lately it's becoming a bad habit. I saw the piece about you on *Celebrity Docket*. It was irresponsible, but it won't make any difference in the long run. It's not important."

She leaned against the head rest. "They won't stop. Everyone connected to Alana Martin will be opened up and sucked dry until they find out who killed her or the next big thing comes along."

Rick took a while to answer. "Are you all right?"

"I'm not going to go inside and have a drink, if that's your question."

"It wasn't," he said. "Maybe you'd like some company. I wouldn't stay long."

"Rick . . . I picked up the witness statements from my investigator today. I'll take them over to Detective Fuentes tomorrow. I hope he'll tell me he's no longer interested in you. In any event, I think I ought to find you another lawyer."

"So you're firing me as your client after all."

"That's not it. I never thought I'd say this, but Noreen Finch was right. My being your attorney is drawing attention, and it's making things more difficult for you. Libi Rodriguez wouldn't have come after you if you'd had any other lawyer."

"You don't know that, C.J."

"It's true. I've been in this game long enough to know how it's played. So what do you say?"

"No, thanks."

"It would be for the best."

"Isn't it up to me, who my attorney is? Or are you afraid of what else they might say about you, and you want out?"

She had no quick answer for him. "None of us wants our lives open to public scrutiny. Even you. You lied to me. Small things, but a lie nonetheless."

"Don't change the subject," he said. "What are you afraid of?"

"Nothing, so drop it. This is not your concern." When she heard silence on the other end, she said, "I'm sorry, Rick. That wasn't me. It was the bitch I turn into sometimes. I should go in."

"Wait. Let's see what shakes out tomorrow. If Fuentes says it's over, you close your case, and we can still be friends. All right?"

"All right."

"So go in and get some rest. Let me know what the detectives say."

"I will. Goodnight."

"Goodnight, Calamity Jane."

She was sitting at the desk in her office on her second cup of coffee, idly stroking Lady Bell, who was purring in her lap, and trying to get some work done before she went to bed, not that she had any hope of sleeping, when her cell phone rang in her tote bag. The irrational thought that it might be Kylie caused her quickly to take it out of its pocket and look at the screen. It was not a number she recognized.

After one more ring, she pressed the button to connect. She listened for a moment to muffled music and conversation in the background, then said, "Yes?"

"Ms. Dunn, this is Jason Wright. You gave me your number."

She sat bolt upright so quickly that Lady Bell leaped off her lap and hid under a chair. "Jason?"

"What time is it?" he asked.

"A quarter after twelve."

"It is? Oops. I'm sorry."

"No, no, it's all right. I wasn't asleep, I was working. Why are you calling me?"

"I want to ask you something. Are you the one who told the police that I murdered Alana?" He sounded as though he found something wildly funny and any second he could break into laughter.

Slowly she rose from her chair. Was he drunk? She said, "No, I haven't talked to the police. Why do you think that? I haven't talked to them at all about you."

"I've been trying to think who it could be. You're the only one I told about having no alibi. Don't you remember?"

"Yes, but I haven't talked to anyone about it." The lie came quickly to her lips, tasting bitter and sharp. "Jason, I never thought you had anything to do with Alana's death."

"I didn't kill her."

"I know that. I know. Listen to me. Call a lawyer. Do it tomorrow."

"I don't know any lawyers. Can you recommend someone?"

"I'm sorry, I can't. Under the circumstances, it wouldn't be ethical. Ask a friend. Or ask your parents."

"They're not speaking to me. My mother is in shock. Oh, oh, my boy is gay. Jason, swear to me that you didn't hurt that girl. It's really funny."

"Don't you have friends you can ask?"

"I'd rather not. They'd want to give an interview about it. Could you please help me? God, I don't mean to sound so fucking pathetic, but I don't know who else to call."

C.J. paced across the cluttered room, looked out the window into the night, then returned to her desk. "All right. I'll make a list for you. Half a dozen, and you choose whichever you like. Put the list on the wall and throw a dart at it. They will all be excellent attorneys, people I trust and respect. Jason, are you listening?"

"Yes."

"So I'll call you tomorrow. Go to bed now. Get some sleep. And don't worry, it's going to be all right." That was probably another lie, but C.J. couldn't stand the tears she heard in his voice. "Jason?"

"Thank you."

He hung up. C.J. stood there with the phone in her hand until it began to beep, then she went to her computer, opened her address file, and started looking for names.

chapter
TWENTY-SIX

the next day, after doing what work she could between returning phone calls and refusing requests for interviews, C.J. went into Henri Pierre's office and asked if he could spare half an hour. She needed a ride to a hearing in the bribery case against a county zoning official. She wanted to avoid the reporters in the lobby, who were more interested in asking her about Richard Slater. Henry cruised by the freight entrance, C.J. got in, and they drove the half mile to the federal courthouse, a soaring modern structure next door to the original Spanish-style building.

When her hearing was over, she had to spend ten minutes chatting with the judge about the Martin case. Coming down the escalator in the atrium, C.J. spotted a fortyish woman with short brown hair catching the up escalator on the other side. Elaine

McCoy had recently been appointed deputy U.S. attorney for the Southern District of Florida. Before that, she'd been head of the banking and money-laundering division and, before that, Internet fraud.

C.J. ran across the atrium and up the steps of the escalator. "Elaine!"

At the top they exchanged a hug and noted how long it had been since they'd gotten together, but their schedules were just impossible, weren't they? When Elaine confirmed that she'd been watching the news lately, C.J. asked if she had time to answer a couple of questions that might bear on the Martin case.

Elaine glanced at her watch and said, "I'll make time. How can I help you?"

C.J. told her she was exploring the possibility that Alana Martin had been murdered by someone with a connection to the porn industry, specifically a producer of DVD's or Internet content using underage girls. She told Elaine about Alana's audition tapes. Alana herself was over eighteen, but she may have known enough to be a problem for someone. C.J. stated what she knew about Harold Vincent and asked Elaine if she had ever heard of him.

That brought a smile to Elaine McCoy's usually serious face. "Oh, yes, we know Harold around here. He was one of the targets of a multi-agency investigation into child pornography. This goes back to the early nineties. Harold Vincent wasn't peddling movies with young children. No, his specialty was teenagers, light-skinned girls primarily from the Netherlands Antilles. Many of them were young prostitutes. Prostitution is legal on Aruba for adults, but younger ones do exist. Back in the eighties, Harold Vincent owned a brothel in Nye County, Nevada. I guess it was in his blood."

Elaine leaned her elbows on the balcony railing. "I wasn't part of the investigation, but I clearly recall the howls of disappointment when Harold slid out of the net. He had a very clever lawyer, no offense intended."

"None taken," C.J. said.

"The filming was done at various locations in the Caribbean, and the videotapes were sold by mail order from Mexico. Later on, when DVD's could be bought on the Internet, his business really took off. Harold had a choice: Keep his products out of the U.S. market and thereby avoid the jurisdictional reach of the federal government. Or he could risk it and make a fortune, because we buy more porn than anybody. He decided the reward was worth the risk. He was making millions, getting away with it until one of the people lower down started talking to us."

"He ratted Harold Vincent out in order to reduce his own sentence," C.J. said.

"We prefer to describe it as an offer of cooperation. Anyway, the defendant rolled over, but we couldn't get to Harold. He had created so many foreign shell corporations that the wall around him was virtually impenetrable. It scared him, though. He was looking at twenty to thirty years easily, with the minimum mandatories. He's gone straight, or as straight as you can get in the business. He does online gaming now, still based in Aruba and highly profitable. He was one of the first to get into it. That Web site is linked to his porn sites, where he charges for downloads and sells DVD's. He uses girls who look young, like Alana Martin, but it states clearly on his Web site: 'Barely Legal Girls. All Eighteen and Over.' The FBI occasionally sends out feelers, but nothing comes back."

"I think you just shot down my theory," C.J. said. "I'd hoped to pin this on a pornographer."

"Sorry." Turning toward her, Elaine said, "This doesn't mean that Alana Martin wasn't trying to get her audition tapes back."

"Yes, but if Harold Vincent was behind it, and he was legal, he'd have no reason to keep them."

"And no reason to kill her," Elaine concluded.

"Maybe. There's always a maybe," C.J. said. "I'm going to see what more I can find out."

"Well, if you hear anything, please share it."

In her tote bag, C.J. had the signed and notarized statements that Judy Mazzio had obtained. She caught a taxi outside the courthouse and told the driver to take her over to the Miami Beach police headquarters on Washington and Eleventh. As the taxi maneuvered slowly through downtown traffic, she stared out the side window. Her reflection came back to her, large sunglasses, a mane of blond hair, and tightly compressed lips. With a sigh, she leaned her head against the seat back.

She had hoped to present George Fuentes with more than two pieces of paper that he might or might not accept: she'd wanted to show him a real motive for murder. Harold Vincent had been a long shot, and the odds had just dropped to near zero. She had hoped to be able to call certain friends in the media and tell them about Vincent, which would certainly get their attention off Slater. The easiest thing now would be to push them toward Jason. It could be done. She had done it in other cases, spinning the story in the direction she wanted it to go. But she wouldn't do it with a man she believed to be innocent. Having stupidly told Paul Shelby about Jason, and knowing that Noreen had probably leaked it to the media, made C.J. feel obligated, guilty for her lapse, unwilling to participate in the bloodfest.

Last night Jason had begged for the name of a lawyer he could go to. C.J. had the list with her, and she intended to meet him and hand it over. If he had any information about Alana's audition tapes, great, but if he didn't want to talk, that was fine too. C.J. took out her BlackBerry and scrolled through the call log for his number, pressed it, and listened to the rings on the other end. Finally someone picked up.

"Club Deuce."

After a moment of confusion, C.J. said she must have dialed the wrong number. She disconnected and looked at the screen, realizing that it was impossible to have dialed the wrong number, as she had simply redialed the telephone that Jason had used. She pressed it again.

"Club Deuce."

"Excuse me, but last night around midnight someone called me from this number. His name is Jason Wright. Do you happen to know how I could reach him?"

"Sorry, I don't. This is a pay phone, and if it rings, we answer it."

She thanked him and hung up. Last night she hadn't bothered to confirm how to reach Jason, and he hadn't been sober enough to think of it either. Now what?

The first time they had talked, Jason had told her he lived near Collins Avenue and . . . and where? C.J. called Judy Mazzio and left a message to get her Jason Wright's address, ASAP. She would leave the list in his mailbox or slide it under his door.

As the taxi came off the causeway and went up the single-lane overpass that would drop them onto Alton Road, C.J. checked in with her secretary. "Shirley, it's me. I'm on the Beach. I should be back in the office before five o'clock. Are there any emergencies I need to know about?"

Shirley replied that things were pretty quiet, but Sarah Finch had called and left a number in Atlanta.

"Let me have it."

A woman on the other end put her on hold for a minute, and then Sarah was on the line. C.J. recognized her warm voice immediately. "C.J., hello, how are you?"

"Having so much fun I can't stand it. It's good to talk to you again, Sarah. What's up?"

"Well, I have been allowed the pleasure of making this call because I know you, and we had such a nice talk the other day. I have good news. Jerry Hazelton, the producer of *Rich, Famous, and Deadly*, would like you to come to Atlanta for a final interview. It's really more of a formality. They're set to offer you the job."

"Oh, my God. Oh, Sarah. This is wonderful. I can't tell you how wonderful."

"There are a lot of details still to be worked out. If you have an agent, they'll want him or her in on the negotiations."

"Yes, of course."

"I think it's all right if I tell you this now," Sarah said. "They were also considering a reporter from Miami, Libertad Rodriguez, the host of *Miami Justice Files*, but I was pulling for you."

No, this could not be better, C.J. thought. "When should I come? Next week?"

"A morning flight on Wednesday if you can. Someone will pick you up at the airport, and Jerry and his assistant will take you to lunch before you meet the big guns. I'd love to get together with you, but I'm flying to New York on Monday. Give Jerry a call."

As C.J. wrote down the number, the taxi pulled up to the drop-off zone at police headquarters. C.J. leaned forward and held up a hand for him to wait. "Got it. I'll call Jerry in the morning, and thank you so very much."

"There's one other thing," Sarah said. "It probably doesn't matter, but some on the staff are concerned about things they've heard. I'll be frank. They mentioned rumors about your juvenile record, a father who died in prison, and the fact you were in an alcohol rehab center."

"Oh, it's all true," C.J. said. "If that's a problem for them—"

"Not at all, but they'll want to talk to you and find out if there's anything else they should know. I'm just giving you a heads-up."

"Thanks." C.J. sighed. "This is such crap. Where is it coming from?"

"No idea. I'm sure it's going to be all right," Sarah said. "Frankly, this makes you all the more interesting. The publicity department will love it. I'm sorry I'll be out of town, but we'll see each other soon."

With Sarah's congratulations still echoing in her ears, C.J. disconnected and laughed aloud.

The driver looked over his shoulder. "Happy news?"

"God, yes. It's everything I've been dreaming of. I'm going to host a show on CNN."

"You are? I should get your autograph. What's your name?"

"C.J. Dunn. I'm a lawyer." The meter said $15.40, and she dug her wallet out of her bag. "For now, the show is called *Rich, Famous, and Deadly,* but that could change."

"Yeah. I heard of you," said the driver. "It was on the news. That girl who was killed over here. They found her body up in Lauderdale without the head. Right?"

"She had a name, Alana Martin."

"That's right. And you're the lawyer for this Special Forces guy they think did it."

"He had nothing to do with it. Nobody ever said he did." C.J. thrust the money over the seat, got out of the taxi, and slammed the door.

"Hey! Take it easy!"

Sergeant Fuentes came down to the lobby and escorted her to the personal crimes bureau on the third floor. A series of glass-fronted offices formed a perimeter around a large center section of desks and file cabinets. There were two holding cells with steel-mesh doors, and in one of them a man sat on the edge of a metal bench with his head in his hands.

Fuentes's office was on the east side, overlooking the apartments on Collins and the Art Deco hotels on Ocean Drive two blocks away. In his knit shirt of eye-scorching green, Fuentes gestured toward a chair, then went behind his desk as C.J. handed him the statements. He rocked slowly back and forth in his chair, reading.

His partner, Raymond Watts, stood by the door, arms resting on his belly, chewing a piece of gum.

C.J. had made the decision to name the girl the witnesses had seen: Kylie Willis. She had not included Kylie's address because she didn't know it. She was correct in assuming that Fuentes would ask her.

"I'm sorry, George. She moved and left no forwarding address. I believe I can find her if it's absolutely necessary."

Watts said, "That's convenient, the girl moving."

"No, detective, it is not," said C.J. "She has made it more difficult for me."

The *café-con-leche* skin on Fuentes's forehead furrowed into lines. "Any chance you can get her to come in and ID your client? If Slater has a solid alibi, we're not going to keep him on our list, obviously."

"I'll see what I can do," C.J. said, "but really, these statements should be enough. The men are now saying it wasn't Alana Martin they saw with Mr. Slater, and that's basically all you had."

Watts grinned around his chewing gum. "We have more than that."

C.J. looked back at Fuentes, who said, "We've been going around to marinas in the area with photographs of several men who were at the party at Mr. Medina's house that night, including your client. A witness at the Redfish Point marina says he saw Mr. Slater getting into a motorboat about nine o'clock on Sunday morning, the day after the party. He had a large cooler with him. Now, I'm not going to sit here and tell you he saw your client loading a body into the boat. If he had, we'd be asking a judge for an arrest warrant. Maybe Slater was fishing. Maybe he was gonna take a scenic cruise. I don't know. I'm telling you this in hopes you can clear it up for us. We could run over to his place and ask him, but you and I both know he'd call you, and we'd be right back here, like we are now. So how about it?"

During this, C.J. had gazed coolly at Fuentes with her brows slightly raised. She said, "Whose boat was it? My client doesn't own a boat."

"Well, we don't know, and the dockmaster couldn't tell us. Mr. Slater didn't sign in or out. They're supposed to, but sometimes people forget."

"Then how can you be certain it was Mr. Slater?"

"It was him. The man who ID'd Slater has seen him around before. Didn't know his name, but he's seen him. We're aware that he doesn't own a boat, because we checked the records; so he must have borrowed it. If you can clear this up for us, it would be helpful."

"Have you divined a motive? Some plausible reason why it would remotely cross Mr. Slater's mind to do away with Alana Martin?"

"His relationship with her would have jeopardized his position with Congressman Shelby."

"That is so lame it's laughable." C.J. stood and shouldered her tote bag. "George, this information, even if true, isn't going anywhere, but I'll get back to you."

Watts, still grinning, moved aside.

C.J. turned around and asked Fuentes, "Just out of curiosity, are you also looking at the young architect who may have been Alana's boyfriend? I believe his name is Jason Wright."

Fuentes said, "If you'd talk to Mr. Slater for us?"

"No comment, George?"

"Sorry, C.J."

As she left, Watts said, "Have a nice day, Counselor."

Even in the shade of the building, with an ocean breeze winding its way across four lanes of traffic, the heat and humidity were sucking the perspiration out of her body. C.J. waited at the curb for traffic to pass, then ran catercorner in her high heels to the Eleventh Street Diner, where she slid onto a stool, took off her sunglasses, and ordered an iced tea.

She checked her messages. Judy Mazzio had called with the address and phone number for Jason Wright. C.J. wrote it down, then called Judy's cell phone. When Judy answered, C.J. said, "I was just talking to Sergeant Fuentes. Guess which of my clients was seen getting into a boat at the Redfish Point marina the morning after Alana Martin disappeared?"

"Who? Oh, my God. Not Rick Slater."

"You'd think he would have mentioned it, wouldn't you?"

"No shit. What does he say?"

"I haven't asked him yet. Judy, I need to know whose boat he was using. Can you get me a list of boat owners from the marina? Never mind sailboats, just motor boats."

"What good will that do?"

"It will make it more difficult for Mr. Slater to lie to me. I'm getting tired of surprises."

When Judy had hung up, promising to send Raul to the marina with a suitably large bribe, C.J. called Jason Wright's cell phone. She sipped some iced tea through the straw and waited. A few moments later Jason's rich, steady baritone was telling her to please leave a message.

"Jason, this is C.J. Dunn." She told him she had an envelope for him but since she couldn't reach him, she would come by and leave it with the landlord.

When she had finished her tea and paid, she called for a taxi. She gave the driver the address, Collins and Twenty-Second, an apartment building called The Farnsworth. Five minutes later the taxi was stopping in front. The boxy, four-story design was from the fifties, updated with new windows and red awnings. Traveler's palms stood flat against the wall. A curved portico extended over a walkway, which led to a white metal gate that was closed and probably locked.

She was looking through the bars of the gate at a courtyard and wondering how to get inside when she spotted a man lying on one of the chaises beside the pool. His skin was like oiled bronze. Mirrored sunglasses turned in her direction as she called out, "Excuse me. I need to leave this for one of your neighbors. Could you let me in?"

He stared back at her for a second, then waved for her to go away.

"It's important." She pushed her sunglasses into her hair so he could see her.

"You're not getting in. We had to lock the gate because of you people."

She was going to ask if he could take the envelope when she saw a movement out of the corner of her eye. She turned and looked into a camera just as the flash went off. It fired two or three more times before she recognized him: Nash Pettigrew.

"Damn it, Nash, get that camera out of my face." She held up a hand.

"What is C.J. Dunn doing outside Jason Wright's apartment, I'd like to know." He raised the camera again.

With effort she stopped herself from screaming at him. She was about to go back to the taxi when the gate opened, and the man in the swimsuit motioned her inside. "Sorry. I thought you were a reporter." He locked the gate and raised his middle finger at Pettigrew. "Bite me."

"Thanks." C.J. held up the envelope. "I need to deliver this."

"Okay. Be sure the gate is closed when you go out." He returned to his sunbathing.

Four floors of open walkways surrounded the courtyard. Jason Wright lived in 210. C.J. took the stairs. The heat of the day radiated from the concrete steps. She found the apartment without difficulty. The blinds were closed. There were several notes stuck between the door and the frame, and someone had taped an envelope above the doorknob. Jason's name was handwritten on the front, and the return address said it had come from Channel Eight, Libi Rodriguez's station.

C.J. took out her cell phone and tried calling him, but again it went to voice mail. She was afraid that if she left her envelope with the others here, it would be overlooked. C.J. put her phone away and knocked. She waited and knocked more loudly. The door of the next apartment came open and a woman walked out with her hands on her hips. "Would you please stop that? He doesn't want to talk to anybody."

"I'm not a reporter," C.J. said. "I'm a friend trying to get in touch with him."

That eased the frown on her face. "Who are you?"

"My name is C.J. Dunn. I'm a lawyer. Jason called me last night and wanted me to recommend an attorney for him, so I've brought him a list." When the woman's eyes fell to the envelope, C.J. said, "I've tried to call him, but he doesn't answer. Do you know where he went?"

"He's home. He's just not answering the door," the woman said. "I heard him come in real late last night, and he hasn't left. I've been here all day. My boy is sick with the flu. Jason's door always scrapes when it opens, and I can hear when he's coming or going. Knock again."

C.J. pounded on the white-painted steel with the edge of her fist, listened, then pounded some more.

The woman said, "If you want me to give him that envelope, I will."

"He has to be there." Moving over to the window, C.J. rapped on the glass. "Jason? It's me, C.J. Dunn!" The blinds had not been lowered all the way to the sill. She crouched down to look through the narrow opening. Except for the light filtering in from outside, the living room was dark.

She stared at a shape that seemed to float in the middle of the room and gradually realized what it was.

The neighbor said, "I guess Jason went out and I didn't hear him."

"No. He's in there." C.J. came away from the window and took out her cell phone. A heaviness had descended into the pit of her stomach. She called 911.

chapter
TWENTY-SEVEN

t he living-room window of Jason's apartment was a gaping hole where the men had broken through with an ax. There had been other noises: blinds falling with a metallic crash, furniture thumping to the floor, then silence. The door opened. A paramedic came out and told everyone to move back.

The neighbor woman put her hands to her mouth to stifle a scream. In an instant, C.J. saw more clearly what she had glimpsed before: the tilted blades of a ceiling fan, a shape suspended underneath—a man, blond hair, wearing khaki pants and a blue oxford shirt. His head rested on his shoulder; the face was turned away. His hands and bare feet were swollen and dark with blood.

C.J. leaned on the balcony railing, catching her breath before walking to a bench by the elevators. She opened her purse for her

cell phone and put it back, too shaken to call anyone. Within minutes, uniformed officers arrived and strung crime-scene tape
around the entrance to the apartment. People stood watching from
the opposite balcony. Nash Pettigrew pushed through and aimed
his long lens at the door. The noise of an engine grew louder, and
the Channel Ten helicopter appeared in the empty square of sky
above the courtyard.

The elevator opened. A lieutenant came out, followed by Sergeant Fuentes, who saw her and backed up.

"Ms. Dunn?"

She explained what she was doing there. He nodded and said to
wait; he would be right back. Fuentes walked toward Jason's apartment and went inside.

C.J. took out her cell phone and called Billy Medina, not sure
even as her fingers pressed the keys why she was doing this, except
that of all the people in her address book, Billy would be the least
likely to demand answers.

He was at a bar on Ocean Drive having drinks with some hotel
developers from Spain. He didn't mind being disturbed; he was
bored to tears. When C.J. told him what had happened and said she
was stuck without a car, he said, "Do you want me to come save
you?"

"That would be wonderful."

"I'll be there in fifteen minutes."

Disconnecting, she noticed the message icon. Rick Slater had returned her call. If it had rung, she hadn't heard it. She slid the cell
phone back into its pocket and waited for Sergeant Fuentes. She
checked her watch. 5:25. She put her chin on a fist and waited
some more.

Footsteps pounded up the stairs. The Channel Seven team
rushed past her, trailed by their cameraman. At the barrier of crime-
scene tape, one of the reporters flipped open his notebook and

started talking to the police. The other stood in front of the camera. A light went on. Some teenage girls waved and giggled, two seconds of fame before the camera shifted to get them out of the picture.

Fuentes finally returned. "Ms. Dunn, you mind if I ask you a few more questions?"

"Go ahead."

"You said Jason called you at midnight."

"That's right, from the Club Deuce."

"Why'd he call C.J. Dunn? If he was looking for a lawyer, why ask the lawyer representing a man who might have killed his girlfriend? You know what I mean?"

"George, I have no idea why Jason called me," she lied. "I think he was drunk."

"He had your private number at home?"

"He had my mobile number. I'd given him my card at a reception for Milo Cahill. By the way, he wasn't Alana's boyfriend. They were close friends, but he was gay. You shouldn't believe everything you hear on the news."

"Who told you he was gay?"

"Mr. Cahill. Jason hadn't come out yet because his family couldn't have handled it."

"In this day and age?"

"Not everyone lives on Miami Beach," she said.

Fuentes sat beside her. "What else can you tell me about him?"

"That's about it, unfortunately."

They watched as a reporter and cameraman from Channel 23 came up the stairs and hurried past them, then a man with two big digital cameras and a *Miami Herald* press badge around his neck.

C.J. asked, "Did Jason leave a note?"

"We haven't found anything so far. Might have sent an email, might've dropped a note in the mailbox. They do that sometimes."

"How long has he been dead?"

"The ME will have a better estimate, but I'm going to say at least twelve hours. He stood on a chair and kicked it over. I'm surprised the ceiling fan didn't fall." George sighed. "Twenty-eight years old. Why do they do it? Some people, I'd love to hand them a rope, but not a kid like this. Whole life ahead of him."

They sat there for a moment in gloomy silence. Then C.J. took a breath and stood up. "I need to go. Someone's waiting for me."

Fuentes walked with her to the top of the stairs. "Don't forget to ask your client what he was doing, taking a boat out the day after Alana disappeared."

"Fishing, what else?" C.J. gave Fuentes a little wave as she went down the steps.

She had just reached the bottom when she saw Libi Rodriguez coming through the gate in her sneakers and snug-fitting top, followed by Carlos Moreno with his video camera. Libi's cell phone was pressed to her ear until she noticed C.J. She disconnected and snapped her fingers to get the cameraman's attention. "Carlos!"

C.J. put on her sunglasses. "I have nothing to say to you, Libi." She swerved to go around them, but the reporter blocked her way.

Libi spoke into her cordless microphone. "Defense attorney C.J. Dunn came here to see Jason Wright, and when he didn't respond to her knocks on the door, she notified police. Why did you want to talk to him? What made you suspect that something might be wrong?"

The microphone moved to C.J., who kept walking.

Libi scooted in front of her. "Ms. Dunn, you're representing a person of interest in Alana Martin's murder. What brought you here to see Jason?"

"No comment."

"Some say that Jason Wright might have killed Alana. What effect do you think his suicide will have on the investigation?"

C.J. grabbed the microphone out of Libi's hand and threw it

across the courtyard. It sailed over the pool fence, hit the edge of the pool, and bounced into the water.

"Oh, my God. I don't believe this! Did you see what she did?"

With her back to the lens, C.J. said quietly, "Stay away from me, Libi, or I'll do the same to you."

"Turn on the camera mike! Turn it on! She just threatened me."

But Moreno had lowered his camera. "Let it go, Libi."

"Turn it on, I said!" Libi's cheeks were hot with rage. "I'll have you arrested. I'll file a complaint for destruction of property."

"Go for it, you brainless twit."

Other reporters were looking over the railings, and cameras pointed their way.

Libi walked along beside her. "Don't pretend to be so perfect. I know who you are, Charlotte Josephine Bryan, high school dropout, juvenile arrest record, locked in a rehab hospital, and you have the nerve to call *me* names?"

C.J. felt detached, as though she were observing a complete stranger with no connection to herself. Under the portico she turned around to smile. "Well, Libi, when I'm hosting *Rich, Famous, and Deadly* on CNN next season, and you aren't, be sure to watch. That's right, I got the job, so unpack your suitcase, honey, you're not going anywhere."

Whatever Libi had intended to say next vanished on a sharp intake of breath.

Billy Medina's Jaguar was waiting at the curb. He leaned over and opened the door. It was blissfully cool inside, and C.J. sank into the leather seat. "Thank you."

"What was that about?" Billy asked.

"Nothing. Libi Rodriguez is throwing a tantrum because I wouldn't play with her."

He checked for traffic, then made a U-turn and headed south on Collins. The engine purred. Billy's hair was combed back, and he wore a finely checked black-and-white silk jacket and an open-collar shirt. He pressed a button on his steering wheel, and the radio went from a news station to easy-listening jazz. "I heard the report on Jason Wright. They aren't saying anything more than what you told me. You look warm. Want to come over to my place? What's your pleasure? Diet cola, Gatorade, a joint?"

The image of an icy gin and tonic jumped into her head. "Let me sit here a minute and calm down."

"Poor baby," he said.

"Poor Jason," she corrected.

"Good for your case, though, if he killed Alana like they're saying. He couldn't live with the guilt."

"Yes, I'm sure that theory will be all over the talk shows tonight. Billy, did you happen to mention to Paul Shelby what I told you about Jason having no alibi?"

"No, I haven't talked to Paul since the party. Why?"

"Then Shelby got it from me. Somebody over there leaked it to the media, and Jason is suddenly guilty of murder. I feel so damned bad."

"It wasn't your fault. Don't obsess about it." Billy put his hand on her leg. "You need to relax."

"I was just offered the job at CNN," she said.

"That's great!"

"I don't have it yet. I might not, if the media keep dredging up my past."

"Let them. What have you got to hide? So you were in rehab. Big deal."

"I need this case over with, Billy. I really need it over."

"Come on, baby." He massaged her knee. "You're freaking out. You're not like this."

"Does the name Harold Vincent ring a bell?"

"Why?"

"Harold Vincent is a pornographer. He owns Blue Wave, Limited, based in Aruba. They do online gaming and Web porn. They also make X-rated DVD's. You just got back from Aruba. You went down there to see about investing in a hotel. You must have heard of him."

"I've met him. I wouldn't want to socialize with him. What's this about?"

"Is he still making DVD's with underage girls?"

Billy's dark brows rose over his silver-framed sunglasses. "I don't think he ever did."

"He did. They just couldn't prove it." C.J. lifted her chin to get more cool air on her neck. "I believe that Alana Martin knew Harold Vincent."

"You're correct," Billy said. "I introduced them."

"You what?"

"It was about six months ago. *Tropical Life* threw a party in the Bahamas, the casino on Paradise Island. I took the entire staff over on a cruise ship. Alana was working for me at the time, so she went too. Hal Vincent was there. His company had been buying advertising space, so they put him on the guest list. He showed up with a hooker on each arm, but he saw Alana and his tongue fell out. Alana was getting stoned, laughing too loudly, hanging on my VIP guests, so I went over to her and asked if she wanted to meet a good friend of mine in the movie business. Her eyes lit up, and that was the last I saw of her for the rest of the weekend."

"Why didn't you tell me this before?"

"I didn't think of it," Billy said. "I should've mentioned it to the police. Alana knew too many people like Harold Vincent. She was not, to put it mildly, the kind of person we wanted at the magazine."

With a little laugh, C.J. shook her head. "You see, Billy, this is why I keep telling you to be careful. One disgruntled employee could say something for spite and you'd have the FBI on your ass."

"I have nothing to do with Hal Vincent," he said. "I work damned hard keeping my business squeaky clean. Give me some credit. Let's not talk about this. It's depressing. You've got Jason Wright's suicide on the brain. You need to sit in my hot tub and smoke some weed."

"Billy, please."

"It's a fine idea. I know what. Come with me to Antigua for the weekend. I'm leaving Saturday to check on the hotel, but we can have some time together. Fly back on Monday or whenever you like. I'll be there a week."

"Some of us have eight-to-five jobs," she said. "Billy, I need another favor, and don't say no. Alana auditioned for a DVD, and she was trying to get her tapes back so they wouldn't turn up on the Internet. You've just told me she knew Harold Vincent. Alana was renting a room from Tisha Dulaney, who works for Vincent—and sleeps with him. It's just too cozy not to mean something."

Billy glanced at her, then back at the street. "And?"

"And I'd like for you to ask Harold Vincent about Alana. If she was murdered by someone in the pornography business—"

Billy laughed in disbelief. "I'm not going to do that."

"Why not?"

They were at the light on Alton Road, waiting for traffic to clear so he could take a right onto the causeway, heading for his house on Star Island.

Billy said, "Look. I don't know Harold Vincent. I choose not to know him. If I go over to Harold's place or have any contact with him, people will find out. They will wonder if I am buddies with a man who makes adult movies and runs a quasi-legal gambling operation on the Web. I am not Harold Vincent's friend." When C.J. started to speak, he held up a hand. "No. No. I can't do it. By the grace of God I was admitted into the elite group of investors in The Aquarius. We are waiting for congressional approval. If the media find out that I am in any way connected to a pornographer, even by association, I'm fucked. Can I spell it out for you more clearly?"

C.J. couldn't see Billy's eyes behind the dark glasses, but she didn't like the tone of his voice. "Forget I asked."

A horn sounded. Billy shot the driver the bird and went ahead. "I'm sorry, baby." He picked up her hand and brought it to his lips.

She pulled away.

"Do we have PMS tonight?"

"For God's sake, Billy. Just take me to my office. You're right, I have too much on my mind."

"What is the matter with you lately? Snap out of it."

"Sure. Snap out of it."

He looked at her and shook his head. Neither of them spoke until the car finally stopped at the entrance to the Met Center.

C.J. got out with her briefcase and shoulder bag and leaned back in. "Thanks for the rescue."

"Any time." He smiled. "Hope you feel better soon."

As the Jaguar pulled away, C.J. realized that whether she snapped out of it or not would make no difference to Billy Medina.

chapter
TWENTY-EIGHT

J udy Mazzio lifted the bottle from the ice bucket and refilled
Harold's glass, pouring down the side to keep it from foam-
ing. She topped hers off and touched the glass to his. The
crystal made a soft *ding*.

"Old times, good times," Harold said.

"We already drank to that," Judy reminded him.

"Then you say the toast."

"Let's see. . . . Champagne to your real friends and real pain to
your sham friends."

Laughing, Harold brought the glass to his lips. The bones of his
wrist were like knobs. His curly hair had turned gray and retreated
even farther on his high forehead. But hell, Judy thought, twenty

years hadn't been kind to either of them. Her ass had dropped, and she'd made good friends with Miss Clairol.

They were on the balcony of Harold's penthouse apartment in Surfside. It wrapped around the southeast corner, so you could look down the Intracoastal Waterway arrowing toward Miami, lights everywhere, or you could see the ocean, a nice view in the daytime, no doubt, but, this time of night, kind of a downer. Harold kept his chairs right in the middle, like he couldn't decide.

Judy sipped from her champagne flute. She had brought him a chilled bottle of Dom Perignon, his favorite. "So. You were saying. Alana wanted her tapes, but you didn't want to give them to her."

"Why should I? She didn't ask nicely. She called all hours of the day and night. She came up to me when I was having dinner at a restaurant. She threatened to go to the police. I said, go ahead. You signed a release. You're over eighteen. There is nothing about it that isn't legal, sweetheart, so what are you going to do besides embarrass yourself?"

A sly smile appeared. "And you know, Judy, if she'd made it big in Hollywood—and she had a good shot, in my opinion—those tapes were worth hanging on to."

"For what, the money?"

"Hell no, for the fun of it. Hey, look at this, Alana Martin back in the day."

"Alana's friend said it was an underage role."

"Listen, it started out this way. What she wanted, Alana, was a part in a feature film I was producing. It wasn't porn. It was straight to DVD, but legit. Guns, babes, drug dealers, cops. A solid script, shot on location in the Bahamas. She was already over there for the week, staying at the Paradise Island Hotel. We were introduced, and she says are you doing movies, and I said yes, I am, and she says, oh, I'm an actress. So I said let me pick you up at the hotel tomorrow, let's see how you do. The minute Alana took her clothes off I could see she wasn't right for it. She had no body, this girl. The director said okay, let's try her out for one of the Internet-download bits. It didn't work. You can't fake it. You need to like what you're doing. Her heart wasn't in it. We shot the movie on Andros Island. My friend has a place there, lets me stay whenever I want. You ought to come over sometime. It's right on the beach. Get away from it all. Jesus, I can't believe you're a private investigator." Harold gave a raspy laugh and raised his glass. "Who would've thought? But I always knew you had the brains. Always knew that. Congrats, babe."

"Thanks."

"You're happy? Making enough dough? Getting laid?"

"No complaints. Hal, I'm thinking you ought to burn the tapes. You know, out of respect for the family."

He thought about it. "I will. I will do that. Jesus, what a terrible, terrible thing." He tipped back his glass.

Judy reached for the bottle. "You're a decent guy, Hal. I always thought so." She poured more champagne into their glasses. "You played fair with me. With all the girls. Nobody had anything bad to say about you."

"You were the best, Judy. I say that with all sincerity. You shouldn't have quit."

"It was time."

"To my brown-eyed girl," Harold said. *"L'chaim."*

They touched glasses and drank.

Judy said, "Alana supposedly had a contact in Hollywood. Was it true? Or was it just wishful thinking?"

"Who knows, with that kid? One thing for certain, she had her mind made up she was going to be a star." He shook his head, and his brow furrowed. "They like them skinny these days. I don't get it." He shifted in his chair to put Judy in the light. "God, you're gorgeous."

"I'm pushing fifty, Hal."

"Look at those boobs. Those legs. Gorgeous."

"Look at *you*. Successful, a good business, traveling all over. And grandkids."

"Yeah, they're great. I'll show you their pictures. My son should have turned out so well, and his wife—don't get me started."

Judy said, "Back to Alana. Supposedly there was somebody here in Miami helping her get in the movies. Did she mention that?"

"Yeah, she did."

"Did she say who?"

"You might know this name. Milo Cahill."

"The architect," Judy said. ·

"He fancies himself a player, but you ask me, he was blowing smoke. He promised to personally introduce her to a casting director who could get her a part. Milo used to be in L.A., but come on. That's not how it works. If he wasn't, you know, a little on the fruity side, I'd say he was trying to get in her pants."

"You've met him?"

"When he first got to Miami, we were introduced at a club. He wanted to buy the right property and meet the right people. I offered my guidance. I drove him around, showed him what was what and who was who. I took him and a bunch of his snotty friends to dinner at Joe's for stone crab, cost me over two grand, and you know what? He never reciprocated. Never returned a phone call. He bought a house but I never saw the inside of it. That's some kind of gratitude, isn't it?"

"What a jerk," said Judy.

"I don't give a damn. I don't. This place is full of phonies, Miami, everybody on the make. Except for New York and Vegas, the rest of the country has gotten so uptight it makes you want to cry. I have very few friends here anymore, Judy. I fly up four, five times a year to play some golf, keep my stockbroker honest, and visit my grandkids. If it wasn't for them, I'd never come back, I swear to God. You'd like my place on Aruba. Anytime you want to visit, the door is open."

"I might do that." Judy held up the bottle to the light, then poured the last of it for Harold. "So, do you think Milo Cahill wanted something from Alana?"

"Of course. Milo never gives something for nothing." Harold finished his champagne and set the glass on the table. "How about if I put some more of this on ice? It's not the Dom, but it's good stuff."

"I'd better not, Hal. I'll be too drunk to drive home."

"Drive home? No, you gotta stay a while. We have some catching up to do."

"I need to ask you one more thing. The night Alana disappeared, she was at a party on Star Island, hosted by Billy Medina. You know him, don't you?"

"I've met him a few times. He has a hotel and casino on Antigua, but I hear it's not doing so well. He's another jerk."

"Why do you say that?"

"A couple of weeks ago he comes down to Aruba with his partners, and they wine and dine me. They rent a boat, they buy me a new fishing reel, they take me to every club on the island. Billy invites me to their suite, I bring some girls, and we have a nice time. He says he's interested in online gaming, so what do I do, schmuck that I am? I spend two days showing him my operation, telling him everything I know, like a father to a son almost, thinking we could work out a deal, but he's gone the next morning, checked out of his hotel, and never so much as a thank-you. You know what? I don't care. Life is too short."

"Did Billy ever get into it? Online gaming?"

"He's trying, but I predict he'll fail. I don't think he's got the capital to make a go of it. The man's all show. Anyway, it's getting restricted more and more, the goddamn government trying to control everything we do, their noses up everybody's skirt. Now you make your money in porn. That's where the action is, till they take that away too."

"It's a different world," she agreed.

Harold set his empty glass on the table. "You're not gonna stay, are you?"

"I really can't. I'm sorry." Judy took his hand, entwining their fingers. She gave it a squeeze. "I should be going."

"I'd like to call you sometime," Harold said. "We'll get together."

"That would be nice."

"We always had fun, didn't we?"

"We sure did."

He pushed himself from his chair, shook out his leg, straightened the waist of his trousers, and passed a hand over his head. Judy took his arm as they walked back through the living room. She could feel the bones through his skin, cool and slack. Their reflections moved in the long, mirrored wall, but she didn't look. Twenty-five or thirty years ago she would have seen a man in a shiny silk suit passing out hundreds as tips, and a woman with long black hair, over six feet tall in her platform shoes. He'd have his friends with him, and they'd be going to a table right up front, and after the show Frank Sinatra or Flip Wilson or whoever would come over to say hello, and he'd pull his chair close and whisper in her ear, would she like to come up to his suite later? Sometimes yes, but more often, she would give him a look through her lashes and say thanks, but I'm already occupied.

"It's true, Hal. We did have us some fun," she said.

"Wait, sweetheart. I should tell you this. A reporter, a woman from Channel Eight, some Spanish chick, I forget her name, she came by here and wanted to talk to me. She started asking questions about you. She wanted to confirm that you worked for me in

Nevada. I showed her the door. I didn't tell her anything, but I thought you should know."

Judy sighed.

Harold put an arm over her shoulder. "You're so beautiful. Why don't you stay for a while? Old times."

She held his face and kissed him. "Take care of yourself, Hal."

chapter
TWENTY-NINE

b arefoot, sitting in her desk chair at home, C.J. spent the evening reading depositions on her computer. As she scrolled through, making notes, she listened with one ear to an argument on television about Jason Wright's motive for suicide. The psychologist was sure that Jason had been unable to accept his homosexuality. The spokesman from a gay-rights group took offense. "His sexuality has nothing to do with it. He was clinically depressed. His friend was murdered, he was viciously attacked in the tabloid media, and, on top of that, he was fired from his job."

The host asked them to listen to a comment from a friend of Alana Martin. "We all went out, and it was like really late, so we stayed at Jason's apartment. I slept on the sofa, but they were in the bedroom together. Yeah, I think they had a relationship."

The telephone rang, drowning out the rest of it. Dylan was asleep out on that end of the desk, a mound of gray fur. C.J. had to reach around him to get to the phone. She checked the caller ID before picking up. "Hi, Judy."

"I hope it's not too late to call."

"No, no, I was working. Wait, let me turn down the background noise. I keep the TV on in case they say something I need to respond to. They're talking about Jason at the moment. Alana's parents were on earlier. They've given up on recovering her entire body. Her funeral will be on Sunday. The city expects so many people, they're going to close off the street, and *Entertainment Tonight* will broadcast it live. It's insane." C.J. aimed the remote. "I'm going to turn this off. You called me. I should let you talk."

Judy said, "I just left Harold Vincent's apartment."

"No."

"I told you I knew him. It cost me a bottle of Dom Perignon to find out that Harold has Alana's audition tapes. He said he wouldn't give them to her because she was rude, the way she demanded them."

"My God. What else did he say? Was she causing problems for him?"

"Hal didn't kill her. I'd bet my last dollar on that."

"Damn," C.J. said. "That would have been so nice, if he had. You know what I mean. I was sure when I talked to Billy that Harold Vincent had something to do with it."

She had reported her conversation with Billy Medina to Judy. Most of it. She hadn't told Judy that Billy was being a pain, because she didn't want to hear an I-told-you-so, not even from her friend.

Judy said, "C.J., you want to make me some coffee? I need to come over and talk to you. It really can't wait till tomorrow."

"What's wrong?"

"I'd rather not discuss it on the phone."

C.J. told her to come ahead, and after saving her notes on her computer, she went downstairs to the kitchen. The coffee was hours old, so she poured it out and started a fresh pot. Passing by the kitchen window, she saw that the lights were on in the cottage. Earlier, Edgar had run around the backyard with the hose, dribbling water from C.J.'s shower onto the plants. She could see him now through the open curtains, notebook on his lap, squinting at a photograph. He had asked when Kylie might be over again. C.J. had told him she didn't know. She couldn't bear to tell him the truth: Kylie wouldn't be back at all.

Judy had offered to find her. It would be good to know where she lived, in case . . . in case what? Fran had been clear: *Stay away from her. Kylie is my daughter, not yours.* Since that conversation, C.J. had felt a slow burn. It was unfair. Fran had asked for help with expenses but had never sent a photo, had never put Kylie on the phone to say thank you. Fran had asked C.J. to look after Kylie in Miami, which she had done, and now she was blamed because Kylie had chosen to stay.

Smiling, C.J. realized she was glad Kylie hadn't caved in. She deserved to live in a place where her ambition and intelligence might be rewarded. For all her naïveté, the girl had brains. C.J. had noticed this at her own father's funeral. Fran and C.J.'s mother had been friends, so the Willises had driven from Pensacola to Mayo to attend the services in the town's only funeral home. Kylie was already wearing glasses. She had brought a book, the first Harry Potter. C.J. asked if she could read something so big, and Kylie had looked up at her with steady gray eyes. "Of course. I'm seven."

The telephone rang, breaking into the past. C.J. crossed the kitchen, hesitating only briefly before picking it up.

Rick Slater apologized for calling her at home. He had just dropped off the Shelbys after driving them and some friends to dinner at the Ocean Reef Yacht Club. He said, "I heard about Jason Wright. They said you called nine-one-one when Jason didn't answer the door. It must've been pretty grim for you."

"Yes. It was."

"Shelby told some reporters it was a tragedy for the family, et cetera, but then I hear him tell his mother and Don Finch it was the best thing that could have happened."

"Hypocritical bastard."

Rick asked, "Why were you at Jason's apartment?"

"He wanted me to recommend a lawyer, and I was bringing him a list of names. It's not something I'd ordinarily do, but . . . "

"But what?"

"I had mentioned to Paul Shelby that Jason had no alibi, and at the time I thought Jason was Alana's lover. I never expected that Shelby or somebody on his staff would leak it to the media." C.J. leaned against the counter. "My screwup of the week. I schedule them frequently enough to keep myself humble."

"It's a bitch to have a conscience, isn't it?" Slater said. "I called to ask if I'm still your client."

"Why wouldn't you be?"

"Last night you were ready to turn me over to somebody else, depending on how it went with the police today. So how did it go? Did the witnesses' statements get me off the hook?"

C.J. crossed the kitchen to turn on the coffeemaker. "They might have, except for something else that's come up. They've been showing your photo around at the marinas, and someone at Redfish Point said he saw you getting into a boat the morning after Alana disappeared. You want to tell me about it?"

She had time to take two mugs from the dish drainer before Slater said, "I had that Sunday off, and I went fishing. I didn't have a dead body with me. Did the guy notice that?"

"He said you had a large cooler."

"Sure, big enough for lunch, a six-pack, and Alana Martin."

The doorbell rang. C.J. walked toward the living room. Her white cat dived under the sofa. "Whose boat was it?"

"It belongs to a friend of mine, the one I met in the Army."

"I need his name in order to establish that this wasn't unusual for you, going fishing on a Sunday morning." C.J. pulled the curtain aside far enough to see Judy's Toyota in the driveway.

Slater said, "I'd rather not involve him unless Fuentes makes an issue of it."

"He will. We can stonewall, but a simple explanation would be better."

The bell rang again.

"I'm sorry, Rick, I need to go. Call me tomorrow and we'll set up a time to talk about this. You're going to have to tell me what's going on so I can properly advise you. Do you understand?"

Slater told her he would probably be free to see her in the afternoon.

It was C.J.'s habit lately to keep the porch light off to discourage any reporters who might wander by, so the entrance was dark. When she opened the front door, the light falling from the foyer revealed her tall, black-haired friend. Judy looked stunning in tight jeans, a low-cut white top, and flashy gold earrings. But her mood didn't match.

C.J. pulled her inside. "Coffee's in the kitchen. I'll fix you a cup while you tell me what's wrong."

"If you weren't on the wagon, I would ask for a drink."

"I can get you a glass of wine."

Judy waved the idea away. In the fluorescent lights of the kitchen, the tension on her face became apparent. She set her purse on the counter.

C.J. went over and took her hands. "What is it, sweetie?"

"I wanted to tell you this before you hear it on the news. Libi Rodriguez came by Harold Vincent's apartment the other day wanting to know . . . if it was true that . . . that I worked for him as a prostitute. It's true. Hal owned a brothel west of Las Vegas. It's legal in Nye County, and the state keeps records. Libi could have found out that way. Hal's place was called The Cherry Trap. I was twenty-one, a dumb kid from St. Louis, but not too dumb to know that it paid, and I needed the money. Hal thought I had promise, so he took me to Vegas and set me up as an escort. I never touched drugs, and I didn't get drunk or steal from the customers. I could carry on an intelligent conversation, and I had more business than I could handle. I liked the glamour and the money, but I didn't want to end up as just another aging working girl. I gave it up. I put myself through UNLV, got a degree in business, but what do you do with that? So I started dealing blackjack. I made a decent salary, and the tips were good, but after a while the routine gets a little old. I knew Edgar. He would sit at my table every time he and his friends would come out to Vegas to gamble. He said to me one day, Judy, why don't you move to Miami, invest in real estate, start a business? That's what I did. I never think about those days anymore, C.J. I never told you because I didn't know how you'd take it. I wouldn't be standing here talking about it now, but Libi Rodriguez knows, and she hates you, and boy, won't this make a juicy item for the tabloids?"

Judy covered her face with her hands. "That bitch. I could kill her."

C.J. put her arms around Judy and rested her cheek on her shoulder. "Please, Judy, don't worry. Tomorrow I'm going to give Libi a call and explain how it works. If this gets out, she and the owners of her station will find themselves on the other side of a lawsuit. I will sue them until they bleed. That ought to get her attention."

Laughing, Judy wiped off some tears with the heel of her hand. "Hey, it's good to have you on my side."

"In the bitch contest, I can beat Libi Rodriguez any day of the week." She gave Judy a final squeeze. "Okay, that's that. Tell me what Harold Vincent had to say. Do you want coffee? It's half decaf."

They sat at the bistro table by the window, and Judy told her everything. When she got to the part about Milo Cahill, C.J. asked her to say it again.

"Milo promised to get Alana a part in a movie. He said he would help her in Hollywood. That's what Alana told Harold."

"You're sure Harold told you the truth?"

"Absolutely."

"Can you think of any reason Alana would have lied to him?"

"I can't think of any. Alana really believed she was going to be a star. She'd have done anything to get those tapes back. She was desperate. That's all she wanted, to be famous. Kinda pathetic, isn't it?"

"I try not to think so," C.J. said.

"I wasn't referring to you."

"I know you weren't. Sometimes I wonder if going for the brass ring at CNN is worth it. Never mind me. The later the hour, the darker the thoughts." C.J. went to get the coffeepot. "Do you want more of this?"

"No, I should go home."

C.J. sat back down. "Judy, there's only one thing that bothers me. I don't care what you did in your previous life, you know that, don't you? You're my friend, and I love you. But how would it affect Edgar?"

"What do you mean?"

"Well, if he finds out."

Judy lowered her long lashes. "He knows."

"He knows?"

Judy nodded. "He was one of my first customers. It was a long time ago. His wife had died, and . . . for heaven's sake, don't let on that I told you. It would embarrass him."

C.J.'s smile turned to a laugh. "Edgar. You old scamp."

chapter
THIRTY

On her way to court Thursday morning, C.J. called Channel Eight, gave her name, and asked how to reach Libi Rodriguez. She said it was urgent. She was walking up the steps to the courthouse when Libi called back.

"Well, well," Libi said. "This must be about replacing that microphone you destroyed. Our attorney said he would call you."

"No, Libi, this is about a potential suit for libel against you and the owners of your station." C.J. explained how, if certain information were irresponsibly and maliciously made public, her loyalty to Judy Mazzio would require her to take action. "On principle, I guarantee you years of litigation." Libi was still sputtering when C.J. added, "Send me a bill for the microphone, but never, ever speak to me again."

The rest of the morning was taken up with arguing, and losing, a motion to suppress evidence in a vehicular homicide case. C.J. missed lunch, slammed some overdue pleadings together, fought with her managing partner about some personnel matters, and in the afternoon sat with her younger associate in the conference room trying to work out an alimony settlement in a divorce case. The husband was an importer of sporting goods who said he couldn't pay because of "difficulties with liquidity." Nothing was accomplished, and C.J. finally called a halt and let Henry escort the husband, his accountant, and his two lawyers back to the lobby. The wife put her head down on the table and wept, and C.J. failed utterly to convince her that things would eventually work out.

It was close to four o'clock when C.J. dropped into the extra chair at her secretary's desk and said this was the kind of day that made her want to move to Vermont and buy a pottery shop. She shuffled through the stack of messages Shirley handed her.

"Anything important here?"

"Harnell Robinson says the check will be sent over by courier tomorrow morning."

"I'm not holding my breath," C.J. said.

Shirley said, "Detective Fuentes called twice on the Slater case. He didn't say what he wanted."

C.J. could imagine: Fuentes wanted to know if Richard Slater had put Alana Martin's body into a boat, weighted it, and dropped it a few miles off Miami Beach. She was expecting Slater to call so they could arrange a time to talk about it. It was odd, his reluctance to give the name of the person who owned the boat, but she supposed there was a reason. Even more odd: that she knew Richard Slater wasn't telling her everything, and still she wanted to believe him, that block of a man with a shaved head and bullet scars on his body. She was losing her concentration.

After giving Shirley a list of things to do in the divorce case, C.J.

went into her office, closed the door, and turned on the television. This had become a habit, picking out the useful bits of news in the Martin case from the vast garbage heap of gossip that churned through the media. Alana Martin's MySpace page was being dissected for clues, and somebody had posted on YouTube a fuzzy cell-phone video of Alana at a night club with an alleged cocaine dealer who had flown back to Peru the day after her murder.

It wasn't all trash. At a noon press conference today, the chief medical examiner had given his opinion that Alana's body had not been deliberately dismembered. The pressure of the duct tape on the joints and the action of the ocean currents had caused the damage. He could not determine the manner of her death, except to say there were no traces of poisons in her system, no bullet fragments or knife wounds, and no injury inconsistent with having been in the water for several days, bound tightly to a heavy object. There was some trauma to the larynx but not enough to confirm strangulation. Asked by a reporter if the victim could have died from a blow to the head, the medical examiner smiled patiently and reminded him that the head had not been found. Another reporter asked if they had yet identified the piece of corkscrew-shaped metal found with the body. They had not.

C.J. heard the word "rain" and looked up from her desk. The weatherman was showing a map of the state, a cool front moving south and a tropical wave pushing in from eastern Cuba. This could mean thunderstorms over the weekend, he said, good news for the Everglades. Wildfires had already consumed nearly five thousand acres of dry and exhausted vegetation. No slave to optimism, C.J. imagined the storms sliding through the Straits of Florida and dumping the rain into the Gulf of Mexico.

The intercom line buzzed. Shirley said that Richard Slater was calling.

Slater told her he didn't have much time. He was at Miami City

Hall waiting for Paul Shelby and some local politicians to finish making the rounds.

"Detective Fuentes called me twice today," C.J. said. "No doubt he wants an answer about your boat trip. You don't have to talk to him, Rick. You can keep your friend's name out of it. That's up to you, but we need to discuss it. When will you be here?"

"I can't. I have to take Shelby's wife and kids to the airport. She's visiting her sister in Tampa this weekend. With traffic, there's no way I'm going to be free before seven o'clock. Do you like Mexican food?" He named a hole-in-the-wall on Coral Way that C.J. had heard of but never tried.

She pretended to be thinking about it. "All right. See you at seven."

"Wait. I need to ask you something. That first day we met, after they searched my apartment, you told me you took my case as a favor to Paul Shelby. He's running for reelection, and you said you supported him. Remember that?"

She hesitated.

Slater filled in the silence. "Uh-huh. You don't like Shelby enough to spit on him if he was on fire. What I see is some loyalty to Milo Cahill. You said that after you won his wrongful death case in California, Cahill made sure all his friends knew who you were. Is that why you took my case?"

"I don't see where this is going."

"Did you do it because you're good friends with Cahill?"

"No. I did it for myself. Milo promised to talk to Paul Shelby about a job I wanted with CNN. Shelby's stepfather, Donald Finch, has a sister who's an executive producer. Last weekend I found out they're offering me the job. I may be grateful to Milo, but I don't *owe* him anything and I am certainly not going to put my integrity as a lawyer up for sale."

"I apologize," Slater said.

She walked the phone over to the window and picked up her

orchid mister, as far as the cord would stretch. "Are you going to tell me what this is about?"

"I didn't expect to get into this so soon, but since Fuentes is breathing down my neck, here goes. When the police came back the second time wanting to talk to me, I decided it would be worthwhile to look at everyone who knew Alana Martin. I got around to Milo Cahill. You know that he and Paul Shelby were in the same fraternity at Duke. When people go back that far, I get curious. I went through the list of other men in the fraternity in those years and found three who would talk to me. Put together, the details make an interesting story. Cahill was on scholarship, and Shelby had money. Shelby gave Cahill loans that were never paid back, and he let Cahill use his charge card. There were the usual rumors about sex, but it turns out it wasn't Shelby and Cahill: it was Shelby and the girls that Cahill provided. One of them was fourteen. Her parents found out. Shelby swore he didn't know, and his family paid to keep it quiet."

Rick paused. "Are you with me so far?"

C.J. had been holding her breath. "Yes, go on."

"Paul Shelby, who had been accepted for law school at Yale the next fall, joined the Navy instead, then went to the University of Florida. Was he paying penance? Maybe. He graduated, joined his dad's insurance business, ran for office, had a wife and two kids, and now he's trying to arrange surplus government land for Milo Cahill's pet project, The Aquarius. What if, when Cahill moved to Miami, he and Shelby resumed the arrangement they'd started in college? What if Alana Martin was part of the price Milo was paying to get congressional approval?"

"This is incredible," C.J. said.

"Just listen. After I dropped Shelby off at Billy Medina's house that night, there were so many cars that I had to park down the street. As I was walking toward Medina's place, I noticed Milo Cahill's limousine. It was parked by the front door of your client's house. Harnell Robinson. There were no lights in the house, but the streetlight was shining on that big Mercedes grill. Alana had told me she'd be at the party, but I never saw her. I didn't see Cahill either. When I left about an hour and a half later, the limo was gone."

"Are you saying that Alana Martin left the party in Milo Cahill's limousine?"

"Maybe. Harnell Robinson's house is vacant. Isn't that right? We were in the backyard of Billy Medina's house last week, and you told me—"

"Yes, it's vacant. Harnell is trying to sell it."

"It's really handy, working for a security company," Rick said. "You know who to ask if you want to find out if a certain football player is part of Milo Cahill's crowd. Would you call Harnell for me? Ask him if he let Milo Cahill park his car in the driveway that weekend."

"Why would Milo want to?"

"Well, if you park your vintage Mercedes limo in a driveway down the street instead of leaving it with a valet at your host's house, then no one knows when you arrive, no one knows when you leave, and if you leave with an extra person in the car, they won't know that either."

C.J. went down her row of orchid pots spraying them with mist. "I can't believe this. Why would Milo kill Alana Martin? Give me a motive."

"Alana was a threat to him. If he's a pimp for Paul Shelby and Alana was blackmailing him, he'd want her out of the way."

"Alana couldn't have been blackmailing him," C.J. said. "She was counting on Milo to help her get into the movies. Last night, Judy Mazzio told me that Milo was the one who'd promised Alana a contact in Hollywood."

"Could he have actually done that?"

"I have no idea."

"Was it likely?"

She gave her white vanda a quick burst of mist. "Probably not."

"All right, then. Say Alana found out it was bullshit. She'd still want to get to Hollywood, and where does she get the money from? Milo Cahill. They were both at the party, then they weren't. Why was his limo parked two houses down the street, in Harnell Robinson's driveway? You can find out. I can't."

"And then what? Shall I run over to Milo's and ask him if he strangled her in the backseat?"

"Jesus. I knew it was a mistake talking to you on the phone."

"You just dumped all this on me. Excuse me if I need more than sixty seconds to process it." She exhaled. "Fine. I'll call Harnell."

"And can you ask Milo what he was doing there?"

"No."

"Not directly. Make up something, like the Star Island security people are asking Billy Medina about it. You and Milo are friends, aren't you?"

"Rick, how much TV are you watching lately? There's a story going around that C.J. Dunn was locked up in a psych ward after an alcoholic breakdown, exaggerated but basically true, and the only person who could have told them is Milo Cahill. He would have done it for giggles. So no, I don't think he's going to tell me anything remotely related to Alana Martin."

After a few seconds Rick said, "A psych ward?"

"It was a very civilized clinic in Boca Raton. Three gourmet meals a day, massages, yoga, and counseling."

"You still want Mexican food?"

"Sure. See you at seven."

She lifted a leaf on her phalaenopsis to check on the new spike. It was still green, and she could swear it was a quarter inch taller. Leaving her orchid mister on the window ledge, C.J. went back to her desk and hung up the phone.

A week ago, sitting with Milo Cahill in the backseat of his limousine, C.J. had asked what Paul Shelby was getting in exchange for persuading Congress to sell surplus government land to private developers. Not a thing, Milo had said, beyond earning some points from the environmentalists, which would be helpful to his reelection. C.J. had known it was a lie, but she'd looked past it because Milo had offered to speak to Shelby about the job at CNN. *I know what you want, and I can get it for you.*

Pending the final interviews in Atlanta, the job was now hers. Was it this that made her willing to open her eyes? Or just the fact that she was ticked off at Milo for having betrayed her? It was a flaw in her character, to be sure, to glance away from the truth when it failed to benefit her. But eventually, and painfully, she did come around to it.

Obviously, Paul Shelby was getting something out of the deal. And from whom? From his old fraternity brother at Duke University. Back then, it had been money in exchange for sex. Not just any sex. Sex with a fourteen-year-old girl. Maybe she was mature for her age. Maybe he hadn't known—

Look at it, C.J. told herself. Open your eyes.

Fourteen years old. C.J. wondered how much Noreen had paid to get her boy out of that mess.

Oh, Milo. You always know what we want, don't you?

C.J. buzzed her secretary. "Shirley, get me Harnell Robinson. Tell him it's okay about the check. I just need to talk to him."

In exchange for Shelby's support, Milo had arranged sex with a young woman who could play the part of a girl. Alana wasn't satisfied with Milo's promises. She needed money, enough money to live on until her career in the movies took off. She demanded that Milo help her out, and when he wouldn't—he couldn't, because those things never end—she threatened him. Alana had a temper. She accused Milo of using her, treating her like trash. She screamed at him and threatened to tell the police. He put a hand over her mouth. . . . But Milo had such soft hands. He wouldn't *murder* anyone. He couldn't. C.J. had once seen him jump on a chair and shriek when a garter snake slithered across his pool deck.

The phone rang several times before C.J. heard it. She picked up. Shirley said Harnell Robinson was on the line.

"Hello, Harnell, No, please don't apologize. I understand your situation. The collection department wants me to file a lien, but I'm prepared to tell them they have to wait a couple of weeks. I have a question about your house on Star Island, the one up for sale. It's still vacant?"

"Yeah," Harnell said, "we wanted to live there, but my wife doesn't like the neighborhood, and the pool leaks, so I can't rent it, and I can't sell it, the way the market is. That's part of my problem with your fees—"

"Never mind that now. Did you let anyone park in your driveway within the past month? Let me be specific. It was the weekend that Alana Martin went missing."

There was no reply from Harnell Robinson, but she could hear him breathing in starts and stops, as though he was making up his mind.

"Harnell, I need to know. Whatever you say will remain between us. I'm your lawyer. But if I have to sue you to collect my fees, the press will find out. They will wonder why a man who makes two point eight million a year can't pay his bills. They might find out about your gambling debts."

"Okay, Milo Cahill said he needed to park his car at my place."

"Did he say why?"

"Said it would be safer than leaving it at the party, you know, all those people wanting to touch it and sit in it. He's crazy about that car."

"Yes, he is."

"He didn't go in the house, okay? There wasn't anybody ever in the house. I checked it out, you know, after the police started asking questions about the young lady."

"Because you were suspicious of Milo?"

"No, not Milo, but he has some strange friends. Milo's all right. He said if I let him park in my driveway and didn't say anything, he'd hook me up with some action on a Marlins game."

"How'd you do?"

"I came out a little bit ahead. Couple thousand."

"You should give it up, Harnell. Give it up before it eats you alive."

"You're right. I should."

"Did you ever speak to Milo about it again?"

"Uh-uh. No need to. Everything was fine. Except I've still got a house I need to get rid of."

"All right," C.J. said. "Thanks, Harnell. And don't forget the check. Two weeks."

"You'll have it, no problem."

She disconnected and slowly replaced the handset. A perfectly reasonable explanation. Milo wanted people to stay away from his car. C.J. herself had seen the attention it drew.

Shirley stuck her head around the corner. "Judy Mazzio wants you to call her."

Leaving her office by four-thirty didn't mean escaping the crush of traffic, which was notoriously bad around the criminal courts building. It was close to five o'clock when C.J. parked her car on the wide gravel driveway of Mazzio Investigations. Raul saw her through the bars on the front window and buzzed her in. He took her through the former living room, where half a dozen clients waited to see about their bonds, then to a door. Raul punched in a security code and opened it. A hall led to the back of the house and Judy's office.

C.J. rapped on the doorframe. "You have a present for me?"

Judy pushed the list across the desk, fourteen pages printed out at the Redfish Point marina. C.J. dropped her purse into one of the chairs and sat in the other. "How much did this cost?"

"Three hundred dollars. It's a bargain. Raul went down there with a thousand in his pocket. The list doesn't separate out the power boats from the sailboats, but you can see which is which under each entry. They're listed by the owner's last name." She pointed. "Page ten."

C.J. flipped through, backed up, then came to a page of M's. Judy had helpfully put a checkmark by the name Carlos Moreno. He lived in South Miami and owned a 26-foot Silverton inboard.

"How many names are on this list?"

"Two hundred and six."

"It could be a coincidence."

"I'm sure it is. Carlos Moreno just happened to do Alana Martin's modeling portfolio. He just happened to be a still photographer for Reuters in Central Asia and the Middle East during the same time Rick Slater was over there, employed by Blackwater USA, protecting the press corps."

"What is going on here?"

Judy made an expansive shrug. "I'm a P.I., not God Almighty. That's for you to find out, if you think your client will be straight with you."

"Ha. I'll need a copy of that."

"It's yours." Judy slid the document into a large envelope. "Enjoy your fajitas."

chapter
THIRTY-ONE

eaving the criminal courts building after five o'clock in pre-sobriety days, C.J. and her friends would drive south across the river and zigzag through Miami's flat grid of streets to the Andalusia Hotel in Coral Gables. The hotel bar, glittering with polished brass and antique mirrors, produced the most creative drinks in town with two-ounce pours between five and seven. Seating was also offered near the atrium fountain, and classical guitar music mixed with the soft splash of water. One was not obliged to drink; one could order a virgin cocktail or a coffee.

C.J. had this in mind as she settled into an armchair just outside the entrance to the bar. With over an hour to kill before dinner with Rick Slater, she would have some tea and perhaps an appetizer to hold off her hunger. Out of curiosity to see what had changed, she picked up the card with its long list of cocktails.

The waiter appeared in his white shirt and black vest. C.J. dragged her eyes from the list. "Hi. Bring me . . . a cappuccino. No, wait. Make that a vodka and soda. Grey Goose, squeeze of lime. But only half an ounce. I'll pay for the whole drink, but tell the bartender half an ounce." She smiled. "I'm driving."

He made a slight bow. "One half ounce. Certainly."

"Oh, and I'll have the cheese plate too. Thanks."

Her BlackBerry chimed in her tote bag. It was a number she didn't recognize. Even so, she hit the button to connect. The twangy female voice on the other end said, "Hello, Miss C.J., this is Noreen Finch. Am I catching you at a good time?"

Noreen Finch was the last person C.J. wanted to talk to. She assumed the woman had obtained the cell phone number from her son. "Well, Noreen, I'm with friends at the moment, but what can I do for you?"

"Paul has asked me to take over the running of his office and his campaign. I guess I'm stuck with making phone calls like this. He and Diana have decided they don't need a chauffeur anymore, so we've let Rick Slater go. He'll get a good recommendation and two weeks' severance pay. But that's not why I'm calling—"

"Wait a minute." C.J. drew herself up in her chair. "I talked to Mr. Slater an hour ago. He didn't say anything about this."

"I just now told him."

"You fired him."

"I had to. Paul wants me to cut costs. Campaigns are expensive! The reason I'm calling is to see if we can get you to send a check for the deposit remaining in Mr. Slater's case."

"What deposit?"

"Paul gave you five thousand dollars as a deposit toward expenses to handle public relations. The media aren't interested in Richard

Slater anymore or in Paul. I assume you've closed your file. We'd like an accounting and a check for the balance."

"I've put in over forty hours on this already, and at my rate, that's about sixteen grand. You're getting off lightly, Noreen."

"Well, now, I don't know how you can justify that if you're only charging expenses. That's what you told Paul. Expenses, not fees."

"My expenses have been much heavier than expected."

"We did you a big favor, Miss C.J. Whatever-your-real-name-is. You got the job at CNN because of Paul, and you ought to be damned grateful."

"I'm so sorry, Noreen, but there will be no check for the balance because there is nothing left. Must go now. Have a lovely evening." C.J. disconnected and muttered, "I do not fucking believe this."

Setting down her drink and a plate of cheese and crackers, the waiter pretended not to have heard anything. "Would you like to run a tab?"

"No, I'll just pay for it now." She reached into her wallet for her charge card. "Could I ask you to bring me the rest of this drink, straight up?" She settled back in the chair and sipped her vodka and soda. She could barely taste the vodka, but ate a piece of cheese to put something in her stomach besides alcohol.

Unbidden, unwanted, a memory floated to the surface. Outside a liquor store. Waiting in his black Mustang, Guns N' Roses at full volume on the stereo. The car door opening, Paul handing her the bag. *You bought Popov?* He had laughed. *Come on, Charlie, we're going to mix it. I'm not wasting my money on Absolut.* She had said he was cheap. *Then you fuckin' pay for it,* he had said, turning the key in the ignition.

The waiter returned with the charge slip and a shot glass with the Grey Goose. She signed, took back her card, and picked up the glass, which contained one and one-half ounces. The bar at the Andalusia still had generous pours in the afternoon. She started to add the vodka to the soda, but instead put the shot glass to her lips and tipped it back. The heat burst onto her tongue and filled her mouth. She took a long breath, pulling the warmth into her lungs.

Later that night, a road out in the country: Paul Shelby holding her arms away from her bare chest. *Damn it, don't tease me. I'm so hot for you, baby. You want it, don't you? Don't you?*

Among the disorderly pile of papers on C.J.'s desk she had left the envelope of photographs from Alana Martin's portfolio. Alana with her forefinger in the corner of her mouth. Alana in a bikini, looking at the camera with moist, parted lips and overdone makeup. The thin arms and legs, the narrow hips and small breasts, didn't belong to a woman of twenty. She could have been sixteen. Or younger. Much younger. Put her in front of a pornographer's video camera in knee socks and a short dress, with her hair in pigtails, and she could have passed for twelve.

C.J. held up her hand to signal the waiter. When he saw her, she lifted her empty shot glass. He nodded and went toward the bar.

The guitarist was setting up his music stand. He tuned his guitar. Men and women in office attire were coming in to get buzzed, forget the day, and find someone for the night, if they were lucky. Their laughter rose above the guitar and the splash of water in the fountain.

The waiter came back with the vodka and a rocks glass full of ice.

Her cell phone rang again. C.J. recognized the number and quickly pressed the button to answer. "Kylie?"

"Hi."

"Hi, sweetie. How are you?"

"Great. I'm at work, so I can't talk long. My mother said I shouldn't bother you, but I wanted to say thanks for letting me stay at your house the other night."

"My pleasure. I'm so glad to hear from you. And you're doing well. A job. An apartment. Kylie—How did you get the apartment? You don't have a lot of money."

"I don't have to pay rent. The owner is in Europe right now, so I'm kind of house-sitting."

"Who is he? The owner."

"I don't know. He's friends with a friend of mine. Have you ever heard of a famous architect named Milo Cahill? He fixed it all up for me."

"Yes, I do know Milo Cahill. How did you meet him?"

"Through Alana."

"And he fixed you up with an apartment? Not good. Milo isn't the kind of man you want to be friends with. Trust me. I know him better than you do."

"You're thinking he's going to come on to me, aren't you? He won't. He's gay."

"Milo Cahill is a chameleon."

"What does that mean?"

"Don't believe everything he tells you. He doesn't have your best interests at heart. Promise me you'll be careful."

"I am careful. Don't worry about me. I can take care of myself."

Christ, how naïve, C.J. thought. "Look, Kylie, if you ever need anything, call me, will you? And I'll stay in touch, all right? You know, just to see how you are."

"If you want to, but I'm fine. Ms. Dunn? One other reason I wanted to call you . . . I've been watching TV a lot because of Alana and everything, and it's awful how they talk about you. Last night they had these video clips of you at a nightclub in California, which has nothing to do with anything, then they show pictures of downtown Mayo, Florida? Okay, I get it. Famous attorney comes from humble roots, blah blah. Did you see it?"

"No, I don't believe I did."

"They said you dropped out of high school."

"I did drop out. I wasn't quite sixteen, but the school gave up on me."

"I know, my mother told me; but the point is, they're making you out to be somebody you're not. It's awful, what they're doing, and you shouldn't pay any attention to them. This is why young people today are going more and more to the Internet. I think that by the time I get my journalism degree, there will be no more television, and frankly? I don't care." Kylie paused to take a breath. "Would you please tell Edgar I'm sorry I didn't get to finish his photographs? I hope he goes ahead and gets a new computer."

"Yes, I'll make sure he does."

"I have to hang up. A customer just came in."

"Why don't you call Edgar? Do you have his phone number?"

"I think so."

"Wait. I can give it to you."

"Gotta go. See you later."

There was a click, and Kylie was gone. C.J. held on to the phone, pressed it against her heart. Kylie was worried about her. Kylie gave a damn what happened to her. C.J. let her eyes fall closed. She leaned her forehead against her palm. My God, she thought. Libi Rodriguez. If not Libi, then another in the pack of wolves. They would not stop until every last scrap of information about her, past and present, had been dug up and laid out for everyone to see. They would gnaw her bones clean. C.J. wasn't worried for herself, really. It was all publicity. She could handle it. But Kylie. Sooner or later they would get to Kylie.

She thumbed through the phone's directory. Sarah Finch. She pressed the button, heard it ringing. She bit her lips.

When Sarah's voice mail picked up, C.J. took a breath. "Sarah, it's C.J. Dunn." She paused, laughing a little. "You're going to think this is crazy, but I've changed my mind. I can't take the job.

I don't have time. I'm a working lawyer, and I can't give that up. I appreciate your help. I really do. If you'd pass this message on to the producers?" She could think of nothing else to say except, "I'm sorry."

She turned in her chair to signal the waiter. When he came over, she shook her head and picked up her purse. "No, never mind. I have to leave."

A little while later she was heading into the glare of the sun on South Dixie Highway, the Metrorail on her right, a sea of cars ahead. At Fifty-Seventh Avenue, blowing her horn, she nudged into the left lane and made a quick turn on the red light. A liquor store on the corner of Sunset Drive sold her a pint of Absolut. Getting back into her car, she found a cup from Dunkin' Donuts in the backseat. She unscrewed the bottle cap and poured enough to rinse out the dried coffee, then threw the liquid on the ground in the parking lot before filling the cup with vodka.

She headed south a few miles, cut west to U.S. 1, then north a block to the strip shopping center where Shelby had turned his congressional office into a campaign headquarters.

PAUL SHELBY, WORKING FOR YOU.

They had locked up for the day, but she looked past signs in the window and saw him putting on his suit coat. There were three desks, some cabinets, posters, computer monitors. And two women, but neither was Noreen Finch. One of them came with a key and unlocked the door. She stuck her head out and smiled. "I'm sorry, we're closed, but if you come back tomorrow—"

"I need to talk to Mr. Shelby." C.J. pushed past her.

He turned around, adjusting the cuffs of his jacket. "Ms. Dunn?"

"Mr. Shelby. Your mother called me to demand the unspent portion of the so-called expense deposit for Richard Slater, after you fired him with no notice and a paltry two weeks' severance pay. I wanted to tell you personally what a shitty thing it was."

Shelby looked past her at the two women standing near the door. "Thank you. You can go now. It's all right. Just lock up on your way out. Ms. Dunn, would you like to come into my office?"

It was a carpeted room with a large desk, a sofa, some flags, a color photograph of the president shaking hands with the congressman, more photographs, certificates. On his desk, framed portraits of his wife and their two sons, gray eyes and neatly combed brown hair like daddy.

Paul Shelby stood squarely in the center of his office, his expression a mix of indignation and incredulity. "I am shocked. If you have a complaint, that's fine, but to barge in here spouting profanity shows a lack of manners I'd never have expected from you. I didn't need Mr. Slater's services anymore. Diana's brother is going to drive her from now on. End of story."

C.J. put her sunglasses away, missing twice before getting them into their case. Her hands were shaking. Her chest felt like a cold wind was blowing through it.

"Are we finished, Ms. Dunn? I have a meeting to attend."

She said, "You wanted me to tell you when my client became more of a burden than a duty to you, so you could fire him. That was against my principles and I should have called you on it right there, but I didn't. You made your decision without consulting me. Now you want a refund on your deposit, after I have put in many, many hours of my time. That's not just cheap, it's rude."

With a sigh, Shelby said, "All right. If you want to keep the money, then keep it. I'm not going to argue."

"You know what really ticks me off? Jason Wright. Who leaked his name to the press?"

"I don't know what you mean."

"You fucking do. I told you Jason had no alibi, and he was

Alana's boyfriend, and you, or maybe Noreen, ran with it, and then reporters were all over him like piranhas. Don't you feel any responsibility for what happened? I do. I feel bad as hell."

"Have you been drinking?"

"Do you deny that you told the media about Jason?"

"Yes, I deny it. What is the matter with you? I think you're drunk." Shelby held up a forefinger in warning as he picked up his telephone. "I'm going to call a taxi, and I want you to get in it and go home."

C.J. pressed the button to disconnect. "You don't know who I am, do you? You really have no clue."

"What are you talking about?"

"Look at me. Look at me, I said. What if I told you my name? Charlotte Jo Bryan. They called me Charlie. You said it was cute. Is it coming back to you now?"

He stared at her, squinting slightly.

"Gainesville, Florida. You were a third-year law student. I was working at the Sundowner on West Main. I didn't wear designer suits then. I wore blue jeans and T-shirts and flip-flops because it was what I could afford. I was nineteen and weighed about twenty pounds less than I do now, and I had short brown hair. Look at me."

Paul Shelby was slowly shaking his head.

"You gave me a thousand dollars for an abortion. You can't have forgotten that."

After a few seconds of silence, he said, "Charlie?"

She held out her arms, then let them fall at her sides. "Yeah. Charlie."

Warily he said, "What do you want?"

"What do I *want*? I don't know. I guess I want . . . I want some acknowledgment of what you did. Yes. That would be nice. An apology. Let's start there."

"An apology? For what? For getting you pregnant?"

"No. For what you did to me." Arms crossed tightly over her chest, she paced in front of him. "I'd never been with a guy so much older, almost ten years older, a law student, a former Navy lieutenant, and I couldn't imagine why you'd want *me*. We didn't have normal dates. We never went to dinner or a movie. I never met your friends. We'd go right to your apartment. But then one of your neighbors saw us come out. He laughed and said who's the kid?"

"For God's sake." Shelby turned away and put a hand to his forehead.

C.J. pulled on his sleeve and forced him to look at her. "It took me a while, but I finally got it, what I was to you. The next time you called me, I said no, but you kept calling and said you missed me. Please, Charlie, I miss you, baby. We didn't go to your apartment. We drove out to the country—you had that new Mustang, remember? The front seat went all the way down."

"Stop it!"

"That's funny. I said the same thing. I said it over and over, but you wouldn't stop. You called me your baby doll. You put your hands around my neck and squeezed. You said it would make it better for both of us. I thought I was going to die. After it was over, you threw me out of the car, and I had to walk back to town. How far was that? Five miles?"

He turned and leaned over her. She felt the spittle striking her lips. "I know who you are. You're the little hick who wanted to go out with me because I had money and a fast car and a father who wasn't in jail or drunk. You were all over me. Yes, we had sex. We got stoned, too, on weed that you provided, and we got drunk, but I did not . . . force you. It was consensual. You wanted it. All of it."

"That isn't true! To be asphyxiated? Raped? Are you crazy? I should have called the police, but I was too ashamed."

"They wouldn't have believed you. No one will believe you

now." Paul Shelby gripped her upper arm so tightly she groaned and dug into his fingers. He shook her. "I have a wife and children and a position in this community. If you repeat this to anyone, I will sue you for slander. You will be fired from Tischman Farmer. Believe me, Ms. Dunn, you don't want to try it. You are sick. You need help."

When he pushed her away, C.J. leaned with both hands on the edge of the desk. "I never said I would make it public. I would never tell your wife. I only wanted you to look at me and see who I am, so maybe I could forget it too."

"All right. I've seen you. Now get out."

chapter
THIRTY-TWO

ick was standing at the gate in the side yard of C.J.'s house talking to Edgar Dunn when he heard an engine and the shriek of tires. He had parked his Audi in the driveway, and a silver BMW was swerving to miss it. The wheels went off the driveway into the grass and then corrected to the left, but not fast enough. C.J. didn't make it into the double-wide carport. She hit the corner of the house, smashing the right front headlight.

Edgar lifted the latch on the gate and hurried through. Rick got to her first. She was gripping the top of the steering wheel, and her forehead rested on her hands. He tried the door. Rapping on the window, he said, "C.J.!" It took her some effort to find the lock. He opened the door and reached over her to turn off the ignition and the lights. There was an empty pint bottle of Absolut on the floor of the passenger side.

She was laughing. "Who moved the garage?"

"Is she hurt?" Edgar tried to see.

"No, she's drunk." Rick handed him her tote bag and the keys. "Let's get her inside." She wasn't wearing a seat belt. He pulled her out of the car. With an arm around her waist, he half-carried her up some steps and through the side door of the house, which led to a utility room, then the kitchen. Edgar turned on the lights and Rick followed him. A couple of cats ran out of the way, scooting into a dining room whose table was cluttered with papers and files, then through a wide opening to a living room with a fireplace and high beamed ceilings. Edgar hurried to the sofa and cleared off a week's worth of newspapers and a tray with the remains of a frozen dinner.

C.J. struggled. "Let me go. Please. Bathroom." She staggered down a hall and a door slammed. Water ran, an attempt to disguise the sound of C.J. Dunn being sick.

Her uncle stood by the telephone. "Should we call emergency, do you think?"

Rick walked to the door, knocked, and went in. She was curled up on the tile floor, moaning, her skirt up her thighs and vomit on her blouse. He flushed the toilet and ran some cold water over a hand towel. Edgar stood in the doorway. To give the old man something to do, Rick asked if he'd make a pot of strong coffee.

He crouched beside her and cleaned her face. "C.J. Talk to me, C.J. Who am I? Do you know who I am?"

Her eyes drifted toward his face. "Rick? What are you doing here?"

"You didn't show for dinner, so I came looking for you."

"Oh. I'm sorry. I forgot." She hiccuped.

He took off her high heels and set them under the sink. "We're going for a walk. Come on." He lifted her to her feet. "That's it. I've got you. Walk with me." He took her to the living room, across to the foyer, then back in the other direction.

She buried her face in his shoulder. "I didn't mean to. I'm so embarrassed."

"It's all right. Just keep moving."

"Dizzy. I have to sit down."

"Not yet. Walk it out."

She heaved, and he took her back to the bathroom and let her spit bile into the sink. She shuddered and started to cry and put her forehead on the porcelain. He lifted her face and wiped it off again. He leaned into the hall. "Mr. Dunn? Could you bring a glass of water? No ice, room temperature."

He closed the toilet lid and let her sit there, and when her uncle brought the water, Rick held the glass to her lips. "Not too much. Just sip it." When she turned her head away, he said, "If you don't drink this, you'll be in the hospital with a saline drip in your arm." She drank then leaned over the sink again, but nothing came up. When she had finished half the water in the glass, Rick walked her back to the living room.

Edgar said, "Last year I found her on the floor in the kitchen, passed out cold. I called nine-one-one. I had to sign papers to get her some help. I thought she was okay."

"She's going to fight it the rest of her life. Do you have any antacid?"

"Yup. Got some Pepto-Bismol in my bathroom. I'll be right back."

Rick walked her up and down the hall and around the living room, and C.J. told him how ashamed she was, and she was not a good person, she was weak and a phony, but she was glad he was there, since he knew about taking care of drunks, didn't he, because his brother had been a drunk too, and she would give anything not to go back in the hospital, and she would never never do this again.

"Please don't tell anyone. You won't, will you, Rick?"

"I won't."

"Cross your heart and hope to die?"

"Cross my heart and hope to die."

She grabbed the front of his shirt in both hands to keep her balance. "Rick, I want to tell you what I did. I called Sarah Finch. Left a message. Sorry. Can't do it. *Rich, Famous, and Deadly.* I would've been so good. I would've. But I gave it up, Rick. I left her a message . . . and said I was sorry. Thank you for con—considering me, but I can't."

"Why'd you do that, honey?"

"You called me honey. Oh. You're such a nice man. Please don't leave." C.J. started to cry again, getting his shirt wet. "Please don't."

"I'm not going anywhere."

He wiped the tears off her cheeks, and they walked some more.

C.J. went to sleep on the couch with a pillow and a blanket from her bedroom. Rick had angled an armchair so he could see her if she stirred. A lamp on the end table had three settings, and he'd put it on low. He propped his head on a fist and dozed. His eyes came open. She was looking at him. He didn't know how long she'd been awake. Two of her cats were curled up at her feet. A smaller white cat watched him from the chair near the fireplace. When Rick stretched his arms, it jumped down and hid under the chair.

C.J.'s voice came out on a whisper, like her throat was raw. "I stood you up. I'm sorry. What time is it?"

He glanced at his watch. "About four o'clock." She looked at the dark window. "Four o'clock in the morning," he said.

Struggling to sit up, she noticed what she was wearing—a satin nightgown with thin straps. She pulled the sheet to her chin.

Rick said, "I didn't do that. Judy Mazzio came over. Edgar called her. She's upstairs asleep in the guest room."

"Judy. Yes, I remember."

"What happened to you?" Rick asked.

"I screwed up, obviously."

"It's day one. New day, new start. And it's Friday."

"Aren't you Mr. Sunshine?" She held her head and squeezed her eyes shut. "Oh, God."

He went over to the coffee table and opened the bottle of aspirin. "Here. Take a couple of these and drink the whole glass of water. All of it. Come on, down the hatch. You're going to feel like shit today. You should call in sick to work."

She gave him the empty glass and wiped her mouth with her fingers. "We both get the day off. You don't have a job anymore."

"That's right, I don't. How'd you find out?"

"Noreen Finch called me. She wanted the balance of your deposit. I told her to go to hell."

"Good for you."

C.J.'s smile vanished, replaced by a slit-eyed stare that he couldn't figure out. Her eyes were puffy, her makeup was gone, and her mouth turned down, pale and tight.

"What?"

She raised her knees, covering herself with the blanket. "Did Judy say anything to you about the boat at the Redfish Point marina?"

"No. What would she have said?"

"She got a list of owners. Guess whose name is on it? Carlos Moreno, the cameraman for Libi Rodriguez."

They looked at each other in the dim lamplight. Rick nodded.

"My God. I knew you weren't telling me the whole truth, but this!"

"I couldn't tell you."

"Oh, balls you couldn't. You didn't want to. What are you doing with Moreno?"

Rick came over and sat on the other end of the sofa. "Carlos is helping me with a story about Paul Shelby. I'm a freelance reporter."

Her mouth came open and a small groan of disbelief came out.

"I might as well tell you now," he said. When she continued to stare at him, he said, "Do you want to hear about it?"

She lifted her hands. "I can't wait."

"I've known Carlos a long time. I met him in Karachi, Pakistan. I was in the Army, and he was working for Reuters. After I left the military, I bounced around doing this and that for a while, like I told you, and Carlos and I kept in touch. His wife didn't like his odds of survival, so he came home and started working in TV. I had written some articles when I was in the service and made some contacts among the press corps. I started working with a freelancer, a guy named Larry Everts, on a story about Blackwater. You probably never heard of him, but he's won a Pulitzer. He sold our piece to *The New Yorker*. I was with Blackwater at the time, so obviously my name didn't appear in the credits, but the right people told me that if I ever wanted to sell something, they'd look at it. The problem was, being out of the field I didn't have much to write about, so I said, hell, why not write a novel?

"I went to Mexico and spun my wheels. One day I got a call from Carlos. He said he had a tip from a girl who wanted money for her story, as long as he kept her name out of it. He was the only journalist she knew and trusted, but he's not a writer, so he called me."

C.J. lifted her eyes toward the ceiling. "The girl was Alana Martin."

"Correct. You asked why Carlos didn't sell the pictures in her portfolio. He was working with me, and besides that, he liked Alana. There wasn't any sex between them. He said his wife would kill him. Anyway, Carlos told Alana about me, and I came to Miami to check it out. She said she was having sex with a U.S. congressman. He liked little girls, but he was afraid to go after the real thing. As a story, it had some spice, but it wasn't enough. What did interest me was the fact that the sex had been arranged as a bribe for a five-hundred-million-dollar project on U.S. surplus land. That's a bigger story than a pedophile politician cheating on his wife.

"So I called Larry Everts, and he said he'd be willing to work with me if I did the legwork in Miami. Larry had heard rumors about Shelby already. Whispers of illegal campaign donations, X corporation picking up the tab for Y product or services, and Noreen Finch using her contacts with the present administration to push her son's career. Larry would follow that up, and I'd take care of my part of the story. We knew it would take time, and I needed to get close to Shelby.

"You'd be surprised how many contacts you make in the military. The executive VP of Atlas Security is a former Navy SEAL I'd met on joint task force exercises in Guantanamo. Shelby didn't know he wanted a driver, but my friend at Atlas told him it would be a good idea to protect the family, so bingo, I had a job."

C.J. wasn't saying anything, just staring at him.

"I watched Shelby for two months," Rick said. "I dropped him off at Milo's place three times when the wife was out of town. Shelby said they were talking about The Aquarius, but nobody else seemed to be around. Alana said he never had any girl more than once, except for her. Shelby liked her acting ability, I'll put it that way. Alana gave me the names of other girls who had been with Shelby. There was a pattern. Long hair, skinny, looked young, from out of town. I was able to find and talk to one of them. She says she met Milo Cahill at a party and went to his house several times before he suggested she meet his friend. He didn't say who the friend was. She went to Milo's house, and he took her up into the tower on the third floor. The man was already there. There was some wine, and she thinks it was spiked with something. She has very little memory of what went on. I showed her Shelby's photo without telling her who he was. She couldn't identify him. She wasn't injured, and she refused to say it was rape. She had just turned eighteen. Milo gave her five hundred dollars."

Beyond the window nothing moved. The streetlight put shadows across the yard. The lamp reflected in the window, and he could see a blonde woman watching him from the sofa. Rick had kept these things from her for too long, and it felt good to let them go.

He turned around. "Do you believe me?"

"Yes." She nodded quickly. "Go on."

"Investigating a story like this takes time. Larry and I had patience, but Alana was worried Milo would find out. She was the only one who knew what Milo was doing. He used her to find other girls. I told her to calm down. I needed her. I'd paid her four thousand dollars, and she owed me. I should've stopped it."

"You couldn't have predicted—"

"I knew it was dicey. I would really like to find out who killed her. I would like that a lot."

"I talked to Harnell Robinson."

"What did he say?"

"That Milo asked to park his car in the driveway that night. It would be safer there. That's what Milo told Harnell. It makes sense," C.J. said.

"You can't see Milo as our bad guy."

"No."

Coming away from the window, Rick sat on the other arm of the sofa, facing C.J. "I still say he had a reason."

C.J. shrugged. "So did Paul Shelby. Alana could have decided to blackmail him."

"I thought about that, but I had his car. He wouldn't have left the party with a woman not his wife. There were too many people around. I know the potential for violence when I see it, and he doesn't have it. He wouldn't even hire it done."

"Anyone can turn violent if pushed."

"Alana wouldn't have gone that far. She wouldn't have black-mailed a United States congressman. That's not an easy target. But yes, I did think of him. Milo wanted Alana to bring a girl that night, someone Shelby could check out and see if he liked. Alana hadn't decided if she would or not. We had planned to meet, but she never showed. When I found that girl passed out in the backyard, I thought she might have been the one intended for Shelby. This girl was a runaway from Pensacola. I got her name and address off her driver's license, but I didn't tell you because first I wanted to see what she knew. There wasn't enough evidence against me, so I took a chance on not using her for an alibi. I talked to her, and—" He shook his head. "She didn't know anything about it."

C.J. stared at him for a while, then laughed and dropped her head to her knees. "Kylie Willis."

"Do you read minds?" he asked. "How do *you* know her name?"

"Her parents are Fran and Bob Willis. Fran was a friend of my mother's. Kylie isn't a runaway. She came to Miami for a weekend and decided to stay. She met Alana Martin and got herself a fake ID and became Alana's party pal. I wasn't aware of this until Fran called me and asked me to send Kylie home. Kylie said she'd been at Billy's that night. She never mentioned you."

"I asked her not to. I was undercover." Rick tried for a smile, but C.J. gave him a look that would have cut steel. "I didn't dump her out on the street. I never did that. The night I took her home, I walked her to the lobby of her building. I saw her twice after that. She wanted to be paid for information about Alana, but she didn't know anything. I gave her a hundred and eighty dollars for her time. It was all I had on me. She comes off as a little tough, but I think it's a front. She said she was adopted. One reason she came to Miami was to feel closer to her birth parents. They died in a car crash. She says she might be walking down the street and find a cousin. She wants to be a journalist. How about that?"

"Yes, how about that. You've been quite an example."

"Give me a break, will you? Where is Kylie now? Is she all right?"

"I hope so. She has an apartment and a job on South Beach. Her mother doesn't want me to have anything to do with her, so I'm keeping my distance."

"Why?"

C.J. reached for her water glass. "It's complicated. Would you give me some water, please?" He walked over to fill her glass and hand it to her. She asked, "Do I look horrible?"

"For a lady with a hangover, you're not bad."

"It's the last hangover I will ever have." She glared at him as if he might say something. She held the glass on her knees. "Do you remember my asking you if Alana had ever talked about adult movies? Kylie told me something. She said Alana tried out for what she believed was a feature film, but she was too skinny for the part, so they asked her to try out for an adult movie, playing the role of an underage girl. It was never made, and Alana wanted to get her audition tapes and destroy them. She wanted the tapes because she thought if they turned up on the Internet when she got to Hollywood, she'd be ruined. Judy tracked down the producer, a man named Harold Vincent. Alana didn't tell you any of this?"

"Not a word of it."

"Vincent confirmed that his company was doing the DVD. The

reason he wouldn't give the tapes to Alana is that she didn't ask him nicely enough. She threatened to go to the police, but she had signed a release, so she was stuck." C.J. hesitated a moment, then said, "Billy Medina introduced Alana to Harold Vincent at a party in the Bahamas. Billy had taken the entire staff of *Tropical Life* to Paradise Island. Vincent owns a travel company in Miami, and they bought ad space, so he was invited. Billy asked Alana if she wanted to meet someone in the movie business. That's how Alana hooked up with Vincent, through Billy."

"I wasn't aware that Alana worked for Billy Medina."

"Not directly, and not for more than a few months," C.J. said. "She was in advertising. He let her go because she wasn't doing her job, that's basically it. I only learned about this yesterday. I was expecting to find something pointing to Harold Vincent as the guilty party, but Judy is certain he had nothing to do with it. She knows him from Las Vegas. The man actually has a conscience. He's going to destroy the tapes so her parents never find out."

C.J. leaned over to put the glass on the table. "Mr. Slater. Despite the fact that you lied to me—"

"I'm sorry about that."

"Pay attention. You are still my client. I should go over to the Miami Beach Police homicide department and tell them everything I just heard, but not yet, not until you are completely in the clear. Detective Fuentes wants to know about the boat. Will Carlos Moreno make a statement on your behalf?"

"No problem."

"I need his phone number. Tell him that Judy Mazzio is going to call him to set something up. I believe this time it will work." C.J. looked around. "Did she bring my robe down here?"

"You need to get up?"

"I have to go to the bathroom. Turn around. Please?"

He turned to face the dining room and heard a shifting of blankets and sheets.

"Are you still working on the story?" C.J. asked.

"Yes. I have enough to make a good start. With what Larry Everts has, we can keep going, keep looking into it, even without Alana."

"Will you leave me out of it?"

When he turned around, C.J. stood there with the sheet wrapped around her, holding the fabric to her breasts. Her bare feet showed where the fabric overlapped at the bottom, and the rest of the sheet trailed behind her. One of the straps of her nightgown had fallen off her shoulder. She said, "Rick? Will you?"

"Will I what?"

"Leave me out of the story. I have nothing to do with Alana, and you don't need Kylie in it either."

"You're right. There's no reason to mention you at all."

She nodded and walked past him, moving for a moment into the lamp light. He wasn't sure at first what he saw, but he reached out and stopped her. There were four purple ovals on the pale skin of her upper arm. "What is this? This. These bruises."

She tried to see. "I don't know. I must have bumped into something."

"No, these are finger marks." He looked more closely. "And a thumb print on the other side." He lined them up with his own fingers. "Smaller than mine, but definitely a man's hand. Who was it?" She pulled, but he held on. "Who did this?"

"I don't know. I was drunk. Maybe I fell and someone grabbed me."

"Bullshit. Who is he, C.J.? Are you afraid I might break the guy's neck?"

"Stop being such a Neanderthal!"

"Yeah, maybe you'd better not tell me." He let her go. "Did Billy Medina do that to you?"

"No." She walked toward the hall, her sheet billowing behind her.

Rick followed. "Were you over at his house drinking?"

"Leave me alone, Rick."

"Was it Medina?"

"I said no!"

"You wouldn't lie to me, would you?"

She kept going, closing the bathroom door and turning the lock.

chapter
THIRTY-THREE

C J. swept up the glass from the broken headlight and
emptied it into a heavy plastic bag. She collected the
chunks of concrete and stucco that her BMW had
knocked off the corner of the house. Judy Mazzio had just brought
her home from taking the car to a body shop. Repairs were going to
put a thousand-dollar dent in C.J.'s checking account. Edgar had
said she could drive his car in the meantime.

Rick had left at dawn, politely declining Edgar's offer of pancakes
and eggs. C.J. had gone back to bed, leaving only Judy to share breakfast with Edgar.

At the moment, Judy was leaning against the old Buick's fender
in the relative cool of the carport, talking on her cell phone to Carlos Moreno, arranging a time to meet him. He would sign the

statement that C.J. had drafted and printed in her office upstairs, in which he would swear that it was not unusual for Richard Slater to borrow his boat on a Sunday morning. With luck, this might put Slater in the clear. C.J. had already phoned George Fuentes, and he'd said he would look at it. He was working another homicide and expected to be around the Beach until God only knew when. Just fax it, he'd told her.

C.J. tied the bag and carried it over to the trash can. She was sweating. Her sleeves were too long for this weather, but she wanted to hide the bruises on her left arm. Judy hadn't asked, which meant she hadn't seen them. C.J. adjusted the clip holding up her hair. The humidity was thick enough to suck through a straw. Rain was predicted for later in the evening. There was not the slightest breeze. It seemed that the earth was holding its breath, waiting.

Judy slid her cell phone into the pocket of her capri pants. "We're meeting at five-thirty at a Cuban restaurant on Southwest Eighth. Carlos said Rick would meet us there. Come with me, why don't you?"

"No, I want to give him a few more days to forget the sight of his attorney lying on the bathroom floor, smashed out of her mind."

"He took good care of you last night. All I had to do was get you into your nightie. I thought maybe I'd find you both tucked into bed when I woke up. Don't give me that look. He's a lot sexier than Señor Wonderful, in my humble opinion."

C.J. smiled. "I'll let you know." She was reaching for the handle on the side door when she saw a small brown car cruising by. She muttered a curse under her breath, and Judy turned around to look.

The car stopped, and Nash Pettigrew leaned out the window. "C.J.! Is that where you crashed your BMW? The body shop says it looks like you ran into a wall. Were you drunk?"

Judy started toward him, but C.J. grabbed her arm and pulled her back. "You don't want your face on the cover of a tabloid." C.J. yelled back at him, "Have a nice day, Mr. Pettigrew."

"I will!"

Judy fumed, "I'm going to shoot that little bastard some day."

"No, you won't." C.J. held the door open for her.

"You're awfully mellow today."

"It's the Xanax. I couldn't bear the hangover."

"Yeah, well, when you're on CNN, you can tell Nash Pettigrew and the rest of them to go straight to hell."

C.J. went inside and closed the door. "I'm not taking the job. I called CNN and said I couldn't do it."

"You what?" Judy squinted as if she hadn't heard.

Walking ahead of her into the kitchen, C.J. said, "I had to make a choice. Be a lawyer or be a part of the info-tainment circus that I've come to despise. I refuse to sell out."

"Sell out? What the fuck?" Judy's eyes pursued her. "Hosting that show was all you ever talked about. Are you running scared? Is that it? Have they finally gotten to you?"

"It isn't that." C.J. took her hands, hesitated, then shook her head. "We'll talk about it later. Please?"

"Okay."

Opening the refrigerator, C.J. found a bottle of root beer. "You want this? I'll share it with you."

"No, thanks." Judy was still staring at her, waiting to hear an explanation.

C.J. looked in a drawer for the bottle opener. "Judy, I'm going to accept your offer to find Kylie."

"You're worried about her and Milo, aren't you?"

"I think she has more sense than that, but yes. God, I would love to go straight to the police. The girls are supposedly over eighteen, but it's still prostitution, and if they were drugged, it's rape."

"What do you use for proof?"

"That is a problem." C.J. opened one drawer after another for the bottle opener. Someone had done too good a job cleaning the place. A vase of freshly cut yellow croton leaves was on the table. The dishes had been washed and put away, and the floor mopped. Coming downstairs at noon, C.J. had nearly wept from gratitude.

"Rick could tell the police what he knows," Judy suggested.

"No, I don't want him saying anything until we get Fuentes off his back. I keep wavering between being a lawyer and wanting to forget my client so I can tear Milo's throat out. Rick thinks Milo is guilty of murder. I can't see it, but I just don't know." C.J. found the opener. The other end was a corkscrew. She stared at it for a while, then slowly unfolded it.

Judy said, "I think you want to use the bottle opener part."

C.J. turned around. "Do you remember that photograph in the paper of the piece of metal found with Alana's body? Do you have time to fax it to me? Now?"

After Judy left, C.J. ran up to her office and went online to find every Mercedes dealer and upscale auto upholstery shop in the Miami area. She started calling and got a hit on the fourth one. The name of the shop was Wunder-Kar. *Vunder.* They specialized in luxury German makes.

C.J. parked Edgar's Buick across the street and walked through the gate in the high chain-link fence. One of the workers, a Hispanic man in his twenties, said there was no way he could let her into the shop. She tucked a fifty-dollar bill into his shirt pocket. After looking around to see who might be watching, he said he would have to stand by the car and make sure she didn't damage anything.

The garage smelled of leather and oil. The ceiling lights gleamed on chrome and expensive paint jobs. The other men barely nodded when her new friend said she owned the Mercedes limo and had to look for something. The front seats had been taken out, but the passenger area hadn't yet been touched. The man told her to hurry up. In her white cotton slacks, C.J. slid across the backseat.

From the ceiling hung the bizarre little lamp that Milo had bought in Berlin, made of antique doll's heads and halogen lamps on metal rods that curled in long silver spirals. From her purse C.J. withdrew the fax that Judy had sent. She held up the page and compared the photograph to the lamp. The sharp point of a coil of metal had been embedded in the duct tape around Alana Martin's headless torso, but the metal had not come from this lamp. The rods were too long and too shiny, and all six of them were still firmly screwed into the base.

C.J. folded the page, put it back into her purse, and found the small but powerful flashlight she'd brought with her. Two weeks ago, there had been a blanket of fake leopard skin across the backseat. What could it have hidden? C.J. passed the beam of the flashlight over every square inch of the backseat, the brown leather worn with age, the holes where some of the stitching had come loose.

She crawled on the floor, picking at the carpet. She pulled down the jump seats. She opened the door in the bar and let down the shelf, finding a corkscrew. The shape in the photograph was more like this, but even this wasn't right.

Finally, exhausted, she sat in the middle of the floor, thinking.

A tap came on the window. C.J. got out and asked the man to open the trunk. She saw a tire jack, a box of brochures for The Aquarius, and dust. She turned off her flashlight, thanked the man, and left.

The fifty dollars would have been a waste except that she felt slightly better about Milo.

Starting the Buick, she had to pump the gas to get it going. Sweat dripped down the side of her face, and she wiped it on her sleeve. Clouds completely hid the sun, but it didn't matter. The air conditioner was as feeble as its owner. C.J. took her cell phone out of its pocket and hit the speed dial for Billy Medina, thinking as she did so that she needed to find some other person to correspond with button number five.

"Hello, *chica*." His smooth baritone filled her ear. "To tell you the truth, I'm a little surprised to hear from you."

"I know. I'm sorry, Billy. Last time we spoke I was pretty shaken up. Not every day you see a man who's hanged himself. Thanks again for the rescue. So. Are you busy later on?"

"No. What's up?"

"Could I come over?"

"Oh, is this the 'we need to talk' talk?"

"Not at all." She didn't want him to think he could take her to bed, but honesty would end the conversation. "Aren't you leaving for Antigua tomorrow? Let me come say good-bye. Bring you some takeout?"

"Well, actually, I have a meeting at the Delano for cocktails, but I'll be home about eight o'clock. Is that too late?"

"No, it's fine."

"Wear something sexy."

He hung up before she could say anything more. She put the car into gear. The transmission clunked, and the power steering groaned, but not loudly enough to drown out the chimes from her BlackBerry.

It was Judy. C.J. put the car back in park. Judy told her that she had just found Kylie's address, both the apartment and her work address, a shop called Shiva Sun on Washington Avenue.

"Wait," C.J. said. "Let me get my memo book. I'll write it down.

I'm going over to the Beach anyway later on. Maybe I'll drop in and buy something."

"Kylie may not be there. She took the day off. Her boss isn't happy about it. She suspects a party. That's why most of her employees don't last. They're always skipping work to party. It's South Beach, and you're only young once."

C.J. wrote down the addresses and put the memo book away. "If they fired her, she might learn something."

"So, did you look at Milo's car?"

She described her search of the limousine. "Even you, Judy, wouldn't have found so much as a hair. Alana wasn't in that car. If Milo had wanted her out of the way, he would have simply paid her. She needed money to move to L.A., and she would have kept her mouth shut. Everyone said she was discreet."

"But she wouldn't have left without getting her audition tapes," Judy pointed out.

"Milo had nothing to do with the tapes," C.J. replied. "Milo had no motive at all."

"Well, Harold Vincent didn't kill her."

"I'm not saying he did." C.J. watched the German and American flags on top of the upholstery shop move in a sudden gust of wind, sink, and lift once more, curling around the poles. The clouds were ragged pieces of a sodden gray blanket.

C.J. said, "Let me run something by you." She angled the AC vent toward her face. "Alana told Kylie she had to meet someone, that she'd be right back. What if she was going to see Paul Shelby? They wouldn't have met in the house. They could have gone next door. That house is vacant, and you just step around the wall and you're there. I don't think Shelby would have planned to kill her. It just happened. They argued, and he grabbed her. He shook her too hard, or she screamed, and he had to stop her. She was a small woman. Fragile." C.J. paused. "Of course, I could be wrong."

There was some silence from Judy's end before she said, "Hate to point this out, hon, but how did he get Alana, dead or alive, off the island? He took a taxi home."

"Yes, that's what he told Rick he would do, but I remember something Jason Wright told me. Taxis are hard to get on Star Island that time of night. You can wait an hour. I've been to parties at Billy's, and people complain about it all the time. So how did Shelby leave? I don't think he used Milo's car. He couldn't catch a ride with a friend. They just wouldn't have understood why he had a body over his shoulder. So what did he do? He had to call someone to rescue him. Who would do that? Who could he trust that far?"

A quick intake of breath told her that Judy got it. "Noreen Finch. She saved his ass from an arrest for statutory rape in college."

"This is a very wild guess," C.J. admitted.

"Noreen could've been there in fifteen minutes." Then Judy said, "You have no evidence. You can make all the guesses you like, and it won't get you anywhere. They're too wealthy, too connected. Who's going to believe it?"

C.J. laughed as Paul Shelby's words came back to her: *No one will believe you.* "All you have to do, Judy, is drop a few suggestions into the right ears. You can't make it all up, of course, but if it's about people who matter in this world, or seem to, then you've suddenly got this ball rolling downhill, and you just get out of the way and let it roll. I do despise the tabloid media, but they can be useful sometimes. Even the mainstream media, like the story Rick is doing. He's going to reveal that Paul Shelby is hot for little girls. It's not a big jump to assume that Shelby strangled a girl who could play the part so very well."

The flags on the building were snapping toward the east. The afternoon sunlight had dimmed. It seemed much later than five o'clock.

"Why don't you go talk to Rick about this?" Judy asked.

"Not yet. I'm going over to Billy's house. I have to be there at eight o'clock."

"I wish you wouldn't," Judy said.

"Not for *that*," C.J. said. "You'll be happy to know that Billy and I are sort of finished."

"Sort of?"

"Definitely finished. I have a hard time saying it. A hard time believing it. Billy Medina was habit-forming."

"Then why are you going over there?"

"To ask him how Paul Shelby left the party. It wasn't in a taxi. Did someone pick him up? What did Shelby say about it, if anything? You don't leave a party without thanking the host, especially if he's one of your biggest campaign donors. I need to ask Billy about it. He's leaving for Antigua tomorrow, and he won't be back for two weeks."

"Be careful. Old habits die hard."

"Not to worry. Do me a favor: don't tell Rick where I am. He doesn't like Billy, and it would be hard to explain."

"Hon, if you want to lie to him, do it yourself," Judy said.

"You're right. He isn't Billy. I was never completely truthful with Billy, and . . . and I think I could be with Rick. He's that kind of man. So if he asks about me, tell him—you know, in an offhand way—that it's over with me and Billy. And that he really ought to overlook what happened last night. Tell him I'm a lot more down-to-earth than I seem. That isn't a lie, is it?"

chapter
THIRTY-FOUR

rick sat in a corner of the booth, Carlos across from him. It was the same Cuban diner that he'd taken C.J. to that first day. Rick wasn't hungry, but Carlos ordered a *media noche* to hold him until dinner. They talked about this and that and had some espresso, and finally Judy Mazzio came in about a quarter to six. Carlos scooted over and made room for her.

After Carlos signed the original and two copies of his statement, Judy signed as notary and stamped the papers with her seal. Carlos looked at his watch and said he had to get home. Rick stood up and gave him a quick hug. "Thanks, man. I'll let you know if it works."

Judy Mazzio was about to leave too, but Rick said, "Can you stay a few minutes? I'd like to ask you something."

"I need to get this faxed to the Beach . . . sure, I have time. Fuentes will be there a while." She sat back down, watching him. Her black hair was held in place on top of her head with a purple ribbon.

He asked her, "How's C.J.? I haven't heard from her."

"She's fine. We took her car to the shop and had lunch."

"Maybe I'll go over later and check on her."

Like a lot of older women, the ones who knew what was what, Judy had eyes that could look farther into you than the front of your face. She said, "C.J. is a good person. She might have some issues, but she's my best friend. If you mess her up, I will come after you."

He might have smiled, but the brown eyes were pinning him. "I'm not going to mess her up. I hope not to."

Judy Mazzio studied him for a minute before she crossed her arms and sat back against the booth. "Don't go over there now. She's getting ready to go out. Call her mobile at eight-fifteen. She'll be at Billy Medina's house at eight o'clock to ask him some questions about your case. I think it would be neat if Billy knew you were on the phone." Judy made a smile he couldn't read. "It's over between her and Billy."

Rick looked at her a while longer. "Good."

Judy had apparently decided she liked Rick Slater well enough to say, "He's cheating on her. That's not why she called it off. She called it off because, basically, he's an asshole. I haven't told her yet about the other women, but I will. I just found out a couple of days ago from Harold Vincent. He was telling me about it."

"The pornographer."

"Well . . . yeah. And he was complaining about Billy Medina. A funny world, huh? C.J. met Billy in AA, and he's the reason she stopped going. After he quit, she quit. He was never any good for her."

Rick was folding a napkin into a tight square. He'd heard that no matter how thin the paper, it wouldn't fold in half more than eight times. "Has he ever hit her?"

Judy showed some surprise. "No. If he had, I'd have known, trust me. Why are you asking me that?"

"No reason."

"I'll tell you about Billy. He has a hotel and casino on Antigua, him and a couple of other guys. He wants to get into online gaming, that's why he hooked up with Harold, so he could learn about it, but after Harold taught him everything he knew, Billy would have nothing more to do with him. I mean, an upstanding citizen like Guillermo Medina does not associate with pornographers, does he? C.J. wanted Billy to ask Harold about Alana, and he wouldn't do it. He's afraid the other investors of The Aquarius would find out he knows people like Harold Vincent, and they'd kick him off the team. They probably would. Billy wants to open a casino in The Aquarius when it's legal, and he thinks someday it will be. That's why he invested in it and threw money at Paul Shelby's campaign. Asshole."

Rick folded the napkin six, then seven times. "C.J. told me that Billy introduced Alana to Harold Vincent. Is that right?"

Judy nodded. "Billy told her. There's a lot about Billy Medina that doesn't show on the surface. C.J. is finally starting to get it."

The paper wouldn't go into a ninth fold. The muscles in Rick's forearms stood out. Giving up, he twisted the paper apart and tossed the pieces into his empty coffee cup. "What's she going to talk to Billy about? You said my case. What does that mean?" When Judy only looked back at him, he said, "I'm the client. You work for me, too, technically."

She twirled a strand of hair around her finger, waiting for someone to walk by. "C.J. believes that Paul Shelby did it. You know. Alana went there to meet someone, right? C.J. thinks it was him, and they argued or she said she wanted money, whatever. C.J. told me how you can get to the property next door, and she thinks it happened there. Except how did Shelby leave afterward? Not in a taxi, because you have to wait too long that time of night. She thinks he called someone. His mother. They put Alana in the car and took off. What C.J. wants to ask Billy is, did he see Shelby leave? Or did Shelby just split and not say anything? You can tell a lot from a person's actions."

"Alana was taken out in the back of Milo's limousine," Rick said.

Judy shook her head. "C.J. doesn't think so."

Even after listening to Judy Mazzio explain it, Rick wasn't convinced. No bloodstains in the backseat or the trunk. No hairs. Someone could have cleaned it. After she'd left, heading for the Beach with the statements, Rick got into his car and called Carlos Moreno.

Inez answered, and he got the frosty treatment for a minute before she relented and asked if he wanted to come over for dinner. "Gee, Inez, I'd love to but I have to go somewhere. Could you put Carlos on?" While he waited, he heard a TV in the background, sounded like a weatherman showing where the band of thunderstorms would come through. Carlos picked up.

"Carlos, I need you to go into my files and get a phone number for me."

Julio Sandoval had been Milo Cahill's masseur for five years. He was a wiry man with blue-tinted glasses and a narrow black beard. Rick had first talked to Julio about six weeks ago, getting a general sense of what it was like, working for Milo Cahill. Julio was quick to roll his eyes and dish the dirt. He couldn't be too picky about his clients, though. He and his wife were expecting a baby and needed the cash.

Julio had said, "I've been in this business for fifteen years, and I am very, very good. I am the only one who can work the knots out of Milo Cahill's back. He wants me over there almost every freaking day. I bring my table, but half the time Milo is never on it. Oh, Julio, would you run over to Epicure and pick up some steaks? I am a licensed massage therapist, and I have to put up with this shit? Julio, would you fix me some tea? Would you give Princess a bath? That dog. I've never hated an animal so much in my life."

Rick got in touch with Julio and asked if he could come by. Julio said sure, but he didn't have much time. They were going out to a movie with some friends. "I'll come down to the lobby, okay?"

"You're lucky I'm here at all," Julio said as he directed Rick to a corner away from the entrance. They sat on a bench done in turquoise vinyl. "I was supposed to be at Milo's tonight, but he cancelled. He has a business meeting, that hideous resort he's designing. He gave everyone the night off. He does that, cancels at the last minute, which is fine with me because he has to pay for it anyway."

Rick said he wanted to ask Julio about the weekend that Alana Martin had disappeared. Had he been at Milo's house that Sunday and the few days after that? If so, had Milo asked him to clean the interior of the limousine? Had Julio seen anyone else do it? Maybe even Milo?

"I wasn't there on Sunday. I stayed home. I'd been out so late the night before, taking Milo to the party, I said fuck it, I am not coming over there today, and he said fine, don't."

"You drove him to Medina's house?"

"Yes. He asked me, and I said not unless you pay me two hundred dollars. And he did! I called my wife. We had plans to go out, but she said take the money, fool. Milo has a room full of costumes, I kid you not, and he made me wear a black suit and a cap. I drove him to the party in that ridiculous car, ten miles to the gallon.

Someone should throw a match into the gas tank. We got there about eleven o'clock. I couldn't just stop on the street and wait for Milo to get out, could I? No, I had to go around the circular driveway, under the portico, and jump out and open his door so he could properly greet his fans and admirers. He didn't want me to go in, of course, his *chauffeur*. How would it look?"

"You stayed with the car?"

"I parked it down the street and listened to my iPod. Milo didn't want the valets touching his precious vehicle. When Milo called me, I picked him up and took him home. He was whining that he needed his back massaged. He gave me another hundred bucks. I didn't get home until two in the morning. There was no way I was going to run over there again on Sunday."

"Jesus Christ." Elbows on his knees, Rick dropped his forehead into his hands.

After a while Julio said, "Is that all? I need to get back upstairs."

Arching over downtown Miami on the Interstate, Rick had to turn on his windshield wipers in a light drizzle. As he turned more toward the west, he could see the thunderheads moving in, before the trees blotted out his view.

Ten minutes later, he was parking alongside the wall outside Noreen and Donald Finch's house in Coral Gables. He had a key to Paul Shelby's office that Noreen had asked him to return. As an excuse, it wasn't brilliant, but it would do.

Donald Finch opened the door holding a rocks glass. His sandy blond hair was rumpled, and his eyes were bloodshot. "Rick! Come in." In the living room Finch put a hand on his shoulder. "I'm sorry about everything. It wasn't my decision to let you go. I hope you know that."

"Absolutely. No hard feelings. Is Mrs. Finch around? I'll give her my regards. I have something to drop off."

"She's upstairs. Do you want a drink?"

"No, thanks, I'm on my way home."

Donald Finch walked to the bottom of the stairs and called up, "Noreen! Noreen, my sweet, you have company." A muffled voice floated down. Finch said, "Richard Slater."

The living room had some French doors on the other side that opened onto a wide terrace under a roof and, beyond that, a pool on the right and, straight ahead, one of the canals in Coral Gables that led out to the bay. Rick walked over to the doors and looked through. Raindrops were dotting the surface of the pool, and he could see slashes of rain against the darker water of the canal. The boat was up on davits, about a twenty-four-footer, with a cover tied over it.

Finch gestured with his drink. "They say it's going to rain all weekend. Good for the flowers, bad for my golf game."

"I see you've got a boat back there. Do you fish?"

"God, no. Never liked it."

"When was the last time you cranked the engine? You can't let them sit."

"We don't. Noreen takes it out sometimes, just putt-putting around with our friends. Good party boat, actually."

"She knows boats, does she?"

"Noreen can do everything. She can rope a calf. I swear. I've seen her." Donald Finch took a sip of his drink. "My wife."

"Mr. Finch, I'm curious about something. The night of the party at Guillermo Medina's house, when that girl disappeared, I had Mr. Shelby's Cadillac. How did he get home? I felt kind of bad leaving him there, but he said I could go."

"Well, I don't know. Paul didn't say anything about it to me." He looked past Rick and said, "There she is, my lovely, calf-roping bride."

How long had she been standing there? Noreen Finch's platinum hair was swept back on one side, and her lips were a slash of red. She wore a white silk top and blue jeans with sequins down the sides. They didn't do much for her figure.

"Mr. Slater, I said you could pick up your check on Monday. We don't keep the checkbook here."

He held up the key. "I wanted to return this. It's for the front door of Mr. Shelby's office."

She didn't blink. He had noticed that about her; she rarely blinked her eyes. She came over and held out her hand, and Rick dropped the key into it. He said, "I was just asking your husband how Mr. Shelby got home from the party. Do you know?"

"What kind of question is that?"

"I feel bad about stranding him."

"No, he got home all right, so don't you worry about it. Donald, I'm going to walk Rick out. Fix me a drink, will you?" She took Rick's arm and turned him toward the front door. "You're such a mystery to me."

"I am?"

"You are. I never know what you're thinking. It would be nice to believe that people who work for us have some degree of loyalty, but it's not always that way. When you're in the public arena, in politics, there are always those who, for one reason or another, want to bring you down. That's a sad fact. I have a real good sense about people, and when my alarm goes off, I listen. That's why we let you go. I don't know who you are."

She opened the door. "Let me save you a trip to the office. Your lawyer still owes us some money for the deposit we gave her, so you just tell Ms. Dunn to take your two weeks' severance out of that and send us what's left."

The light in the left-turn lane on Twenty-Second was yellow when he got to it, red as he went through. The pickup truck behind him went through as well, not unusual for Miami. You couldn't proceed on a green light without first checking to see what idiot was running the red light.

The truck was a fairly recent Ford 150, black or dark blue. Rick would have ignored it if it hadn't kept a steady distance behind him, speeding up to make the light, then slowing not to come too close. The humidity had fogged his rear window, making it impossible to see the driver's face. Another vehicle came up close behind the truck. Its headlights shone through, turning the driver into a silhouette. Eyes on his rearview mirror, Rick studied the shape. The shoulders were wide, and hair hung to his collar. The rest of it was combed straight up. It made the top of his head look like a paintbrush.

"Hey, Dennis. What are you doing back there?"

When Rick reached the gate of his apartment complex, he kept on going and took a right onto *Calle Ocho*. The pickup fell back, and a car cut in ahead of it, but a few blocks later Rick saw it again.

chapter

THIRTY-FIVE

billy came to the door barefoot, wearing loose straw-colored linen slacks and an unbuttoned long-sleeved guayabera that he might have just thrown on. His silver hair was damp from a shower, the comb marks still in it. The hair on his chest was black, and a heavy gold chain gleamed at his neck. He was beautiful, and from habit, or some fatal weakness, she felt pulled toward him like a moth to flame, and despised herself for it. Billy kissed her cheek, then stood back and took inventory of what she was wearing: pink crop pants and a white top with three-quarter sleeves.

"You look like you're on your way to a PTA meeting."

"Be kind to me, Billy. I woke up with a hangover." She moved past him into the living room.

"Did you? Welcome back to the real world. What can I fix you? Hair of the dog? Milk of magnesia on the rocks?"

"Nothing right now, thanks."

The clouds obscured what sun remained, and halogens in the ceiling lit the white marble floors, the leather-covered furniture, the polished railing that curved up the stairs to the balcony on the second level. C.J. put her purse on one of the sofas that made a U-shape, facing the pool.

Billy would want her to stay tonight. In the past, when she had refused, it had been lack of time, or a bad mood, not because she hadn't wanted him. Did she still? Or was the wanting a sudden awareness that something was gone? Like putting the tip of her tongue to the place in her jaw where a molar had been wrenched out. What was it? Desire or its absence?

He stood behind her. She could see his reflection in the glass. Tall and slender, hands in his pockets, the light on his hair. Waiting for her to make the first move. Billy never pushed.

C.J. said, "I turned down the job hosting the show on CNN. They offered it to me, but I called them back and said no. You were right, Billy. It's no good being in the spotlight."

"Just when I was getting used to the idea of having a famous girlfriend. That's all right. Something else may come along you like better." He put his hands on her shoulders, his thumbs digging into the tight muscles up her spine, the way she liked it. "You haven't called since our spat. I guess it was a spat. When I let you in just now, I realized I've missed you. I'll be gone for two weeks. Are you sure you can't come with me? Or fly down next weekend? My treat."

She was afraid if she turned around he would kiss her. She said, "I'm sorry, Billy. I have more to do than I can handle right now."

"You make too much to do. You need to let it go and enjoy life." He lifted her hair and put his lips to the back of her neck.

"Please don't," she said, drawing away.

His dark eyes studied her for a time. "That's it, then."

"I'm sorry, Billy."

"Yeah, me too. Things were getting a little stale." A flicker of dissatisfaction pulled his lips down. He'd rather have been the one to pull the plug.

"You won't be alone for long," she said.

Billy asked, "Have you been fucking your client?" When a breath left her lips, and she turned away, Billy's smile followed her. "You have, haven't you?"

"No."

"Oh, baby, I knew you liked it down and dirty, but Slater is so beneath you."

"Shut up, Billy. I haven't slept with him, not that it's any of your business." To avoid his penetrating gaze, C.J. took some steps toward the windows. She stopped, her attention caught by something that hadn't been there before. She pointed across the room. "What is that?"

At the bottom of the stairs, between the vast living room and the hall that led toward the dining room, she had noticed a white marble statue, an abstract female form. The top curled over itself, leaving an empty oval for a face.

Billy followed her when she went to look at it. "It's a replacement for the one you bought me. I thought about calling you to come look at it in the gallery, but I wasn't sure you'd want to."

She slid her hand down the surface. "This is so you, Billy."

"Hard?"

"I was thinking smooth. Cool. Impenetrable."

"Do you like it?"

"I'm not sure. Obviously carved by a man."

"How can you tell?"

She smiled. "Women do not carve female figures with a hole where their head should be." She slid her hand over the top. "Was it very expensive?"

"Twenty-five thousand."

"My God."

"As I told you, things are looking up for me." He walked around it, and she went the other way. He leaned down and peered at her through the hole. "You're being elusive tonight. Why did you come over? Fess up."

"I have a question about Paul Shelby."

"Aha. You're playing lawyer again. Does this mean we're not going upstairs later, for old time's sake?"

"It means I have a question. The night of your party, how did he leave? I suppose he came to say good-bye to you. Was he with anyone? Did he take a taxi?"

"Why?"

"Humor me."

"No, I'm not going to humor you. When someone asks me questions, I like knowing what the purpose is."

"The police are still looking at my client as a possible suspect in the murder of Alana Martin, and I want to clear him. I believe Paul Shelby killed her."

Billy laughed; then, when she didn't join him in laughter, said, "Paul Shelby? Have you gone nuts?"

"He was having sex with Alana Martin. I believe she blackmailed him, and he killed her."

"Paul Shelby and . . . that girl?" Billy stared at her. "Paul wouldn't touch a girl like that."

"Well, he did. Milo Cahill was arranging it. Alana was Shelby's payment for supporting The Aquarius."

"Milo? Now I know you've gone crazy."

"It's true. I think Alana wanted money from Paul Shelby to get out of Miami. They argued. Maybe he didn't intend in advance to kill her, but it happened."

"Here? In my house?"

"Not in your house. I don't know where, somewhere outside, possibly next door. He panicked. His driver had left. He had to call someone to come get him. I don't know who. But if he left in a taxi, then I'm wrong."

"Oh, baby." Billy laughed again. "You are wrong."

"Tell me."

"Paul came to me and said he was stuck. His driver had left, and he couldn't seem to get a taxi. I asked one of my security people to take him home. Uh-oh. That's not what you wanted to hear."

"You didn't tell me about this when we talked before!"

Billy spread his arms wide. "Well, maybe you didn't ask."

C.J. went over and sat down and put her head in her hands.

He sat beside her and patted her knee. "Cheer up, baby. Our politicians might be thieves and liars, but they rarely commit murder."

"I was so sure."

"You need a drink."

"No."

"A teeny one. Medicinal purposes. You overdid it last night, but you look none the worse for wear. I won't let you go too far." He nudged her playfully. "How about it? Don't let me drink alone. Bombay Sapphire and tonic, twist of lime?"

She shook her head. "A club soda."

With a laugh, he said, "Your problem is, you can't take anything in moderation. Sit there and relax. I'll get it."

His soft linen trousers flowed around his legs. She had already noticed that he wasn't wearing underwear, leaving everything to move around under the fabric. He had done this for her. It used to turn her on. He was waiting for her to change her mind, to get on her knees, to say she must've been crazy, letting him go.

The statue without a face seemed to gaze back at her. The one she had bought for Billy had deserved to be thrown out. Of course he hadn't liked it. He hated flowers, and those had been so phony and cheap. She had thought the shine of the leaves and petals would fit with his house, but he had stuck the statue in a dark corner of his dining room where, forgotten, the bolts through the plaster base had left rust spots on his marble floor. Dennis Murphy had chipped out the tiles and replaced them.

C.J. turned her head and for several seconds stared in the direction of the dining room. She could see the wide arch from where she sat. Without looking away from it, she reached for her purse and felt around for the piece of paper she had put in there earlier, the fax from Judy Mazzio. As if pulled, she got up and crossed the living room, her heels clicking softly on the floor.

Standing in the entrance, she looked at the oriental carpet, the silver-framed Rufino Tamayo paintings of women over the buffet, the chandelier that reflected in the surface of the long table. The corner was empty. The new tiles were exactly the same as the old ones.

At the art show last February, C.J. had touched the petals and leaves, then the curling stamens of the flowers, how whimsical to make such a delicate thing out of steel. She had even talked to the artist and asked how he'd done it. C.J. had paid the money, and the artist and his son had loaded the statue into her trunk and tied the lid down with some rope. By the time they reached Billy's house, Dennis was there, and he carried it into the house by himself as easily as he had lifted the poured-concrete cherub in the backyard of Noreen Finch's house.

C.J. held the unfolded page at arm's length. The medical examiner had laid the piece of metal next to a ruler, but she could see it coming out of the center of a flower, a curl of steel, something like a corkscrew, but longer and more delicate.

From behind her, Billy asked, "What are you doing?"

chapter
THIRTY-SIX

On the south side of the Miami River, just before the last drawbridge, lay a mostly-forgotten area of boat-repair shops, rusted-out warehouses, and cramped concrete-block houses. The people who lived in the houses were too poor to move. Or maybe they liked the fact that city inspectors overlooked the chickens in the backyard and roofs with mismatched tiles. One of the few businesses still hanging on was an off-brand service station with a convenience store inside. The place smelled of stale coffee and hot-dog grease, and the owner kept a shotgun behind the counter. Rick didn't mind this. The fuel prices were low, they carried his brands of beer in the cooler, and he liked to kid around with the owner's sister, Nelia, who ran the cash register. The owner himself was a former flyweight boxer with wrist-to-shoulder tattoos and a crucifix on a heavy gold chain. Fernando had been born in the same general area of Mexico where Rick had spent the past two years. He had offered to hook Rick up with whatever he wanted. Rick hadn't asked what that might be, but he assumed a wide selection to choose from.

Rick nosed his Audi up to the front windows and cut his lights and windshield wipers. It had started to rain, a light drizzle. An old man shuffled out the heavy, smudged glass door and wandered off down the street. Glancing through his tinted side window, Rick could see the front end of a Ford pickup truck drift to a stop at the curb, lights off. He leaned over and unlocked the glove compartment and took his Smith and Wesson out of its holster. After routinely checking the magazine and making sure the safety was on, he jammed the gun into the waist of his trousers and pulled his Hawaiian print shirt down to cover it.

Nelia saw him through the glass and hit the buzzer. She waved and smiled. Her skin was marked with acne scars, but her body justified the bulletproof glass separating her cubicle from the customers outside.

Rick lifted a hand in greeting. "Hey, sweetheart. Is Fernando around?"

"In the back with the mop. *Ese maricón* that just left? He peed on the floor."

"I'm surprised you didn't shoot him."

"Yeah, if I'd seen him doing it."

Rick found Fernando by the coolers with a mop and bucket, spraying the floor with industrial disinfectant. "What's up, my man?" Fernando said. "I seen you on TV. You're famous."

"I could do without it," Rick said. "Listen, I've got a guy following me. He's parked on the street. I want to go ask him about it. Could you unlock the back door for me?"

Fernando's eyes lit up. "You want some help?"

"No, thanks. I can handle it. You wouldn't have any duct tape, would you?"

"Aisle three, next to the motor oil." Fernando took the mop out of the bucket. "Just don't leave him on the premises when you're done, okay?"

Rick took a roll of heavy-duty duct tape to the counter to pay for it. "Nelia, how would you like to do me a favor?"

A minute later, when the steel delivery door had quietly closed behind him and the lock had turned, Rick looked around. Darkness was falling early due to the heavy clouds, but shreds of daylight remained. A wooden fence went around the property, and beyond that a vacant lot sloped down to the river. Somebody had kicked enough boards out of the fence to make a shortcut. He walked past the Dumpster, crouched down, and went to the corner of the building. Looking toward the street, Rick estimated ten yards from the building to the sidewalk, which was heavily shaded with trees. Beyond that, the Ford sat with its engine idling. A couple of cars went by. An arm came out of the window with a cigarette and flicked some ashes. A humid breeze took the smoke.

Rick lifted the edge on the duct tape and pulled. It made a soft ripping noise. He pressed the tape to the side of the building, which was still dry, and the roll dangled there. He took his pistol from under his shirt and held it next to his thigh and waited. Nelia appeared, swaying her molten hips. She wore tight jeans and a low-cut pink top, and the circles of her earrings gleamed against her dark skin. As she walked, she looked up at the sky and popped open an umbrella. She moved on an angle toward the truck, close enough to touch the hood. She twirled the umbrella and waited for a car to pass, then stepped off the curb. In the truck, Dennis Murphy watched her, his head turning toward the street.

Rick moved fast. He came up to the driver's side, pinned Murphy's arm to the door, and put the barrel of the gun to his neck, snugging it tight under the curve of his skull.

Murphy jerked, and the cigarette dropped to the pavement. "What the fuck?" Rick's fingers were clamped hard above his left elbow.

"Don't move. I have a forty-five calibur pistol that could blow your brains through the roof of this truck. Take the keys out of the ignition and toss them out the window. Easy."

Murphy's eyes darted side to side as if someone might be around to witness this. No one was. "What do you want?"

"The keys. Throw them out."

Murphy laughed. "You're putting yourself in a bad spot, man." The keys jangled on the cracked concrete.

"Now you. Get out. Slow." Murphy reached across with his right hand for the door release. Shifting as the door slowly came open, Rick moved the pistol around the window frame and pressed it again to Murphy's head. One sneaker hit the ground, then the other. "Turn around, face the door." Murphy was a couple of inches shorter. This worked to Rick's advantage as he quickly slid his left arm around the other man's throat and squeezed hard, using pressure on his carotid arteries to cut off his blood supply.

Murphy struggled, but after a few seconds his body sagged. Rick maintained the pressure a while longer, and, when he was sure Murphy was out, dragged him toward the rear of the building. Nelia was coming back. She glanced Rick's way and kept walking.

Raindrops whispered in the tall weeds that had grown up through the pitted rocks along the river bank. Past the chain-link fence, the hammering of metal on metal and the hiss of acetylene torches came from the night shift at the boat works. The scent of diesel fuel, rotting vegetation, and muck drifted downwind. Rick crouched next to Dennis Murphy and waited for him to wake up.

Murphy lay face up on a ragged sheet of plywood, feet on land, head a few inches from the oily water. His ankles and knees were bound with duct tape; his arms were behind him, secured at the wrist. Across the river a two-story office building had closed for the night: nobody over there looking out a window.

When he woke up, it took a minute for Murphy to grasp his situation. Rick poked his shoulder. "Why were you following me?"

Murphy lifted his head off the plywood. "Fuck you."

Rick stood up, put a foot on Murphy's chest, and shifted his weight toward the downhill end of the plywood. It went under, and the water swirled up, reaching Murphy's head, then his shoulders. "Did Noreen Finch send you after me?"

Murphy took a lung full of air and screamed, "Help!" Rick leaned forward and Murphy went under. Bubbles came up. He counted to ten. When Murphy's head reappeared, his spiked red hair was flattened to his skull. He spat out water.

"Talk to me, Dennis. Maybe you'd rather go swimming. Nobody would notice. You'd drift out to the bay, probably be cut up by boat propellers, turned into fish food." Rick sat on his heels beside him. "Did Noreen tell you to follow me?"

"No!"

Rick slapped him across the face. Then again. When he thought he had his attention, he leaned closer. "Did she tell you to kill Alana Martin? Or did Shelby do it?"

"You're crazy. Let me go."

"See if this makes sense to you, Dennis. Paul Shelby killed her, and Noreen Finch drove over and helped him get the body off the island. Did you help them? Is that what happened?"

"No! Jesus Fucking Christ, no."

He tried to roll away, but Rick dragged him toward the water. His shoes lost some traction on the algae-slick wood, and he slipped to his knees. Water rushed over his legs. He put both hands on Dennis Murphy's chest and counted slowly to ten, then hooked his belt and hauled him out. "Who murdered Alana? Was it Paul Shelby?"

A spray of water came from Murphy's mouth. He dragged in some air and coughed on it. "No! Fuck! Let me go. I don't know anything about it!" A scrap of sodden plastic bag stuck to his cheek, and Rick lifted it off.

"Did you help them put Alana's body in Noreen's boat that night? Maybe the next morning? What did you tie the body to so it would sink? You didn't do a very good job. She floated up again."

Murphy wheezed. "I didn't kill her. I swear."

"If it wasn't you, was it Shelby? or Noreen? Had to be one or the other, Dennis. Which one?"

"I don't know, man. I don't know anything."

"Let's see how long you can hold your breath." Rick stepped on the end of the board and Murphy went under. When he came up again, Rick said, "Showtime, Dennis. No more bullshit. I'm ready to push you in. Was it Shelby? Yes or no?"

"I don't know!"

A blow across his cheekbone sent his head whiplashing to one side. The next blow split his lip. "What happened to Alana Martin? I'll fucking put you in the river."

"Don't! I didn't kill her. Don't put me in there. It was Billy. He did it."

"Medina?" Rick sat there a minute thinking, then gave Murphy a shove. "Were you there? Did he cut her up?"

Murphy shook his head. "Nobody cut her up. She came to the party. They went upstairs to talk. It was an accident. I helped him get rid of her body. That's all I did. Tied her to a metal statue. Took it out on his boat."

"Jesus." Rick had to take a breath. "Why did he do it? Why did Billy kill her?"

"She was threatening him." Murphy coughed. "She acted in some porno movie. A friend of Billy's had the tapes. She thought Billy could get them back."

"This friend of Billy's. Is his name Harold Vincent?"

"Yeah."

"She threatened Billy. How?"

"Alana said if he didn't get her the tapes, she'd go to the newspaper, the TV, shit like that. I don't know. They were upstairs during the party. She went after him, and he pushed her. She hit her head. It was an accident."

"You believe that?"

"I don't know."

Rain ticked on the wood and dotted the slow-moving surface of the river. Rick could feel it on his shoulders and back. "Did Billy send you after me?"

"Yeah. Didn't trust you. Too many questions about Alana."

"What did Billy tell you to do to me?"

"Fuck you up." Dennis Murphy laughed through bloody teeth. "I was supposed to fuck you up."

"That's nice. Fuck me up, huh? Maybe send me to the Everglades in pieces? Is that what he had in mind?"

"I wouldn't have."

"Uh-huh."

Murphy spat out some blood. "I told you everything. Untie me. How about it?"

"Can't let you go, Dennis."

"What are you going to do?"

Rick grabbed him by the ankles and dragged him into the weeds. His shirt came up, and he moaned when his back scraped the rocks. Holding him under the arms, Rick hauled him over to a twisted tree trunk near the fence and propped him against it. He found the roll of duct tape where he'd left it, picked at the free end, and spun it out. He wrapped the tape around the tree trunk and Murphy's torso, pinning his arms. He tore off another piece and got it over Murphy's mouth and twice around his head.

The rain was coming down, and the wind bent the tall grasses. In the dim light Rick could see a pair of small, pale blue eyes glittering with rage. Rick patted Murphy on the shoulder. "The cops will be coming by later on to pick you up."

Breathing hard, more from nerves than exertion, Rick trotted back through the vacant lot behind the gas station, went around, and left Dennis Murphy's keys on the seat of the truck. It might be there later, it might not. Fuck him. Rick got into his car. He wiped the rain off his face and put his pistol back into the glove compartment. He didn't lock it. He wanted to be able to get to the gun easily when he arrived at Billy Medina's house. C.J. would be there. He thought about the bruises on her arm. If Billy had touched her, Rick would break both his knees and then shoot him.

His hands were shaking as he jammed the key into the ignition.

chapter
THIRTY-SEVEN

as Billy stood there with a glass in each hand, waiting for her to explain, C.J. folded the page.

"It's just a picture of a piece of metal they found with Alana Martin's body. They don't know what it is. I thought of the flowers that used to be here, but it's not the same."

"Let me see it."

"It's nothing. I had that statue on my mind. You didn't like it. That's all right." She walked past him.

His bare feet were silent on the smooth floor, but in the windows she could see him behind her. The buildings downtown were gone, swallowed up in rain. Lightning flickered. "There's a storm. It's coming this way. You know, I really ought to get home before it breaks."

The car keys were in her purse, which seemed impossibly distant, a white dot on the black leather sofa.

Two slight thuds, Billy setting the drinks on the coffee table. "If you leave now, you'll drive right into it." He reached for her hand. "Stay and have a drink with me, a real drink."

"I really can't."

"Why is your hand so cold?"

"Is it?"

"Yes, very cold." He squeezed her fingers.

"It's your house. And the rain—I was chilled coming in."

"Show me the picture. Come on, C.J. Let's see what you have in your pocket." He caught her around the waist and had the paper in his hand before she could swivel away. He shook the page open. "Yes. I saw this too. You're wrong. There's no way in hell this piece of metal, whatever it is, came off my statue."

"I just said that, Billy." The muscles in her legs were quivering. She wondered if they would carry her outside. "The flowers, I mean that part of the flowers, was much curlier. And different metal. Not at all the same."

"But you're wondering about it." He tossed the page to the sofa. "Aren't you? I've been wondering about it too. I had the statue in the garage and then it was gone. I asked Dennis, and he said he had taken it to his house. He asked me if that was okay, and I said sure. I didn't want it anymore."

"Dennis took it?"

"I think . . . this sounds crazy, but I think he may have had something to do with Alana's disappearance."

"You do?" C.J.'s purse was out of reach on the middle of the three sofas, formed into a square, with a large coffee table in the middle, blocking her way.

Billy said, "I think Dennis used that statue to sink her body."

C.J. nodded. "It was heavy enough. Why did he do it?"

"Dennis knows Harold Vincent. Did some handyman jobs for his travel agency. I recommended him."

"Did you?" C.J. walked casually, slowly across the floor. "So Harold Vincent was in it too?"

Billy was behind her. "I think you were right about Harold. The pornography. Alana was involved with him. He knows dangerous people. Desperate people. You asked me to talk to him, and I did. Remember you asked me? I talked to Harold, and he said that Alana was causing major, major problems for him, wanting her audition tapes. I tried to get some answers, but he wouldn't elaborate. I didn't call you about it because, well, I didn't think you wanted to see me anymore."

"The tapes," she said. "That must be it." Her heart was beating so fast and hard she was afraid he could hear it. She took a breath to calm herself. It didn't work. Her purse was straight ahead. The car keys inside it. She kept moving. "I never liked Dennis. Something about him. If, as you say, he worked for Harold Vincent, and Alana was causing Vincent major problems, then he had a reason to get rid of her, so he sent Dennis, and . . . and Dennis kidnapped and murdered her."

"But we can't prove anything, can we?" Billy took C.J.'s elbow and turned her around.

She didn't want to look in his face, afraid he would see too much, but she lifted her chin and said, "No, we can't prove it. We have no evidence. Even the statue is gone. We can't do anything."

"Oh, C.J." Billy's black brows came together as though he'd felt a sudden pain.

"We can't tell anyone," she said again. "I think all we can do . . . is let it go. We can't accuse Harold Vincent or Dennis either, without proof. They would sue us for slander."

"You know, don't you? You know."

"About lawsuits, you mean. Oh, yes. My advice is, do nothing

for the moment. We'll talk when you come back from Antigua."
C.J. was walking backward now, Billy holding on to her fingertips.
"Call me when you get there. I should leave and let you finish pack-
ing. Billy, let go."

"I'm so sorry." And then he turned her around, and his arm was
across her throat. "Sorrier than you can imagine, C.J."

Her scream stopped as her breathing was cut off.

He kissed the side of her face, letting his lips linger there. "Alana
wanted the audition tapes. She wanted me to tell Harold to give
them to her. She thought he was my friend, and he'd do it for me.
He told me to go to hell. When I told her that, she didn't believe
it. She thought I had some influence over him. I'm not in the porn
business, but she was threatening me, and I knew it would get out.
She would have told someone. I'd have lost The Aquarius. I'd have
lost everything. Do you see? I couldn't let it go on."

C.J. dragged in a breath. "Billy, please."

"That damned statue. The base was plaster. It fell apart in the
ocean. I didn't think about that, but you would have. You'd have
used marble."

"Billy, there's no evidence. There's nothing. The statue is gone.
Whatever you did, nobody can prove it."

"Can I trust you not to say anything? Can I, *chica?* Would you
do that for me?"

"Of course I would. Yes, Billy. I won't say anything. How could
I? We mean too much to each other."

"My sweet, sweet liar." His lips were at her ear. "You just broke
up with me. Good-bye, Billy. It's over. You wanted Rick Slater. Yes,
you did. When I saw you and him together, I could smell the sex
between you. What a slut you are. But I liked that about you."

Her shoes slid across the floor as he dragged her across the room.

"I promise you one thing. It will be quick. No pain."

When she tried to speak again, his arm tightened, choking off her words.

Billy said, "Yes, Detective, when she came over tonight I could see she was depressed. She'd been offered a job on CNN, and she gave it up. She said she couldn't handle it. I went to the kitchen to make us some drinks, and when I came back, she was in the pool. I never heard her calling for help. I think she didn't want any help. I think she just wanted to end it."

C.J. grabbed for the back of a chair as they passed it, but she couldn't hold on. They had reached the last of the sliding doors leading out to the terrace. The pool glowed blue through the glass.

He would drag her outside, put her head under, and wait for her to drown.

"It's so sad. I loved her."

The edges of her vision softened, and she started to drift. Was this what it was like, dying? This easy surrender, this letting go? She wouldn't feel the water, wouldn't feel anything. No pain. It was what Paul had said. This won't hurt. You'll like it.

How strange. She could see Paul's face over her, and his hands were on her throat, squeezing gently, then harder, harder, and his knee was pushing her legs apart. But she didn't want it. She didn't want this.

C.J. twisted her head and was rewarded with a small gasp of air. The will to live surged through her like a jolt of pure oxygen. She would not die, not like this, not a quiet victim, not letting it happen without a fight.

C.J. dug her fingers into Billy's arm, but the sleeve prevented her nails from getting through. She tried to reach up and claw his eyes, but he jerked his face out of the way and tightened his grip.

She bucked and twisted and kicked her feet. They came off the floor as she hung onto his arm.

Billy stopped at the panel of light switches and reached around to turn off the pool lights. She knew what he wanted, to drown her in darkness where no one could see, and to turn the lights on again before he called the police.

"No!" C.J. lifted a knee and with all her strength brought her heel down on his instep.

He screamed and bent over, and in that brief moment she wrenched herself away from him. She sped through the living room, calculating that it wouldn't do any good to reach her keys because he could drag her out of her car before she started the engine. She grabbed a brass bowl off the coffee table and threw it at him. As it clanged on the floor, she abruptly turned left into a long hallway, past the media center, past a bathroom, past the downstairs guest suite. Another turn, she would be at the side door.

It was locked. Billy was moving toward her; reaching. She felt his hand slide off her shoulder, felt some of her hair rip from her scalp. She could hear her own ragged breathing.

The hall led left again. Stairs going up. Another door to the garage, a dead end. The kitchen with the gleaming stainless steel and long, black granite counters. A knife block near the stove.

C.J. reached for the handle of the chef's knife and turned to face him. Billy stopped, one hand on the refrigerator for balance. The knife bobbled out of her hand. "Oh!"

He came for her. She grabbed the knife block and threw it. Then blindly reached toward the island in the center of the kitchen and grabbed a bottle—his Dutch gin—and threw that. The bottle smashed on the tile floor. Billy was running, couldn't stop in time, and stepped into the broken glass.

"Ahhhh!" One of the shards had gone into his foot. He bent to pull it out, then his eyes were on her again. "Bitch. You can't get away." But she was already gone, moving past the dining room and into the living room, where the white floor was a vast expanse of winter tundra, a rectangle of bright red at the other side, the front door. She skidded into the door and pulled on the handle, looking over her shoulder.

Billy was limping badly, and his teeth were bared. He had left a trail of blood behind him.

She couldn't get the door open. She swerved away from him. He caught her by the stairs, tripped, and they both went down. She couldn't scream. Billy's hands were on her throat.

chapter
THIRTY-EIGHT

ick Slater stood on the front porch staring at the red entrance doors of Billy Medina's house. He pressed the button again and heard the chimes. Edgar Dunn's old Buick
was in the driveway. C.J. had to be here. Rain bounced off the black
slate in the circular driveway and slanted through the landscaping
lights.

He put his ear to the door. Nothing. Had they gone out? Were
they upstairs in bed? That thought gave him pause. He stood there,
undecided, then walked into the rain and went around the side of
the house. Before he reached the back terrace, his shirt was soaked
and clinging to the pistol he'd stuck into his waistband. The surface
of the pool seemed to vibrate in the rain. He stepped under the
patio roof. The back wall of the house was mostly glass. The inside

lights were on. Billy Medina had a lot of square furniture, low black sofas and chairs, and most of it was turned to face the windows. Lamps arched over the sofas on curved silver poles. Rick saw a marble statue shaped like a woman. He didn't remember it from the last, and only, time he'd been here. He saw the stairs, which floated on metal supports. A balcony above the stairs. Nobody up there.

It might have been the color that caught his attention, a smear of red showing through two of the sofas where they'd been angled into a square. He walked farther to his left, saw more blood. Followed it with his eyes and saw two people on the floor at the bottom of the stairs. Billy Medina and C.J., and she was struggling to get away.

Stepping back, Rick put two bullets into the window. They made two neat holes. The heavy, hurricane-proof glass wouldn't shatter. He aimed at one of the sliding doors and took out the lock. The bullet sparked on the metal. He shoved on the frame.

As he sped across the room, he focused on Billy Medina. Time expanded. He reached them, raised his right arm, and smashed the butt of the pistol against Medina's head, down low where the bone curved into the spine. As Medina collapsed, Rick dropped the gun, grabbed Medina's shoulders, and threw him off C.J. He drew back his fist. Medina wasn't moving.

Rick left him there and shouted, "C.J.!"

She was coughing, wheezing, taking huge gasps of air. He sat her up and propped her against his knee. He pushed her hair off her face, felt her back, her neck. Red marks flamed on the delicate white skin.

"I'm fine. I'm okay," she whispered.

He picked her up off the floor and took her to the nearest sofa. She put her arms around him and held on. "Rick! I thought—I thought I was dying. I found out—he killed Alana."

"I know. I know." Rick smoothed her hair. "I just had a run-in with Dennis Murphy. I had to beat the shit out of him to get the truth. I knew you'd be here. Judy Mazzio told me. I was worried about you and Medina, so I came over."

C.J. looked past him at the man on the floor. "Is he dead?"

Rick could see Medina's chest rising and falling. "He's alive, but his foot's cut. He's bleeding pretty bad. What happened?"

"I threw a bottle, and he stepped on the broken glass." C.J. continued to look at Medina. "Call nine-one-one."

"Why? Let him bleed."

"I need him alive," she said. "You're still a suspect until we can show why not."

"Shit." Rick stripped off one of his shoes, then the sock, which was still wet from the river. He wrapped it around Medina's ankle, knotting it as tightly as it would go. He pulled Medina closer to the stairs, positioning him so his bloody foot would be on one of the steps, above the level of his heart.

He made the call. He gave his name and told them to send an ambulance to Guillermo Medina's house on Star Island. He didn't have the address. The dispatcher said she could look it up. He told her to hurry, a man had stepped on some glass and lost a lot of blood.

Rick found his pistol and dropped it into the thigh pocket of his cargo pants. He sat on the sofa next to C.J. to put his shoe back on, lacing it tightly, jerking hard on the shoelace. He was angry, not with her, but the rage was close to making him want to go pound Medina's head into the floor.

C.J. said, "Where is Dennis Murphy now?"

"I left him duct-taped to a tree by the Miami River. Billy told him to follow me. I think they were planning to send me where they sent Alana. Should I tell the cops to go pick him up now, or wait till we explain about Billy?"

C.J. stared at him, then said, "Is Dennis badly injured?"

"Not really."

"We should tell them when they come for Billy."

Rick said, "Dennis told me that Billy wanted Alana Martin out of the way because she was threatening to link him to Harold Vincent. Is that right?"

"Yes. My God. What a fool I've been." With a little moan, C.J. put her hands lightly on her neck.

"You're going to hurt later on," Rick said.

"I'm fine. If you hadn't come when you did, I wouldn't be."

Rick kissed her arm where he'd seen the bruises. "I should have come after him last night."

"No, I told you, it wasn't Billy."

"Who, then?"

"Paul Shelby. I went over to his office, and we argued—It's not worth talking about. You won't put that in your story, will you?"

Rick shook his head. "No. I'm going after him for the girls that Milo bribed him with. Billy Medina had to be in on that, too. Shelby is going down."

C.J. held Rick's hand tightly. "Write it, Rick. Show Paul Shelby for the snake he is. That's what I want."

"You got it. He's over at Milo's tonight. Yeah. Another of their so-called business meetings. I have a contact in Milo's house. Seems Milo gave everyone the night off. Shelby's wife and kids are out of town. What a coincidence." Rick reached for his phone again. "I'm going to send Carlos over there to take some pictures of Shelby's car. If we can get him coming out, even better. I want to go after the girl, persuade her to talk, pay her if I have to. It's the proof we need to nail Shelby to the wall."

"What girl?"

"I don't know. Whatever girl Milo set him up with." Rick put the phone to his ear.

"We have to stop him," C.J. said.

"Hold on. Let me talk to Carlos."

"Rick, we have to stop him!"

He held up his hand. "Carlos, it's me. There's a lot happening tonight, man. I'll fill you in later, but get right over to Milo Cahill's place. Shelby is there with a girl—" Rick watched C.J. pick up her purse and walk toward the door. "C.J.! What are you doing? Hold on, Carlos."

"I have to go to Milo's. I have to go."

"Carlos, I'll call you back." He caught up with C.J. and held onto her arm. "You can't leave. I want the paramedics to check you out."

"I'm fine. Get out of my way, Rick. I have to go."

"If you go over there now, they'll deny everything." He blocked C.J. when she tried to go around him. "There's nothing you can do. The girl is over eighteen."

"What if it's Kylie? Milo got her an apartment and a job. She trusts him. She had to work tonight, but she didn't go in. I tried to call her and got no answer. Where is she? Where?" C.J.'s voice was trembling.

Rick heard sirens in the distance. "We can't leave now. It's too late. We have to explain to the police—"

"You explain!" She hit him in the chest. "Let me go!"

"What is the matter with you?" He caught her wrists.

"It could be Kylie!"

"Wait for the police!"

"Kylie is my daughter! She's my daughter!" C.J. pulled in a breath. "Let me go. Rick, for God's sake, let me go. It could be Kylie."

"What are you saying?" Rick stared into her eyes.

"Please. Let me go. She's my daughter."

chapter
THIRTY-NINE

n his rearview mirror, Rick watched the emergency response vehicle, siren screaming, lights flashing, turn into the driveway of Billy Medina's house. They wouldn't have a problem getting through the front door. It had been left wide open. Rick went over the bridge and took a fast left on the causeway heading to the beach. For a Friday night, traffic was thin, possibly because of the storm. The rain was coming down in sheets.

"Hurry. Please hurry." C.J. stared out the windshield as if her eyes could get them there faster.

Rick put his hand over hers. "Just tell me where to turn." He knew the way, but it gave her something to concentrate on. Whatever she wanted to say about Kylie, and maybe that was nothing, she could say later.

Finally he got out of the business district and headed into some residential streets. "Kylie's probably not even there," he said.

"If he has touched her, I will kill him."

It took under five minutes to get to Milo Cahill's house. C.J. had her door open before Rick stopped the car. The gate was closed. C.J. ran to a smaller door in the wall just as a flash of lightning lit up the street. She rattled the handle, jerked on it. Rick moved her aside and gave it a couple of kicks, then slammed into it with his shoulder. It finally gave.

A dark green SUV was parked by the garage. Shelby was here. C.J. pointed toward the side yard. They ran around back, pushing past wet foliage between the house and the wall. The terrace shone white in another burst of lightning, then went dim when it faded. Across the Intracoastal, the big condos on Collins Avenue glowed through the downpour.

Rick followed C.J. under a striped canvas awning, where they tried to see through the windows of a room that curved out from the back of the house. The room was lit only by a small lamp beside a rattan chair. The rain beat on the awning like a drum. Rick thought he heard the yapping of a dog. A moment later, a white Panama hat seemed to float across the room, materializing into a man dressed in dark trousers and shirt. Picking up the dog, he came a little closer to the window. The face stared back at them, the mouth making a small O of surprise.

"Milo!" C.J. yelled, "Let us in!" She went over and tugged on the door knob.

"Go away!"

Rick picked up a porch chair to smash the plate glass window.

"No, there's a key!" C.J. ran her hand over the top of the door and found it. She flung the door open. Milo turned and ran. Rick caught up with him halfway across the living room. A great many candles flickered on tables and in niches and in holders on the walls.

"Stop! What are you doing in my house?" Milo was furious. The dog yapped and snarled and struggled to get down.

C.J. closed in on Milo from the other side. "Is Kylie here? Is she?"

"Get out! Get out! I'm calling the police!"

She slapped him across the face so hard that his hat flew off. "Is she?"

. He held his cheek. "I don't know what you mean! Get out of my house, both of you."

She ran for the stairs. When Milo followed, Rick shoved him onto a sofa and told him if he moved from there, he would break his legs. The sofa was red, shaped exactly like a big pair of lips. C.J.'s footsteps faded on the steps to the second floor. Rick caught up with her. Music was coming faintly from somewhere. Frank Sinatra, singing about it being a very good year. They looked up a narrow, circular staircase with a metal railing.

"Shelby takes them to the tower room," Rick said. "Stay here, I'll go."

But C.J. pushed ahead of him, her feet almost a blur. Rick followed her. They turned around the iron column supporting the steps. At the top, a yellow light in a small brass chandelier illuminated the landing and a wooden door.

The music was louder. C.J. beat on the door with her fist. "Paul Shelby! I know you're in there!" She turned the knob.

It was dim inside, only a few candles, but not too dim to see a man in a dark-colored knit shirt with his back turned zipping his pants. He was looking over his shoulder, yelling, "Get out! How dare you come in here!"

There were silk floor pillows and a low wooden table with wine and what looked like some rolling papers and a baggie of weed.

The girl was on the floor, slumped against the pillows with her legs straight out in front of her. She lifted her head and tried to focus, but her eyes weren't connecting with her brain. She was still dressed, if you could call it that: a short plaid skirt and a white polo shirt, like a private prep school uniform.

C.J. cried out and ran to her. "Kylie, it's me. It's C.J. Don't be afraid."

Rick saw the portable stereo in a corner and went over to shut it off. Now the only noise was Paul Shelby shouting, "What are you doing here? Get out, I said."

Rick pushed him against the wall. He grinned and felt his jaw lock before he said, "You sick fuck. She's a child."

"She's twenty-one!"

"She's seventeen, and she's dressed like she's twelve."

"If she's under twenty-one, she lied to me. She came here of her own free will—"

"Shut up."

"You're angry that we fired you? What do you want? Name a figure, I'll double it." Shelby looked past Rick. "C.J., I don't understand. Whatever it is, we can fix it. Just tell me what you want."

Rick gave him another shove. "I said be quiet."

"Nothing was happening! We were talking. She's a friend of Milo's."

Rick took his pistol from his waist and held it under Shelby's chin. The safety was on, but Shelby didn't know that. His eyes shone with a primordial terror that Rick hadn't seen in a long time. "Shut the fuck up."

C.J. hauled Kylie to her feet. "Rick, take her downstairs and stay with her. I want to talk to him."

"I'm not leaving you up here alone with him."

"Take her out of here, Rick. Please." C.J. nodded. "I'll be all right."

"Just a second." Rick leaned closer to Shelby. "One hair. You touch one hair on that woman's head, I will rip you apart, and then I will kill you. Do we understand each other?"

Shelby nodded. He was taking some deep breaths now, patting his hair into place, thinking of a way he could get out of this.

Rick lifted the girl and carried her down the steps. She laughed and hung onto his neck going around and around the circular stairs. In the living room, Milo Cahill was on the lip-shaped sofa, hugging his dog. Rick carried Kylie to the back room, put her in a chair, and knelt beside her. "Kylie. You okay?"

"Hi." She smiled.

"You know who I am?"

Her head moved slowly side to side.

"That's all right. You just sit there. We're leaving in a minute."

"Okay."

Rick patted her shoulder, not knowing what else to do. When he heard the back door open, he looked around and saw Carlos Moreno peering in. He wore a rain-drenched yellow poncho, and there were bulges underneath, where his cameras hung at his hips.

He came in and pushed the hood back. "I got some pictures of Shelby's car. Where's Shelby?"

"Upstairs with C.J. They're having a talk."

He saw Kylie and whispered, "Is that her? The girl? What's the matter with her?"

"She's been drugged, probably by Milo before Shelby got here."

"Did Shelby—you know?"

"No, we got here in time."

"How old is she, fourteen? Oh, man, we've got him by the balls. Do you know her name? Who is she?" Carlos opened his poncho and turned on his digital camera.

Rick pulled him across the room. "No pictures. The girl will be gone in five minutes, and so will we."

"Her face won't be in it."

"You were never here, Carlos. You never saw her."

"But the story—"

"There will be no story."

"Why? Rick, you can't let it go. It's what you wanted."

Rick shook his head. "I'm letting it go."

C.J. could hear the rain on the roof. It streaked the dark glass of the windows. She leaned against the door and watched Paul Shelby. In the candlelight, she saw him gradually recovering his composure. The tension in his spine releasing. Color returning to his face. Straightening his shirt collar. Then forcing a slight smile.

"What next?" he said. "You have me in a difficult situation, I admit. What are you and Rick Slater doing here? Did you drop in to see Milo? What did he say to you? Talk to me." Shelby laughed nervously. "You're not saying anything, C.J."

She didn't move from her place by the door. "Two days ago, Rick told me why he got a job with you. He's a freelance reporter. He's been investigating you. Alana Martin came to him and said that Milo Cahill had arranged for her to have sex with you. She met you here in this room several times. She wasn't the first."

"That's a vicious lie!"

"It was for your support of The Aquarius. Milo gave you Alana Martin as a payoff."

Paul Shelby was still smiling, but he looked sick. "You've been against me from the start, haven't you? I felt the hostility but didn't know why. Okay, I get it now. You hate me because of what you say I did to you. It's in the past. Let it go. There is no profit to you, or to Rick Slater, in spreading these rumors. You will hurt innocent people. My wife. My sons. The girl who was just here—"

"Don't you even know her name?"

"She said it was Traci."

"Her name is Kylie Willis."

"Good for her. If you want to throw guilt around, throw some in her direction. She came here willingly. I have resources, C.J. I will fight you all the way. Think very carefully before you try to bring me down."

"Do you like little girls, Paul?"

"I didn't know she was seventeen! She lied to me. Milo won't tell you anything, because he would be damning himself. All right." Shelby raised his hands, a gesture of surrender. "What are we going to do about this? Do you want me to resign from office? Is that it? Do you want money? Does Rick want money? Talk to me!"

"Do little girls turn you on? Tell me. I want to hear you say it."

Slowly, as if something might break, Paul Shelby sat on the window ledge and crossed his arms. "I have desires. Everyone does. You ask any man, or any woman for that matter, about their fantasies. We all have our weaknesses."

"Stop making excuses for yourself! Open your eyes and see who you are, Paul. A pedophile. A man nearly fifty who likes sex with little girls."

"All right, I admit it! Does that make you happy?" He added, "I'm seeking therapy."

C.J. shook her head. "You're pathetic."

"I would like to have assurances that Rick Slater isn't going to smear me in the press. I tried to help him, getting him a good lawyer—"

"Shut up and listen," C.J. said. "I have something to tell you. I never had the abortion. That's right. I spent most of the money you gave me, then I had to go to my mother and ask her for help. I thought of suicide. It would have been easier, I thought, than telling her what I'd done. She was a religious woman. She said the only way God would forgive me was if I gave the baby to a good home. She had some friends. They couldn't have children. Fran and Bob Willis. They lived in Pensacola. They still do."

Shelby was staring at her, frozen. His face was pale against the dark window behind him. A flicker of lightning put him for an instant in silhouette, and rain slid down the glass.

"I had a baby girl. They named her, but Kylie was—she is—the most painful, the most beautiful thing that ever happened to me. You never noticed her eyes? They're gray, like yours. She's your daughter, Paul."

The silence stretched out. He cleared his throat. "If that's true—and maybe it is—what do you want me to do about it? Do you want me to support her? Is that what this is about?"

"My God." C.J. laughed. "No. I don't want you to have anything to do with Kylie. Ever. I just thought you ought to know where your—your *fantasies* almost took you."

"I didn't know who she was!" He breathed through his teeth and said slowly, "What do you *want*?"

She paced back and forth in front of him, and he followed her with his eyes. "Tonight Rick and I found out that Billy Medina is the one who murdered Alana Martin. He admitted it. He killed her at his house the night of the party, and he threw her body into the Atlantic. She was getting to be an embarrassment, and he was afraid he would lose his investment in The Aquarius. This is the project that *you* have been pushing in Congress."

"My God." Paul Shelby's face was hidden behind his hands now. "C.J., I'm begging you. I'll do anything. No one has to know. For our daughter's sake—"

"You make me sick. You don't give a damn about her. No, I

won't tell them about Kylie, but when the police come for Milo Cahill, he will try to save himself. He might say you brought the girls here. He might give their names. I will exert what pressure I can on Milo to leave Kylie out of it, but he might not listen to me."

"The world is coming apart," he groaned. "What am I going to do?"

"What you will do," C.J. said, "is deny she was ever here, even if Milo says otherwise. That is what I want. You came tonight to discuss business with Milo. No other reason. If you ever mention her name, if you ever use her to try to cut a deal for yourself, I will destroy you. That is a promise. I can do it. You hired me because I knew how to work the media. Watch me. I would turn them loose on you, and I wouldn't care if I went down in flames too. Do you understand?"

"Yes." He was crying.

She crossed the small room, then glanced back over her shoulder. Paul Shelby had turned to face the window. His arms were outstretched as if he was holding on.

"Paul, our lives as we knew them are over. Yours. Mine. Kylie's is just beginning. If you have a shred of decency left, you will do the right thing."

C.J. went out, quietly closing the door behind her.

Rick Slater looked around when he heard quick heel taps coming across the terrazzo floor. He met her halfway. Her eyes were on Kylie.

He spoke softly. "She's all right. Drugged, but that's not a bad thing, under the circumstances. Carlos is here. No, no, it's fine. I told him, no story, no photos. He'll do whatever you want."

C.J. leaned against him. "Thank you."

"Does Shelby know who she is?"

C.J. pulled away a little to look at him, to see what he meant, and in that long, wordless moment the truth flowed between them like an electrical current.

"It explains a lot of things," Rick said. "You and Shelby."

She nodded. "I told him. If her name comes up, he's going to deny she was ever here. It's Milo I'm worried about."

"Deal with it later. We need to go. I have to get back to Billy's place and tell them what happened. You take care of Kylie. I'll ask Carlos to take you home."

"Wait."

C.J. went back through the living room, walking quickly toward the red sofa. She picked up Milo's hat and tossed it into his lap. Rick could hear the murmur of voices.

Then from outside there was the breaking of glass. A half second later, a heavy thud. Then a girl's high-pitched laughter.

Kylie stood at the window looking out, her hands at her mouth. Carlos opened the door and ran onto the terrace. He looked up, then came back inside and announced, "He jumped. Shelby jumped!"

C.J. ran into the room. Milo followed with his dog, which had started barking again. C.J. pulled Kylie away from the window and held the girl tightly to prevent her from seeing anything more. Paul Shelby lay in a crumpled heap among shards of glass. The rain washed the blood into the cracks between the paving stones, sloping gently toward the dock, toward the water.

Milo screamed, "Oh, my God. Oh, my God." The dog was yapping and struggling to get down.

Rick said, "Shut that dog up."

"Hush, baby. Oh, my God." Milo scurried to a door and shoved the dog through it.

C.J. took Kylie to the armchair, covered her with a throw, and told her to sit there and not to move. Kylie curled up, put her head on her arm, and closed her eyes. C.J. walked over to the three men and whispered fiercely, "Paul Shelby didn't jump. Why would he do that? It was an accident. He came over to talk to Milo about The Aquarius. Didn't he, Milo? They always went up there to talk. Paul liked the view. He liked to sit on the ledge. You had warned him not to; he could lose his balance. Rick and I came by to see you, but you told us you had company. That was when it happened. A tragedy. I feel so sorry for his family."

Milo was staring at her.

C.J. said, "We know nothing about the girls who were here. Do we? Nothing at all."

He mutely shook his head.

Rick pulled C.J. aside. "Can we do this? What about Medina?"

C.J. put her fingers to her forehead. "We rushed over here to see if Milo was safe. We were afraid something had happened to him. Let me think."

Milo cried, "What are you talking about?"

"Be quiet," C.J. ordered. "I'll tell you in a minute. Rick, can Carlos take Kylie? I need her out of here right now. You'll have to put her in his car."

"Sure. He and Inez can take good care of her. I think she'll sleep for a while."

Carlos looked back and forth between them before saying, "It's no problem."

"What is going *on?*" Milo said.

"In a *minute!* If you want to save yourself from being arrested when the police get here, you will do as I say." C.J. put a hand on his arm. "Why don't you run upstairs and tidy up? Make sure there's nothing there that shouldn't be. Hurry. We need to report this."

Milo backed away, turned, and ran for the stairs.

C.J. went to Kylie and roused her. "Kylie? You have to go now. This is Carlos. He's our friend." She hugged her tightly, then moved aside so Rick could pick her up. "Thank you, Carlos. Take care of her for me."

"I'll be right back," Rick said. He scooped the girl out of the chair.

Kylie smiled. Her eyes were half closed. "Hi, Rick."

C.J. followed them to the front door. "It's so dark in here. We should turn on some lights and blow out the candles."

It was picked up on the police scanner, and within an hour satellite trucks were parked up and down the street, reporters were swarming the front yard, and the spotlights of news helicopters swept over the house. The street was a sea of flashing blue and red lights.

Detective George Fuentes asked what the hell was going on. They were going to get this sorted out. C.J. talked to him. He wasn't satisfied, but he couldn't find any cracks to put his fingers in and pull. He told her that in view of the fact that it was a U.S. congressman who had died, the FBI would be asking questions too. And what was the deal with Billy Medina? C.J. told him she and Rick would come over and see him in the morning.

It was past midnight and the rain had stopped when they finally came out the front door. The camera flashes were like strobes, and reporters shouted their questions. C.J. made a short statement about what a loss this would be to Congressman Shelby's family and friends and to the community. When she was finished, Rick put an arm around her and guided her through the crowd.

chapter

FORTY

C. J. noticed that Rick had a quarter inch of dark fuzz on his head. She touched it lightly, not enough to wake him. She loved looking at him. The big arms, his back, his legs, the way the muscles moved, everything. There was a tattoo on his shoulder blade, an eagle with open claws. She had counted eighteen scars on his body and had kissed them all. It was a different kind of compulsion, and C.J. didn't care to get over it. She needed him. She had told him so one night, throwing caution away, and he had said he wasn't going anywhere. He didn't lie about the important things. He could have made money off his story, and been famous for a little while, but he said it didn't matter. She believed he meant it.

He opened one hazel eye, squinting at her. His smile lifted his mustache. He had a little chip out of one front tooth. He pulled her closer and stroked her back. Finally he gave her bottom a pinch.

"It's eight-thirty, Sunshine."

It was not in his nature to sleep late, and today they couldn't. Rick was taking her and Kylie to the airport at noon to catch a flight to Pensacola. Kylie had been here two weeks, and she was leaving today. She would go back to high school—late, but she would finish. She would start community college in the spring. She was okay with that, so she'd said. C.J. was going to pay for it, and for the university to follow. After some argument, Fran had agreed, for Kylie's sake.

Rick rolled over and sat on the edge of the bed, reaching for his shorts on the floor. He put on a T-shirt and jeans and his sandals. "I'll make coffee." His footsteps thumped down the steps.

C.J. dreaded this trip. A few days ago, she had finally gathered the words and the courage to call Kylie's parents and tell them she wanted to be part of Kylie's life. It hadn't been easy, but it was something that C.J. admitted should have been done years ago. The three of them, she and Fran and Bob, would talk to Kylie. The thought of it made C.J. want to run the other way. How would Kylie react? Would she feel betrayed? Would she ever want to speak to C.J. again?

C.J. went across the hall, tying her robe. Kylie's door was open, and the sheets were folded neatly at the foot of the bed. She went to the window. Kylie and Edgar were on the front porch of the cottage. They had finished Edgar's photographs, but he would miss her terribly, till she came back for a visit over Christmas.

C.J. touched the glass. Kylie would be all right. She had not grown up in a household fueled on shame. Fran and Bob were good people. They were willing to share their daughter with a woman who was virtually a stranger to her. This gave C.J. hope that there could be something in the future.

The first night Rick stayed with her, and Kylie across the hall, C.J. couldn't sleep. She had lain awake listening to the patter of rain on the leaves. They had talked and talked, and Rick had finally closed his eyes, but her mind wouldn't stop, and she had whispered:

I never held her. I never kissed her or told her I loved her. Except once. Only once, when they brought her to me in the hospital. Her head smelled like heaven, and I wanted to unwrap her and see everything about her, but my mother said don't get attached. She said that's enough, give her to me. I wanted so much to hang on to her, but I let go. I got out of bed and went to the window, and I could see them driving away.

For a long time I dreamed about my baby. I would look at every stroller that passed. The only way I could stand it was to say that I'd never had a child at all, that she wasn't mine. Gradually she faded away. I got on with my life. I became someone else, and she became an echo.

Rick wasn't asleep after all. He had put his arms around her and rolled over so he could look up at her. "Come on, C.J. She's right across the hall, and she'll be back to see you over winter break."

"She'll find out who I am one day. It's not a pretty story. I hope I'm ready."

"You will be," Rick had said. The moonlight had come through the window on his ugly, beautiful face. "Kylie is yours. She's going to love you just fine."

ACKNOWLEDGMENTS

A writer depends on the generosity of others. I am grateful to Sam Richards, for stories of old Miami; Dana Vitantonio, for a unique perspective on Las Vegas; Reid Vogelhut, for his recollections of the lush life; Milton Hirsch, for legal matters; Mel Taylor for a glimpse inside TV news; and Nicholas Windler, for choosing the right wine. As ever, my sister Laura had 20-20 vision.

Many thanks also to my agent, Richard Curtis, and to all the folks at Vanguard Press, especially my freelance editor, Kevin Smith.